Betsy von Furstenberg

A LAVISH ESTATE in the Bahamas, a grand Venetian palazzo, and an opulent Parisian apartment are the settings of the debut novel by a woman who knows them intimately—Betsy von Furstenberg. An accomplished actress who garnered rave reviews over three decades on Broadway, in film, and on television, Ms. von Furstenberg has now turned her talent and unique experience to writing fiction. In *Mirror, Mirror,* she depicts with intuitive skill the dark emotions that lie beneath the glamorous facade of high society.

Descended from nobility whose roots lie in the Middle Ages, Betsy von Furstenberg was born in a castle which still overlooks the Rhine and is now the home of her uncle. Her father, Count Franz Egon von Furstenberg, was a member of the Westphalian line of Furstenbergs. After her parents divorced, Ms. von Furstenberg was raised by her mother, an American from Alabama. They lived first in Italy, then in New York City, though Betsy spent several summers as a child in a palazzo in Venice.

Ms. von Furstenberg began dancing at the age of four under the tutelage of Anton Dolin, and, at the age of seven, became the youngest dancer featured by the American Ballet Theater, in a production of "The Raymond Scott Quintet." At the age of fourteen, she became a model, and at an age when her friends were concerned with debutante balls, Betsy von Furstenberg had chosen her career and was acting in the Italian film that would win highest honors at the Venice Film Festival in 1951, *Women Without Names*, starring Simone Simon and Valentina Cortese.

The face of the blond beauty then appeared on major European magazine covers such as *Elle* and *Realité*. And, as a result of her Broadway debut the following year in Philip Barry's play *Second Threshold*, she appeared on the covers of *Life* and *Look* magazines, posing before the cameras of such renowned photographers as Louise Dahl-Wolfe, Horst, and Slim Aarons.

On Broadway, she was swept into the glittering world of a New York stage actress, thinking it normal to do at least one Broadway play each year. Ms. von Furstenberg appeared in dozens of plays, including *Oh, Men! Oh, Women!* with Franchot Tone; *The Chalk Garden* by Enid Bagnold; *Nature's Way* by Herman Wouk; Jean Kerr's *Mary, Mary*; Neil Simon's *The Gingerbread Lady*; *What Every Woman Knows* with Helen Hayes; *Much Ado About Nothing* with John Gielgud and Margaret Leighton; and *The King of Hearts* directed by Walter Kerr. She has performed extensively on television, from drama to westerns and soap operas.

Betsy von Furstenberg is also a successful journalist who has published articles in the *New York Times*, the *Daily News*, *People*, *Saturday Review*, *Ladies Home Journal*, *Good Housekeeping*, and *Playbill*.

Ms. von Furstenberg was recently married to John J. Reynolds. By a former marriage, she has a son, Glyn Vincent, who is a playwright; and a daughter, Gay Caroline Vincent, an artist.

BETSY VON FURSTENBERG

MIRROR MIRROR

J

JOVE BOOKS, NEW YORK

For my husband, Jack, who came into my life unwittingly in the middle of the book, but whose humor and enthusiasm carried me to the end

Thank you to Jeanne Drewson; Mel Parker; my children, Caroline and Glyn Vincent; and, especially, Virginia Gardner

MIRROR, MIRROR

A Jove Book / published by arrangement with the author

PRINTING HISTORY
Jove edition / January 1988

ISBN: 0-515-09243-6

Jove Books are published by The Berkley Publishing Group, 200 Madison Avenue, New York, New York 10016.
The name "JOVE" and the "J" logo are trademarks belonging to Jove Publications, Inc.

PRINTED IN THE UNITED STATES OF AMERICA

10 9 8 7 6 5 4 3 2 1

PART ONE
Venice
1968

Legend has it that in Venice when a good soul dies the winged Lion of San Marco carries him up to heaven.

Chapter One

THE MORNING MIST lifted, and the canals bared their mirrors to the sky. A flock of pigeons clattered awake. They slowly rose and circled above the broad, cobbled Piazza San Marco, then wheeled about the dome of the cathedral before settling on the rooftops.

Across the Grand Canal, a ray of sunlight pierced a partly opened leaded-glass window in the Palazzo Nordonia. The scent of the Adriatic, wild and sweet, wafted in with the breeze. Antonia dreamed for a moment that she was flying, her body suffused with sun like a cloud.

The man beside her stirred and circled her with his arm. The familiar weight reassured her. "Antonia." He urged her awake, pressing his lips to her eyelids.

The breeze felt cool on her skin. Overnight the sheet had slipped off her body. She shivered in the spring air.

"Antonia, wake up. It's late."

It was true. She could hear the vaporetto engines down on the canal and the sound of water lapping at the walls of the canal. Downstairs the servants were rousing, slamming shutters back. The city was going to work. She groaned and turned toward the count.

He looked down at Toni. The small, intense woman had the Mediterranean coloring—black hair and soft olive skin. Her narrow face was serious beyond her years, and her swiftly etched body, taut with muscles, was more like a boy's than a young woman's. Even after ten months, Carlo Nordonia was still tantalized. He was a man who was used to getting what he wanted, but some secret pride in her intelligent black eyes eluded him. She was like quicksilver; she might disappear if he held her too close. Yet now he did, running his palm down her narrow, silky back, over her high, round buttocks. She awakened beneath his touch. Her body began to move slowly and pliantly, but her sleepy eyes watched his from a still point that seemed unreachable.

The flat morning light revealed every line in Carlo's face, Toni noticed detachedly, deepening the furrows in his high forehead, accenting his strong cheekbones and the thinness of his aristocratic face. She arched slightly to meet his mouth, kissing him.

Toni loved waking beside Carlo in the morning, as if she belonged here in his palazzo on the Grand Canal. For a moment, as she held him, the intensity of her feelings surprised her, for she had willfully defied her parents by choosing a lover who would never marry her. She pressed herself against him and stretched out her legs, drawing her foot down his calf.

Suddenly she felt something cold and wet press against her foot.

"*Va via, cattiva cane!*" she cried.

Carlo's body rumbled with laughter. "That won't work, Antonia. Hush Puppy responds only to English commands. Surely you know that by now."

Aware that she was being discussed, Carlo's aged basset hound regarded Toni with baleful yellow eyes, obviously insulted at the reprimand but certain of her master's approval.

"Hush Puppy always wakes me up in the mornings," Carlo reminded Antonia. "You mustn't scold her for doing her job."

He rubbed the old dog's head fondly, and sat up with a reluctant sigh. "Speaking of doing one's job, Toni, we must get to work on the catalog for the Renaissance art exhibit."

Antonia smiled fondly. "Carlo Nordonia, surely you don't intend to work today."

Carlo slapped the heel of his hand against his forehead. "What time is it? She'll be here any minute." He threw back the sheet and climbed out of the bed.

Toni looked at the tall man admiringly as he stood erect, his skin pale in the early light. The year's concentrated work had taken a toll. Though his face had aged dramatically, his body was still lean and strong. Sometimes he looked even boyish to Antonia, and that pleased her. The warm, familiar sense of pride filled her as she realized that she, an ordinary girl of twenty, held this powerful man enthralled.

"My daughter could walk in any minute," he said as he threw on a robe and put on his tortoiseshell glasses.

Toni laughed at the thought. ''Your daughter would be shocked! I can't be much older than she is.''

Immediately she regretted the tactless remark as the count frowned and turned away from her. His strong puritanical streak made it impossible for him to admit to himself that he loved and needed a woman who was less than half his age—a woman who had made it clear from the beginning that she admired his intellect, and desired him as a lover. But when she had finished the research for his book, Toni would leave him. She would seek a husband who could give her children, who could grow old with her, who was not haunted by memories.

A sound from outside the palazzo caught Carlo's attention. ''There's a boat at the landing,'' he said. ''Surely she can't have arrived already.'' He swung open the French doors and went out on the small balcony that overlooked the Grand Canal. Seconds later he returned, cursing softly in Italian. ''My daughter is here,'' he said to Antonia. ''Out of my bed, lazybones!''

Toni laughed at the count's consternation. She leaped up, threw her arms around his waist from behind him, and kissed the nape of his neck. He stiffened and drew away.

''You're so funny, worried as a mother hen,'' she said. ''No one will let your daughter into this room; you know that. Has anyone ever seen me? For almost a year I've been your mistress, and not one of the servants even suspects.''

She wrapped the sheet around her body and paused to look through the French doors on her way to the shower. It was a brilliant morning; for a few moments it seemed the canal and the sky were the same clear azure. Last night's cool rain seemed to have washed the ancient city clean, and now it sparkled in the sunlight. Down below on the small landing a servant was tethering a motor launch to one of the stone lions that served as landing posts. Two young women were seated in the boat, their knees pressed against a couple of suitcases. It was a pitifully small amount of luggage, Toni thought, for the daughter of Count Carlo Nordonia.

One of the girls was willowy and fair, with a cloud of golden red hair. Even from a distance Antonia knew that this was Francesca Nordonia, for Carlo's daughter bore a striking resemblance to her mother, the beautiful red-haired woman whose life-size portrait dominated the grand staircase of the palazzo.

Since she had been working for Carlo in the palazzo, Toni had heard many tales about his late wife. An American, she had captured the imagination of society and the press on both sides of the Atlantic. Venetians still talked about her as if she were alive, about her daring exploits and the scandal she had brought down on herself and her husband.

Susannah Nordonia. Even her name was beautiful, Toni thought. As beautiful as the imperious eyes that looked down from the portrait. The eyes of a beguiling but independent woman, not to be controlled by the reins of a husband, a child, or a rigidly moralistic society. A woman who still held Carlo Nordonia's heart in her hands, Toni had long ago realized, who was still alive in the servants' gossip and in the carefully preserved rooms of the palazzo, which she had restored in meticulous detail.

Toni had sensed the count's unwillingness to talk about Susannah, and she had never pressed him for information. But now her exiled daughter was coming home, and it almost seemed as if Susannah herself had alighted from the launch to reclaim her home.

Then the young woman with the golden hair raised her head to look up at the palazzo, and even though Toni noticed the resemblance to the portrait downstairs of her mother, this girl looked serene and gentle, like Botticelli's Venus rising from the water.

Antonia turned her attention to her companion. Darker skinned and apparently older than Francesca, the young woman crackled with energy and glowed with an exotic loveliness that didn't strike Toni as Italian, or even European. She seized the two suitcases and danced up the algae-carpeted marble steps of the landing with a natural grace and elegance that looked totally unselfconscious.

Toni could hear the older girl's clear, strong voice as she spoke to Carlo's daughter. "This place is a castle! You've been keeping secrets from me, Francesca. Why didn't you tell me your father was a king?"

"He's not a king, silly," Francesca said, her voice so delicate that Toni had difficulty making out her words. "He's just a count. You know that." She looked around uncertainly, as if she, too, were seeing the palazzo for the first time.

How odd, Antonia thought, that she's so unsure of her surroundings. Carlo had said that Francesca spent much of her early childhood in the palazzo.

"Hurry up," the dark girl said with friendly impatience. "I want to see the inside of the château."

"Josie, it's a *palazzo*. This is Italy, not France."

Carlo joined Antonia at the open doorway to the balcony. "That's Josephine, my daughter's maid," he said. "Francesca begged me to let her bring the girl along. I finally agreed, mostly because I was afraid Francesca would be homesick without her." The smile faded from his face.

He turned around, taking Antonia's hand and pulling her with him. "Come, we've got to scramble. Just time enough for a quick shower."

But still the young voices echoed up from below. "*Non, non, m'sieur! Ne touchez pas!*"

"Good God!" Carlo growled. "Will you listen to that accent?"

Antonia laughed. "I take it Josie is Haitian."

"Her mother is from Haiti, yes. Lord, I hope my daughter hasn't picked up the patois."

"Josie," they heard Francesca say bluntly, "it won't do you a bit of good to speak French. These people are Italians."

"Well, then tell the boatman to take his grubby hands off my guitar. I'll carry it myself."

"Oooh." Antonia laughed. "That one is a character!"

"She is a Bahamian servant," Carlo said with unnecessary abruptness, tugging her away from the window.

"But she's beautiful in her way, Carlo. And quite funny and charming."

Seeing that the conversation was at an end whether she liked it or not, Antonia walked back into the bathroom and turned on the antiquated faucets. The water rumbled through the old plumbing, then gushed forth with a great, discontented roar.

Antonia stood under the pounding water. She didn't understand Carlo's attitude toward his daughter, whom he had virtually abandoned after his wife's death. This seemed incomprehensible in an Italian to whom family love and pride were so important. He had visited her only at Christmastime.

She wondered if Francesca looked so much like her mother that it pained Carlo to see her. After his wife's death, Carlo had become something of a recluse, living by himself in the cavernous palazzo while Francesca was brought up on his estate in the Bahamas with the housekeeper and her daughter. Carlo spent most of his time in his library or his comfortable office on the Campo San Polo, studying and writing about the art and history of Venice, as if to block out more deeply personal thoughts.

"Enough," Carlo announced, turning off the water and pulling her out onto a thick rug. "We really have to hurry, Toni. What will my daughter think if she sees you?"

"She'll think you're a handsome devil enjoying the company of a sexy young woman." She snatched the towel from him and began to dry her short hair.

"What on earth shall I do with her today?" Carlo asked, half to himself. "Send her off shopping, I suppose. I've got to finish editing that catalog; the publisher expects it by the end of the week."

"I'll help you."

"No, I've got a better idea. Will you take charge of Francesca? You're close enough in age to be friends. Take her under your wing, Toni. That would be an enormous help to me. I'm afraid I'm at a loss with young girls."

"You aren't at a loss with me," Toni said slyly.

Carlo gave her a wry look as he lathered his face.

"I'll take her on an expedition to the Piazza San Marco. I'll give her the grand tour," Toni said.

"And you must order her a gown. I plan to open the palazzo for a ball on her birthday, to introduce her to society."

"A *ball*?" Toni looked so astonished that Carlo laughed.

"Yes, my love, a grand event that will be attended by half of the nobility of Western Europe." In the mirror he caught Antonia's suspicious expression. "Don't worry, Antonia. I've hired a social secretary to attend to the details. The invitations were sent out some time ago, and the acceptances have been coming in nicely."

Toni wrapped a dry towel around her body and sat down on the edge of the old-fashioned tub. "When is this great event going to occur?"

"The date is June eighteenth. I have only a month to get ready."

"It won't take that long to have a dress made, Carlo."

"That's not all I have to do. Remember, she has been brought up by servants in the Bahamas, so she has no idea how to behave. I had my secretary arrange for a virtual army of coaches to work with her, teaching her to dance, to talk with important people, protocol, to carry herself properly, to . . . oh, a dozen other things."

"You couldn't have let me in on this little secret?"

"So that you could plague me with questions as you are doing now? No, Antonia, I could not."

"And just where am I to take her to buy a ball gown?"

"To Renata." He waited for her astonished reaction to his mention of the famous designer. "She won't design clothes for just anyone. I see you are aware of that. But for this ball, she will do the gown for the guest of honor. Will you go with Francesca for her fitting this afternoon?"

"Only if you promise to invite me to the ball."

"You may come to the ball," Carlo said cautiously, "but I cannot escort you; you must realize that."

"I'll find my own escort," Antonia said. "Don't worry!" She flounced out of the bathroom with exaggerated dignity.

When he finished shaving, Carlo found Antonia dressed and seated on the edge of the bed, twirling her sunglasses in one hand.

"So, then, it is settled. Your task this morning is to accompany my daughter to her fitting. Make sure she has everything she needs. I don't want her running around town in her blue jeans. You might find a way of suggesting that she take a stab at looking like a young lady. Who knows? She might even enjoy it."

Toni paused for a moment before an antique mirror to quickly brush out her tangled black hair. Her life was about to become more interesting, she realized as she silently let herself out of the count's bedroom.

In order to get out of the palazzo unseen at this busy hour, she had to walk along the vast indoor balcony that swooped around the high entrance, which was dominated by the grand staircase. From Carlo's doorway, she saw that the hallway leading to the balcony was deserted; she hurried along it until she reached the entrance to the balcony itself. There she paused, catching her breath as she realized that Francesca and Josephine were standing at the foot of the grand staircase near the portrait of Francesca's mother; from their air of concentration Antonia knew they were likely to linger. She was caught there; if she sprinted quickly, they were sure to catch a glimpse of her. But since they had no idea who she was, they'd probably assume she was only a servant passing overhead.

The darker girl was talking in her strong, clear voice. Antonia didn't stop to listen. She slipped forward onto the balcony and fled toward the safety of a huge marble column, pressing herself into its shadow. Below her, Josie stopped talking suddenly as Toni's sunglasses fell to the stone floor with a clatter. Holding her breath, she waited until Josie and Francesca resumed their conversation, then ducked down behind the balustrade and scampered for the back stairway.

Francesca looked at the portrait of her mother. Susannah's green eyes were just as she remembered them—defiant, mischievous, and beautiful. "I remember so few things about her," she murmured.

At a discreet distance behind the two visitors stood Emilio, the count's majordomo. Ramrod straight in his burgundy and gold uniform, he pretended not to see the count's young mistress scurrying along toward the servants' exit. He was widely experienced at protecting his master's privacy as well as his own acute sense of propriety in moments such as this. Emilio knew he had no right to disapprove of Count Nordonia's actions, but it distressed him that Carlo had once again brought a woman into the household. For years, the palazzo had been a safe masculine preserve. What a relief that had been, after the contessa's hectic reign. Now, however, the years of peace and quiet had ended, and Emilio had to put up with the presence of young Antonia, who at that moment was scurrying along the balcony like a squirrel with Count Nordonia's innocent young daughter just below.

Emilio's disapproval of women did not extend to Francesca Nordonia, of course. Indeed, the majordomo had always believed that the little contessa belonged in her father's home. Surely such a sweet, submissive child would not repeat her mother's indiscretions. Remembering the notorious escapades of the count's late wife, the usually impassive servant could not help but frown at the antics of the young Antonia. Surely the count did not mean to marry this one! Emilio shuddered delicately at the thought.

Emilio felt that he shared a personal bond with the count, and practically an umbilical one as well. The two had grown up together. They were best friends until the day Emilio assumed his role as Carlo's servant.

They had gone everywhere together as children, climbing to the top of the campanile in the Piazza San Marco, stealing oranges from the fruit stands by the Rialto Bridge. How many times had they slipped off in the Nordonia gondola at midnight, rowed to the Lido, and returned home by dawn. But then, when they reached the age of manhood, they suddenly became awkward with each other. Their future was clear by then: Carlo was destined to be the head of a great family, Emilio his servant. Emilio never resented his position. He was too loyal for that. He had managed Carlo's household with economy, efficiency, and great style all his adult life, and in the years since the death of the contessa, Emilio had been, for all practical purposes, the master of the Palazzo Nordonia. He ran the large palace exactly as the count wanted—by instinct, without being told. He kept its furnishings preserved, its servants quiet and industrious, its fruit and wine cellars stocked for the guests who seldom visited. But one day Emilio noticed that Antonia was sharing Carlo's bed and his bath. Carlo could easily be forgiven a female companion for the night; Emilio had looked the other way countless times. But this girl was different. She was too young, and for all her boyish élan she had a catlike inscrutability that Carlo probably perceived as a challenge. Emilio knew the count would not quickly grow tired of her.

Her presence encouraged him to spend more and more time writing and less and less time on his business interests. The count may have grown to be the world's greatest expert on the art and history of Venice but he had neglected the source of the family's fortune, the vineyards.

Without supervision, the attorneys and financial advisers had let the estate deteriorate dangerously; Emilio himself did a better job of tracking the Nordonia losses in the financial section of the papers than the count did. The anarchist political climate and the antibusiness actions of the government raised doubts about the advisability of investing here in Italy. But the count refused to seek out safer business markets abroad. This decision frustrated Emilio, for he knew that Carlo was not without business sense; he just refused to use it.

All of it was puzzling, Emilio thought. Daughters, wives, mistresses! Now the count was even planning a ball, the likes of which these old walls had not seen in many years. His frugality was all in vain. Emilio shrugged and heaved a weary sigh, wondering what other surprises lay ahead.

He glanced up at the interior balcony to make certain that Antonia had safely fled, then directed a less exalted servant to carry the visitors' luggage up the stairs. Young Francesca and her friend ran ahead and waited at the first landing. "Another flight, Contessina,'' Emilio said, straining to hide the fact that the climb had winded him.

''Isn't this where my father's rooms are? I'd like to see him now.''

Already these complications, Emilio thought. The count never saw anyone before noon. Even the maid left his breakfast tray outside his door. Only Antonia, his researcher, had permission to join him in his study. The majordomo looked at Francesca curiously. The soft blue-green eyes and hair the color of flame were as he remembered from years before, but she was clearly no longer a child. She had become a very pretty young woman, although she lacked her mother's vibrant presence. She was nervous and ill at ease, and some sadness lingered beneath the clear turquoise of her eyes. Emilio had always despaired of the way Carlo neglected the child. It was the majordomo, not the count, who had chosen Francesca's Christmas presents and who had seen that a birthday check was sent to her every June. Carlo would have forgotten. Emilio looked at his watch. The count would need a little time to dress and have his coffee. ''It is nine o'clock. You and the signorina will have some breakfast and freshen up. Your father will see you in exactly one hour.''

As the procession made its way up the long marble staircase, Emilio was surprised to notice that Francesca Nordonia moved tentatively, almost fearfully, while her young companion leaped joyously ahead, taking two steps at a time. It was almost as if this Josephine, rather than the count's daughter, were the mistress of the household, returning home after a long exile abroad.

Chapter Two

"HERE IS YOUR room, Contessina." Emilio swung open a door and gestured the two young women into a large, sunny bedroom.

Francesca hung back for a moment at the sight of such splendor, but Josie put a firm hand on the small of her back and shoved her over the threshold, muttering a respectful "Wow" as she followed.

Astonished at the delicate beauty of the bedroom, Francesca walked slowly into the center and then stood looking around her. Ever since the plane landed, she had been flooded with memories. The city rose out of the sea like a gilded mirage, at once vivid and insubstantial. The familiar Byzantine facades, the strong smell of the acid-green canals, the golden palazzo itself, appeared before her like an enchanted stage set for an Arabian fairy tale. The palazzo, all velvet, gilt, and Tiepolo ceilings, was more beautiful than she remembered, but it seemed to have shrunk with age, like a childhood toy. She had few conscious memories of the paneled rooms and long, marble corridors, yet when she walked through them, she recognized them at once. She could have found her way about blindfolded. She even recalled the exact number of steps from the piano nobile to the second floor; there were twenty-nine. She had learned to count while climbing those stairs. But she knew she had never before seen the room that Emilio now showed her.

Its walls were covered in rose damask. A delicate gold and crystal chandelier hung from a bronze medallion in the center of the vaulted ceiling. The bed of carved gilded wood shone with a rose counterpane, and the draperies, the armchairs, and the small curved couch before the windows were of white damask with floral tracery. The small fireplace was covered with white and green tile; the French doors to the balcony gleamed with ivory enamel. The delicate crowned lion, which dominated the family crest, was embroidered on the deep rose counterpane and pillow covers. Francesca's own monogram had been woven into the design.

"Did my father prepare this room for me?"

"No, Contessina." Emilio paused. "It was your mother. This was the last room she designed. We carried out her plans after she died."

"It's beautiful!" Francesca was thrilled to hear that her mother had taken such care in designing a room just for her. "But I seem to remember sleeping upstairs."

"*Sì*. With your nurse. The contessa planned this room for you when you outgrew the nursery. This door is the closet; the other is the bath and dressing room."

Francesca was stunned by the splendor of her surroundings. She had never allowed herself to dream of sharing her father's home. Even when Carlo had written her and asked her to come to Venice to celebrate her eighteenth birthday, she had not dared to believe that such a miracle could really come about.

Emilio stepped across the corridor and opened another door. "For you, signorina," he said to Josie as he revealed like a magician a small bedroom ringed with tall windows and painted a pretty apple green. Two of the windows looked out onto the side canal, and the others faced the palazzo's rear courtyard, which was filled with olive trees whose dull-faced leaves turned their silvery backs to the breeze.

Josie let out a shriek of delight, ran into the room, and hurled herself headfirst into the high, soft bed. "Wait until my mother hears about this, Francesca! She won't believe it."

Francesca, always more reserved than Josie, walked sedately to the bed and sat down cautiously on the edge. "After all those years in our beach house, this does seem . . . unbelievable," she admitted.

The two girls had grown up together in much humbler surroundings. Carlo's mansion in Lyford Cay, near Nassau, had been closed since his wife's death. Francesca, Josie, and Marianne Lapoiret had shared a comfortable beach house on the edge of the estate. Marianne, Carlo's Haitian housekeeper, had raised Francesca like her own daughter. At Carlo's expense, she had sent her and Josie, in drab gray uniforms, to an exclusive convent school, a strict and spartan citadel for the daughters of the island's middle class and aspiring poor. The girls certainly hadn't been deprived, but they'd both sensed a lack in their lives. They knew they were different from their classmates, whose parents' lives seemed to center on their children. Josie's father had been killed in a fishing accident when she was an infant; and for all the attention she got from Carlo, Francesca might as well have been an orphan. Now their hands touched in a bond of sympathetic wonder. They were both overwhelmed by their new surroundings.

After a moment, Josie sat up and thanked Emilio in an uncharacteristically humble tone of voice.

Emilio nodded, then turned to Francesca. "Will that be all, Contessina?"

"Yes, thank you, Emilio."

As soon as the majordomo was out of earshot, she fell back on the soft bed and pulled Josie down next to her. "I feel like Cinderella."

Josie gave her a violent hug. "*P'tite soeur*, the best thing you ever did for me was to bring me here."

Francesca giggled. "And you didn't want to come! I practically had to drag you on board that plane. You couldn't bear to leave that dreadful boyfriend of yours." Francesca refused even to speak the name of the young musician Josie had been dating in Nassau.

"Look down there," Josie cried, ignoring the taunt. She had flown across the narrow corridor back into Francesca's room and flung open one of the windows. "There's another lion. He's fabulous!" She turned to Francesca, her amber eyes aglow with pleasure. "And to think I almost turned this down just because of some man!"

Francesca crossed her arms and raised one eyebrow. "So Lucas Caswell is suddenly only 'some man,' is he? You swore you'd be heartbroken all the time you were here, Josie, but now even stone lions are more interesting than he is."

Josie beckoned her to the balcony.

From this vantage point, drinking in the strange mixture of smells that were at once new but familiar, Francesca felt that she owned the city. What had Emilio called her? "Contessina." Little Countess. She rolled her head back and gave a whoop of joy.

"What is it?" Josie asked.

Francesca blushed shyly. Her hair had fallen about her

shoulders. Josie took one look at her happy, disheveled face, and relaxed. "Just laughing to yourself about it all?"

"I don't think I've ever been this happy before. I could die laughing."

"Well, don't die laughing while you're hanging over the balcony, if you don't mind. You're liable to fall. I'd have to jump in after you, and that water's no joke. I saw garbage floating down there," she said in a faked exasperation. She leaned over the balcony and took a whiff. "It smells!" She pinched her small nostrils shut and flailed the air to dispel the imaginary odor. "That settles it. I'd have to let you sink."

"You'd let me drown before your very eyes?" Francesca asked.

"Maybe," Josie answered, teasing her, and stepped back inside. "I'm going to try on my new peignoir," she added, dashing from the room.

Francesca was hanging up her clothes when Josie returned, pirouetting before the mirror in her new black lace dressing gown. She was convinced it made her look irresistible.

Francesca couldn't help but laugh, although she felt a twinge of something like envy as the lovely, amber-skinned girl swirled gracefully, the lace falling loosely over her breasts. This was the new Josie—obsessed with men, suddenly sophisticated, Francesca thought.

After her graduation from the convent last year, Josie had enrolled in music courses at the University of Nassau. As a favor to friends, she sang at weddings, where her rich contralto and her self-possession impressed everyone. Francesca envied her her vivaciousness. She had always been an audience for Josie; she held back and watched.

Then last month for the first time, after singing at a funeral, Josie was paid for her work. "*P'tite soeur!* We're rich!" she had cried, running into the beach house.

Francesca was uncomprehending. "How can you be so happy after going to Sister Alicia's funeral?" The nun had been a teacher of Josie's.

"You're right," she answered, momentarily sad. "Everyone was devastated. The service was interminable. I felt so sorry for them. After all, what good can singing do?" Then she grinned. "But it did me a lot of good. Look at this!"

She held out five ten-dollar bills. It was the first money Josie had ever earned. Francesca was impressed. "That's wonderful. What will you do with it?"

"Let's go into town and celebrate."

"Does Marianne know?"

"No, I want to surprise her. Besides, I'm afraid she'd make me stick it in a bank. How boring! Let's get going before she comes home."

The two girls took the car to the main shopping street in Nassau and Josie bought the dressing gown that now sloped low over her creamy shoulders.

Josie pulled back from the mirror, but still gazed at her reflection. "If only Lucas could see me now. Would he be impressed!"

"Isn't he impressed enough already?" Francesca asked dryly.

What Francesca meant, but could not say, was that Josie was too good for Lucas. He was a tall, rawboned native from "over the hill," the black section of Nassau. He played saxophone in one of the clubs there. Francesca had gone to hear him once, and felt distinctly out of place in the black crowd; there were only a few whites present. Lucas, when introduced to her, gave her a cool nod and then ignored her. It was a sudden reminder of the new tension that was growing. That was the first time Francesca had realized that she might lose Josie, who was so pale that she could pass for white, to this alien and possibly hostile world.

Josie looked over her shoulder. "This place makes me feel like a Renaissance princess."

Francesca laughed. "I keep getting the feeling that someone's going to walk through that door and take this all away from us if we're not careful. We mustn't let them hear us laughing. They might realize we don't belong and send us packing."

Just then they heard a scraping at the door, followed by a sharp knock.

"It's them!" Francesca cried in mock alarm.

"Over my dead body," said Josie. She waited a moment, then pulled the door open.

The hallway was empty. At Josie's feet were two gilt breakfast trays bright with geraniums, coffee, and freshly baked bread.

"Strawberry jam. How did they know?"

"They're only serving us in our rooms because we're under house arrest," said Francesca.

The two girls plunged into silence and quickly devoured

their first Venetian meal. When they had eaten the last crumb, Josie got up.

"I've got to write that letter."

"I'm exhausted," said Francesca, pulling down the cover of her bed.

"How can you sleep now? Aren't you too excited?"

"I'm not going to sleep. I'm just going to lie down for five minutes. I'm too nervous about seeing my father to sleep. Besides, I'm afraid that I'd wake up and discover this was all a beautiful dream."

Josie impulsively hugged Francesca at the door. "Thank you for bringing me," she said. "Without you I never would have known that all of this existed."

Alone, Francesca stripped off her clothes and lay down on the high bed. Its curved posts spiraled into the air. It was a bed that could not help but inspire sweet dreams. She closed her eyes.

The room turned the light to rose behind Francesca's eyelids. Her memories of her mother, so long suppressed, came flooding back. When she was five it had been easy to blank out the details of a tragedy she didn't understand. Now she remembered the mansion at Lyford Cay, boarded and shuttered, a ghost house overgrown with vines as it had been in those days before her father began his yearly Christmas visits. The fingers of her mind tugged at the undergrowth, undid the latches, and threw open the windows until the house was restored to its bright and airy dominion overlooking the sea. Everything was as it had been during her mother's life.

Francesca was playing on the glossy black and white tiles of the veranda, utterly absorbed with her dolls. Her mother was away in Venice, but that was hardly unusual. Francesca knew she would soon reappear, striding through the house and shaking out her long red hair. Her father's voice would lighten, and the servants would bustle about purposefully as a sign of her arrival. But there had been no sign yet.

One of the servants was brushing a feather duster over the wicker furniture. Francesca suddenly laughed out loud. She was imitating her mother at a party, and her dolls were her guests as well as her audience. She had often watched with fascination from the top of the stairs as Susannah dazzled a roomful of glittering visitors.

"Child, how can you laugh like that?" the servant asked,

her expression one of shock. "Don't you understand that your mama's dead?"

Francesca threw the doll at the servant and cried out as if she had been slapped. Nothing could undo the words that the woman had said, but at least Josie was there to comfort her. She was only seven, two and a half years older then Francesca, yet she hugged her and tried to console her. "Shh, now. That won't do any good."

"Isn't my mother coming back?" Francesca asked her.

Josie, with instinctive sensitivity, didn't answer, and Francesca cried louder. In sympathy Josie began to cry as well.

"My father will bring her home," Francesca protested.

Then Marianne was there, hugging them both. She took Francesca on her lap. "Not even your father can bring someone back from heaven, child," she said in her soft voice. She had avoided telling Francesca the truth. It had been a mistake, but three months after the fact it was still impossible to believe Susannah was gone. Carlo had not come back to tell Francesca himself that her mother was dead, as Marianne had hoped he would. She sighed deeply and, rocking Francesca in her arms, explained to her as gently as possible, answered her unanswerable questions, and held her until she had cried herself to sleep.

A loud knock startled Francesca awake. The graceful chandelier above the bed swayed slightly in the breeze from the open French doors, casting prisms of light on the walls.

Francesca struggled to wakefulness and found Emilio at the door.

"Your father will see you now. He's waiting in the library."

She dismissed him, taking care to hide the mixture of pleasure and fear his words stirred up in her, and put on the only dress she thought suitable for the occasion. Its square neckline seemed too low-cut for daytime, and the full skirt was meant for dancing, but it wasn't too badly wrinkled. It would have to do. She quickly brushed out her hair, then hurried to the library.

Carlo was standing beside his desk when Emilio ushered Francesca into the room. He took off his glasses and studied her distractedly as she walked across the Oriental rug to stand before him. She was like Susannah, of course, alarmingly so in many ways, though the differences were still there. Francesca was more eager to please, less certain of her beauty, more air than fire.

She looked to him like the frail maiden in a medieval tapestry. The shaft of light that fell through the high panes of the tall windows turned her hair to a halo of gold and made her pale blue dress shimmer like water. For a moment he imagined her as a child blinking in the light, and he felt an odd impulse to take her in his arms. But he wasn't sure enough of her for that. She had grown too lovely, and for all her awkwardness, she was a woman now. Every time he encountered his daughter, she presented herself as a stranger all over again.

"Francesca, *cara mia,* how was your trip?" He reached out for one of her hands and clasped it in both of his. It was slim and fragile. She made him think of a statue, her pale, translucent skin as smooth as alabaster. He felt the coolness in her greeting. Was she glad to see him? he wondered. Probably not. Grateful, certainly, for a chance to stay at the palazzo, but glad? No. She hardly knew him, this child he had kept in exile all her life.

He leaned forward and pressed a kiss on her high brow. "You've grown into a lovely woman."

"Thank you, Papa."

"You must be tired from your journey, *piccola.*"

"Josie and I are both rested, Papa."

He offered her a chair near the windows, and as she sat down, the basset hound trundled out from under his desk.

"Oh, Mama's dog!" Francesca clamped her lips shut almost before the words were out, but it was too late. Carlo had seen the excitement in her face.

"No, your mother's dog died a long time ago. This is the last of her puppies. Her name is Hush Puppy," he said. "She is the best dog I have ever had. Go ahead and pet her. She loves attention."

"She looks so sad," Francesca murmured, bending over to stroke the dog's head.

Carlo chuckled. "*Cara,* they all look like that."

Francesca let a ringing laugh escape as the basset rolled over on the carpet and presented her belly for stroking, and Carlo felt himself relax. He had found a way to break through to her after all.

"She has the run of the palazzo," he explained.

"I think she's beautiful."

Carlo looked down at the long-bodied, droopy-eyed basset. "Yes. So do I."

He took a pack of cigarettes from his jacket and tapped one out. The smell of Gauloises filled the air, and Francesca smiled and relaxed a little. She pulled the heavy dog onto her lap. Suddenly it was all so familiar, her father with his thick tortoiseshell glasses that enlarged his kind dark eyes, the sallow face, the long line of his mouth twisting humorously.

She remembered now as a child playing for hours outside the library door while her father was locked inside, murmuring quietly to her doll, waiting for her father to emerge so that he would take her for a ride in a gondola or walk with her to get an ice cream—anything to be with him. At the same time, she feared his attention. But, inevitably, when she heard his step approaching the door she snatched up her doll and ran for the stairs.

He chatted politely for a few minutes, asking about Marianne and about Francesca's graduation from the convent school. "Next year perhaps you would like to study here in Italy. That is, if you haven't forgotten all your Italian," he said, smiling.

"*Mai,* Papa. *Io capisco tutto,* even if I'm not used to speaking it anymore."

"*Bene*. But there is an even more important matter that we must discuss."

"What, Papa? Tell me."

"Your birthday. You'll be eighteen next month and that's the age when a young lady should be presented to society. I thought a ball would be the best way to introduce you to our friends. A ball on your birthday. Do you agree?" he asked, straightfaced.

"A ball? Oh, Father!"

"In your honor, here at the palazzo."

"It's too much! It would be magnificent." She jumped up in excitement, then clapped a hand over her mouth. "But I have nothing to wear, not a thing. Not a dress, or those long white gloves—you see, we can't." As thrilled as she was, she was also terrified.

Carlo dismissed her objection with an amused wave of his hand. "I will take care of everything, Francesca. Your dress, dancing instruction, all that needs to be done. We have plenty of time, but I suspect you would like to get started right away. Am I correct?"

"Yes, Papa."

"All right, then. There is someone I want you to meet now." He reached up and pulled a tasseled bell rope. A moment later the door opened and Emilio entered.

"Emilio, *prego,* bring me Signorina Antonia and Josephine Lapoiret."

The majordomo nodded and left the room, and the count turned back to Francesca. "Antonia is my research assistant. She has been helping me with the catalog for an exhibition of Renaissance art, which will travel to museums all over the world. She's not much older than you are, and I'm sure you'll enjoy spending the afternoon with her. She will take you to a fine dressmaker to be fitted for a ball gown. Then she will show you around Venice. You may take Josephine with you." He drew a hand through his hair. "I would escort you myself, but I have a deadline to meet."

"I understand, Papa." Francesca smiled wryly. She'd had long years of practice at hearing her father say he had no time for her. His excuses for keeping her away from him were so familiar that she no longer wondered how valid they were.

"I want to show you a list of the people I've invited to the ball." He was rummaging through the papers on his desk, looking for the list, muttering to himself, thinking that the guest list was the sort of detail Susannah would have handled effortlessly.

Susannah, in fact, would have delighted in preparing her daughter for the ball—teaching her to dance, taking her for fittings, coaching her in the social graces that were expected of a young woman of Francesca's standing. Carlo sighed softly. No need to dwell on what might have been. Such a shy, awkward child, he thought. Would she even be able to cope with something as simple as a reception line? Well, he had hired a good coach, a gentlewoman whose fortune had dwindled, but who could turn this frightened girl into a countess in time for the gala.

"Ah, here is the list! You see how long it is, *cara?* I've invited half of Europe to meet you—the important half. I want you to familiarize yourself with these names, and over dinner I'll discuss them with you."

"Discuss them?"

"Of course! Who they are, their families, what they've done, so you'll know what topics of conversation to choose, which guests you should bring together or keep apart, who their enemies are—a ball is full of intrigues and possibilities, you know. And I'm going to depend on you to make it run smoothly."

"Oh, no, Papa. I'll disappoint you," she blurted out before she could stop herself.

He smiled at her. "I know you're shy, *cara mia*. You must take after me. Your mother was the gregarious one."

So that was it; Francesca understood at last. He wanted her to take Susannah's place as mistress of the palazzo and hostess of the Nordonia social gatherings, but he was afraid she would prove unequal to such a challenge. Perhaps he was right, she admitted silently. Perhaps she would never be as confident and dazzling as her mother had been . . . but she could certainly try.

She looked into her father's worried face and felt her spine stiffen. Maybe she could never make him proud of her, but she knew she had to make the attempt.

"Show me the list, Papa," she said, forcing her voice to remain strong and steady. "By tonight I'll know it backwards and forwards."

Before he could answer, the heavy door swung open and Antonia entered. She had gone home to change. She was now dressed appropriately for her role as the count's assistant in a tailored skirt and blouse. She approached them and regarded father and daughter gravely.

Her father was right; the girl was not much older than she was, but she had the serious demeanor of an older woman.

Francesca held out her hand. "*Piacere*, Antonia," she said, feigning a regal confidence she did not feel.

"*Piacere*, Francesca," Antonia said. Her voice was surprisingly deep.

"Antonia is an expert on the glories of Venice," Carlo told her. "She also knows many of its darkest secrets. You could not have a better guide."

"We could start here in this room," Antonia began brightly. "Has your father shown you his sketches by Leonardo, or Palladio's architectural folio? The palazzo is a museum in itself, you know."

"First you should take her to Renata for her fitting," Carlo said. "You can show her around the palazzo after you return."

Francesca thought it strange that her father never looked directly at Antonia when he spoke, yet they seemed vitally aware of each other.

Josie walked into the room, and the uncomfortable tension broke.

"Josephine Lapoiret, how good to see you," said Carlo, striding toward her. As she stood smiling in the circle of sunlight on the thick carpet, she seemed part of its delicate and exotic design. She took in the room with its patterns of sun and shadow, its rows of leather-bound volumes, and then turned her attention to the count.

"Antonia," he said, "this is Josephine, my daughter's maid and traveling companion."

At the word "maid," a leaden silence fell over the room. Josie blinked and then stiffened. Francesca was stunned into speechlessness, her father's words echoing in her mind: *my daughter's maid . . .*

Sensing the reason for their shock, Antonia carefully changed the subject. "We should leave right away. We must be at Renata's shop in one hour. I'll take you along the side streets, so you can see the real Venice."

"I must get back to work on the catalog," Carlo announced dismissively. "Do you need anything before you leave?"

"The guest list," Francesca said. "I want to take it with me." Her father handed her the list, and after kissing him coolly on the cheek, she bent down to give the basset hound a good-bye pat. Then she turned to her lifelong friend. "Are you ready, Josie?"

She knew the count had hurt Josie deeply, but this was neither the time nor the place to talk about it. "Imagine, Josie. A ball gown designed especially for me!"

In a gesture that was both defiant and sympathetic, she put one arm around Josie's shoulders and led her out of the room.

Antonia followed them into the corridor, throwing Carlo a withering look before she closed the door.

"Go without me, *p'tite soeur,*" Josie said shakily. "I feel as if I should stay here."

"My father's old-fashioned," Francesca assured her. "He doesn't understand that you and I are best friends."

Antonia took Josie's hand and pulled her along the marble corridor. "You *must* come with us, Josie. I have in mind the exact shop in which we shall buy you a gown for the ball as well."

"We're abducting you." Francesca laughed. "You have

no choice, so come along or we'll have to use force."
Francesca reached down and pinched Josie's bottom.

Far down the hall, Emilio winced at the shrieks and giggles that followed. Everyone in the palazzo—the major-domo, the other servants, and Count Carlo Nordonia himself—paused momentarily to listen to the sound. It had been a long time since they had heard shouts of laughter in these corridors. Too long.

Chapter Three

ANTONIA LED HER two charges through a maze of streets as crazily mapped as the lines on the palm of a hand. Francesca had no conscious memory of this side of Venice, its dark, medieval alleys where the night fog that rolled from the sea was still trapped at midday, and yet she seemed to know her way. The sunlight could not penetrate these narrow passageways, and the worn facades with their secretive window slits held a clammy chill. Time had also been trapped here; for all the centuries that had intervened since these fortress walls were raised from the moat of the lagoon, they might still mask the terrors of the plagues or the treason of scheming doges.

They rounded a corner and found themselves on a narrow street cluttered with attached buildings. Antonia stopped short and looked around in confusion. "I thought I knew this shortcut, but all of a sudden, nothing looks familiar. I hope I haven't gotten you both lost!" She turned and looked behind her at a maze of alleys that curved away from the stone pathway they had followed.

But Francesca had the opposite sensation. This ancient quarter of Venice felt like a country in a dream where she knew every brick, every doorway.

Her feet knew their way over the stones, and she confidently took the lead.

Toni put a hand on her arm. "Wait, Francesca, don't go any farther in that direction. I don't think it's the right way. Maybe we should stop and ask for help."

"No, no. It *is* the way, I'm sure of it."

"The way to Renata's?"

"No, the way through this maze. I must have been here many times when I was a child. I know the way with my eyes closed." And she reached out her arms like a sleepwalker and led her hesitant companions down a back alley that opened onto yet another pinched corridor.

"Follow me," she said as she began to run.

Antonia and Josie had no choice but to run after her; not wanting to be deserted in this strange place, they trailed along. Ahead of them Francesca's hair beckoned them onward like a bright flag against the dark gray stone walls that closed them in. But Antonia felt Josie's reluctance like a brake holding them back. She looked at the girl's solemn face and realized just how deeply Carlo's harsh remark had cut into her feelings.

"Hurry, Josie!" she said cheerfully, catching her cold hand. "This is no place for you to get left behind."

Ahead of them Francesca was overcome with a strong, peculiar sense of déjà vu. She suddenly remembered her mother leading her urgently by her hand, cased in its delicate white glove. "Do you want to see the woman with the pigeons?" she had said, pulling Francesca along as fast as her legs could carry her. Why had her mother led her so many times through this maze? And today Francesca was as breathless and all atremble as she had been then, as if she were still under the influence of her mother's mood, as if Susannah, her mother, ran just ahead of her.

Francesca turned a corner and stopped. Through a low archway came a blaze of light, and the little group emerged into a piazza bathed in brilliant late-morning sunlight and filled with waddling pigeons. Above their heads hung row upon row of broad arched windows brightened by scarlet geraniums, and behind the tall houses white streamers of laundry snapped in the sea breeze. Stumbling into the strong sunlight, they were momentarily blinded. This was one of Venice's oldest piazzas. A low marble fountain, the stone worn as soap, played merrily in its center.

As a child, Francesca had pressed her fists to her eyes at the shock of the sun, but today she was blinded by the light of memory, by a flood of images of her mother gliding across the stone piazza. This had been Susannah's favorite spot, a hidden and secret meeting place. Susannah would scan the pale, elegant facades of the houses as if to make sure no one watched them, and then she would lead Francesca to the benches that circled the pretty fountain. An older woman would be waiting on one of the benches scattering bread crumbs to the cooing pigeons that tottered over the uneven stones, which formed a delicate Byzantine design around the fountain.

The woman would always greet them silently by handing them some crusts of bread. Francesca remembered the day she grew brave enough to allow the pigeons to peck at the crust in her hand. When she reached out to touch the bobbing white head of one of the birds, it squawked in anger and fluttered away. She remembered the silvery cascade of her mother's laughter, her sudden confident happiness. And the strange woman's throaty voice: "Be careful that fat one doesn't bite your hand, child. He'd just as soon eat fingers as bread."

"This place is beautiful," Josie now said in wonder. "However did you find it?"

"My mother brought me here so many times I could find my way just by trailing my fingers along the walls in the dark."

Francesca looked around her, marveling at the scene. It was all so familiar—the air pure as water, a faint scent of the sea, the clean laundry streaming across the sky, windows decked with bold-colored geraniums.

"If only that woman were still here."

"What woman?"

"A friend my mother always came to meet. I don't know her name." She remembered seeing their fingers interlaced. Friends who barely spoke, who seemed to understand each other with a glance.

After a while, mother and daughter would rise and pass through the hot sunlight to the narrow archway, on a walk home that was leisurely and calm.

Suddenly Antonia broke into her musing. "We must hurry now to Renata's. She's very much—how would you say? —Old World. It's no good to be late with such a one. *Andiamo.*"

As Toni herded them forward, Josie and Francesca both insisted on buying postcards.

"They are for Marianne," Francesca explained, "Josie's mother."

Antonia looked from one to the other in exasperation. In the face of such splendor all they could think of was sending postcards home, like any other tourist. Was it possible that Francesca, this awkward girl still caught up on memories of her childhood, was really Carlo's daughter? She was pretty,

Antonia admitted, and she had the fine, elongated bone structure of an aristocrat, but she was impossibly awkward and self-conscious. Josephine Lapoiret, on the other hand, was at ease with her body and her exotic beauty.

When they stopped to buy postcards at an open stand, a small boy chased a red ball among the three of them and lost it in the tangle of their feet. Francesca picked it up and handed it to him. In surprise he let his eyes follow her long frame to her face, and dissolved into giggles. "*Una giraffa!*" he cried.

The child's remark broke through Josie's mood, and she burst into laughter.

Francesca turned to her in dismay. "How can you laugh, Josie? He called me a *giraffe!*"

"But Italian men love giraffes," Toni said placatingly. She took both girls by the elbow and tugged them forward. Renata's place was not far.

What an odd trio, Antonia thought as she marched them along: Francesca . . . an innocent abroad in her own birthplace, whose ancestors had ruled this city for a thousand years. What potential lay in those ancient bloodlines. And the mulatto, Josie, who imagined herself Francesca's equal; her sunny, simple personality had already suffered a culture shock. As for herself, Toni thought, she exemplified the liberated Italian woman. She, at least, was as free as anyone could be to direct her own destiny.

Soon the skein of little streets and canals opened on Campo San Fantin, a tiny square behind the Teatro La Fenice. Across the plaza between two shops was a narrow gateway nearly hidden from the street. Toni pushed open the iron gate and led her two wards along a roofed passageway to an enclosed garden, which quietly thrived in the sunlight. Unlike the showy display of Venice proper, this garden was private and untended, a little corner of Mediterranean wilderness. Beyond it stood a tiny two-story house of faded yellow stucco, its arcade of stone columns rising out of the wild garden. Thick ocher walls surrounded the property.

Francesca stepped forward, delighted. The garden was in full bloom, a riot of white flowers that were almost tropical in their snowy profusion. The arcade was lined with enormous terra-cotta pots of day lilies blooming in the sun. Jubilantly she turned to Josie, who nodded her approval.

"It smells so sweet, like home."

"Venice has many kinds of beauty," Antonia said, leading them along a curved stone path to the terrace. "But I must warn you about the dressmaker. Renata is a bit of a recluse, and we mustn't upset her. She rarely takes on new clients anymore, but she wanted to fit you as a favor to your mother. It was the contessa who made Renata famous."

"My mother?" Francesca restrained Toni's hand from knocking on the little blue door. "How? Tell me."

"Renata trained with Fortuny, who was a Venetian, and in his day the most famous dress designer in the world. When he retired, the contessa wore Renata's designs exclusively. It brought Renata to the attention of the *haute monde*. She had very few clients, just a handful of the most famous women in the world, and your mother made that possible. Then"—here Toni paused, cautious about mentioning Susannah's death—"Renata went into semiretirement. Princess Grace still wears her dresses, and also Jacqueline Kennedy, but Renata no longer issues collections every year. Many of her earlier dresses are now museum pieces." Toni turned and knocked. Then she added, "You're very lucky, Francesca. Renata truly loved your mother. She practically lived at the palazzo, and often she flew all the way to the Bahamas to fit her."

The door finally opened on a tiny woman whose deeply lined face was the color of a walnut. She wore a neat black dress, its only ornament a tape measure that dangled around her neck. Her graying hair was scraped back into a severe chignon. But her eyes weren't old. They were cool gray under their deep hoods, and they were filled with an infinite, shrewd wisdom. Before those assessing eyes, Francesca felt too tall, too thin, and too awkward. Yet the woman was smiling kindly as she beckoned the three visitors inside.

"*Benvenuto,* Contessina. I am Renata. I have been expecting you for years."

As she drew them into her cluttered workroom, Francesca was overwhelmed with the feeling that she had seen Renata before. Something about the look of deep concentration in the woman's eyes rang true and familiar to her.

"We've met before," Francesca said. It was not a question.

"Many times, but I am surprised that you remember. You were a very small child the last time I saw you, but even then I knew you would grow up to be beautiful, like your mother." She gestured Francesca toward a large mirror in an ornate Victorian frame. "Let me see you in the light." She pulled back the heavy draperies and let the sunlight pour into the fitting room. After studying Francesca from several angles, she went to a partly open door at one end of the room. "Maria," she called, "kindly bring us some coffee."

A young assistant entered the room bearing a tray. While Antonia helped her serve coffee Renata began a slow, twisting dance around Francesca, who was still struggling with her memory. When had she felt the brush of those hands before? If she could only remember, perhaps she could also summon up some image of her mother, who must have stood in this spot, before this very mirror, countless times.

While Renata continued to study her, Francesca looked around the workroom. The studio was alive with color, filled with velvet and satin and bolts of silk and cashmere, tended by headless dummies and cluttered with the tools of Renata's trade. The dressmaker's strong hands traced patterns in the air, as if imagining Francesca in this design or that. Finally she partially unrolled several bolts of fabric in different shades of white and placed the ends on Francesca's arm, then her face, testing the colors against her pale skin.

"I have it, Contessina. Now please be so kind as to step behind the screen and take off your dress."

While Francesca undressed, Renata turned to the other young women. Josephine, the more spectacular of the two, demanded her complete attention. She looked older and more sophisticated than Francesca, perhaps also more aware of her unusually striking beauty. The full, well-shaped lips, the wide amber eyes, the café-au-lait skin, and the finely modeled face made Renata wonder if this young woman would someday be a professional beauty—an actress, perhaps? Certainly she was too short to be a model, more's the pity. A mixture of races had produced in this one an exotic beauty that spoke of earthy sensuousness in sharp contrast to the ethereal loveliness of Susannah Nordonia's daughter.

When Renata let her eyes drift from Josie to Antonia, she felt a small, knowing smile tug at the corners of her mouth. A small, slim girl with a boy's narrow hips, she was dressed plainly, but even so, Renata admitted, with such style! From the clean planes of her small face to the careless swing of her trim hips to the tilt of her high breasts, this was a young woman who begged to be touched. So Carlo still had a weakness for lean, athletic women, she thought. Some things never changed.

She turned as Francesca came out from behind the screen in her white cotton underpants, trying to cover her breasts with her folded arms. "That little boy was right," she said as she stepped up on the small dais in front of the mirror. "I *do* look like a giraffe."

Renata chuckled, studying her figure with the eye of a sculptor. "Yes, Contessina, a beautiful, willowy giraffe who will turn into a swan when she wears my dress to her ball."

Accepting Francesca's grateful smile with a slight nod, Renata whipped her tape measure from around her neck and called for her assistant to write down the figures as she called them out. As the sun passed overhead, the room grew hushed and shadows played in the corners where the dummies clustered like sheaves of cut flowers, drooping in the cool shade. Francesca hugged her breasts in the chill; then, at Renata's command, she dropped her arms and straightened her spine. Through the dust motes, the huge mirror reflected the pale luster of her cleft back, the delicate pattern of her ribs through the fabric of skin.

Renata, finished at last with her measuring, disappeared through a small green door and returned bearing a bolt of creamy silk almost as big as she was. This fabric would be perfect—no strong, vivid colors for this little countess. Her features and her complexion were understated and delicate, like her personality. She had none of her mother's flamboyance. Ivory silk would be cameo-perfect. Unrolling a length of the luxurious fabric on the work table, she held one end up to Francesca's body.

"This is what I see you in," she said. "A low-cut bodice that will bare those lovely shoulders, a bell-shaped skirt with a dropped waist to show off your slimness. The hem of the skirt will be caught up lightly with a bow here and there." She put the fabric down and made a sweeping circular gesture with both hands. "And everywhere seed pearls. Thousands of seed pearls. You will be a vision, my dear, even more exquisite than your mother!"

She dismissed Francesca's sputter of disbelief. Clearly the child was unused to being favorably compared with her spectacular mother. But Renata sensed in her a tremendously appealing softness and vulnerability that the glorious Susannah had never possessed.

If only she could speak more openly to this girl about her mother. But some secrets, she knew, were meant to be kept forever. She tore her mind away from the past and began to work in earnest, racing against the fading light.

At a sign from Renata, the assistant carried off the bolt of gleaming material. She brought back a roll of muslin, which Renata quickly unwound and cut into sections. Then, her mouth bristling with pins, she quickly placed the pieces over Francesca's body so that the gown took substance before them.

"Turn now."

Bewildered, Francesca revolved slowly before the mirror. She had wanted a garment spun of Renata's absolute confidence, an armor of beauty that would shield her at the ball. Instead, she stood revealed and vulnerable in this wispy, nearly transparent dress, the gossamer film of a ghost, through which her legs showed. The pins circled her waist like a belt of tiny daggers. Under Renata's nimble fingers she felt her body being prepared for some perilous ritual she didn't yet understand.

Outside the sun wheeled away. The room stood eclipsed in shadow now. "*Finito, bella,*" said Renata. The assistant quickly began to remove the muslin shroud with her cold hands.

"You may get dressed."

Francesca stepped into the roomy alcove behind the screen and scrambled into her clothes. As she turned to leave, her eye fell on a leather portfolio tucked under the window seat. It was embossed with a gold Florentine design, and in the center, in elegant scrollwork, was Renata's name. Francesca sat down and opened the book. Encased in transparent plastic were drawings of dresses with swatches of fabric, signed and dated from the 1950s. On the facing pages were photographs of beautiful movie stars and socialites wearing the elegant gowns and tailored suits. There was Princess Grace before her marriage in a traveling ensemble, and on a facing page Princess Margaret in a regal gown. Francesca stopped at a full-page photograph of two oddly matched women entering an elegant room. Their eyes were dazed and happy. One gazed defiantly into the camera; the other looked serenely beyond it. That woman, Francesca realized with a thrill of surprise, was her mother. She and her friend were dressed exactly alike in matching sequined sheaths, but Susannah's was pure white and the other woman's was solid black. Behind them photographers juggled elaborate paraphernalia.

Francesca studied the picture intently. The woman in black was younger than her mother—a girl, really—and her arm was thrown around Susannah's shoulders. It seemed a spontaneous gesture of affection but something about it arrested Francesca's eye. The woman's possessive posture and defiant expression seemed strangely familiar.

"Renata, I've found a picture of my mother wearing one of your dresses," Francesca called. She picked up the portfolio and carried it out to the seamstress, who was talking animatedly to Toni and Josie. "When was this taken, signorina?"

Renata took the book from Francesca's hands just as footsteps sounded in another room, as of someone running urgently toward the back of the little house. Francesca looked up, startled, but when Renata said nothing, she decided that perhaps Maria, the assistant, had run to the kitchen or the back garden on some important errand.

Renata paled slightly and then tried to laugh. "Such a dreadful picture," she said dismissively. "Taken at a silly costume party. I don't know why I've kept it all these years." She closed the album abruptly and set it down on a table. "At one time I had many truly beautiful pictures of your mother, my dear. But right now it is late, and I am very tired."

"Oh, please," Francesca pleaded, "just tell me the name of the other woman in the photograph. She looks so familiar to me."

"So many years ago, Contessina," the dressmaker said. "She was just a nobody. I have no memory of her at all." She clapped her hands for her assistant. "Clear away the materials, Maria. I shall go to the Palazzo Nordonia in a few days for you to have a fitting."

With surprising strength for one so tiny, Renata herded the three young women toward the front door and out into the garden, promising once again to come to the palazzo during the next few days.

"How odd," Antonia said when they were out of earshot.

Francesca thought that if given another moment or two she might have recognized the woman with her mother in the picture.

Toni shot Francesca a look. She found their dismissal abrupt, even rude. The dressmaker had practically thrown them out. No wonder Carlo seemed reserved about Renata when he spoke of her, his voice banked with as much fear as respect.

As they passed the cathedral of San Marco in all its glory and crossed the *piazzetta* on the lagoon, Francesca suddenly looked up and saw the winged lion standing high up on his pillar.

"That's the lion, Josie! My favorite, the one I told you about."

"Ah yes," Toni interrupted, "the lion of San Marco who carries the good souls who die in Venice to heaven."

Francesca laughed delightedly. "He only flies at night; my mother used to tell me that story." Suddenly she was overwhelmed with memories of herself and Susannah: hot afternoons sitting in the outdoor café letting her chocolate ice cream slowly melt in her mouth, as she stared up at the winged lion visualizing him flying toward the moon. Did he stretch his great paws out in front of him or did he tuck them under? she wondered. Did the dead person ride on his back? Francesca wanted to ask her mother a thousand questions but Susannah would be leaning back in her chair smoking, squinting a little in the sun, dreaming her own dreams; and Francesca didn't like to interrupt. Nevertheless she had felt very close to her mother those rare times they had been alone together.

When the three came to Calle Vallaresso, Josie found her own perfect dress. For Venetians who love beautiful clothes, the narrow street between Harry's Bar and the Hotel Monaco on the Grand Canal is where the heart of Venice beats. Here the finest shops in Europe display their wares in a peacock's iridescent display of wealth. Josie's somber mood had been completely dispelled by the delicious tortellini at Florian's outdoor café, and now her spirits soared. She and Francesca pressed their noses to the store windows like children hugging the bars at a zoo, tantalized by the dangerous and beautiful animals within. But Francesca held back at Missoni's door.

"No, don't be silly!" Antonia pushed her toward the door. "You must have a proper wardrobe for your life here in Venice. The count wants you to spend plenty of his money so he can be proud of you." She had been relieved to find that Francesca wasn't spoiled, but the girl's timidity had begun to wear on her. She was baffled by the contessina's unwillingness to claim what was due to her. Antonia herself, although merely a member of the striving middle class, had been more confident of her own worth as a toddler than Francesca was as a young woman.

With the able assistance of the infinitely self-confident Josephine, Toni finally talked Francesca into buying a Missoni skirt and sweater of a beautiful gold knit that brought out the gold in her hair and, at another store, several simple cotton dresses for daytime wear. Antonia would present the count's card, and the salesmen would cart the boxes out to the canal, where the Nordonia gondola awaited them. Meanwhile, Josie browsed among exotic gowns of glittering sequins, rich brocade, and gleaming satin, unable to choose precisely the right dress for the ball. Antonia had struggled to keep a straight face when she sauntered out of a dressing room wearing a floor-length sheath that sparkled with Venetian beads.

"It's beautiful, Josie!" Francesca insisted.

"Too gaudy for the count's ball," Antonia decreed.

"Next, please," said Josie.

"Surely you don't need to try on every dress in the store, Josie," Toni remarked.

"Yes, I do. This may be my only chance to play the princess."

"Come, then," Toni offered. "I'll take you to a shop where you're sure to find the perfect gown."

The promised shop specialized in ball gowns, and it was shockingly expensive. When Toni presented the count's card and indicated that she was looking for a ballgown for Josie, the salesman leaped to the conclusion that the beautiful girl was the count's daughter.

"Contessa Nordonia, I am greatly honored that you have chosen to wear one of my gowns. All Venice is preparing for your ball. *Che onore!*"

Josie and Francesca exchanged a look. Josie lifted an eyebrow and replied haughtily, "Yes. I'm inviting all my closest friends, so of course I must have the most beautiful gown you have to offer."

The man didn't recognize Josie's pretentiousness as poor acting, and with a hurried, "But, of course," he scurried around the racks. He returned with a handsome white gown. Josie eyed it with disdain.

"Too pale and conventional," she said, flattening the Bahamian lilt in her voice.

"But Countess, to be presented to society, it is customary—"

"Show me something in red."

"But, Contessina, surely for your presentation—"

"*Red*," Josie said.

The bewildered salesman disappeared and soon returned with a silk dress the color of raspberries, which he presented rather tentatively. But there was nothing tentative about the gown's style and shade. The deep red enhanced the tawny velvet of Josie's complexion. The design was both romantic and bold. Its tightly fitted bodice was softened by a ruffled neckline and bell-shaped sleeves that were gathered at the wrist.

"Oh, Francesca," Josie cried, forgetting about her ruse, "isn't it gorgeous?" She held the dress up in front of her. "It's the most beautiful dress I've ever laid eyes on."

The salesman, wary now, looked at her as if he thought she intended to steal it. He even tried to take it away, but Toni restrained him. The gown was a bit more expensive than Toni had expected—after all, she didn't have Carlo's permission—but once she saw Josie swirling in the full skirt in front of the mirror, she didn't have the heart to tell her to send it back. It was wrapped and dispatched to the waiting gondola.

The girls followed the package out of the store with a new sense of self-importance. Francesca pointed out an expensive pair of crocodile shoes in the store window, but Josie pulled her away instead to a gelato stand. Their newfound glamour quickly disappeared behind a couple of large chocolate ice cream cones.

Antonia looked at her watch uncomfortably. Emilio himself was waiting in the Nordonia gondola to escort them back to the palazzo, and she knew he had little patience with women's weakness for shopping. Anxiously she nudged Francesca and Josie toward the landing where, to her dismay, they found the majordomo wearing his most theatrical scowl.

He'd had every intention of scolding them for making him wait so long, but one look at their childlike excitement and he was charmed out of his anger. He also realized that Francesca and Josie would not be appearing together as friends in public for much longer. He had heard, on the palazzo grapevine, the story of Carlo's harsh introduction of Josie as a maid and lady's companion, and Emilio commiserated with her. She and Francesca were like the count and himself when they were boys together, a lifetime ago. He watched Josie drape an arm around Francesca as if they were still girls in Nassau. Neither of them understood yet. But Josie would be made to feel her place soon, and there would be no more larks like this shopping trip. Let her enjoy it. There would never be another.

Josie, thrilled to be taking her first ride in a gondola, charged toward the landing and scrambled recklessly into the graceful boat. Behind her, Francesca stepped gingerly aboard after handing her packages to Vieri, a household servant who also served as Carlo's gondolier.

As the gondola glided easily through the watery streets, Antonia pointed ahead to the beautiful Renaissance church of Santa Maria della Salute. "Look there! Can you see all those people in front of the church? They are making a movie. Isn't it exciting?"

A thick cluster of boats clotted the canal in front of the church as people looked at the odd scaffolds that had been erected at the water's edge. Huge cameras were positioned along the quay, and men were scrambling up the scaffolds to rig lights. Actors in full eighteenth-century regalia fanned themselves in front of the church while the countless stage-hands below them struggled to cover the water with billowing green plastic. "For the movies, real water isn't good enough," Toni explained. High on a scaffold, a thickset man with a lined, dramatic face barked orders through a megaphone.

Antonia said he was one of Italy's foremost directors; he had come to Venice to make an elaborate costume film based on the story of Casanova. For the project, the director had assembled an international cast that included several of the most famous stars in the world.

"No wonder the canal is jammed full of boats," Josie commented. "Look at those gorgeous costumes."

"Who is that beautiful woman?" Francesca asked, pointing to a shapely actress who was dressed in an extremely low-cut gown.

"That's Nadia Baldini. You must have heard of her. She's our most famous actress after Sophia Loren." Toni indicated a tall, blond man who stood talking to the actress, his face turned away from the canal. "There's the actor who's playing Casanova. Wait until he turns around; you won't have to ask who he is!"

Vieri managed to move the boat forward, away from the traffic jam, and it jutted so close to the scaffold that Francesca caught sight of the strikingly handsome man's blue eyes as he turned from the actress. She grabbed Josie's arm and cried excitedly, "It's Jack Westman!"

Josie shrieked and lunged toward the back of the boat.

Francesca scrambled along behind her so frantically that the two of them nearly succeeded in capsizing the gondola.

Emilio was thrown across a seat, losing both his balance and his dignity. By the time he had regained his footing, he was infuriated. He swore violently under his breath. Francesca and her friend had attracted almost as much attention as the actors. The majordomo, regretting his decision to allow Vieri to come in closer to the church, looked for a way out of the traffic.

"Who would ever dream that we'd find the most gorgeous man in America right here in Italy!" Josie exclaimed.

"I can't believe this," Francesca chimed in. "It's really, really him! Vieri, pull us closer. Hurry."

Suddenly the girls fell silent. Toni saw why: Westman had noticed them and returned their stare. Josie reclined on an elbow self-consciously and Francesca dissolved in blushes and sank low in her seat. Westman was staring so hard that Francesca had the sensation that his eyes were pulling her closer.

In fact, the boat was jutting forward just beneath the scaffolding. It was the only path out of the jam; the boats behind them had blocked any other exit. Tony knew Vieri was only trying to get them away from the church as quickly as possible, but he was drawing them deeper into trouble.

There was a strange intensity in the American's stare. It made Toni nervous and she laughed uneasily. Luckily Emilio was still unaware of what was going on just over his head. Busily supervising Vieri's attempts to slip the boat around the jam, he missed the man's blatant stare. The actor stared at the count's daughter as if she had just robbed him and he meant to catch her before she got any farther away.

Westman shouted at the director and pointed to the gondola below. "Paulo, look, the blond! She's the extra for the church scene. The Madonna you've been looking for!"

Emilio looked up in alarm. His face became a mask of fury, as if some strange older man had insulted his own daughter. "Vieri! *Presto*."

The director glanced over his shoulder at the young woman in the swaying gondola. Then he turned full face and squinted as if to evaluate Francesca through the lens of a camera. "Hire her!" he shouted.

Francesca held her head high. "He means *me*," she whispered. She clutched at Josie's hand as all the muscles in her body tensed.

Ignoring Emilio's protestations, Josie raised Francesca's hand and held it high in the air. "She accepts!" Josie cried.

A roar echoed across the traffic jam. Passengers in the neighboring boats who had witnessed the impromptu audition had begun to cheer.

Appalled, Emilio reached for the girls' hands and pulled them down. "For shame, Contessina! Remember yourself." Then he turned and glowered at Vieri, who was poling frantically to free them, and at last making some progress. The boat shot forward.

Francesca watched, fascinated, as Jack Westman leaped from the scaffolding, jumped into a boat, and tried to pursue them, using the swaying gondolas as stepping stones. Their amazed passengers roared with delight as he hopped from one precariously tipping boat to the next. The actor was agile, but Vieri was faster. Urged forward by Emilio's outraged bellowing, he soon left Westman far behind. "Stay, *bella ragazza*. Let the American catch you."

Josie was chattering excitedly about the thrill of the chase, but Francesca sat as if mesmerized, unable to take her eyes off the handsome actor even when they had left him so far behind that she could no longer see his face.

Chapter Four

JOSIE WAS STANDING before the mirror in her bedroom holding her new evening dress up in front of her when a brisk knock made her turn sharply toward the door. "It's open," she called, expecting a visit from Francesca.

Emilio stepped inside the room, looking uncomfortable. "It's time for supper, signorina."

"I'll get Francesca."

"No," he said gravely. "You and the contessina will be dining separately."

For a moment Josie thought he meant they would be served dinner in their rooms. That seemed wildly informal for the palazzo, which was a thicket of rules and barbarous propriety. Yet Emilio had said "supper."

Josie stared at the majordomo in stunned disbelief as her mind grappled with the situation. Emilio, she realized, was trying to tell her that she was to eat her meal, not with Francesca and her father, but with Emilio, Vieri, and the other household servants. Slowly and carefully, she spread the crimson ball gown out on the bed, then faced the majordomo. She could feel the heat of embarrassment burning in her face. How she had looked forward to eating dinner at the long, formal table in the ornate dining room, being served by Carlo's army of servants, chatting with Francesca and the count about the afternoon of shopping. She glanced down at the pretty floral-print cotton dress she had put on for the occasion. Her mother had designed and sewed it especially for the trip to Venice. Now, after having seen Renata's creations and the dresses displayed in the gleaming boutiques on the Calle Vallaresso, the simple print seemed crudely made, almost shabby. If only Marianne had known what she was sending her daughter to! Josie suspected that as a servant she would have no need of pretty dresses, and wondered if the next insult served up to her would be a cap and a trim black uniform.

"I'm not hungry," she said proudly.

"Please," Emilio urged. "You must eat. The food is delicious. And we are not such bad company." He gave her a warm smile, and Josie suddenly wanted to fling herself against his chest and cry. Instead she stepped out the door ahead of him.

"Oh, there you are!" Francesca called from across the hallway. "I left my door open just to hear you practice your guitar. I never heard you play that piece with so much expression."

Josie stood not six feet from Francesca, but could see only her outline against the blur of light from the doorway. It was as if the corridor were a mile wide.

"Where are you going? Did you come to tell us dinner is ready, Emilio?" Francesca asked, her voice gaining urgency as she saw the pained look on Josie's face.

"No," Josie said stonily. "He only came for me. Your father has decided that I'm not fit to eat with you anymore."

"Oh, Josie, no. Emilio, she's having dinner with us."

Emilio turned red and shrugged slightly. "Contessina, what does it matter? This is life in the palazzo; your father does not mean any harm."

"But Josie's my guest."

"Contessina, *prego*—"

"I won't stand for it."

"Never mind, Francesca," Josie said. "I'm leaving tomorrow. That will settle the matter."

"Leave?" Alarmed, Francesca interrupted, "Leave, don't be silly, you can't leave. What about the ball . . . your beautiful dress . . ." Seeing Josie's air of stubborn determination, Francesca went on desperately, "Look, I bet I can get my father to let you sing at the ball." Francesca brushed past Emilio and went to Josie's side. "My father simply doesn't understand that we're such close friends. He didn't mean to hurt you. I know he wants you to stay, and so do I."

"No, I've got to go."

"I'll straighten it out with my father tonight, and he'll treat you like royalty tomorrow. Think how wonderful that would be if you could sing at the ball! I can't let you go now, not when we've got the whole world at our feet." Francesca gripped Josie's hand.

It was true. Josie thought she ought to give Francesca a chance to explain their friendship to Carlo. "You're right, *p'tite soeur*. How could I give up the chance to dance the night away in that red dress?" Josie pressed both of Francesca's hands in hers. "No, I won't desert you. I know you'll make him see . . ."

Francesca kissed her. Josie drew a deep breath and turned back to the confused Emilio. He clearly hated to upset his young female charges. She gave him a forgiving smile and let him lead her away from Francesca.

As she followed Emilio down the stone staircase that twisted along the outside wall of the courtyard, she forced herself to consider her position unemotionally. All her life she had accepted the fact that, in Nassau, her mother was the count's housekeeper—his servant—and that Francesca, in reality, was not her *p'tite soeur* at all, but Carlo's aristocratic daughter.

To be sure, Josie and her mother had not dined with Carlo when he was at Lyford Cay. The thought of doing so, in fact, would not have occurred to Josie, who had never sought the company of the solitary and aloof Count Nordonia. And yet here in Venice, she had expected him to treat her as his daughter's equal. Her mother's words of warning—that things would be different in Venice—came back to Josie as Emilio led her into the servants' dining room behind the tremendous kitchen. Marianne had been trying to prepare her for this . . . this humiliation, which she had no choice but to accept for the present at least.

Five servants were sitting at a large oak table when Emilio and Josie entered the room. Each bowed graciously when the majordomo made the introductions, and Josie, in spite of herself, was pleased at their friendly acceptance of her. In Nassau, she suddenly realized, these people would have been her friends. Vieri gave her a wink as Emilio led her past him to an empty chair. Augustus, the man beside her, was old. He had warm brown skin and curly gray hair.

"You must be from back home," she said.

Augustus laughed delightedly and answered her in English. "I am from Nassau, sure enough, girl. I know your mama, that pretty Marianne. And you as pretty as she, in a flowered dress!"

Josie was warmed by the rippling island accent. "How long have you been here?"

Like a child he held up the fingers of both hands. "Ten,

more twelve years—I lose count. I am with the count after Countess Susannah died. What a sad time that was! I'll never forget that year."

"I remember it, too," Josie said.

"You were just a grasshopper then." He smiled broadly, but then the smile faded. "Long time here, Lord." He shook his head.

Josie silently finished the thought for him: *In this cold place. In the sun's shadow instead of its glory.* In spite of the welcoming faces, she felt a heavy sadness settle over her. Looking at the old man, she wondered how long she was destined to remain in this Venetian exile. Her gaze wandered from his gray hair to his knotted hands, and she shivered. What was this twist the course of her life had taken, and how could it be undone?

Francesca nervously waited for her father to come down to dinner. She used the time to rehearse a speech about Josie, but the entrance of a servant stopped her short. The stout woman lit the large silver candelabras at the ends of the long mahogany banquet table, and two silver peacocks seemed to leap out of the darkness. In a moment the servant left the room and almost immediately reappeared, carrying a water pitcher.

Distracted now, Francesca examined the tapestries that lined the walls. Antonia had explained that they presented an illustrated history of Venice, but by the soft light of the candles their detail dissolved into a blur of gold and red. It occurred to her that she didn't know a fraction of what Toni did about her father's city. Antonia was native; but then, so was she.

Footsteps echoed on the hard marble floor of the grand hallway. The palazzo was a landscape of stony echoes and glassy half-light, and she found it hard to think of it as home.

"Good evening, Francesca," her father said, brushing her cheek with his lips. He was wearing a dark velvet smoking jacket, and she was glad that she had put on the new gold Missoni knit. Would they keep up this formality day after day?

As he sat down, she fidgeted, wondering how to begin the conversation. She supposed she ought to thank him for his generosity first.

"Father, Antonia bought us such beautiful clothes today. We're so grateful."

"We? For Josie as well?" His face was expressionless.

A waiter entered and poured the water. Francesca was not used to being waited on. At home she did this herself. She waited until the butler had left the room. "Father, Emilio took Josie down to the servants' quarters to eat dinner. I told him it must be a mistake."

A raised eyebrow, a troubled look as the count fingered one of the heavy silver spoons. The rich expanse of mahogany table seemed to widen between them. She felt terribly far away from him. Reflections of the candle flames danced across the polished surface, and the grain of the wood looked as deep as a lake.

Carlo gave her a wary smile and said, "What is the mistake?"

"Josie and I always eat together. She's my best friend—"

"And your servant," he interrupted her.

"My family," she contradicted.

He looked down briefly, his expression so private that he seemed unaware of her presence. She remembered that about him now: Whenever she disagreed with him, he would pretend not to hear her, or would answer with exaggerated politeness. That way they could go on making believe she was the perfect daughter who would never make the mistake of disappointing him.

But Carlo looked up again, and she saw that tonight he would hear her out. He said sadly, "I know this is difficult for you both, but you and Josie are no longer children. It is time for each of you to assume your proper place in the world. You must let me know what I can do to make the transition easier for both of you." He paused as if searching for words. "I see no reason why Josie should not accompany you when you go out in public; that, in fact, is part of her job as your companion. If you wish it—and I must assume that you do—you may invite her to your ball. But, *cara*, she must learn that from now on, her place is not at your side but in your shadow. And you also must try to understand that."

Francesca shook her head, determined to stand up to this intimidating stranger. "No, Papa. Josie's place will always be at my side. I invited her to Venice as my friend and my guest."

"Your *maid*, Francesca, not your guest."

"Papa," she answered, surprised by the anger in her soft voice, "during all the years when you wanted nothing to do with me, it was Josie who loved me and took care of me. Surely—''

''Enough!'' Carlo roared. ''Josephine Lapoiret is my housekeeper's daughter. Her social standing is very different from yours. Ever since you were a very young child Marianne has lived under my roof in Lyford Cay for one reason only: to take care of you. I provided for her and for her daughter, and in exchange they looked after you. Now, Josie may leave my employ and try to make something of herself. If she chooses to do that, I certainly wish her well. But I brought her here as your maid and companion, and as long as she's on my staff, she'll be treated as an employee should be treated—with respect, but not as a guest at the dinner table.''

''But we were equals in Nassau. We always ate together there,'' Francesca protested.

Her father would not be stopped. ''Francesca, it's time you assumed the responsibilities that accompany your rank. Marianne made an understandable mistake; she was overly familiar with you, and your friendship with her daughter went on too long. She should have prepared Josie to accept her position.''

Francesca felt confused and frustrated. She had come home to the palazzo for her eighteenth birthday—now, about to assume the responsibilities of a grown woman. Why, then, would her father not allow her to organize her life as she wished? Were his standards so medieval that he regarded women as incapable of making even the simplest decisions on their own? How long would he expect her willingly to bend before his iron will? ''Papa, please listen to my side of—''

The count raised his hand for silence. ''One simply does not dine with the servants.''

The tone of his voice told Francesca that the subject was closed, quite possibly forever.

Two servants were placing silver dishes on the table. Francesca closed her eyes briefly when Emilio removed a heavy lid to reveal the main course. *Uccellini con polenta*. Tiny brown birds so tender that the flesh fell away from the frail bones. She would make a meal of polenta and vegetables and push the *uccellini* to one side.

''How was your fitting with Renata?'' the count asked.

Francesca talked for a few moments and then, seeing that her father wasn't listening, decided to shock him into attention. "In Renata's picture album I found a photograph of Mama."

Carlo glanced sharply at her.

"She was wearing a white sequined sheath, and the other woman in the picture . . . was in exactly the same dress but all in black—"

"Renata's taste is unassailablc," Carlo said, cutting her off. "You can trust her absolutely."

"Who was the other woman in the photo, Papa?"

The count's face had grown pale, and a sheen of perspiration had appeared on his high forehead. "Probably some socialite she met at a party. Nobody important, certainly."

"She looked familiar to me," Francesca persisted.

"Perhaps you saw her when you were a child. You saw most of your mother's friends at one time or another, and heaven knows, she had an army of them. Now, tell me about your gown for the ball."

Francesca realized she would get no more information from her father about the woman in the black sequined sheath. What was there about that woman, that photograph, that people didn't want her to know? Renata had literally thrown her out onto the street after she asked about the picture. Now her father was stubbornly insisting the woman in black wasn't "important."

The Palazzo Nordonia was thick with secrets, she was discovering, and Susannah seemed to be at the heart of its dark mysteries.

When Emilio entered with a bottle of wine, he immediately noticed Carlo's pallor, and glanced at Francesca in search of the cause. She was speaking almost mechanically about her shopping trip, but the count seemed not to be listening.

Worried, the majordomo poured the wine. Carlo's face was beaded with sweat, and the look in his eyes was distracted. Again, Emilio cast a glance at the daughter. What had she said to upset the count?

Emilio knew—and only he knew—that Count Carlo Nordonia had plenty to worry about already. The last thing he needed was more problems. Lately he had been drinking too much, working too hard on his writing, locking himself in his study for too many hours of research. He ignored his business affairs, including the vineyards, which were one of the few remaining reliable sources of income to replenish the Nordonia fortune.

Now that the contessina had come home, all Emilio's meticulous efforts to maintain a budget were being thrown to the wind. On the count's orders, no expense was to be spared to make her presentation to society the most brilliant occasion of the season in Europe. Her gown, the orchestra, the dinner, the champagne—all must be the finest, and Emilio began to tick off in his head the instructions he must give to the staff tomorrow. Every room must be opened and restored down to the tiniest thread, the smallest tile. His army of servants would bring life back to the palazzo. But that life, Emilio knew, could only last a night. The palazzo would blaze for an hour of stunning glory. Afterward, Carlo and his daughter would at least have that night to remember.

Carlo signaled for dessert. Emilio placed a silver bowl of black cherries and brandy in the center of the table and set it aflame with a flourish. The blue flames spurted high, and the silver peacocks glittered with life.

Francesca saw that the count was searching her face with troubled eyes. She knew she had displeased him by asking about the photograph of her mother, but now she sensed a deeper, more pervasive displeasure in his gaze. It was as if he had analyzed her, observed her, and concluded that she did not measure up to his idea of what the daughter of Carlo Nordonia should be.

She looked down at her dessert plate, ashamed to meet his gaze. She was neither as beautiful nor as fascinating as her mother had been, and for that her father would certainly never forgive her. Even when she tried to please him, he seemed uninterested in her, preferring the solitude of his study to her company. Her silence seemed to grate on him, her conversation obviously bored him, and he made no secret of his doubt about her ability to do honor to her title. No wonder he had kept her away from him for so many years, even failing to show up last winter for his Christmas visit. Her heart sank when she heard his next words.

"Forgive me, Francesca. I won't stay for dessert, but you must enjoy yours." Carlo rose and motioned Emilio to bring his brandy to his room. He circled the long table and stood at Francesca's side. "*A domani, cara mia.*" He kissed her forehead lightly.

"But, Papa, I haven't recited the guest list for you. I know all of the names by heart. There's Prince Rainier and Princess

Grace, and Aga Khan—" She felt like a schoolgirl showing off before her teacher, but she couldn't stop herself.

"At breakfast, *cara*." The count turned and strode out of the room.

Francesca sat in silence, her cherries jubilee untouched. Never in all her years with Marianne and Josie had she been left alone at the table to finish her meal in solitude. The stout woman came in to remove all of the dishes except the silver serving bowl of dessert that still stood on the table in front of Francesca, who felt like the last remaining patron in a restaurant being given a strong hint to leave by a busy waiter. In the base of the candelabras, the peacocks gleamed hypnotically in the candlelight; she wished dully that Josie were there to see them.

Thoroughly dejected, she stood up and, carrying the bowl of brandied cherries, walked straight up the grand staircase and knocked tentatively on Josie's door. She knew how inadequate a gift the cherries were, and she dreaded confessing that she had gotten nowhere with her father, almost wishing she could go to bed without talking to her friend. But it was too late. The door swung wide and Josie faced her, resplendent in her lace peignoir, her eyes red from crying.

"What is it?" Francesca asked. "You're still upset about my father's shabby treatment of you. Oh, Josie, I'm so sorry."

"No." Josie flicked a stray tear off her cheek. "I—I'm just homesick, that's all."

Francesca held out the delicate silver bowl. "I brought you some cherries jubilee."

Josie took the bowl and set it down on the dresser. "We had them, too," she lied.

Francesca blushed. Her thoughtful gift now seemed condescending.

"How did it go with your father?" Josie asked.

"Not very well, I'm afraid. He's impossible," Francesca said, indirectly pleading for understanding. "He's always run this place one way, and he doesn't seem capable of change."

"Did you explain that I'm not a maid?"

"Of course I did, but he's simply inflexible. He's used to having absolute power over his life and everyone else's. He just doesn't listen."

"I see," Josie said, although she really didn't see at all. If she had been there, she knew she would have made Carlo listen and understand. She doubted Francesca's willingness to fight for what she believed; Josie felt she simply lacked the courage to stand up to her father.

"Don't blame me," Francesca said urgently, reading her friend's mind. "Please. I can't bear it when you're angry with me, Josie. I know I won't make it through the ball without you. How could I face all those strangers?"

Josie turned back to her, angry now. "You need *me?* I'm supposed to give you moral support, right? What kind of support do you give me? Can't you understand how hard it is for me to face strangers and be introduced as a maid?"

The bitterness in her voice brought tears to Francesca's eyes. "I promise you I'll never let that happen again."

"Unless your father tells you to."

"Never," vowed Francesca.

"But in the meantime I'll take my meals downstairs, right?"

Francesca tightened her throat to choke down the tears, trying to balance her fear of Carlo against her fear of losing Josie forever. "Josie, I'll try again tomorrow to talk to my father, but it's hard for me. You know how I am, *p'tite soeur*. I could never be brave unless you were standing behind me telling me I could dive off the rocks or swim out into the deep water."

Josie's anger wavered slightly when she saw the terror in Francesca's eyes. "And *you* know, *p'tite soeur,* that your father is separating us for that very reason. You're too brave when I'm behind you. The last thing the imperial Count Nordonia wants is a reckless, courageous daughter." She took Francesca's shoulders and shook her gently. "*Chérie,* if you won't stand up to him for my sake, then please do it for your own before he marries you off to some fat, rich, seventy-year-old duke just to show the rest of his tight little aristocratic world how grand he is."

She let go of Francesca and looked questioningly into her eyes. "You can't do it, can you, *p'tite soeur?*"

"I don't know, Josie. He's so aloof and so . . . scary; I just start to tremble when I'm alone with him."

Josie's steady gaze made Francesca uncomfortable. Here she was depending on Josie's help and support when she herself didn't even have enough courage to stand up to her own father.

"I'm going to pack you off to bed," Josie said. "We both need a good night's sleep."

As soon as Francesca had left the room Josie took the bowl of cherries and, sitting on her bed cross-legged, began to eat them with the big serving spoon, slowly savoring every bite. She imagined herself singing, wearing her new red dress on the night of the ball. The audience would be full of the most beautiful women in Europe but she would be the envy of them all, and every man would ycarn for her. There would be waves of applause and cries of ''bravo'' when she finished, because as she sang she would cast a spell—a voodoo spell. That would teach them! Josie giggled, and, raising the big silver bowl to her lips, she drained the last drops of liquid.

Chapter Five

EMILIO APPEARED WITH a decanter of brandy. He set the bottle and a crystal glass on the stand next to Carlo's favorite chair. The count nodded good night as the door closed behind his majordomo. His pajamas and cashmere robe were laid out on the bed; the fire was a heap of glowing embers. Hush Puppy, fed and brushed, lay sound asleep beside the deep leather chair. Automatically, the count undressed, pulled on his robe, and sank down into the comfort of his chair.

On any other night he would have held his breath in anticipation. Now was the moment when the doorknob would turn and Antonia would creep into the room like a thief. But not tonight. He lit a cigarette and thought of how he would sit here watching her approach in silence, their eyes locked. He had asked her not to come tonight, but now he regretted it. If anything, he needed Antonia more now that the girl was here. He needed Toni to ward off the past, which Francesca unknowingly embodied.

His daughter was like an unwanted gift sent to remind him of a woman who was best left forgotten. Her eyes, her smile, her mannerisms were all Susannah's. It was as if his wife were staring at him across the chasm of thirteen lonely years. The child's resemblance to her mother was so remarkable that when Francesca was most herself, her tone of voice or her laughter struck him as discordant. Susannah doesn't laugh like that, part of him would protest. No, that's not her southern accent. Susannah had never been gentle or shy. She had never struggled to please him, as their daughter seemed to be doing, and yet everything Susannah did had fascinated him. Even at the end, when he knew she would bring disgrace down on all of them.

He took a long swallow of brandy. Francesca—thank God! —did not seem to have inherited her mother's strong will.

Oh, she had tried to buck up against him at dinner, but a single sharp word had made her realize that it would do her no good to forget her place.

Susannah, unfortunately, had never been able to learn that one simple lesson. What a shame, he thought as he stamped out his cigarette and reached down to stroke the faithful basset hound as she stretched and pressed her head against his knee. "Go to bed, Hushie," he said, smiling into the drooping eyes. "I'll survive for a while without your company." He watched the old dog walk in circles around and around the hearth rug, then stretch out before the fire and close her eyes.

As he stared beyond the dog into the dying embers in the fireplace, he wondered what his daughter would have been like if Susannah hadn't disappeared from her life when she was only five years old. Would Francesca have been as full of fun? Would she have been as beguiling?

Carlo doubted that anyone, even Susannah's own daughter, could charm people as his wife had so often done. He took another sip of brandy and let his mind drift back through the years.

1949

CARLO CAUGHT HIS first glimpse of Susannah at the annual horse show at Madison Square Garden. The crowd was hushed in wonder at the sight of a nineteen-year-old girl taking the treacherous course, the first time a woman was favored to win the coveted leading rider award. Although it was unheard of in Italy for a woman to ride professionally, the count couldn't help but be mesmerized by her poise, her self-assured beauty. Her neat hips were poised over the saddle, though never touching it; the stallion's hooves barely nicked the ground. From his box, Carlo could see the determination in the girl's wide-set eyes, the defiant urging of her pointed chin, as if she couldn't get enough speed from the horse.

When the event was over, she had cleared the course in the fastest time of the evening; and, breathless and exhilarated, she received her trophy in front of Carlo's box. She peeled off her velvet cap and her red hair spilled down her back like a river of fire.

"I'd like to meet her," Carlo said to the man sitting next to him.

"That won't be easy, old man," he replied, shaking his head.

Carlo's friend, Claude, was an English business acquaintance who, in the course of arranging tax shelters for an international clientele, had established a network of the famous and infamous. Claude didn't discriminate between the notorious and the noteworthy; so long as they had ambitions or artistic aspirations or too much money, they were his sort. He knew everything there was to know about offshore investments and he could get his friends into the best parties. But when it came to penetrating Susannah Lee Ingraham's social circle, even Claude was out of his depth.

"A bit of a maverick, that one," Claude said. "A good southern family, the best, but she's turned against them. Can't blame her. They're much too conservative for my taste, too."

That could be a problem, Carlo thought. Although he was known as an astute businessman in those days, because he had never married he was regarded as something of a playboy, even though he wasn't. He was simply too busy with his work to find a suitable wife. Or so he thought. But just as it was his task to modernize the vast empire he would inherit, he realized that it was his responsibility to marry eventually. Women amused him, and a few even stimulated him intellectually, but none seemed to share his life. He had his pick of socialites, but they struck him as vacuous. When his family urged him to settle down and lead a normal life, Carlo replied that he didn't ask much, just that the lady had to have an aristocratic spirit. But that proved a quality hard to define, even harder to find.

It was Claude, with his gambler's instinct, who led Carlo to Susannah. Months after the horse show, at a cocktail party at the Italian embassy in Washington, Claude went out of his way to introduce the count to a member of the prestigious Virginia hunt club. Over his protests, Claude accepted an invitation to a meet for Carlo. "You've never seen the country in this part of the world," Claude explained a little too quickly. "Besides, you'll like Southerners. They're more civilized than other Americans."

When Carlo saw Susannah again, he knew her by the cascade of dark red hair that swept over her shoulders. She was taller than she had appeared in the Garden, and her thinness added to her air of distinction. While the other hunters spent the afternoon scrambling back and forth over green fields after an invisible fox, Carlo kept his personal quarry well in sight.

Once Susannah split off from the scarlet-coated pack and galloped at a jump of breathtaking height, soaring off, it appeared, into thin air. Carlo, a good, if cautious, rider, pursued her right up to the jump, where his horse veered off into the brush. All around, dun fields stretched emptily to the horizon; Susannah was nowhere. She had stranded him in a thicket up to his knees. His horse snorted and sidestepped, trying to break free of the prickly bushes.

"Hold, Caesar. Hold!" Carlo said to the horse. One strong branch caught and tore his glove, drawing blood. "Damn. Ruined a glove. Hold!"

The horse was working up a lather now, rearing and trampling in the high brush, the bit clenched in his teeth. Carlo gripped into his sides with his knees, shortened the reins, and, after an intense struggle in which the sky seemed to circle around him, he managed to jerk the bit free. Caesar reared again and smashed out of the brush, with all his might working his great head and neck against the constraint of the bit. Carlo reached for his whip, but it was gone.

"You bastard," he muttered. The fields locked into place and Caesar calmed to a prance. Carlo grew more relaxed and in control of himself as well. "There, boy. Gentle now." He patted Caesar's black neck and began to search for the stirrups he'd lost. As he felt for them with his toes, he realized how lucky he was that none of the expert hunters had seen him lose mastery of his horse.

"Is this yours?" Susannah asked, practically appearing out of nowhere. The voice was a low-pitched, mischievous drawl.

Carlo swung Caesar around. Susannah had materialized out of the trees. She sat on her mount with crossed arms, as if she'd been watching him for hours.

"Your crop?" She held it forward.

"But how did you get it?" he managed.

She clucked her horse into motion and handed the whip over. "It flew into the air, right over the jump. I'm afraid it scared poor Caesar out of his wits. He's terribly whip-shy."

She was so close to him he could have reached out and touched her cheek. But she was about as touchable as a wild hare or a fawn, approaching him by whim or curiosity, by some inhuman caprice. He thought how strange it was to see this fleet girl emerge from the worn, rounded blue hills, the shorn fields. She was a visitor from a wilder terrain. Her wide-eyed beauty made him catch his breath.

Her eyes grew suddenly derisive at his stillness. "Well, take it," she said. "You may need it again."

"Thank you," he retorted. "I very well may, if you lead me on another wild-goose chase. That jump nearly did me in. I'm lucky Caesar balked."

"Actually, I knew it'd stop you." She laughed.

"You did! Yes, I'll bet you did. You were watching all along." He wheeled Caesar around, turning his back to her.

Her voice rose defiantly, but the long syllables were honeyed with charm. "Yes, I did. I watched you from the embankment. I couldn't help it, that jump was so tempting." She had caught up with him now, and reached out an arm to stall Caesar. She looked back at him flirtatiously. "I thought I'd teach you a lesson, what can happen if you follow strangers. Especially those you can't keep up with." She tossed her head. He watched her athletic back, long and narrow in the waist.

"What do you mean, can't keep up? Would you care to bet?"

It was the right tack to use with her. She flung her head around with a wide, exhilarated grin—almost a smirk—and he saw the determined child in her face. Her horse knew her mood and began to trot ahead. She rose, posting, and he knew he didn't want to catch up to her, he wanted to follow her, watching that graceful back rise and fall. But, with a determined kick, he urged Caesar to shoot forward.

"First one back to the clubhouse!" she shouted.

He didn't know the way, but Caesar did. Fields streamed past, branches whipped his face, and she was always just ahead of him, the auburn waves of her hair leading him on. Then he lost her.

A few minutes later the tall chimneys of the club came into view, with its broad portico. Susannah was lounging against the columns. "Well, there are you, at last! I'd almost given up on you," she scolded him.

"Really," he said dryly. "You make three minutes sound like three hours."

"You're actually quite good, you know," she said, walking over to him.

"I hope not by your standards. I want to ride like a rational human being, with a healthy respect for human life." He swung to the ground and stood next to the girl for the first time. "The winner has to buy the drinks."

"I've never bought a drink for a man before," she said in her lovely drawl. "Is that the custom in England?"

"I'm not English, I'm Italian."

"Oh, you speak English beautifully! But I knew there was something different about you."

"Different?"

She looked at him with cool, assessing green eyes. "Yes, different, but you'll do," she said brazenly, challenging him again.

"Come, let's cool the horses down before we go inside."

They could have left their mounts with the groom at the stable, which was what Carlo under other circumstances would have done. But he remembered that this girl loved horses, lived for them, and sensed that if he wanted to get to know her, there was no better way than to develop a rapport with her horse.

They walked around a shady pasture until the sweat had dried on the horse's backs, and then they toured the stable. Susannah knew each horse intimately, its traumas, its jumping prowess, its bloodlines. He drank in the stories as if the world of horses were all that concerned him; and when, at twilight, they shut the barn door behind them, he felt strangely renewed. The girl's exhilaration had rubbed off on him. Far away, but drawing ever nearer, they heard the voices of the hounds, the horn of the frustrated hunters.

"Let's get away from here," he said. "Let me take you to dinner."

"Good. I couldn't bear it if they've caught a fox."

"And yet you hunt."

"Just for the jumps. I usually go off on my own, like today."

"Did you mind that I followed you?"

"Yes, terribly," she said severely, then laughed at his consternation. "No, I wanted you to. I've always liked Englishmen even when they turn out to be Italian."

* * *

They had spent the summer under the burning southern sun at horse shows and cross-country events as the judges scrutinized Susannah in her black formal habit, searching for flaws in her perfect, driven performances. But always Carlo watched her with fascination. For most of the beautiful women he knew, it was enough to live off one's looks, to enjoy a trivial, pampered existence. But Susannah was different—she craved competition and success the way a man would. She was up at dawn every morning to exercise her horses before the sun ruined the day, driving them to their peak over a course of high jumps before the unforgiving eyes of her trainer. If Carlo had not dragged her away, she would have spent the night in the stable.

Susannah's goal was to place first in eventing, a three-phase competition in dressage, cross-country, and stadium jumping that was held every year for equestrians in the East. Cross-country courses were mapped out with specially designed, sometimes camouflaged, surprise jumps and hairpin turns over varied terrain. Participants were allowed to walk over the course, but had no chance to ride it before the clocked event. Susannah refused to miss any of the important events. The more dangerous, the stiffer the competition, the more determined she was to compete, even if it meant traveling hundreds of miles to New England from her home in Virginia. Every weekend Carlo joined her, driving his Maserati from New York to wherever she was and parking it behind her horse trailer. When he could get away from his business meetings, he would even visit her during the week.

At first Susannah treated him as a nuisance at best. The other competitors gave him sidelong glances as if he were trespassing. But though Carlo may not have been a great rider himself, he knew what it took to make one. He was astute and he had a keen eye. The first time he mildly suggested to Susannah a change in her performance in the ring, she did a double take. She'd had no inkling he was so knowledgeable. When his advice worked and she left the ring triumphant, she gave him a wide grin and a little bow of acknowledgment. From then on, whenever he watched her work out, she would ride up to him after a difficult turn around the ring for his appraisal.

Slowly Carlo's tall frame became a familiar, even popular sight ''backstage'' at the weekly events. And he was welcome in the spectators' tent where the society matrons fawned over the count and their daughters vied for his attention. Carlo tolerated the social scene just long enough to be sure Susannah's competitive spirit was aroused. That accomplished, he was more apt to be found behind the stalls in a circle of male riders and grooms playing poker. Susannah jokingly accused him of following her around the circuit for the gambling opportunities. He was lucky at cards, so lucky a rumor circulated that a slap on the back from Carlo before entering the ring was a good omen.

His courtship of Susannah was restrained, so seemingly casual compared to his young predecessors, that she wondered at times if he were actually courting her and she flirted with him, trying to make him show his hand. But if nothing else, Carlo had learned Susannah only valued what was difficult to acquire. He watched and waited and even stepped back, pretending to ignore his competition. He skipped a weekend here and there, letting Susannah stew, wondering what he was up to in New York, giving her a chance to compare him, favorably he hoped, with the younger men around her.

The first time he didn't show up for a meet, she was surprised at the extent of her disappointment. She didn't do well in the ring and a sadness gripped her till he telephoned in the evening to ask how it was going but offering no explanation of his absence. She was too proud to ask for one. She admired his cleverness and intelligence, and when he took her hand for the first time in the car she knew she never wanted him to let go. His warm confident hand enveloped hers completely; it took everything for granted. She was already his. But when they said good night, he simply brushed her forehead with his lips as usual, as if their hands had not already revealed the depth of their feelings for each other.

She began to ride not only for herself but for him. She had never been so exhilarated, head over heels in love; now she couldn't wait to see him each day. Yet Susannah still played the game, holding her cards up, proving she could be as cool and as proud as he.

"Don't you ever stop?" he asked one morning as she groomed her horse.

"Stop what?" she asked impatiently, currying the high black withers of the thoroughbred. He pawed the ground and Carlo stepped back, out of his way.

"Stop all of this. This stableboy work, this dangerous competing. You've won *everything* in sight. Why do you keep pushing yourself?"

"I do it well and I love winning."

Outside the wide stable doors he saw the low wooded mountains of Connecticut begin to glow a brilliant emerald in the first rays of the sun, the color of Susannah's eyes. He glanced at his watch. It was sunrise at five-fifteen.

"Come with me to Italy. Let me introduce you to my family. If you think the equestrian judges in America are difficult, wait until you meet the Nordonia clan."

She let the horse's hoof go and rose slowly. "What do you mean? Am I going to ride in Italy? Is that what you're suggesting?"

"You know it's not. Once we're married," he said lightly, handing her the hook, "do you think I'm going to share you with a horse?"

She stared at him. "Married?"

"Yes. Didn't you know?"

Carlo's and Susannah's eyes met and held. Though he said the words lightly, almost ironically, she knew they were said in earnest, and she felt a shiver of excitement.

"I—I couldn't give up riding," she stuttered.

"How can you ride when you'll be bearing children?" Carlo demanded in mock seriousness. Out of the corner of his eye, he watched Susannah's reaction and almost burst out laughing.

Her lips barely moved. "I never thought of that."

"Besides, as mistress of the palazzo you'll be too busy to chase after trophies. Don't you know it's time you grew out of horses and thought of becoming a wife and mother?"

"You sound just like my parents now."

"I hope they agree to our marriage."

"*I* haven't agreed."

Carlo came toward her and reached out to push a strand of hair away from her white face. For the first time she looked vulnerable, frightened. She shook her head and pushed him back. She did not want him to notice that she was trembling. The horse snorted and tossed his head. "Marco's skittish. He won't let anyone near him but me."

"You're the skittish one," he said, lifting her chin and kissing her slowly. "You won't let anyone near you either."

"I let you." Her eyes were soft.

"Sometimes you let me." He kissed her again, drawing her against him, realizing she was almost as tall as he was. Slowly he felt the tension ease out of her thighs as they relaxed against his. No woman's perfume had ever aroused him like Susannah's natural one of soap and hay. Even when she was covered with perspiration after competing in the ring, she had the scent of a child who had played too long outdoors.

For a moment she clung to him. He heard her heart pound and he knew he had won her. She leaned back in the circle of his arms and gave him a look of perplexity. "But Carlo, I'm not sure I'm ready to give this up. It's such a blind leap. I've never been to Italy, I have no idea what it's like to live with a man."

"But we're together every day. I follow you everywhere, you know that. You didn't think I came just to be a spectator. You had to know that eventually I'd ask you to come and live with me."

Susannah closed the door of the stall and walked out of the stable slowly. Outside she took a deep breath and turned to Carlo. She knew she had to answer carefully. "As your wife I would be Countess Nordonia, wouldn't I? How on earth would you expect me to behave? I'd have to be more . . . I don't know . . . *formal,*" she said, searching for the words.

"No. I want you just the way you are," Carlo interrupted her. He guessed what was troubling her. Despite her youth, Susannah had always done exactly as she pleased. She took her popularity for granted and often mocked her social success, which came to her so easily; she preferred her riding breeches to her debutante gowns. He had watched her all summer fight and win title after title to stay at the peak of her profession as an equestrian. Now he was offering her a new challenge, one for which she was hardly prepared.

"God help me, I'd be known as your 'American' wife."

"I don't care, as long as you're my wife." He bent to kiss her again, but paused when he saw the way she looked at him, her eyes full of curiosity and enjoyment. Her mercurial moods always took him by surprise.

"You like having me in your power, don't you?" he said, smiling into her eyes.

The thought of her proud head tossed back in conviction, the waves of auburn hair, filled Carlo with a longing she was too innocent to understand. Her slender hands, the teasing green eyes, the fleet body, sleekly muscled as a dancer's, all summoned up a passion he couldn't quell.

Since the Nordonias were one of the oldest Catholic families in Europe, Susannah knew there was no question of a mixed marriage. The day after Carlo's proposal Susannah began studying for conversion to the Catholic faith. Fortunately, religious feelings had already been instilled in her as a child by her black nurse, Cassie, who had taught her prayers and taken her by the hand to mass in the black section of their town. Susannah had remembered and loved the candles and the music and the smell of incense and the sense of mystery. When she died, Cassie had left her her rosary of silver and lapis beads. So, having been brought up by a Catholic nurse, she was not unfamiliar with Catholicism and she studied her catechism eagerly and in secret to surprise Carlo.

September came with a flourish of victories and, much to Carlo's relief, the declaration of Susannah's retirement. Their engagement had been announced reluctantly by her parents a few weeks before.

Carlo's family and friends welcomed his marriage to an American with about as much enthusiasm as Susannah's family did. They were full of dire warnings the couple found easy to ignore. But finally the disapproval of their respective relatives served to draw them even closer together. And they conspired to escape.

In October, they decided to elope to Nassau. On the way they stopped in New York City. Carlo took Susannah to see Bishop Flannery. She was interviewed at length and subsequently the bishop himself baptized and confirmed her in the Lady Chapel of St. Patrick's.

Carlo and Susannah left the cathedral and walked slowly up Fifth Avenue looking in the shop windows. In front of Cartier's, Carlo casually suggested they drop in. There was a lot of bowing and scraping as they were ushered into a small private room, where Jules Glaenzer (the head of the establishment, who was as famous as Cartier's itself) greeted Carlo like an old friend. Susannah was seated at a table as Glaenzer left the room.

"What's going on, Carlo?" she asked as Carlo's eyes twinkled. Glaenzer strode back in and with a flourish placed a small red velvet tray in front of her. On it was a ring with the largest diamond she had ever seen in her life.

"I know it's a little ostentatious," Carlo said, studying it over her shoulder, "but you can carry it off."

"Oh, Carlo, I can't believe it! It's magnificent!"

"Try it on. The ring itself is very old and in a beautiful setting, as you can see. It belonged to my great-grandmother."

"The cabochon ruby it held originally," Glaenzer interrupted, "is being made into a pendant for you, Miss Ingraham."

Susannah slipped the ring on her finger. It fit perfectly. Carlo and Glaenzer exchanged a satisfied glance.

As they left the store Susannah was speechless, staring down at her hand on Carlo's arm.

They were married in a small Catholic church in Nassau. Susannah wore a natural linen suit, and her hair—which she had pulled back into a soft chignon—was covered by a white Venetian lace mantilla Carlo had given her. She carried a bouquet of lilies of the valley and Cassie's rosary.

Since Susannah refused to telephone her parents, Carlo sent them a telegram, feeling guilty about eloping with her but relieved that he had managed to avoid the lavish wedding her parents would have insisted upon. After they had been pronounced man and wife, he brought her to the large Victorian house on Hog Island that his family had owned since he had been a boy.

From the moment she set foot in the huge, oppressively formal house, she was as untouchable as a wild horse, approaching him as if by whim and then darting off with a capricious laugh. In the early days she playacted her way through their lovemaking, trying in her way to please him, but he knew that a part of her remained distant, coolly observing him as he made love to her. Later, as he grew bolder in his attempts to arouse her, he had seen in her green eyes the flicker of something close to contempt. That elation, that force that drove her to win, that fired her great enthusiasm for life, receded in bed like a failing tide. There was no use reaching after it. Susannah was like a deaf mute; she could not speak the language of sexual passion, could not learn it by instinct or by rote. Carlo wished his wife were more of a hypocrite, that she would fake an interest, that her eyes just once would mirror his great hunger so that he could dream about it afterward. He thought that if she could only return a tenth of his longing, they would be the most ecstatic couple in the world.

And yet Carlo never doubted that she loved him. For Susannah didn't just dabble at being a wife and a hostess. She excelled at all these roles as if she were hell-bent for another ribbon. Susannah immersed herself in the history of his family and his city until she became almost as much of an expert as Carlo himself. She restored the Nordonia palazzo in Venice, dwelling meticulously over each tiny detail from the hand-fashioned brass door keys to the blue eyes of the smallest cherub in the Tiepolo ceilings. She surprised him by the refinement of her taste and astonished all of Venice. That an American could perform such an act of homage and exhibit such scholarly depth in restoring one of their monuments moved them profoundly. The American countess had become herself one of the city's treasures.

It was when she died that Carlo began to neglect his business interests, preferring to shutter himself in their palace, her mausoleum, and devote himself to continuing her work. The histories of Venice he wrote were all dedicated to her.

Her devotion to him, to their home, to their daughter, had been single-minded and passionate. Susannah had been passionate about everything, except his lovemaking.

ON THE FLOOR above Carlo's room, Francesca lay listening to the faint sound of water lapping against the stones below her open window. Too keyed up to sleep, she rose and put on slippers and a robe. She listened at the door for a moment and, hearing no sound of human activity, tiptoed down the staircase. Francesca knew her mother's door by sight far down the hall. She practically ran to it, suddenly feeling that this was the true purpose of her voyage to Venice. The heavy brass knob turned silently under her hands, and she stepped inside, closing the door and waiting for her eyes to adjust to the darkness. The shutters of the tall windows were open, and moonlight streamed in, illuminating a small lamp on a table near the door. Holding her breath in the grip of some unnamed fear, she reached out and turned on the light.

Susannah Nordonia's bedroom, perfectly preserved, looked

as if her mother had just stepped out for a moment. Dominating the room was a wide bed covered in deep blue velvet pillows. Francesca remembered the tall silver posts, deeply engraved. The heavy blue and silver brocade draperies were partially drawn, as if awaiting Susannah's return. Pale Tiepolo clouds billowed on the ceiling overhead. Enthroned among them was the full-breasted goddess whom the four-year-old Francesca had assumed was her mother's guardian angel. Out of the corners, nearly lost in the darkness, peeked cherubs and other angelic presences. As a child, Francesca had thought they were hovering there alive.

Francesca stood absolutely still, remembering the last time her mother had left Nassau. Good-bye, always good-bye, Francesca remembered. "Good-bye, my darling, I'll be home soon." She had promised to come home soon, but had held Francesca longer and closer than usual, as if she knew she would never return from Venice.

In the center of the far wall stood a silver dressing table. A small candelabra hung with crystal pendants decorated the table like a miniature, delicate tree. As she pulled its slim gold chain, the lambent glow revealed the silver-topped jars of powders and creams that were dusted and polished as if Susannah had sat here to make up her face only yesterday. Francesca seated herself on the velvet bench before the table. Slim perfume bottles of Venetian glass were stoppered with fans of frosted glass. One of the stoppers, the largest of all, supported a glass filigree in which two maidens were entwined, their slender arms wound gracefully around each other. A second bottle of Murano glass bore a hand-printed label. Francesca lifted the vial and read the words written in her mother's hand: *Lyford Rose*.

Carefully she removed the stopper. Most of the perfume had evaporated, but the fragrance that had been captured in the bottle was astonishingly beautiful. This was the scent Francesca remembered, the flowery fragrance that had surrounded Susannah years ago and that now hung in the atmosphere of this room. Susannah seemed so close at that moment that Francesca felt the back of her neck grow warm with the radiance of her presence. Reluctantly she replaced the stopper and set the bottle in its place.

A small, silver-framed snapshot stood among the bottles. It was a picture of Susannah on the count's arm at her wedding. She looked scarcely older than Francesca herself, and her face beamed joyfully. In the mirror Francesca's drawn and tired face stared back in dismay. Somehow she must make herself into a new person. Perhaps if she could only recreate her mother in her mind, she could learn the secret of that vibrant personality, that enjoyment of the limelight. But her tired mind could barely piece together her mother's features. How could she be expected to emulate a woman she had barely known? Francesca's throat tightened in anger, her hands clenched in frustration. Her love of her mother was too painful and exasperating to remember. She drew a deep breath, gazed at the blue ceiling, and deliberately made herself forget the ball and her father's expectations. She thought of something else entirely—a smile, an intent look, a man pursuing her: Jack Westman. The knot in her chest dissolved.

I wonder what it's like, she thought, to kiss him.

There was a sound from the corridor.

Somebody was at the door. Panicked, she ran for the bathroom, only to find it locked. She spun around, expecting to be confronted by . . . The bedroom door swung slowly open. "Hush Puppy?" She ran to the dog and pushed her the rest of the way in and closed the door quietly behind her. She sat watching Francesca, panting heavily, her tongue lolling and her tail beating contentedly against the floor.

Francesca took a deep breath and pulled herself up. After all, why shouldn't she be in here? She turned back and tried the bathroom door again. It wasn't stuck. It was locked. She went to her mother's dressing table and looked through the meticulously arranged drawers. The more she looked the more determined she was to find the key. She imagined herself ringing for Emilio and simply demanding the door to be opened. It was about time she began playing her proper role. But she knew she never could bring herself to do it and instead she continued searching obstinately through a bureau drawer that held her mother's gloves, dozens of them. Distracted from her search for a moment, she pulled on a long pair of gray suede. As she did, a key fell noiselessly to the floor. What unbelievable luck! Quickly she tried it in the lock. It turned easily and she stepped into the high-ceilinged room. The walls and floor were fashioned of rose-colored Carrara marble and in the center of the floor was a sunken tub the size of a small swimming pool. It was completely inlaid with flower-painted tiles, their brilliant colors dimmed by years of neglect. A fly drummed against the wall searching for the broken pane in the window where it had flown in. The door creaked behind her and Francesca jumped. The icy room brought back a rush of memories but at the same time there was a presence, or rather an absence, of life that made her want to turn and run. Instead she stood mesmerized. Images of her mother and herself as a small child "swimming" flashed through her head. She breathed in the memory of the warm water and the steamy perfume of bath oil and flowering plants that filled the room. They had sailed flower petals like miniature boats, the pink armada against the white. Squealing with delight, she had sunk her mother's ships with a well-aimed bar of soap. She recognized shells her mother must have collected in Nassau arranged around the edge of the tub. The Venetian glass urns, artifacts and antiquities that might have come from the boudoir of Nefertiti, now were covered with dust and cobwebs. She didn't remember the large framed pastel drawings that decorated the walls. Examining them, she realized with a little shock they were nudes of her mother. She couldn't help comparing her own slight frame with Susannah's graceful, voluptuous figure. In each sketch Susannah seemed to be looking at someone with an intimate yet bold expression Francesca didn't remember.

The cold was penetrating; with a shudder she quickly backed out of the room, closed the door, and locked it. Without asking herself why she did it, she dropped the key back into the glove. Folding it with its mate, she shoved the gloves back in the drawer and pushed it firmly shut.

Josie awoke early, put on her floral-print cotton dress, and walked down to the servants' dining room without stopping to rap on the door across the hall. After a week in Venice, she had given up hope that Francesca would make any real attempt to talk her father into changing his mind. Clinging to the dream of establishing a reputation as a singer on the night of the ball, Josie had tried valiantly to swallow her resentment, to treat Francesca as she always had, as a sister and a friend. But Carlo's determination and Francesca's timidity had finally succeeded in driving a wedge between the two young women. Josie and Francesca still talked, laughed together, and teased each other, but only on the rare occasions when Carlo's rigid schedule allowed them to be alone. All day long Francesca was shut up in the ballroom with one of

Carlo's army of coaches. Dancing lessons in the morning, comportment in the afternoon, French instruction in the evening. "I don't want my daughter speaking in that disgraceful Haitian patois," the count had said, not caring that Josie, who spoke the same way, was standing within easy hearing range.

Josie made herself talk pleasantly with the servants; she needed to learn Italian, and her meals downstairs were an excellent opportunity to do so. After breakfast she excused herself and went out, as she did almost every morning, to explore the city where Francesca was born.

Francesca's city, Josie thought with a touch of bitterness. Next week, on her birthday, Carlo would present his daughter to society like a trophy to be won by the man with the best credentials. Then what would become of her friendship with the mulatto, Josie Lapoiret, who spoke bad French and ate with the servants?

A career as a singer, Josie promised herself. Fame and riches and adulation that would raise her to a position equal to, if different from, the one Francesca would hold in the eyes of the world. But Francesca's success had been bestowed on her the day she was born in the Nordonia family. Josephine Lapoiret would have to work for hers.

At the convent school, she had majored in music. She had become known locally by singing at weddings and private parties. But there was much more to be done, and Josie intended to start right here in Venice.

Surely there were great voice teachers here, but Josie would have to get a job in order to pay for lessons.

She would need languages if she wanted to succeed in Europe. From the servants she had learned to make herself understood in Italian, but she could not yet distinguish between their working-class accent and the Italian that Carlo Nordonia spoke. Her French needed to be refined as well.

Josie took her wallet out of her purse and checked her financial situation. She still had some of the money she had earned from her first singing jobs in Nassau, plus a little money her mother had given her. Carlo's "charity" would suffice for ordinary expenses; today was the time to dip into her precious savings.

She walked to a shop she had noticed the day before. In the back she found the section where language books and records were displayed. After studying them carefully, she chose a book and a record in French and another in Italian. She paid for them and carried them back to the palazzo.

In the privacy of her bedroom, she unwrapped her packages and plugged in the rickety old record player. Then she sat down and listened to the French-instruction records over and over until the accent began to sound familiar to her. She began to repeat the phrases exactly as the recorded voice pronounced them.

This, she knew, would take little time; perhaps because of her natural talent for music, languages came easily to her. She would not need a team of coaches to turn her into a cultivated "lady"; she would do it by herself, without Carlo Nordonia's knowledge or help.

She worked with the records all morning. After lunch, she sauntered aimlessly through the palazzo, looking into one sparkling room after another. Around her the other servants bustled importantly, shattering the glacial stillness of the building. Already the marble floors had been polished to a sheen, and the chandeliers in the entrance hallway glittered with the brilliance of summer stars.

A maid stopped before her, arms filled with freshly laundered table linens. "Josie, we just heard that you will sing at the ball!" Her voice was as excited as her dark brown eyes. "Why didn't you tell us?"

Josie smiled, then shrugged. "I don't know, Marta. I guess I still can't believe it will really happen."

"It will happen if the count says so, Josie. He has given all of us permission to come into the ballroom to listen to you. It will be very exciting for us, you understand."

Touched by the young woman's words, Josie promised to sing her first song especially for the other servants. Then she watched Marta bustle away, marveling at the pride she took in her position as a servant in the Nordonia household. She had started up the stairs to practice some of her songs when another maid stopped her.

"Ah, there you are, Josie! The contessina wants to know if you wish to join her for a special dancing lesson. Her instructor has come back for an hour to work with her on the waltz."

"Tell her no, Giulia, but thank her for inviting me."

The maid looked astonished at her refusal of such a wonderful invitation.

"This is Francesca's ball," Josie said, keeping her voice

steady and her smile in place. "I don't want to take any attention away from her." She didn't add that she had seen Carlo Nordonia enter the ballroom and that she had no wish to join Francesca under his icy stare. In an attempt to change the subject, she added, "Such a fuss, Giulia. You'd think they were crowning her queen of Italy!"

The maid leaned close to speak confidentially. "There will be two real queens at the ball, Josie, from Spain and Holland. Emilio told us the count has received their acceptance notes. So exciting, is it not? We haven't had such guests in the ten years I've been here."

The maid went off to tend to her chores, and Josie turned away from the stairway, heading for the open ballroom door as if drawn there by some magnetic force. Perhaps she would sit in on the dancing lesson after all.

She watched the count and his daughter dance, and when the music ended Francesca impulsively stood on tiptoe and kissed her father's cheek. That kiss gripped Josie with anguish. She felt deserted, betrayed.

Francesca had changed almost beyond recognition. There was a new confidence in the way she stood, a new assurance in her gestures—even her voice had grown stronger since she had begun to work with Carlo's coaches. She wore her new poise like a royal cloak. She and the count were two of a kind now, and nothing could have been more natural than the way they'd spun around the ballroom in each other's arms. Ashamed of her envy, Josie quickly fled up the stairs to her room.

Chapter Six

THE PALAZZO WAS a cage of light. As the purple night rose out of the east, the enormous flares that lit the marble steps down to the water cast rich black shadows. The delicate palace swirled behind the flames like a mirage. The first guests glided up to the landing in a long gondola gilded with an ornate family crest. The paparazzi shot forward and the guests gathered the folds of their velvet evening capes and stepped into the rosy path of the flares and flashbulbs.

Josie watched as they made their way up the steps and into the grand entranceway of the palazzo. Then she followed the other guests inside and joined the throng that stood near the foot of the grand stairway. She felt an unaccountable thrill of excitement as she realized that this was the moment when Francesca was to make her entrance. Through the open door of the ballroom, she heard the orchestra begin to play. Along with the other guests, she glanced up just as Francesca appeared at the top of the long marble stairway on the arm of her father. For a long moment, the two of them stood absolutely still. Then they began a long, slow descent, which Josie knew she would remember for the rest of her life. Tears filled her throat and burned behind her eyelids as she watched Francesca walk down those stairs and away from the life they had lived together.

Francesca floated down the steps in the glorious ivory silk gown Renata had designed for her. The fabric shimmered as the graceful belled skirt flowed around her long legs. The beaded bodice glittered under the warm light from the huge chandeliers. Her golden red hair, pinned up softly with white tuberoses, framed her pale face like a halo of torchlight. The guests murmured their admiration, and Josie found herself joining them in a long, incredulous "Oooh!" as the count swept Francesca across the entranceway to take her place beside him in the reception line.

Josie remained in the hallway, unwilling to subject herself to a brief, cool handshake from her lifelong friend. Instead, she wandered through the rooms, then out onto the palazzo steps to watch the last of the guests arrive.

It was nearly an hour later when Francesca entered the ballroom at her father's side. She felt herself hang on air for a second, suspended above the ground by the force of the guests' palpable admiration. Then her father took her in his arms and the room swirled into color and noise.

Everyone was curious about Susannah's daughter, this lost, forgotten child who had burst upon them after so many years. She was almost the same age now as Susannah had been when she first blazed into their path. No one had expected Francesca to be as beautiful as her mother, or to have as startling a presence. More delicate than Susannah, she lacked the bold look that could stamp its will on a roomful of strangers. But she cast a spell that was just as arresting. She had entered the ballroom like a golden sylph, full of joy and grace. If Susannah reminded one of the lush allegories of summer the Renaissance painters loved, her daughter was spring, fresh and sweet and innocent as a Parma violet. She was not Susannah, but no less a queen; a May queen bringing hope after a dark season.

"She's so young," the duchess of Balfour exclaimed. "Her mother all over again."

"Hopefully not!" Her companion, a sharp-featured older woman in magnificent diamonds, winked at the duchess. The duke put a warning hand on his wife's shoulder.

"*Tais-toi,* Antoinette. There'll be no talk of scandal tonight. Do you hear, *chérie?*" he added, softening his tone for the benefit of their friends clustered around them. But it was too late.

" 'Scandal'! What 'scandal,' Antoinette?"

She shrugged off her husband's hand and turned defiantly to the group. "*Cette pauvre petite,*" the duchess declared, indicating Francesca on the dance floor, "has a lot to live down as well as live up to." With that she smiled suggestively and swept away, leaving them all clucking curiously among themselves.

The duke strode off resignedly in the opposite direction in search of a drink. No use warning his old friend Nordonia.

What harm could those old bags do? Plenty, he admitted to himself with a sigh.

Even the meanest among these illustrious guests were hard pressed to cast a shadow of past misfortune on such innocence, but Antoinette de Balfour, like a wicked fairy godmother, managed it. Like a tiny flame, the word "scandal" spread through the crowded rooms of the palazzo, causing Francesca's appearance to be greeted with more than ordinary curiosity, and sometimes even with whispers, which Francesca was happily oblivious to. Some guests stood staring long and hard at Susannah's portrait in the hallway, searching their memories for the details of old newspaper headlines.

Carlo and the duke stood watching a woman examining the portrait through her lorgnette as if she were hoping to find a lost clue in the very consistency of the paint. When she saw she was being observed, she tittered with embarrassment, mouthed the word "magnificent" at Carlo and, with a little wave, rejoined the other guests.

"They are in the minority, you can be sure; those who remember." The duke clapped Carlo on the back. "Don't let it spoil your evening."

Feeling desperately lonely, Josie walked outside to stand on the steps of the palazzo. A gondola pulled away from the landing. An instant later, another one took its place, tilting in the water as its passengers stepped out. A stout gray-haired woman steadied herself on the arm of a tall, lean man. "Hold on tight, Maggie," Josie heard him say. "The last foot of this journey is the most dangerous. Be careful or we'll both end up waltzing in the canal."

A cheerful American voice. Where had she heard it before? Josie looked at the man and saw a shock of blond hair and a craggy profile. "There you go," he said as he helped the woman to the landing, and Josie knew him. It was Jack Westman, the actor who had chased Francesca on their first day in Venice, jumping from one gondola to another.

"Maggie Strauss," Josie heard someone behind her say. "And that's Westman, the American actor."

"She has good taste in men," another woman's voice answered.

"She collects them like works of art." The two women lowered their voices as the couple drew closer.

"Maybe, but he's also a connoisseur, quite a collector himself."

"Strictly contemporary, I suppose, the younger the better."

"No, not really. He and that actress, Nadia Baldini, have been having an affair for years but I hear it's off at the moment. That's how Maggie happened to snare him for tonight."

The voices ceased as Westman paused on the steps. The light fell on his tanned face as he helped his famous friend up the stairs. Josie was directly above him, close enough to make out his angular face and bright blue eyes. He wore his formal clothing almost too easily; there was something of the outlaw about him that reminded her of a cat burglar in tie and tails. Politely he maneuvered his way around the two women. He gave Maggie Strauss a devilish grin and whispered something in her ear. They were laughing as they stepped indoors.

No sooner had they entered the palazzo than they were surrounded by friends. Maggie Strauss was as popular in Venice as she was in New York or Paris. A plain-looking, good-hearted woman, she had dedicated her life to art and even built a fine museum in her native America. The entire world linked her name to beauty, yet for all the masterpieces she owned, she was said to be ashamed of her own reflection in the mirror. The expression in her eyes, Josie noticed, was full of warm intelligence and humor, but the features were coarse and homely.

"I'll introduce you to anyone you want to meet," Maggie said to Jack in her strong Texas accent. "With one exception: the count's daughter. She's an innocent young thing, I hear, and I won't have you corrupting her. Carlo had her educated in some convent at the end of the world, and he'd murder me if I let someone as disreputable as you put sinful ideas into her head."

"Maggie!" Jack raised his eyebrows in feigned incredulity. "How can you imagine that I, of all people, would be the one to despoil an innocent Italian virgin?"

Maggie Strauss waved away the comment dismissively. She turned away from him as the majordomo walked past them. "Ah, Emilio, there you are. Where is the count?"

The majordomo began to point down the hallway but Jack pulled away from her. He was staring, along with most of the men in the foyer, at an extremely beautiful dark girl who was walking, or rather parading, down the grand staircase. Maggie noticed the rich quality of her skin, like café au lait, and the stunning dress that accentuated her narrow waist and high bosom. There was something deliberately provocative in her languorous descent; Maggie immediately thought of *Nude Descending a Staircase* juxtaposed with a nineteenth-century photograph of the creole mistress of a plantation owner. She had displayed it in a photography exhibit.

"Carlo's in the ballroom." She nudged Jack, who was transfixed.

"What? Will you excuse me a moment? I'll meet him later, Maggie. You go prepare the way."

The young woman reached the lower stairs and Maggie saw her face clearly. "Oh Jack, she's nothing more than a girl."

"She handles herself like a woman. Will you be all right without me?"

"Of course. Everyone I know is here tonight. Promise you'll come along later."

"Sure," he said.

Maggie hid her pang of jealousy under a determined smile and turned toward the ballroom.

Chapter Seven

JOSIE WOULD NOT meet Jack Westman's eyes, though she could feel them leading her on. She wanted to plunge down the stairs, out the front door and away, but she paced herself, smiling into the upturned faces beneath her. She made herself survey the foyer slowly, looking away only when she came across Westman. She knew it annoyed him; she could see him frown out of the corner of her eye. Courage, she thought to herself. It was difficult enough to try to lure such a famous man into paying attention to her; worse was her sudden sense of guilt, for she realized she was trying to reach this man before her best friend did. At the bottom of the stair she drew a deep breath and decided to walk right past him.

She had already sighed with relief—or disappointment, she didn't know which—when she felt a hand on her arm.

"Hello, I'm Jack Westman," he said, staring intently into her eyes.

"Josie . . ." she replied and awkwardly shook his hand.

"Why were you running away from me?"

"Bad habit," she answered lightly as he pulled her toward the ballroom.

"I don't usually dance, but for you . . ."

Josie stopped dead in her tracks. "I'm sorry," she stammered, "I don't waltz." She recovered her dignity slightly.

"Then we'll have a drink," he said, not missing a beat, and swung her around to lead her back through the throng. A waiter passed with a tray of glasses.

"Champagne?" Jack asked.

"Please." Josie took a big gulp of the ice-cold wine as Jack led her firmly to a less crowded spot near the windows.

"Now, what is an exotic-looking woman like you doing in a place like this?" he asked as he took a flask out of his pocket and, giving her a wink, poured the dark liquid into his already empty champagne glass.

"I'm from Nassau," she began. "Francesca lives with my mother and me."

"Oh," he said, and for the first time he seemed to be at a loss for words.

"We're like sisters . . . or rather we were," she added under her breath. She drained her glass and a lovely giddy feeling came over her. She laughed at the confused expression on his face. "Francesca Nordonia, silly," she said boldly. "This party is in her honor."

"Ah, yes, I've been warned she's quite a catch."

"Wait till you see her . . . *Maman,* my mother used to call us her two kittens."

"*Mes petites chattes?*" Jack translated.

"That's right. You speak French?" Josie asked, surprised.

"*Très peu,*" Jack admitted. "I have a terrible accent."

"So do I!" Josie gave a shout of glee and immediately clapped her hand over her mouth as a couple turned and looked at her curiously. Her "disgraceful" accent seemed suddenly so unimportant.

"You have a beautiful smile." Jack was leaning very close to her with an unmistakable look in his eyes.

"You sound like the wolf in 'Little Red Riding Hood.' " Josie laughed but her heart thumped. "May I have some more champagne?" she asked.

A waiter was passing close by. Jack caught up to the servant and brought her back a glass. Just as he handed her the champagne with a little bow somebody jostled him from behind and the wine splashed onto her skirt. He whipped out his handkerchief and Josie leaned down to dry the stain. As she straightened up again and offered him back his handkerchief, she caught the expression on his face and she knew without following his gaze that he had spotted Francesca. Her gaiety evaporated, and turned to stone inside her. Francesca was standing at the entrance of the ballroom, surrounded by people, and yet she seemed alone like a night-blooming lily in a dark garden. Her hands in their long white gloves were open and seemed to be stretched out toward them a little. But it was the look in her eyes that Josie had never seen before, a look of recognition somehow as Jack stepped away from her. She didn't wait to see any more but turned and, pushing through the crowd, bolted for the stairs.

Francesca thought it took him forever to cross the distance that separated them. When he finally reached her they looked at each other for a moment. Then without a word he put his arm around her lightly and they began to dance. It was a slow tune; neither could remember later what it was. Minutes passed and they were lost in the sensation of each other's being. He felt her sensitivity and her highly strung nerves. A blue vein in her delicate wrist was throbbing when he held her hand near his cheek. She sensed his warmth and vitality under the starched shirt.

"My Madonna," he said at last and had to clear his throat. "So while I was looking for you in every hotel lobby and restaurant in Venice you were right here hiding in this old fortress."

Francesca smiled. "Rather a magnificent old fortress, you have to admit?"

"The countess in her palazzo—just as it should be."

"Oh, please, I hate that . . ."

Jack laughed. "You don't like being a countess?"

Francesca blushed. "Well, it really doesn't matter, does it?" she finished lamely.

Jack stared down at her. Then, gently, he pulled her close. "No, no, it doesn't matter, not in the least," he murmured slowly.

The music changed tempo and Jack gave her a little hug and twirled her around.

Francesca knew the lyrics by heart. "You mustn't kick it around." It had been an old record of her mother's. She and Josie had practiced dancing barefoot to it in Nassau.

"I saw you were talking to Josie . . ."

"The other 'little cat'?"

"She told you . . . ?"

"About her mother and about Nassau. I'd already been warned about your father and if I'm not mistaken, here he comes now," Jack said through his teeth.

There was no mistaking Carlo. Taller than either of them, he appeared at their side like a thundercloud glaring down at them from under his brows.

"You don't mind, Mr. Westman, if I dance with my daughter?"

"Not at all, not at all." Jack gave her hand a squeeze, bowed with a flourish, and was gone.

The electricity flowed out of her arms when he let go of her. She turned to her father in exasperation but one look at his expression silenced her instantly. He took her in his arms and she followed him through the steps automatically.

"That man certainly impressed you," Carlo said sarcastically. "I thought you were going to faint in the middle of the dance floor."

Francesca said nothing.

"Right in front of everyone. It's a good thing I rescued you." He spoke teasingly but the effort to control his annoyance was obvious.

"Yes, Papa."

"I didn't know you had such a soft spot for American cowboys."

"Mama was an American."

"A movie star!" he went on as if he hadn't heard her. "One of Maggie Strauss's friends. I'm not saying I object to his coming here tonight. Far from it. I'm willing to extend my hospitality to any friend of Maggie's. But remember your position, Francesca. You must be polite to everyone, no matter how trying. But you also must take care not to encourage suitors who may not be worthy."

"But, Papa, I simply danced with the man. I don't even know him."

"It's best to keep it that way. Remember, not all men are serious or sincere about women. I just want to protect you, *piccola*."

"It's all right, Papa. I'll remember."

Francesca no longer heard her father. She kept her gaze fixed over his shoulder, and, while seeming not to, she scanned the large, crowded room for a glimpse of Jack. He can't have gone, she prayed soundlessly. But he was nowhere.

The music died for a moment, and the guests turned toward the windows. A muted chanting filled the night. Pulling back the draperies, they stared down at the canal where dozens of paparazzi shouted from their speedboats, demanding a glimpse of the young countess.

Carlo sought out Emilio and ordered him to get rid of the photographers before they disrupted the party. The moment he relinquished Francesca, Jack was at her elbow.

"May I see you tomorrow?"

"I'd like to, but my father won't let me go out alone."

"Your father doesn't much like me, does he?"

"My father is very old-fashioned, very strict."

"I have to see you."

"Maybe there's a way," Francesca said slowly. "Josie and I are going to the Lido tomorrow afternoon. Perhaps you could meet us there."

"Tomorrow afternoon. I'll wait for you in front of the Excelsior Hotel. Don't disappoint me."

When Carlo turned back to Francesca, Jack was immersed in conversation with the Earl of Leicester. They stood several feet away from Francesca. The earl was impressed with Westman's film work, and he took it upon himself to introduce the actor to the count.

"We've already met," Carlo said coldly.

"May I make a suggestion?" Jack said. "The only way to get rid of the paparazzi is to give them what they want. Usually a very brief appearance will satisfy them. If I may offer some advice from my own experience, let them see Francesca and take her picture. Once satisfied, they'll go home."

The count listened skeptically, but the Englishman urged him on. Francesca, who had joined them, reluctantly nodded her assent to the idea.

"I suppose it won't hurt to try it," Carlo said at last.

"But there are so many people on the balcony here, it's ready to collapse. You'd better go to the second floor."

"It might be best if I escort your daughter," Jack said quickly, taking Francesca by the elbow. Before Carlo had time to object, the two were gone.

The second floor was deserted, awash with moonlight and distant music. The roar of the paparazzi frightened Francesca when Jack opened the French doors. She reached for his hand, and together they stepped out on the stone balcony, into the cool night air. Francesca waved into the flash of light.

For a moment Jack's strategy seemed to have misfired. When the crowd of photographers recognized Westman, their roar grew even louder. Their flashbulbs burned fiercely and the noise was deafening, but the uproar only served to seal off Francesca and Jack from the jostling mass beneath them. Francesca clung to Jack's hand until finally he pulled her indoors and forced her, with the intensity of his gaze, to look into his eyes. He pressed his lips to her forehead. Then he was gone.

Francesca stood still for a moment, smiling into the darkness. Looking around to make sure no one saw her, she did a little jig of joy on the marble floor. It was her own version of a waltz, and it gathered the moonlight and the music and the soft summer night into the shining folds of her skirt.

From the staircase above, Josie watched as Francesca twirled. In the dark her face and dress seemed to radiate with their own silver light. Josie shrank back behind a pillar. Although she could not be seen in the shadows, she feared somehow her envy would give her away. Once she would have been happy to see Francesca's lilting dance, but now it drained her own strength from her. Earlier, when she had spied on Jack Westman and Francesca in the ballroom and saw Westman come to life in Francesca's arms, all she could think was that she would never be close to Francesca again. Now Josie welcomed the darkness that bored into her breast, and found the courage to name Francesca her enemy. It made her feel strong once again.

It grew late. Just before midnight, liveried servants brought out the platters of delicate seafood antipasto, a splendid Venetian array of giant crab, clams, octopus, and caviar; this was followed by the pièce de résistance, a long *rosa salmone* in a delicate lemon sauce, served with angel-hair pasta tossed with a local delicacy, *seppia*—cuttlefish—and its ink. For less adventurous guests, there were platters of pheasant and quail on beds of risotto, mushrooms, and chestnuts; and to clear the palate, blood-orange *sorbetto*.

Outside the windows, colored light cascaded through the sky as the fireworks celebration to mark Francesca's eighteenth birthday began. Maggie Strauss had reclaimed Westman, much to Carlo's relief. Francesca was again surrounded by the sons of the finest families in Europe, who gave her no time to look for Westman. She had never been happier; the mere remembrance of that moment of intimacy on the balcony in the blaze of flashbulbs made her ecstatic.

At the stroke of midnight the count separated Francesca from her new friends and led her upstairs to his library. He took a gray velvet box from a desk drawer. "This is from your mother. She wanted you to have it when you reached eighteen."

Francesca opened the box under the desk lamp and saw, gleaming on the satin bed, a strand of luminous pearls. When Carlo held the necklace up to the light, its sheen made her gasp. A delicate pendant hung from the strand. It was a blossom, its petals carved from freshwater pearls, the diamond stamens sparkling as brilliantly as the fireworks outside. Wordlessly, Francesca balanced the delicate sprays of light on her fingertips.

"I commissioned Boucheron to make it for Susannah." Carlo's voice held a hint of pride. "It was my gift to her on the day you were born."

Overwhelmed, Francesca wanted to express her pleasure, but some new rift had opened between her and her father that not even this gift from the past could bridge. Carlo fastened the necklace around her neck and kissed her cheek, his dry lips barely touching her.

"It's as lovely on you as it was on your mother."

She raised a hand to touch the necklace. She tried to summon up enough courage to tell her father how much the necklace meant to her, but he turned toward the window, and the moment was lost.

"Now, *cara mia*, run along and attend to your guests. I'll be down soon."

When Francesca reached the foyer, Jack Westman was there helping Maggie Strauss into her cape. He stopped short in the middle of his sentence when he caught Francesca's eye.

"What is it?" his companion demanded, her hands drawing the cape around her neck.

Westman, remembering her warning about Carlo's daughter, said quickly, "Nothing, really," as he smiled at the girl and herded Maggie toward the door. Maggie could sense that his attention had been suddenly diverted and she swept around to face Francesca. The girl stood dazed beneath the portrait of her mother, as still as if she were part of the painting.

"There you are! Just a moment, Jack, don't rush me. It's late enough, another minute won't make any difference. There's Francesca. Let's say good night to her."

She approached Francesca. "Darling, I've been raving about you all night to everyone, Jack here will testify to it. I want to thank you and Carlo for a wonderful evening. It looks like Venice will be interesting again. Where is your father, by the way?" Maggie gushed, reaching for the girl's hands. Then her eye traveled from the girl's tremulous face to Jack's. The older woman straightened and crooked her arm through the man's. The gesture broke the lock of the young lovers' eyes. "Now make sure to tell Carlo that I'll be calling him," she insisted, and with Jack firmly in tow she marched out of the foyer.

Jack's head shot around the door a split second later. His lips shaped one word, "Tomorrow." Francesca, laughing, ran up to the door to wave good-bye.

There was shouting on the boat landing. Below the guests a man in jeans and a plaid shirt stood in a motorboat nudging the landing. "Jack!" he slurred the name drunkenly. "Get your carcass out here!"

Westman looked with embarrassment at Maggie and shrugged his shoulders apologetically. "He's a friend of mine from the film, Arkansas Whalen, my stand-in. It looks like he stood in for me tonight at every bar in town."

"Get the hell down here, Westman, and let's go have a drink!" Arkansas yelled.

Jack excused himself from Maggie and recklessly bolted down the steps to the landing to stop Arkansas from coming any farther. But he slipped on the last steps and shot through the air.

A drunken cry of "Man overboard!" echoed across the water. As Francesca watched Jack plummet beneath the canal's surface, a terrible fear clutched her heart. It seemed as if the cold darkness were closing over her own heart; a fleeting deadly premonition that was gone the second Jack's head surfaced.

Arkansas leaned over to lift him out of the water by the nape of the neck, but Jack grabbed his friend's shoulder and playfully pitched him overboard into the gloom. Francesca and the remaining guests crowded onto the balcony to clap and laugh.

Upstairs, at the sound of the roughhousing on the landing, the count came to the window of his study to survey the night spread out before him. He closed the leaded-glass windows in disgust at the sight of the men splashing in the water, making buffoons of themselves. Still, though the ball had been marred by the paparazzi and this American playboy, it didn't matter. Tonight, Francesca had had her triumph. He was proud of his daughter.

Chapter Eight

In the darkened ballroom the last stragglers chatted quietly among themselves at small candlelit tables. Josie stood watching from the doorway while the five-piece orchestra packed up their instruments to go home. She had been told that she would sing with the orchestra, but Emilio had put her off. "You'll sing later," he had said, and now it was too late. Westman had left, Carlo had gone off upstairs, and Francesca was out on the portico saying good-bye to the most influential guests. The only audience that mattered wasn't there to hear her.

Someone began to play the piano. She threaded her way through the remaining guests and approached the piano player, a black man, slight and handsome in a white dinner jacket. His heavy tortoiseshell glasses gave him a learned air.

"Go right ahead; I don't mind if you stare." He smiled at her. "I'm Charles Cash."

"I'm sorry. It's just that I never expected to see another colored person here tonight."

"You've never been to the European music festivals in the summer, then. Lots of us come to play. The Europeans like American jazz. Are you the girl who's going to sing?"

She nodded.

"The majordomo says you're good. Let's see what you can do."

He led the way on the piano. Josie sang the first few bars tentatively, getting a feel for the room and for the pianist. The ballroom, now a sea of glistening candles, was an acoustical dream, and Charles played with such sensitivity to her phrasing that she soon relaxed. She stood next to the glossy piano, oblivious to the crowd, and sang for herself, feeling isolated here among strangers, exotic and alone. She realized that solitude was a country as foreign to her as Europe. She had not been raised for it. She had never been a stranger as she was tonight. She was used to the open friendliness of the island, the daily communion of happiness.

But the music slowly dissolved her unhappiness. Charles charmed her, encouraged her with his attentive playing, and she began to sing for him. For all his devoutly intellectual air, he played the piano with a rapture that grew impassioned. He modulated into a higher key to explore the range of her voice. When she strained for a note, he reassured her with his warm smile, rescuing her with another graceful change of key.

"There, you made it that time," he said to her a second later.

She was surprised; she hadn't realized how high he'd taken her.

"Your voice is warmed up now. Let's try another tune."

He lifted his hands from the piano, and the room filled with applause. Josie was startled. The sound of clapping elated her. The knowledge that she had impressed a roomful of strangers eased the tight knot in her breast. As Charles began to play again, Josie forgot about Westman and Francesca and lost herself in the melody. "Wading in the Water." Charles joined her in singing the last chorus, and before they had even finished, the room rang with applause.

Josie saw shapes moving through the darkness. Guests were coming back into the room to hear her. Was it so easy to move people? She had felt like an outcast all night, but now the room was hushed in anticipation, and her first European audience appeared to love her.

"That was great," Charles said.

She smiled, then deliberately changed her mood. "Do you know 'In My Solitude'?"

She could tell by the way he caressed the keys that it was the kind of song he wanted to play. Josie felt that she had earned the right to sing this song, that Venice had taught her the way.

As she sang about loneliness, she thought of Francesca and the slow disintegration of their long friendship. She saw her *p'tite soeur*'s face before her, innocent and loving at first, then growing distracted, turning away, fading and dimming until it almost disappeared.

The dramatic lighting in the room accentuated the high bones of Josie's face. Her eyes seemed larger and more expressive than usual. Attentive silence fell over the room as her mellow contralto held the audience spellbound; her voice was unusual, combining the warm tone of the alto with the range and brightness of the soprano.

When the stirring song ended, fresh waves of applause washed over her, warming her and renewing her spirit and energy. The ballroom was filled with people now—where had they all come from?—and their shouts of encouragement told her they had no intention of letting her stop singing.

For nearly an hour she flooded the room with sound, reaching into her memory for the lilting calypso tunes of the Caribbean, letting Charles lead her through an occasional blues number, and ending with a rollicking gospel song. That set the whole roomful of sophisticated Europeans stomping their feet.

She left the room to a standing ovation and noticed, with a catch in her throat, that every face she saw was wreathed in a smile. Accepting congratulations and shaking hands on every side, she made her way out of the ballroom, knowing that, despite her own misery, she had made a roomful of people very happy.

Behind her as she reached the stairway, Charles said, "Let me take you to lunch tomorrow, to celebrate your triumph."

"*Our* triumph," she corrected. "You were wonderful." She turned to see him smiling down at her, not so handsome as Jack Westman, perhaps, but handsome enough to have lunch with. "Pick me up at noon? I'll be waiting out in front."

"Great." Charles gave her a friendly peck on the cheek and disappeared into the departing crowd.

Josie turned to go upstairs and found herself face-to-face with a glowing Francesca. "*Petite soeur*," she burst out, "wasn't it wonderful? So much applause!"

Francesca looked embarrassed. "I was outside saying good-bye to the guests," she said uncomfortably. "Then Papa insisted that I go with him to the Gold Room to talk with the people from Spain. I'm very sorry I didn't hear you sing, Josie. All the guests are raving about you."

"It doesn't matter," Josie said, brushing past her and rushing up the stairs. But it did matter, Josie realized; it mattered terribly. At least Francesca understood what she had missed; Carlo wouldn't even know about her success. Why did his opinion matter? she asked herself. Why did his dismissal of her hurt so deeply?

"So what?" she said to her reflection in the mirror when she had shut herself in her room. "Even if Carlo heard you were half nightingale, he wouldn't care. He'd still send you downstairs to eat with the servants. You don't need his pat on the head any more than you need Francesca's."

But the sad amber eyes that looked out at her from the gilt frame on the apple green wall told her she was lying to herself. Wearily, she took off the beautiful red dress, hung it lovingly in the closet, and climbed into the soft, high bed.

Dawn was breaking when Francesca waved the last guests good-bye on the portico. Even the paparazzi had abandoned the canal and only a single servant moved among the debris of the buffet, bearing away the last empty glasses. The tinkling crystal reminded her it was morning, but she didn't feel the hour at all. She could barely keep her feet still. *I've carried it off*, she thought, tapping her feet in a nervous pattern across the grand hallway. She came to a halt in front of her mother's portrait and looked up at the painting with pride. A million hours ago, she had descended these stairs in trepidation, but now she would fly up with joy.

She must sleep. She must. In a few hours she would meet Jack Westman at the Lido. The thought made her knees weak. Who was he, really? She realized she was grinning like an idiot at the thin dawn air. She ran upstairs. But instead of continuing up to the third floor, Francesca paused, then headed for her mother's room. This was another dawn she wanted to spend with Susannah.

The room was as peaceful as when Francesca had left it two weeks before. She slipped across the Aubusson carpet to the dressing table and pulled the chain of the little silver tree. The mirror burst into light. Francesca saw her hair was tousled and her cheeks feverish, her eyes glistening. I've had too much champagne, she thought. A hand went to her neck where the delicate rose of pearls gleamed.

"Oh, Mama, you should see me now," she breathed. "I *am* beautiful." Not just beautiful, but incandescent, glowing with excitement. She soundlessly opened the dressing table drawer and took out a round disk of eye shadow. She dabbed a finger in the silvery green powder and brushed it across her eyelids, then leaned back to admire herself. She looked far older and more mysterious. Then she applied her mother's lipstick and smiled seductively at her reflection. The vivid color brought out the shape of her mouth. Arching her neck, she tried to catch the exact expression of the woman in the portrait downstairs, a look in which pride and excitement and warmth ignited the features. She had never seen that look of triumph glitter in her eyes before. For the first time, it looked like Susannah facing her in the glass.

Inspired now, Francesca sought out the hidden door in the wall that opened on a mirrored dressing room she remembered from her childhood. It was camouflaged among the lacquered panels, but after a moment she found the spring. The wall gave way beneath her fingers to reveal a small room, its light triggered by the door hinge. She beheld row upon row of Susannah's clothes. The smell of her mother's perfume flooded the room with her presence. Francesca opened the closets. There were Susannah's winter coats, soft and fur-collared, sliplike dresses fragile with lace, and a rack of sequined ball gowns and satin robes. One wall was lined with transparent boxes of shoes, shiny lizard and gleaming leather.

Francesca touched the dresses, fearing for a moment that, like flowers dried between the pages of a book, they might crumble at her touch into pools of dust. But they were smooth and creamy beneath her fingers. Among them hung a long sequined evening cape of blue velvet, and she couldn't resist slipping it on. It was as soft as a kitten. She stepped back into the bedroom and pirouetted before the mirror.

"I am you, Susannah," she said.

A pale face appeared over her shoulder in the mirror. She gasped and whirled around.

Carlo stood in the doorway, his eyes filled with grief and shock. He held himself stiffly, as if afraid to move. Francesca's heart pounded in her ears, but over its din she heard him whisper, "Susannah . . ." Slowly he moved toward her, scarcely breathing, reaching out one hand, as if to touch a memory.

Frightened now, Francesca took a step away from him, bumping into the dressing table and making the delicate lamp tingle musically. The slight movement and sound jarred Carlo back into the present. His features hardened as reality sparked behind his glazed eyes, and Francesca knew she'd done something terribly wrong.

"Take that cape off and get out of here," Carlo thundered. "You are not to come into these rooms again."

Francesca fled to the dressing room, shedding the velvet cape. Her cheeks reddened as if Carlo had slapped her. She peeked around the door. Her father stood before the dressing table, staring at the glittering candelabra, consumed by his own tragic thoughts. She tried to escape to the privacy of her bedroom, but as she slipped past him he reached out and gripped her arm. She twisted in fear as he swung her around, and was amazed to find his eyes gentle with tears. Immediately she relaxed and placed both hands on his chest as if to comfort him.

"Papa," she said, her voice barely audible, "I'm so sorry. I didn't know . . ."

He bent his head, and the sorrow in his dark eyes wrenched at her heart. She had not realized that Carlo still loved her mother after all these years, still mourned her.

"I miss her, too," she said in a small voice. "I didn't mean any harm."

Carlo raised his hand to smooth back her hair. "I know you didn't, *cara mia*."

She felt a tremor of grief shake his body. For a moment he closed his eyes, but when he raised his head, he was composed again. "Forgive me, Francesca. For a moment you looked so much like her . . ." He slipped his arms around her and held her. After a long pause, he cleared his throat. "I am not angry with you, Francesca, just unused to so many reminders of the past, and then to see you in this room, wearing that cape . . ." He held her away from him and took both her hands in his. "You are the one who should be angry, *cara mia*, at a father who kept you away from him for so many years. Be angry, if you must, but please believe that I did not stay away out of a lack of love for you."

"I believe you."

"Hard as this may be to understand," Carlo continued, "nothing means more to me than my family, and you are my family." He squeezed her hands, then let them go. "You were perfect tonight, *piccola*. Everyone fell in love with you. You have become a beauty in your own right."

"Thank you, Papa." Francesca's face, like her father's, was wet with tears.

"Such terrible late hours these Venetians keep," he said with a crooked smile. "Come, I'll walk you to your room."

She clicked out the lamp. Through the windows, she saw that the sky was streaked with red. They walked down the hallway to the staircase, their arms around each other. At the door of her bedroom, Carlo kissed her brow. "Good night, *cara mia.*"

"Good night, Papa." Through a film of tears she watched her father walk down the hall. There was in his bearing a new assurance, born perhaps of the knowledge that his daughter loved him in spite of everything.

Carlo stood for a long time at his bedroom window, watching the sky turn from red to gray to blue, wondering how his child could have ripened and blossomed so quickly. Only weeks ago she had arrived in Venice, shy and awkward, a mere schoolgirl who seemed incapable of assuming ownership of the palazzo one day. Then he had wished her more confident, more self-assured.

Carlo's wish had been granted. Francesca had dazzled his guests tonight and made him proud, but he had deep misgivings about her new self-possession, and especially her frightening resemblance to her mother.

He wondered whether a personality could be transmitted from mother to daughter biologically. Was there a gene for aberration and adventure that determined fate as surely as skin and bone were handed down from mother to daughter? After all, when he met Susannah she seemed nearly as innocent as Francesca in her white gown, but the strange tendency was already part of her, waiting to astonish and confound them both. "But I must have always been this way," Susannah had protested to him once. "I just never knew it. I can't help it. It's part of me, like my hands or my feet. It's an instinct, like breathing air."

1952

CARLO STRODE THROUGH the half-finished mansion in Lyford Cay. Every room seemed to be full of Bahamians, hammering, scraping, or sawing away. He had to give Susannah credit; she had gotten more work done in less time than he ever thought possible. The modern structure, airy and filled with light, took advantage of its tropical environment instead of walling it out. Its open corridors and glass walls were in exact contrast with the palazzo or the Victorian home he had sold on Hog Island. He walked under the trees through the torn-up part of the garden, nodding to the half a dozen gardeners busily carrying out Susannah's horticultural plans. At last the din and racket was behind him and the white sands stretched under his feet down to the sea. The sound of the gentle waves soothed his ears. After swimming for a long time he stretched out on the beach. The hammering in the distance had finally stopped. The men must have quit for lunch. Susannah should be back. She had left early to go to see her new English friend who lived nearby; an artist, someone whom she had met before he'd arrived. He was glad she had found some company; the cay was deserted at this time of year, and he spent too much of his time in Italy on business to be here all the time. Still, his plan had been successful. The house was serving its purpose. Supervising the work together from drawing board to laying the roof had eased the tensions of their marriage. The renovation on the palazzo completed, he had wanted to find a new way to keep Susannah happily at home with him, and creating a new home together had recaptured her imagination. Best of all, Susannah had at last professed that she wanted another child, a companion for Francesca.

As he lay on his stomach with his head on his arms, he noticed far up the beach two dark stick figures against the sky. Half-asleep, he watched them approach through his lashes. Heat waves rose from the sand between him and them. They looked like long-legged birds dancing on the light as they playfully separated and converged. He had decided they were natives trespassing on the deserted beach. But as they came closer, one figure darted away abruptly and he heard a tinkle of laughter and a flash of red hair that, he realized with a little shock, was unmistakably Susannah's. But she was behaving so unlike herself, like a child. He suddenly felt he was spying on her. They were standing still now, facing each other. Susannah and the other woman. He could see now it was a woman—or rather a girl, almost as tall and thinner even than Susannah. They were talking, talking endlessly. What could they be discussing at such length? Didn't she care that he might be waiting lunch for her? he thought peevishly—Susannah, who was always hungry and never on time for a meal. He watched as they took each other's hands, kissed, and one started upward toward the tree line as the other watched. But then she ran back, gave Susannah another embrace. Again the laughter. Finally she was coming toward him. He waited, his throat constricted. Why should he be so alarmed? Ridiculous. He reminded himself that jealousy of Susannah was not a new sensation, only one that he simply didn't admit he felt even to himself. He rolled over on his back, forcing himself to keep his eyes shut until he felt Susannah's shadow fall across him and her breath on his cheek.

"Hi."

Her face was close to his. Her teeth gleamed white as she grinned down at him. Her hair was tied up and her freckles and sunbleached lashes made her look like a very young boy.

"Was that your friend?" he asked casually after she had settled down next to him.

"Mmmm," she nodded.

She was leaning on her elbows looking thoughtfully out at the sea. He could see the swell of her breast under the halter where her tan stopped, white as the fruit of the litchi nut.

"Well, what's she like?" he asked.

"Sybilla? Remarkable," Susannah said slowly, "really remarkable. She's twenty-three and she's already had her first exhibit in Paris."

"She paints?"

"She's a glorious painter. You must take a trip next door and see what her mother has got hanging on her wall."

"Lady Jane, that ogre? She and her daughter seem to call you up on any pretext ever since we installed the telephone last week. I've regretted that we put it in."

"Lady Jane is a bit pushy," Susannah agreed. "Poor woman, I'm afraid that's the way she makes her living, from latching on to important people and giving parties."

"I thought she had a lot of money of her own. What about the grand manor in England you told me about?"

"The lord is in his manor drinking up the last of the fortune. He hates Nassau."

"So, she's been confiding in you."

"A little. And the rest is easy to see. I don't think she's got much beyond what she sank into her new house next door. Appearances are everything with her. But Sybilla is completely different, natural and innocent and remarkably talented. I think we'll enjoy getting to know her."

There was a long pause.

"Where's Francesca?" Susannah asked suddenly.

"It's too hot for her at this time of day," Carlo said. "I keep telling you that."

"Fiddlesticks!" Susannah jumped up. Carlo reached for her hand.

"No. Wait a minute."

"What?" Susannah squatted back down. She combed his hair back from his forehead with her fingers. "What?" she repeated more gently. Her bottom lip was parched from the sun and he yearned to run his tongue over it.

"How about a kiss?"

Her face blotted out the sun and her mouth tasted of salt and fruit. She didn't pull away. Instead he felt her breasts heavy against him as she breathed evenly, leaning over him. Looking up into her eyes, he wondered for the thousandth time at the contradiction between her calm and his own intense excitement.

"Do you really want another child, Susannah?"

"I told you I did, didn't I?" She ran a finger over his lips and poked it teasingly into his mouth. He caught it in his teeth quickly, sucked it, and then took her hand in his, ending the game.

"You know I do, darling. I want a son as much as you do." She sounded too insistent to herself. It was a sore point between them.

"But you were so housebound with Francesca. Have you forgotten so quickly?"

"Why are you playing devil's advocate with me, Carlo? You've been after me for two years to try to conceive again. Now that I've decided, don't try to talk me out of it."

He loved it when she took up a cause. He always imagined her striding out of the clouds leading a celestial army, like an incarnation of the Winged Victory. "I won't, don't worry. No one ever talked you out of anything. I'm just so glad you've had this change of heart."

"It's not a change of heart, really. I love children, once they're old enough so that I can have some freedom." But, she thought, if it's not a boy this time, how many times will he expect me to try?

That evening Sybilla Hillford came to dinner. Susannah dragged a couple of borrowed wicker chairs out onto the raw planks of the new veranda. Carlo sat on the steps and Francesca clambered into her mother's lap as Marianne brought them gin and tonic.

"Here you are, so civilized, and the roof is barely raised," Sybilla said.

She took a sip of her drink while Carlo smiled at her. Carlo watched the two women's polite exchange. Remembering their behavior on the beach that morning, he remarked to himself that they were really children playing at being grown women, or was it the other way around?

He found Sybilla's presence grating, an intrusion in this peaceful hour when the workmen left. He wondered at her tension; she exuded a kind of taut mental energy, as if she were in the middle of an exam instead of having a cocktail. She was an attractive girl—perhaps a little too thin, with dark brown hair and eyes and a creamy English complexion—though she made no effort to make herself pretty. She wore a loose black linen dress, already wrinkled, that nearly disguised her boyish, flat torso. Although the breeze was cool she looked uncomfortable; she had already slipped her long feet out of her patent leather shoes. He saw she had faint traces of blue paint on her hands. She looked at them nervously and he realized she resented his attention. She blushed and he turned away, sorry to have embarrassed her.

"Oh, that reminds me," Susannah moaned, "I forgot to go into town to buy plates. Another night of those dreadful paper things, I'm afraid. I just hope Marianne isn't serving pasta."

"As long as we've got wineglasses," said Carlo.

"I don't mind," said Sybilla. "After my mother's formality, it's rather a relief."

"Your mother doesn't make you dress for dinner out here, for God's sake?" Susannah asked.

"Of course. We mustn't let our standards slip just because this is a resort. I don't think you fully understand my mother yet."

"Did she really have other plans? I feel terrible about leaving her next door alone."

"She was really busy. She's already jumping into the social whirl out here, or rather, creating a social whirl. But I could tell she was dying to come over and see your new house. I'm warning you, she'll give you lots of advice."

Carlo rolled his eyes at Susannah. The daughter was quite enough. Susannah ignored him and went right on.

"Tell your mother we'll invite her for dinner the minute

we've finished the dining room, or the china arrives, whichever comes first."

Carlo tried to change the subject. He wanted to be alone with his wife. He was hardly looking forward to another surprise dinner guest like this; if Susannah was too generous, they'd have both mother and daughter on their hands all the time.

As they sat having coffee after their meal, Carlo said, "I understand you're an accomplished painter."

"A painter, yes. Accomplished? I'm not sure."

"Oh, Carlo, you must walk over to Lady Jane's tomorrow and take a look at Sybilla's work. It's so impressive."

"Perhaps I shall," said Carlo with reserve.

"I've brought something to show you tonight," Sybilla said.

Susannah turned to Sybilla brightly. "What did you bring?"

Sybilla immediately launched into an academic discussion about modern art. "I just want to prepare you for what you're going to see," she finished as she brushed back a strand of her straight hair.

Carlo thought he could do without the preparation. Sybilla was pretentious, and though Carlo found his wife's conversation amusing and full of insight, Sybilla talked like a pedantic graduate student about the new abstract expressionists. He sneaked a glance at his watch. He'd been waiting all day to be alone with his wife, who in the candlelight looked warm and flushed. He reached his foot over to hers, but when he nudged her, she moved her foot away and shot him a quizzical, absorbed smile.

"I'll have more coffee, if I may," Carlo said.

Susannah ignored him. "Show us your painting now, Sybilla. I can't wait."

"Yes, let's see it," said Carlo, as if asking to see the color of her money. Both of the women laughed.

"Are you sure? I'm afraid I've been a bit of a bore," Sybilla said.

"Not at all," demurred Susannah.

The girl went out to her car and returned with a small, unframed canvas. When she turned it toward them, Carlo was surprised. It was an oil painting of bright rhythms of color. After a moment the colors took shape and he saw flowers twisting and bursting with life, vivid beyond his imagination. They were flowers in a dream that had suddenly come to life and taken on a will of their own. But in all that beauty there was a sense of menace, its luxuriance revealing a kind of deliberate sexuality. He was drawn to the painting, yet on another level its depth repelled him.

"Did you really paint that?" he said. He looked up and saw both women hanging on his words.

"Oh, Carlo, do you like it? I think it's wonderful!" Susannah exclaimed.

"It's clear you're very talented," said Carlo.

Susannah put her arm around Sybilla's shoulders, dwarfing her. "You've just got to keep it up and really dedicate yourself! If you're capable of this, you can do anything."

"If you really like the painting, you may keep it, Susannah. It's a housewarming present."

Carlo looked at her dubiously, but Susannah leaped at the opportunity. "What a wonderful gift! Thank you! And you'll loan us another one, too, as soon as you've done it?"

"Of course," Sybilla said, rising to leave. It was late; they had lingered over dinner. Carlo did not protest her leaving, but Susannah did.

"Come over tomorrow, then. You can paint the ridge, before the bulldozer has a go at it."

"All right," Sybilla promised, slipping her shoes back on.

When he heard the car jolting over the dirt outside, Carlo reached for his wife's hand. "I can't believe she's gone at last."

"Oh, you're a terror. You intimidated that poor girl to death. Thank heavens you liked the painting."

"I'm not so sure," Carlo said.

"But you do see how extraordinary she is. If only she'd work harder."

"I don't know. She's awfully young to have dedicated herself to an artist's lonely life."

"You're right, but I was glad to see that at least she wasn't drinking much tonight."

"She drinks?"

"I didn't tell you? Actually, it's the drugs that worry me. In Paris she tried everything, apparently. She came back here to stay with her mother to get better."

They looked in on Francesca. The child looked angelic below Carlo's outstretched candle, her delicate pink mouth heavy with sleep, her eyelids waxy and golden. Susannah bent over and kissed her brow.

"I love the way she smells," she said. "So clean, like wildflowers. Oh, Carlo, I do want her to be happy. As happy as I am tonight."

They strolled down the wide corridor that spanned the top of the living room and peered down into its dark chasm. Carlo held her hand in his.

"This place seems so eerily quiet at night. The sky is much darker than it ever is in Venice. I'll be glad when we start bringing guests here."

"Susannah, the beach house won't be ready for another six months."

"Oh, they'll come sooner. I'll have them camping out on the lawn if need be. This will be the most marvelous home for entertaining!"

Carlo looked at her disconsolately.

"What's the matter, darling, doesn't that make you happy? I thought it was what you wanted."

"I want it if it will make you happy," Carlo said. "Besides, the Lyford Cay Club looks like it will be quite a draw. That ought to keep you busy."

She snuggled against him. "Oh, admit it, Carlo. You want me for yourself."

He kissed her softly in the dark, then flicked on the light in the master bedroom. The king-size bed was one of the few pieces of furniture they had installed; the rest of the room was a maze of half-opened trunks and cases of books. "Look at that! The light actually works."

"Turn it back off, darling. I prefer the dark."

Carlo turned back to the door and flicked off the switch, as his hand reached out for her and she moved closer to him. His fingers touched her cheek, tracing the curve of her mouth, her skin cool and smooth to his touch. As he pulled her to him, her lips brushed against his and he felt her hands fumbling with the buttons of her blouse, her yielding breasts softly pressing against him.

"Why are you in such a hurry?" he said as she pulled him toward the bed.

"Tonight is the night I will conceive, I know it," she murmured.

SHE HAD NEVER been able to conceive again, yet she had tried to make him happy, Carlo remembered, his memories keeping sleep at bay. Lord, how she had worked to make him happy. Carlo thought of Francesca's infancy as the happiest time in his life.

But as the child grew more independent, Susannah had changed. Something was released in the mother, some yearning for adventure. Sure that in a crucial way she had pleased Carlo, Susannah now felt free to leave him. Oh, there was always a pressing reason: an important auction of antiquities in London, an art dealer to see in Paris, a friend ill in a hospital in New York.

When the house was finally completed, Carlo remembered, she led him through the finished rooms, walking gingerly over the Miró rug that had been woven especially for them. Sunlight poured into the spectacular two-story living room, around which the rest of the house was built. Susannah had filled the room with comfortable contemporary furniture upholstered in sand and white linens. The only vivid colors were the reds and greens and oranges that flashed and glowed in the de Koonings and Rothkos she had hung on the walls. At one end of the room a magnificent Modigliani nude looked down on a Zulu wood carving. Degas horses brightened the walls of the smaller rooms.

Carlo genuinely liked most of the paintings. Only Dalí's portrait of Susannah disturbed him. Like everything else in the Lyford Cay house, it stood in sharp contrast to the portrait that hung in the palazzo. The new portrait upset Susannah, too, though she couldn't say why, and, like Carlo, she couldn't bear to look at it. Only years later did the count realize that Dalí had seen, and had painted, a dark side of his wife that he had not been willing to admit existed. There had been no question of refusing the Dalí, of course, since he had commissioned it, and so it had hung in an upstairs guest room until several years after Susannah's death. Then Carlo had had it taken down and sold it anonymously.

And then there had been Sybilla . . .

Giving up the notion of going to sleep, Carlo rose from his bed and poured a snifter of brandy. Passing through the connecting door to his study, he took a small key out of a finely carved ebony box and opened a hidden drawer in his desk. The notebook was still there, having lain untouched, unopened, all these years. He ought to tell someone about it—whom? Antonia, perhaps?—in case something happened to him. Repelled by the sight of the small book and the memories it evoked, he closed and locked the drawer and returned the key to its box.

Lady Sybilla Hillford. Carlo's lips curled in disgust. *Lady*, indeed.

Carlo drained the brandy snifter as the first rays of light began to filter into the room. That dark side of Susannah—could she have passed it on to Francesca?

He shook his head in an attempt to banish the thought. Francesca was a child, an innocent who wanted desperately to please the father who had for so long ignored her. No need to fear that she, too, would plunge the Nordonia name into disgrace.

Chapter Nine

THE LIDO WAS the barrier of sand that protected the scores of islands in the lagoon upon which Venice was built. Francesca hurried across the packed wet sand past the long rows of deserted white cabanas as a dense mist billowed up from the sea. She had put on a rose-colored dress as light as the petals of a flower, but the "flower" had wilted and her hair hung in damp tendrils. The weather had turned foggy and cool. She was a mess and she was furious. The day after the ball was turning into a nightmare. She was sure she had missed Jack, for she was an hour late. There had been endless delays.

Josie had announced grandly that she would not be able to accompany Francesca on the excursion to the Lido because she had a lunch date with her new friend, Charles Cash. Francesca had suggested that she bring him along, but Josie would have none of it. Despite Francesca's objections, Josie had stalked out of the palazzo to meet Charles.

Carlo had insisted that Emilio go with her in the motorboat and stay in sight of her all afternoon. The majordomo, apparently believing that he was cut out for higher purposes, had consented with a grumble and a scowl. Then, soon after they left the palazzo, the motorboat had broken down. They'd had to run to catch the vaporetto. And Emilio, of course, had considered running beneath his dignity. It had taken them forever, and although every inch of the trip had been unpleasant, it had yielded one happy result: It had made Emilio thirsty. Francesca had cajoled him into going and having a drink while she strolled along the beach.

"But, Contessina, it is so foggy you will see nothing," he had pointed out.

"Oh, Emilio, I love the fog!" she had lied.

And so he had disappeared into a café while she pretended to head up the beach. If Jack had waited for her this long, he would most certainly have gone inside. The Excelsior Hotel, on the beach, was the nearest and most obvious place he could have gone. Dripping wet now and thoroughly discouraged, Francesca approached the pseudo-Moorish hotel and pushed through the doors to the lobby. For a moment, she stood still, looking around at the ornate decor.

"Francesca, I was worried about you!"

She felt her heart lurch at the sound of Jack's voice. He took her hands and dropped a gentle kiss on her cheek. "All sorts of things happened, Jack." At the compassionate look in his eyes, she began to babble. "It was awful. My father was awful, Josie refused to come, and Emilio—"

"Come, sit down over here," Jack invited her. "You're all wet, darling girl. You must be cold."

"Y-yes," she stammered, feeling her heart stop entirely at his use of the simple endearment.

Jack hailed a waiter and spoke to him in Italian. He disappeared and returned a moment later with a pot of hot chocolate, which he placed on a small table between her and Jack. "Now, tell me about the awful things that all these people did to you, Francesca."

She started to enumerate her grievances, but found her annoyance waning as she looked into his blue eyes.

"This Emilio," Jack said. "Who is he?"

"My father's majordomo. Very 'grand,' unutterably correct, and absolutely loyal to my father."

"I can't wait to meet him. He sounds like fun."

Francesca surprised herself by laughing. "Don't worry. You will, if I don't meet him on the boardwalk in fifteen minutes."

Jack's disappointment showed in his face. "I take it he came along for the specific purpose of keeping you away from me."

"Or any other man who might try to take advantage of an innocent convent girl," Francesca said mischievously. Then she sobered. "I'm sorry about all this."

"Don't be. It isn't your fault. Maybe we can meet somewhere tomorrow, if your friend Josie gets over her snit by then."

"She will. She's very good-natured, Jack. It's just that I hurt her feelings last night by not going inside to hear her sing."

"Oh," Jack said. "What kept you away?"

"My father. I feel terrible about it, but he said I could hear Josie sing any time and that I had a greater duty to my guests." She drank the last of her hot chocolate and put the cup down thoughtfully. "He doesn't like it that Josie and I are so close."

"Because she's colored?"

"Partly, I guess, but mostly because he says we are of a different class."

Jack guffawed. "Oh dear! Does he really say things like that?"

"You shouldn't laugh too hard, Jack." Francesca nodded. "He thinks you're 'beneath my station,' too," she added mischievously.

Jack winced. "Ouch. Nobody's ever said that about me before." He raised his eyebrows questioningly. "Does that mean you won't ever meet me again?"

"No. I'll sneak out of the palazzo if necessary."

"I don't want to come between you and your father, Francesca. It might be better if we just stop seeing each other."

"No!"

Westman smiled. "Okay. I was hoping you'd say that." He searched through his pockets until he found a pencil stub and a matchbook. "Here. I'll write down my phone number for you."

She took the matchbook from him and held it in her hand as if it were a talisman. It was red, with a lightning bolt logo and the words *Il Pipistrello* emblazoned across its cover. She wrote the palazzo phone number on a paper napkin and handed it to him. "You can try to call me, but if my father picks up the phone, don't expect a welcome."

He caught her hand, raised it to his lips, and kissed her palm, then folded her fingers around the kiss. A second after he let go, she felt a firm hand on her elbow and turned to find Emilio scowling down at her. Jack lunged to his feet and started to speak, but Francesca interrupted him. "It's been nice talking to you, Mr. Van Camp. I hope you and your wife enjoy your visit to Venice." She turned to Emilio and, seeing that he obviously didn't recognize Jack, tried another maneuver. "Emilio, Mr. Van Camp and his wife visited the Bahamas last year. I got so interested in talking about Nassau that I forgot the time."

As the majordomo led her out of the hotel, she glanced back over her shoulder and caught a thumbs-up gesture from Jack. Emilio did not speak as he hurried her toward the waiting vaporetto, and she wondered if she had succeeded in fooling him. He had hardly glanced at Jack. Still, she could tell he was angry that she had managed to talk him into letting her out of his sight.

As the vaporetto crossed the lagoon, the mist lifted, revealing the ancient city hovering on the waterline in a haze of golden light. She looked down at the matchbook she still held in one hand, stealthily opening it to look at the precious telephone number. She had memorized only the first three digits when Emilio took it gently but firmly out of her hand.

"Il Pipistrello," he said, glancing at the cover. "This means 'The Bat.' What sort of place is this?"

"I don't know. I found it. I picked it up because I thought it was pretty." She reached out to take it from him, but he deliberately let go of it, letting the wind catch it and send it swirling away behind the vaporetto to be swallowed up by the dark water. She turned to glare at Emilio, but he didn't give her a chance to speak.

"You should not have spoken to that stranger, Contessina. The count will not be pleased."

Francesca felt the sting of tears behind her eyelids. Without the telephone number, she had no way of reaching Jack. He hadn't even told her the name of his hotel. She turned on the majordomo. "How could you do such a cruel thing?"

He had the grace to look miserable. "Please, Contessina, it was an accident. I did not mean to drop the matchbook in the water." He turned away as if he couldn't bear to meet her accusing eyes. "The count would be very angry if he knew you had contrived to meet that man today. He is a nobody. An American film star? This is not the sort of man your father would have chosen for you."

Francesca bowed her head resignedly. Emilio *had* recognized Jack. "You're going to tell my father, aren't you?"

After a long pause, the majordomo said carefully, "Perhaps it would be best not to deal the count an upset so soon after such a successful ball." He turned his wise brown eyes on Francesca's frightened face. "But you must understand, Contessina, that my loyalty is to your father. He knows better than you do what will make you happy in the long run."

Francesca looked at him speculatively. She would never manage to see Jack unless she got Emilio on her side.

"Thank you, Emilio, I'll remember that," she said gratefully, adding a pathetic little sigh for effect.

Francesca hesitated for a moment before rapping on the door to Josie's bedroom. She knew her friend was in; she had heard her return to the palazzo as she sat over dinner with her father in the stony silence of the dining room. Eager to be away from his somber mood, she had excused herself immediately after the dessert dishes were cleared away.

"I'm glad to see that you have grown less dependent on Josie's company, *cara*," Carlo had said during dinner. "It is good to be kind and friendly to everyone, but you must learn to—"

"Papa," Francesca had said, interrupting a lecture she had heard too many times already, "I've been seeing less of Josie for one reason only: You have shipped her off to the servants' dining room and filled my days with lessons and coaching. Now that the ball is behind us, I intend to see as much of my closest friend as possible."

She had stalked out of the dining room and hurried upstairs, but now she wondered if Josie would welcome her visit or turn cold and hostile, as she had been this morning. Rapping on the door she called out, "Josie, it's me. I want to hear about your afternoon."

Josie, she discovered to her relief, was buoyant with happiness, her earlier resentment forgotten in the thrill of an afternoon of Venetian adventure.

She launched into a description of the restaurant where she and Charles had eaten lunch and then, almost without stopping for breath, began to talk about the rest of her afternoon. "He took me all over Venice. We went to the Isola di San Michele. It's a *cimitero*, where the dead are buried in tombs above the ground, and then we went to the Ghetto Nuovo, where the Jews were all cramped into tiny houses on a single island. And Charles told me some fascinating stories about Venice and took me to three of his favorite churches. You've got to see the Church of Saints John and Paul—San Zanipolo, the Venetians call it. It's full of statues of all the doges of Venice. You'll probably find some of your bloodthirsty ancestors there. We could go to mass there on Sunday, couldn't we?''

''Of course, Josie. What a good idea,'' Francesca replied, puzzled by Josie's sudden affability after the hostility she had vented earlier in the day. She listened with half of her mind as Josie went on to describe the other spots she had visited with Charles. The other part of Francesca's mind was occupied with thoughts of Jack Westman. How long would he wait for her to call? Would he give up on her and try to reach her here at the palazzo? She had no hope that his call, or even a message from him, would be passed on to her. How, she wondered, could Josie babble on so giddily when she herself was so troubled? The disasters of the afternoon would not have occurred at all if Josie had kept her promise to accompany her to the Lido.

Something in the tone of Josie's voice caught Francesca's complete attention.

''And he thinks I should take voice lessons while I'm here,'' she was saying. ''Charles says that I'm wasting my voice by singing only popular songs. He even recommended a teacher for me—a famous diva, retired now, who coaches just a few promising students. He says he's sure she'll accept me, because I have the kind of voice she likes to work with, but of course I can't afford more than one or two lessons.''

Suddenly Francesca understood everything—Josie's sudden affability, the suggestion that they go to mass together on Sunday, this unexplained spurt of sisterly chatter. Josie wanted her to talk her father into paying for her voice lessons. She mulled the situation over in her mind, half listening to Josie's nonstop narrative.

In the old days, Josie would have come right out and asked her to speak to Carlo, but she wouldn't do that now, not after he had humiliated her and separated the two of them. For that, Francesca felt she was at least partly to blame. She, after all, had virtually begged Josie to come to Venice with her, and she had lacked the courage to insist that her father treat Josie with respect. Perhaps she owed Josie this one favor.

She watched Josie as she described still another Venetian treasure. Her amber eyes were glowing with excitement, her expressive hands drawing pictures in the air. There could be no doubt that she was sincere in her enthusiasm, nor did Francesca question her musical talent. Surely she could convince her father that he owed Josie the voice lessons in return for making her so suddenly and acutely aware of what he referred to as "her place." The lessons might even provide Francesca with an excuse to get away from the palazzo to meet Jack.

She suddenly realized that her mind was made up; she would speak to her father the next morning.

"And Charles is taking me out to dinner tomorrow night," Josie was saying. "If you can get out from under your father's thumb for one evening, you could come with us, Francesca."

"No. I'd feel like a third wheel."

"You wouldn't be. I'd like you to come along."

Francesca studied Josie's expression carefully, but could find no insincerity in her eyes. "Why?" she asked. "Don't you want to be alone with Charles?"

Josie's cheeks reddened, and she dropped her eyes. "Not just yet, I guess." She seemed to be waiting for Francesca to speak, but when that didn't happen, she went on cautiously, "Maybe later on I'll want to be alone with him, Francesca. Really alone. But I'm not ready yet."

Francesca covered Josie's hand with her own. She suddenly understood her friend's hesitation; she felt the same way sometimes when Jack Westman looked at her. She longed to be with him, but at the same time she felt a flutter of panic at the thought of taking that huge step out of childhood and into a man's arms. "I know what you mean, Josie. I'd love to come with you and Charles."

Josie reached out with all of the old sisterly warmth that was so familiar and looped her arm around Francesca's neck. "Oh, Francesca, it's so exciting, but at the same time it's so scary!"

Francesca felt her heart swell with love for this girl who had shared her childhood and who now faced womanhood with all of the same excitement and panic.

"Josie, are you *sure* Charles won't mind if you drag me along to dinner with you?"

Josie started to shake her head, but at that moment there was a knock on the door.

Relieved at the interruption, Francesca rose to open it. She found her father, looking grave. "Can I speak to you alone, Francesca?"

Josie slipped out of the room as Francesca faced her father.

"There was a telephone call for you, *piccola*," Carlo said. "Jack Westman called you."

Francesca said nothing.

"I thought we'd seen the last of him last night. Really, Francesca, is that the kind of man you want? He's too old for you, far too worldly. A man like that may seem impressive to a young girl . . ."

As Carlo detailed all the reasons why Jack was unsuitable, Francesca's mind reeled. Jack must have grown impatient waiting for her call. She hoped her father had not driven him away. At last Carlo finished his speech.

"What did you tell him, Papa?"

"I told him that you weren't available."

He saw the disappointment in her face. Francesca had one last hope. "Did he leave a number?"

"Of course not. He understood me. I don't think he'll call again. And if he does, Francesca, I must forbid you to see him." Carlo was annoyed. He knew that when he grew angry he sounded impossibly stiff and old-fashioned, but he couldn't help himself.

Francesca's disappointment was overwhelming. Forcing herself to remain composed, she looked directly at her father. How could he tell her how much he loved her one day and then ruin her life the next? "You will not listen to what I have to say about this, Papa?"

Carlo sighed. "About a man like this, *cara*, you can have nothing to say. At least, nothing I care to hear. You will not see this American again, Francesca. Is that clear?"

Francesca nodded, assuming a surrender she had no intention of honoring. "Yes, Papa."

The count nodded, apparently satisfied with his daughter's submission. "Fine," he said. "I have also spoken to Franco Mdvani, with whom you danced several times last night."

Francesca searched through her mind, matching names with faces. Mdvani, yes, the son of the Italian ambassador to—

"He was most impressed with you," Carlo interrupted, "and he has my permission to call you tomorrow morning. He wishes to invite you to dinner. You have my permission to accept."

The wheels of Francesca's mind began to whirl. She knew better than to ask her father's "permission" to join Josie and Charles tomorrow evening for dinner. "One simply does not dine with the servants," he would say. Again. But there was no reason that she and Franco Mdvani couldn't just happen to run into Josie and Charles.

"If I go out with Franco," she said quietly, being careful to sound meek and passive, "will I have to be chaperoned?"

Carlo shook his head. "The son of Giorgio Mdvani can be trusted to behave in a manner that is above reproach," he said.

But the daughter of Carlo Nordonia most assuredly cannot, Francesca thought slyly.

"I would be happy to have dinner with him," she said.

Carlo's smile was genuine, and Francesca decided to seize the moment.

"Papa," she said sweetly, "I think Josie should have voice lessons while she's here in Venice . . ."

Francesca had easily persuaded Franco to take her to meet Charles and Josie at the Café Oriental, a trattoria with a terrace along a back canal. Franco Mdvani was terribly thin and terribly nervous. He looked slightly like an overbred wolfhound. His hand, when he helped her down the stairs of the restaurant, was icy cold. But he was a gentleman and he was nice. After the initial surprise of finding he was not to dine with Francesca alone, he had adjusted to the unusual company. Over *tiramisu*, a dessert of bittersweet chocolate mousse, Francesca asked the question she had been withholding until the right moment: "What's Pipistrello?"

"Ah, yes, Pipistrello," Franco replied. "It's a nightclub. The name means 'bat.' It's mentioned in the newspaper columns all the time. Is that where you heard about it?"

Francesca looked at him blankly, but Josie—who had been carefully coached—jumped in to save the moment. "Yes, I saw something about it and mentioned it to Francesca. Have you been there? What's it like?"

"It's a jet-set nightclub, a hangout for Americans, movie people, publicity-seeking Europeans. People go there to be seen and to have their pictures taken with the celebrities." He shrugged. "I've been there once or twice. It's very noisy, very crowded, but it's worth seeing once. Would you like to step in there after dinner?"

Josie shook her head. "Doesn't sound like our sort of place." She looked at Charles, as if seeking his opinion.

"Not my style either," he said, "but thanks for the offer."

Franco raised his eyebrows at Francesca.

"No, thank you, Franco," she said, pressing her temples. "I have a terrible headache; it must be the wine. I think I'll make this an early evening."

They parted from Josie and Charles outside the restaurant.

"I'll go in the back way," Francesca insisted when they arrived at the palazzo. Franco kissed her hand outside the kitchen door and, backing away, tripped over a cat. Francesca suppressed a giggle. She slipped inside and stood in the silence of the dark empty kitchen, counting the minutes until she judged it safe to slip back out through the garden and into the winding streets.

She had to ask several times before she found her way to the famous nightclub. It was in the cellar of an ancient stone house at the dead end of a canal. She groped her way down the stairs into a low-ceilinged room. An Italian band was playing rock and roll and the air was thick with smoke. She stood, blinking, waiting for her eyes to adjust to the gloom. A hand was at her elbow and she looked up into Charles's smiling face. He winked at her conspiratorially. "We're over here."

She followed him to the table and exchanged a few words with Josie, feeling suddenly exultant at the renewal of their friendship. It was wonderful to conspire in whispers with her as they had done as children in Nassau. And her happiness was intensified by her certainty that she would be with Jack before this night had ended. He would come to this place; of that her heart was certain. He had to come.

Fluttering with nervous energy, she stood up. "Excuse me. I want to walk around. Maybe he's here already and we just didn't see him."

Charles shook his head. "It's still too early, Francesca. The celebrities rarely show up before twelve."

"Charles plays in clubs like this one," Josie said, "so he knows what he's talking about. Why don't you have a glass of wine and relax for a few minutes?"

Francesca shook her head. "I'll wander around. Be back soon."

She got up and circled the large room, fascinated by the oddly dressed patrons who gyrated on the small dance floor or stood in clusters around the tables. Nothing in her experience had prepared her for such a gathering; it was almost as if a casting director had sought out actors to play a scene in a motion picture. Each person in the crowd seemed to have gone out of the way to find the most bizarre hairstyle, the oddest outfit, the most outlandish makeup. These, she concluded, were the acolytes of the famous, the ones who came to Pipistrello in the hope of being noticed by a director or being caught in a photograph with some well-known patron.

Unsurprised that Jack Westman was not among them, she summoned up her nerve and walked over to the bar, growing more confident when she realized that no one was paying any attention to her. She leaned forward and caught the eye of a young bartender. "Does Jack Westman ever come in here?"

The man nodded. "Whenever he's in Venice," he said. "He usually shows up around midnight, so you've got a few minutes to wait. Would you like a drink?"

Francesca shook her head and wandered off. At the corner table, Charles and Josie were holding hands, their heads together in what appeared to be an intimate conversation. Unwilling to interrupt them, she found her way up the stairs and out into the street, longing for a few minutes of silence and fresh air. She walked over a little stone bridge and sat down on the other side to wait, her feet dangling over the water, and watched as gondolas began to glide silently up to the club's landing, certain that she would spot Jack any minute.

As the hour grew later a crowd of fans began to form at the entrance, waiting for the celebrities who had made the club famous. A twinge in her back reminded Francesca that she had been sitting on the stone ledge for a long time. She stood up and walked back and forth past the end of the small bridge, easing the tension in her muscles and trying to warm up, but keeping an eager eye on the club's entrance.

The sound of a gondola shushing up to the landing caught her attention, and she watched as its passenger alighted. A tall man, blond hair, cleft chin. He had arrived at last!

She ran toward the other end of the bridge, long silken hair flying behind her like red-gold fire. "Jack," she called, "Jack!"

He turned and looked toward her voice, but he was standing in the light from the entrance to the club and couldn't see into the darkness across the water. "Francesca?" He smiled incredulously and took a few steps toward the edge of the canal.

Francesca stopped running and froze, horrified at her impulsive greeting. What if Jack had planned to meet someone inside? What if that beautiful Italian actress was at this minute making her way to Pipistrello to join him?

But Jack was calling her name again. "Francesca, where are you?"

"Here, on the bridge," she called, her heart hammering. "I lost your matchbook. I couldn't call."

They both began to run. Then he was swinging her high in his arms. It was if they had struggled to meet each other half their lives; his arms, as he pulled her into them, felt like a lost part of herself. He kissed her mouth, lightly at first, then pressed his lips to her eyelids, her forehead, her cheek, the hollow of her throat, as if he could not get enough of her. Finally he covered her mouth with his, and she instinctively parted her lips. Overwhelmed with the sensations that surged through her, she gave herself up to the kiss, enfolding him in her arms, glorying in the feeling of his heart pounding so close to hers, the spicy scent of his tanned skin, the sound of his ragged breathing and the soft murmurs that stole from his throat.

Jack was the first to draw away, but he pressed his lips to her forehead before tucking her head into the hollow of his shoulder and stroking her hair slowly. "There, now, my darling," he said. "You know how I feel about you."

She nodded silently, enjoying the soft, grainy feeling of his jacket against the skin of her cheek.

Jack went on, "We have to talk, you and I."

She raised her head and lifted her brows at him. "Talk?"

Jack laughed softly at her surprise and disappointment. Then he dropped a kiss on the tip of hcr nosc and, keeping one arm firmly around her, pushed her away until they were side by side. "Let's go."

"Where to?"

"Not Pipistrello," Jack said, bobbing his head toward the entrance to the disco. "The paparazzi will be buzzing around that door in a few minutes. Anyway, it's too noisy in there."

"I have to leave a message for Josie and Charles!"

Jack translated Francesca's message to the doorman and tipped him.

"We could walk for a while," Francesca suggested, slipping her arm around his waist. Even in the darkness she could see the brightness of his blue eyes. The warmth and strength of his body seemed to fill her field of vision, engulfing her like a protective and loving presence. A light, happy laugh bubbled up in her throat, surprising her. "I was afraid my father had chased you off forever."

"He gave it his best shot," Jack admitted. "I couldn't even get a call through." He bent his head, and she felt his warm breath on her forehead. "How did you sneak out tonight? I know the count didn't give you permission to wander around Venice all alone at this hour."

She told him about the scheme she had concocted, then let his surprised laughter ripple over her like the dappled moonlight.

They threaded their way through the narrow streets and along the labyrinth of *rii* toward the Ponte dell'Accademia, meandering down long detours and lingering here and there to lose themselves in touching and whispering.

Near the entrance to a brightly lit nightclub, they skirted a cluster of paparazzi waiting with noisy impatience for some unsuspecting celebrity to appear in the doorway. Jack kept his head turned away from them until Francesca pulled him around a corner and out of sight.

"Those guys drive me crazy," he said, "but they got some great pictures of you after the ball." His voice broke on a self-deprecating laugh. "I was so desperate for word of you that I read the newspaper accounts over and over. I even cut out your picture. It's in the frame of my bedroom mirror. That's how besotted I am."

"I cut out the one of us standing together on the balcony," Francesca confessed. "I love it because we look like a couple. Like two lovers, we belong together."

He pulled her into a dark doorway and took her face between his hands. His lips touched her mouth. Francesca felt her legs begin to tremble as a fresh current of desire flowed through her body. The sound of the water lapping against the canal walls seemed to keep pace with her pounding heart.

Gently he placed his hands on her shoulders and pushed her away. Then he laced his fingers into hers and began to walk her slowly along the shadowy street. "I want to take you back to my room and spend the rest of this night holding you and making love to you. I want to keep you with me for the rest of my life, and I want to tell the whole world we belong to each other."

Francesca moved closer to him, warming as he caught her arm beneath his and pressed it to his side. She nudged his shoulder playfully with her chin. "I hear a 'but' coming."

Jack nodded, unsmiling. "But," he said, "I'm too—"

Pressing the fingers of her free hand against his lips to end the speech, she said, "If you say you're too old, too celebrated, too foreign, or too far beneath my station, I'll climb up on the steps of that church over there and scream until the police come and haul me off to prison. I've heard all those ridiculous arguments from my father. Twice!" She kept her hand over his mouth until she felt his lips relax into a smile.

"But I *am* too old for you, Francesca."

"You're thirty-two, Jack, if the newspapers are right. That's no older than my father was when he married my mother." She cupped his face between her hands and pressed her lips to his. "I'm a woman now," she said, her voice husky and intense. "And I'm ready. You know I am."

He nodded, his eyes grave, concerned. "Point taken," he said. "I won't mention the subject of age again."

Francesca held her breath in the silence. "But . . . ?" she said.

"But your father despises me and will go to great lengths to keep you out of my evil presence." Jack smiled grimly. "And he strikes me as a man who doesn't give up easily."

"We can meet without his ever finding out."

"I don't want to make you sneak around."

Francesca heaved an exaggerated sigh. "Indulge me," she said. "Stop playing hard to get." At Jack's shout of laughter, she snatched his hand again and began to cajole him like an adult trying to bring an errant child into line. "Here I am on the loose in the most romantic city in the world, and I can't even talk an American movie star into a few secret trysts. How do you think that makes me feel?"

"You," he said with mock solemnity, "are scandalous. I'm shocked, Francesca."

She let out a joyous shriek and threw her arms around his neck. "Then you'll pursue me secretly? Promise?"

"Promise," he murmured, burying his face in her soft hair.

Francesca's mind reeled with thoughts of what lay ahead. She began to chatter happily, planning, suggesting places and times to meet, all the time wondering giddily what had happened to the timid, frightened girl who had arrived in Venice a few short weeks ago. Walking beside him, his arm heavy across her shoulders, she stretched up to place a quick, bold kiss on the hollow under his jaw. With Jack she had never been afraid, had never wondered for even a moment if she would measure up to his standards. He had made it clear from the start that he wanted her, and his desire had made her brave.

Ahead of them, the Palazzo Nordonia stood bathed in moonlight, its windows staring at them in silent accusation, its lions scowling in fierce disapproval. Inside the palace, the count would be asleep. She would deal with him tomorrow.

She led Jack to the dark entrance to the rear courtyard. "Tomorrow Josie and I are going to mass at San Zanipolo. Meet me there?"

He nodded and kissed her lightly. "Until tomorrow, my love."

She turned on her most innocent smile. "See you in church," she said.

His laugh followed her through the gate and into the deep shadows of the orchard. She stood still for a moment to let her eyes adjust to the darkness. As she started to move toward the back door of the palazzo, the sound of voices cut through the silence. She backed into the cover of the trees and stood as if frozen. The voices were coming from the outside staircase that led from the upper floors of the palace to the courtyard below. She knew immediately whom they belonged to: her father and Antonia.

When they reached the lower part of the staircase, she could make out their words.

"*Piccola,* don't leave yet, please. There's no reason—"

"It's better this way, Carlo."

The next few sentences were lost in the tremor of fury that swept through Francesca as she stood in the darkness below. So this was how her pious father spent his free time! No wonder he had been so eager for her to have dinner with Franco Mdvani: He wanted her out from under foot while he met with his young mistress for a few hours.

"Tomorrow, then," she heard Carlo say.

"*Domattina*, Carlo," Antonia replied. "*Fino allora . . .*"

The courtyard fell silent as Toni made her way through the trees, passing within a few feet of Francesca, who hid herself still and invisible in the darkness. She began to breathe again when the gate creaked open and clanked shut, but she didn't move until she heard her father's footsteps reach the top of the staircase and the door snap closed behind him.

Domattina, Carlo. *Fino allora*. The words rang in her brain. *Tomorrow morning. Until then . . .*

Tomorrow morning, while she and Josie were in church, Carlo would slip out of the palazzo to meet his young lover.

What a naive child she had been! She had believed her father's story about working for a few hours each day in his office in the business section of the city, away from the bustle of servants and the distraction of the household. Working indeed, Francesca thought. He was making love to a middle-class woman only a few years older than she. A woman even more "inferior" than Josie. And after his hours of pleasure, Carlo would come back to the palazzo to stand guard over his daughter's virtue, to tell her that Jack Westman was too old for her, too low-born, too worldly. Count Nordonia was not only an autocrat, she realized, but a hypocrite as well.

Filled with a new, deeper resentment of her father, she climbed the stairs to her room on the third floor.

Tomorrow, she told herself. Think about meeting Jack tomorrow at San Zanipolo. Imagine how it will be to look into his blue eyes and feel the strength of his arms.

But as she undressed and got into the soft bed, her thoughts of Jack kept ending in the echo of those two voices making intimate promises on the outside staircase in the darkness.

Chapter Ten

FRANCESCA SCANNED THE seats of the outdoor café in the Campo Santi Giovanni e Paolo. Flocks of tourists crowded the tables and filed through the portals of the church. There was no sign of Jack, but Francesca felt her pulse begin to pound nevertheless, as if she could sense his arrival.

Beside the ancient church with its fifteenth-century Gothic facade stood Andrea Verrocchio's equestrian monument to Bartolomeo Colleoni. The juxtaposition of the man of war and the soaring flying buttresses of the church seemed an emblem of her father's Roman contradictions—the severe Catholicism he had imposed on her and the hypocrisy and self-centered view of life that she had begun to discover.

"I'll wait for you at the café," Josie suddenly said.

"Don't you want to come to mass?"

"I haven't been to confession," Josie said.

"Neither have I."

"You don't need it," Josie scoffed.

"How do you know?" Francesca asked dryly. "Besides, you could hear the mass without taking communion."

"I'm meeting Charles here," Josie admitted. "I told him we might go to Murano after mass, and he asked to come along. I hope you don't mind."

Francesca smiled. "Of course not. In fact, I'm glad you two are seeing each other. You might as well go on to Murano without me. I feel like I'm chaperoning you instead of the other way around."

"Francesca, if this goes much further I *will* need a chaperon."

Francesca slipped a lace mantilla over her hair and stepped through the high portals of San Zanipolo. She felt lost in the immense solidity of the church. The Lombardo statues on the marble tombs of the statesmen made her feel she was being spied on by ancestors who know only too well all her family secrets. She crossed herself as she passed the altar of Saint Vincent Ferrer, too distracted to marvel at Giovanni Bellini's work and took a conspicuous place before the main altar.

"Hail Mary," she prayed, but it was hard for her to concentrate. She kept seeing her father at breakfast leaning over to kiss her with lips that had caressed his mistress a few hours before. "Blessed art thou among women and blessed is the fruit of thy womb . . ."

Distracted despite her attempts to pray, she found herself wondering if Jack would be able to find her in this crowded church. The mass began, and she glanced around at the throngs of people filling the massive nave, their eyes on the priest who was officiating. Perhaps Jack wasn't religious and would not even come inside during the service. Or perhaps he was devout and would be attending to the mass rather than searching for her. When another glance around the nave yielded no sign of him, she forced herself to concentrate on the ancient ritual and was soon caught up in the murmured prayers, the gleaming vestments, the heady incense. She began to pray silently and in earnest: Dear God, forgive me if I've done wrong by disobeying my father and by feeling so much anger and bitterness toward him. But how can I not resent his hypocrisy? How can I let him forbid me to see Jack, who is so good and who loves me so much?

She squeezed her eyes shut as the communicants filed forward to take the host. She stayed behind, on her knees. She had not gone to confession and did not take communion because she knew she would become Jack Westman's lover the moment he asked her to. But although she had sincerely begged forgiveness for resenting her father, she could not feel any guilt over wanting to love Jack.

As the congregation stood to receive the priest's blessing, Jack slipped into place beside her. When she turned toward him wanting to fling her arms around him, he pressed a soft kiss on her hair and took her hand in his.

"I meant to wait at the back of the church until the mass was over," he whispered, "but I couldn't stay away from you another minute."

They stood together, hands and eyes locked, as the congregants shuffled past them into the campo. Finally, when the aisles were nearly clear, they genuflected and walked out into the sunlight.

"I'm famished," Jack announced. "Let's find your friend Josie and grab some lunch."

"Josie skipped mass and ran off to Murano with her friend, Charles." Francesca smiled mischievously. "You'll have to settle for spending the afternoon alone with me. Can you endure that?"

"Such a disappointment." Jack pulled a long face. "Alone in Venice with the most beautiful woman in Europe."

Francesca plucked his dark glasses out of the breast pocket of his jacket and handed them to him. "Put on your disguise, Mr. Humility. I won't be responsible if all these tourists try to tear your clothes off." She waved a hand at the camera-toting vacationers who crowded the square. "You're not safe here, Jack Westman. Can we find a quieter place to eat lunch?"

"This way." He closed his fingers around her upper arm and guided her easily through the crowd and out of the square. "We'll have lunch at a little café near the Piazza San Marco. Then I'll give you a tour of the city. We'll end the afternoon at a tiny place near the Frari where they have the most delicious tea and pastry in Venice, and then I'll toss you into a gondola and send you home to your palace before your father can even miss you."

Francesca felt a twinge of disappointment, but at the same time her admiration of him increased enormously. He was refusing to rush her into his bed. He was giving her time to get used to him, to be sure she wanted him, even to change her mind and walk away from him, if she wished to do that. She looped her arm through his, amazed and delighted to realize that he looked as happy as she felt.

Across the campo, Josie watched over the rim of her coffee cup as Francesca and Jack made their way through the crowd. Charles, sitting next to her, was planning their afternoon in meticulous detail, but she had stopped listening when she caught sight of Westman and Francesca. The golden couple, tall and beautiful, attracted the stares of passersby, even those who apparently didn't recognize him as an actor or her as a member of the Italian elite. Francesca, her golden-red hair shining in the sunlight, displayed a new grace and confidence, Josie noted again. Part of that was due to Carlo's coaches, part of it to her success at the ball, and the rest of it—most of it, Josie suspected—to her certainty that Jack

Westman loved her, although she had confessed to Josie that he had not yet told her so.

Josie's heart constricted as she saw Jack dip his head and place a light kiss on Francesca's cheek. Even from a distance she could see the happiness in his face. He did love her, Josie admitted to herself. He had loved Francesca from the moment he first saw her. The flattering attention he had paid to Josie at the ball had been nothing but the mindless flirtation of an attractive man whose eye had been caught by a pretty young woman in a red dress. When that same eye had fallen on Francesca later in the evening, all thoughts of Josie had vanished from Jack Westman's mind.

Her throat tightened with disappointment, Josie sipped at the bitter coffee and made automatic responses to Charles's questions. Carlo would have a spasm if he knew what his daughter was up to, she told herself.

Charles's soft voice suddenly broke through her musings. "Afterward, maybe we can go somewhere and just be alone together. Would you like that, Josie?"

She caught the glint of eagerness in his warm brown eyes and forced herself to smile. Why not? she asked herself. Francesca had Jack Westman wrapped around her little finger for the moment. Charles was no Jack Westman, granted. He didn't make Josie's blood pound in her veins. He couldn't melt her heart with a touch, a look. But he was attractive, sexy even, and he would be gentle and patient. He knew, or at least suspected, that she was a virgin, and he would take care to please her as well as himself. Who better than Charles, in fact, to prepare her for someone like Westman?

"Yes," she said quietly. "I think I would like to be alone with you, Charles."

Mirella Varchi no longer sang in public. She had retired when she was still in her prime to leave her admirers with the memory of her voice at its peak. Now the renowned diva lived through her students, whom she chose with meticulous care.

Seated in a thronelike chair, eyes closed in concentration, she listened to the dark-haired girl sing. Josephine Lapoiret's voice, though immature and crudely trained, excited her. Its quality was unique; her rich contralto, the rarest of voices, would cut through an orchestra as well as a strong soprano.

She had in abundance the qualities that could not be taught: an extraordinary ear, graceful stage presence, and strong instincts for emotional expression. She was at the right age to begin the serious, slow training that would develop her voice into a great instrument and preserve its rare beauty. There was no doubt that this voice was unusual and exotic enough to capture the imagination of the public, if she proved to have the stamina and discipline she would need to fulfill her potential. Without that discipline, it was pointless to teach her. Mirella Varchi didn't know whether Josephine Lapoiret was capable of hard work. She knew only that Count Nordonia had sent her this marvelous child, and that tipped the balance in the girl's favor. She assumed the count must be Josephine's patron, a guarantee of the best tutelage the Continent could offer.

Josie stopped singing, and the room settled into silence. After a moment, Mirella Varchi opened her eyes. "You will spend each weekday afternoon here with me, Josephine. You will sing for one hour. Then you will sit in on my master class. You'll learn more from my advanced students than you would from listening to concerts. The musicianship of my students is nearly beyond reproach. By the end of the summer, you'll know what you must aim for, and you will have learned to work hard. You will be a singer someday, Josephine."

Josie felt the thrill of acceptance run from her scalp down along her spine to the tips of her fingers. She felt like dancing joyously around the room, but she simply bowed her thanks and said, "I'm honored, Signorina Varchi."

"Yes, you are," the diva replied with disarming honesty. "I hope you realize, Josephine, that despite my respect for Carlo Nordonia I would have turned you away without a second thought if I had not been excited by your voice. I granted you an audition as a courtesy to him. His mother, as you undoubtedly know, was my close friend and patron. She had one of the most remarkable voices I have ever heard, but of course her position made it impossible for her to sing professionally. Like you, she had a rich, flexible contralto that was perfect for every kind of music from opera to jazz." Mirella smiled nostalgically. "How shocked her family would have been if they had known that she and I used to shut ourselves up in this room and sing blues songs from America!"

All of Josie's carefully nurtured reserve vanished in a

lusty shout of laughter. "You must have been wonderful, signorina! I wish I could have heard those songs."

"You will sing that sort of thing perfectly someday, Josephine, better than I ever did, I suspect. Oh, you could probably sing opera and oratoria, and perhaps you will, if you want to. We'll see. At any rate, those decisions lie ahead of you. For now we have to work on the head tones and explore your range and—oh, so many things we have to do."

She stood and held out both hands to Josie, who felt sudden, unexpected tears behind her eyelids at the diva's warm touch. "I'll do anything you say, signorina. I'd like to sing classical as well as popular someday, if you think that's possible, but I'll do whatever you tell me to. I'll work harder than any student you've ever taught. I promise."

Mirella Varchi smiled and squeezed Josie's hands. She murmured, as if to herself, "So many dreams. Such a great gift." Suddenly she seemed to shake away whatever memories were misting her eyes. "Now, young lady, stand over here. We begin today. Now." She poked Josie between the shoulder blades, ordering, "Straighten up. Is this the way a great singer stands? Head up . . . no. *Up,* not back . . ."

Carlo bent to place a kiss on Francesca's forehead. "I'm off to meet with my banker, *cara*. After that I'll spend a few hours working in my office."

Francesca noticed that his eyes wavered only very slightly as he repeated the half-truth. He undoubtedly would spend the afternoon in his office, but Antonia would be there "working" with him.

"If you go with Josie to her lesson," Carlo went on, "you will take care to come directly home."

"Of course, Papa," she replied, trying to sound submissive. If the count could lie to his daughter, she had decided, then the daughter was perfectly justified in indulging in a bit of deception herself. "Have a nice afternoon, Papa," she added smoothly as Carlo turned and left the palazzo.

"Ah, Francesca, there you are." Josie was hurrying down the stairs. "When I realized you weren't in your room, I was afraid you wouldn't be ready. Come on. We have to hurry or I'll be late for my lesson."

They left the palazzo together, as they had done every day for the past two weeks, and headed toward Signorina Varchi's house as if they meant to spend the afternoon there. But when they were out of sight of the Nordonia servants, they parted, Josie continuing toward her singing lesson, Francesca darting into a side street to meet Jack.

"I'll meet you right here at the usual time," Francesca promised, "so we can go back to the palazzo together." Giving Josie's hand a squeeze of gratitude, she dashed off toward the Basilica di San Marco.

Jack was waiting for her on the upper terrace where the four bronze horses looked out over the piazza. She ran to him, and he caught her in his arms before one of the blind arches and began to kiss her as if he hadn't seen her in weeks.

"I want to take you to the Church of Santa Maria Gloriosa dei Frari."

"Here we are, two outlaws on the lam from my father, and you're dragging me to a priest."

"In the Frari there's someone who looks just like you." He kissed her again, but she pushed him away. A guide had stepped out on the terrace, followed by a crowd of tourists. While the guide droned about the gilded bronze horses dating from the fourth century and brought to Venice from Constantinople during the Fourth Crusade, the tourists aimed their cameras at Jack and began to snap away.

"Mr. Westman, please, can I have your autograph?"

"Could you stand closer to the horses?"

"Shake my wife's hand, will you, Westman? She talks about you all the time."

"Who are you?" someone said to Francesca. "Are you an actress or what?"

Francesca took a step back and let Jack satisfy the people's curiosity with a few smiles and handshakes, but then someone reached past him and touched Francesca's shining hair, and Jack flew into action.

"Let's go," he said, taking Francesca's hand and pulling her behind him. "Excuse us. Out of the way, please." Politely but inexorably, he forced his way through the crowd, ignoring the hands that reached out to touch him. In seconds he had maneuvered Francesca out into the open. Still holding her hand, he led her down the stairs at a run, across the uneven marble floor, past the gold and enamel mosaics and the marbles veined like sumptuous fabric.

Together they ran outdoors again and across the piazzetta to the Doges' Palace, not stopping until they stood in the cool shadow of the loggia. Shaking, Francesca looked out at the turquoise harbor, the pool of Saint Mark's.

Jack put his arm around her shoulders. "It frightens me, too, sometimes, but they don't mean any harm."

"Why do you court that kind of attention?"

"I need those people, Francesca. When the public stops loving me, I'll be out of work. But I'm not courting them; I'm courting you." He shook her gently. "Come on, now; that wasn't so bad. We're both still in one piece, aren't we? They didn't get any of my flesh or hair to keep as relics."

She moved closer to him. "If they had, I'd have scratched their eyes out."

"Well, I should hope so."

Francesca tucked her hair up under her straw hat and put on her sunglasses. There were too many people who knew her father who might recognize her. She loved sitting in the Piazza San Marco with Jack just where she had sat as a child with her mother and telling him all she remembered about her childhood and the winged lion of San Marco. Jack brought her hand to his mouth and kissed it.

"If I die of love for you, will the lion come for a sinful old man like me?"

Francesca wondered if you died with your lover in a state of sin, would the lion take mercy and carry you together on his back to heaven? Suddenly she felt very sad; why did she have to lie and to hide? She wanted her father to love her as she was in love with Jack. She wanted to confide in him and laugh with him as she had briefly before the ball. Why did she have to give up one love to have another? She sighed so deeply, Jack chuckled. But he seemed to know what she was thinking. He lifted her face and looked into her eyes. "Chin up, little one." Francesca's eyes filled. "Little one"—that's what Papa called her. "*Piccola.*" They got up to leave.

They caught the vaporetto and, after disembarking, wandered along a narrow street to the Church of Santa Maria Gloriosa. Known as the Frari, for the Franciscan friars who built an earlier, smaller structure on the same site, the fifteenth-century Gothic building contained some of Venice's most remarkable paintings, including Bellini's *Madonna and Child,* which hung over the altar in the sacristy.

"The Renaissance painters really loved to portray the Madonna, didn't they," Francesca commented. "Look at her features, Jack. So delicate and so perfect."

"Titian's best Madonna looks exactly like you. That's why I brought you to see it." Jack led her into the nave, which was dominated by Titian's *Assumption of the Virgin*, a twenty-foot-high altarpiece. Framed by gilded columns, it depicted the Virgin, her yearning face uplifted as she ascended heaven surrounded by clouds of robust *putti*. Below them, strong-limbed peasants reached out to touch her skirts, astonished by the miracle.

"That first day I saw you on the canal, I recognized your resemblance to this Madonna. This is your face, your hair, Francesca, don't you see? Titian used the same model for *Sacred and Profane Love*, but I'll have to take you to Rome to see that."

The sun had disappeared, and thick gray clouds scudded across the sky. They walked aimlessly through the streets, Jack's thumb caressing the back of Francesca's hand. She grew so contented in their companionable silence that she was startled when he finally spoke.

"Have you ever been to Paris?"

"No. I've never been anywhere but Venice and Nassau."

"Then I'll take you to Paris someday soon. It's not as magical and golden as Venice. It's grayer and more intellectual. But for us it'd be perfect."

"Why?"

"Three reasons. First, the French rarely recognize me. Second, they'd *never* recognize you. Third, your father would be hundreds of miles away."

Francesca laughed, delighted with the idea of going to Paris with Jack.

"In Paris I'll build you a castle on the Seine. We'll lock ourselves inside, away from the tourists, for weeks at a time."

"It sounds perfect. When do we leave?"

He sighed. "I'd go tomorrow if the film were finished. But I have to do some scenes next week and a few more in August. I can't possibly leave before the middle of next month."

"I wonder if we can keep our meetings a secret that long. My father wants to take me to the Greek Islands on his yacht. Soon I'll run out of excuses not to go with him."

"Tell him the truth."

"Jack, that would ruin everything. He'd send me back to

the Bahamas and then what would we do? You have to stay here. We'll just have to wait."

He took her hand. "I'm not sure I can wait any longer, Francesca."

She understood, and realized that she, too, had waited long enough. She squeezed his hand. "Today, then," she said softly.

"Now," Jack whispered.

She looked up, surprised, as a raindrop hit her forehead and trickled down along her temple. Jack bent toward her and licked it neatly off her skin. The warmth and wetness of his tongue made her catch her breath. He dipped his head lower and kissed her open mouth, and the brief contact sent a shock of desire to that place deep inside Francesca that only Jack seemed capable of touching. She tilted her face up to him, inviting another such kiss. She stood on tiptoe, trying to get closer to his mouth, but he took hold of her upper arms and gently steadied her. He turned her toward the canal, one arm around her shoulders. They started to run as it began to rain harder and harder. He helped her into a gondola and gave directions to his hotel.

While the gondolier poled them through the rain Jack began to make love to her. Francesca could sense the difference in intent in his caresses. She could not move her mouth beneath his. In the tiny cabin they were thrown together uncomfortably, but he moved his body against hers and she was surprised to see how neatly they fit together. He lifted her dress, and her lace slip rose on her thighs. His hands on her breasts aroused her, startling her with the intensity of her own feeling.

"What is it?" she whispered in alarm.

He shook his head at her and she looked into his dilated eyes. "You want me." He smiled.

"Yes."

She stroked her hands over his shoulders and slim back, feeling the lean muscles tense. His hand caressed her knee and thigh, and then the tender space between her legs. She heard the rain on the water, felt the waves rock against her spine. Jack's warmth seemed to absorb her, as if they shared a single skin.

In the dim light from the little side windows Francesca watched through half-closed lids as Jack's mouth left her own and his dark golden head bent over her breast. She breathed in the perfume of his hair, damp from the fog. As his lips found her nipple she closed her eyes and put her head back, giving herself over to the waves of feeling that grew more and more intense. When she finally opened her eyes Jack was smiling at her. They had both been surprised at her new abandon. Glancing down, she caught sight of her breast, so white against the shiny black raincoat, the nipple erect and crimson. She gave a little shiver but Jack was already gently buttoning her blouse and gathering her coat around her. He pulled her head onto his shoulder and kissed her brow. "We need a breath of air." He chuckled and pushed one side of the door open with his foot. The rain had subsided and a breeze cooled their faces. This gentle protective side of Jack made Francesca's love for him all the stronger.

During their times together Jack had always been affectionate, but he had held himself under rigid control and taken care to stay in places too public for anything more intimate than a kiss. His reticence had begun to wear on her as her need for him grew stronger and more urgent. Often she had boldly held herself against him when he kissed her, wanting, needing to feel the pressure of his physical desire for her. On most of those occasions he had squelched her teasing with a hard kiss and sent her home. But this afternoon their teasing courtship would end, and they would become lovers.

He led her through the puddles of rain to his hotel, whisking her quickly up to his room, speaking to no one on the way.

Inside the room, he closed the door and leaned back against it, looking at her intently. After a moment he said gently, "No second thoughts, Francesca? I want you to be absolutely certain."

Fór answer she unbuttoned her blouse, pushed it off her shoulders, and let it slip to the floor. She held out her arms to Jack, and he clasped her to him, holding her gently for a moment. Francesca rubbed herself against him, thrilling to the roughness of his linen jacket as it brushed her bare breasts. Then Jack was peeling off the rest of her clothes and leading her to the bed. He threw off the spread, and they sank down onto the cool sheet, clinging to each other. He kissed her until she moaned beneath him and began to fumble with the buttons of his shirt, longing to feel him naked against her.

Quickly he undressed and stretched out beside her, stroking her breasts and flat belly as he kissed her mouth again. Then with one warm hand, he eased her legs apart and pressed his palm against the secret place between her thighs, kneading her flesh until she began to writhe beneath his hand. The tight coil within her loins tensed and hovered as if on the verge of bursting open, and she cried out.

He eased himself over her, and with one swift, smooth move he was inside her—holding himself motionless as he studied her face. "My darling, I'm sorry if I hurt you."

"It's all right. I love to feel you inside me." She moved beneath him, wanting somehow to burst that coil of tension inside her, not knowing how to please him, feeling awkward and inexpert, wondering why he remained so still.

"Wait a moment, Francesca." He pushed a strand of hair away from her face and kissed her lightly. "Take a few seconds to get used to me."

She lay still, letting him caress her with his warm hands and lips. Then she stirred beneath him, letting her body tell him what she wanted. He began to move against her, gently at first, then faster when he saw that she was all right. Wanting more of him, she braced her feet against the mattress and thrust herself up to meet him, feeling that coil pull itself still tighter together, aware that he was watching her face. There was no pain now, she realized, and no more anxiety about pleasing Jack. There was only the wanting, the urgency. Then she knew the coil was about to explode, and she threw her head back as her body began to stiffen. Above her, Jack increased the speed of his thrusts, and suddenly the tension inside her shattered into a sunburst of sensations that left her mindless and weak with pleasure. Jack grew tense, moaned deep inside his throat, and then relaxed, letting his weight down gently on top of her.

Breathless, she clung to him, enjoying the sleekness of sweat on his back under her hands. When he rolled away from her, she felt suddenly alone. He pulled the top sheet over them and then gathered her into his arms and held her close against him. After a while, he tilted her face up to his. "As soon as I can get loose from this picture, I'm going to Paris. Do you still want to come with me or have I scared you away for good?"

"I'll go with you; you know that, Jack."

"And you'll marry me?"

She nodded, then flung her arms around him and hugged

him with all her strength. "I didn't know I could be this happy."

"Neither did I, Francesca."

She pushed away from him and studied his face, wondering if perhaps he had said the same thing to other women. But his eyes—those open, honest, almost innocent blue eyes—she decided, were full of exactly the same emotion she was feeling.

"I love you, Francesca."

"And I love you."

"Even though I'm too far below your station?"

She nodded. "And too old and too foreign—"

He dropped a kiss on her nose, and before he could raise his head, she had taken his face in her hands and pulled his mouth down to hers. She put into the kiss all the tricks and flourishes she had picked up from him, and she was thoroughly pleased with herself when she felt the beginnings of his arousal against her stomach.

"Don't get me excited again, vixen. We have to shower and sneak you back to the palace."

He got out of bed and pulled her to her feet. They showered and dressed together, Francesca teasing him shamelessly, Jack playing the outraged innocent. Before they left the room, Jack removed a gold signet ring from his finger and pressed it into her hand. "Will you wear this on a chain around your neck until I can get you a ring of your own?"

Francesca's answer was another kiss, but Jack pulled away after only a moment.

He locked the door behind them and steered her out of the hotel. As they reached the main door, she gave him a good slap on the rear end, and he bent down to whisper in her ear. "I don't know why I worried so much about despoiling you. I should have spent more time worrying about my own virtue and good name. You, my love, are a corrupting influence."

As he hugged her to him a photographer rose from a crouch on the sidewalk, his camera aimed directly at them. Jack lunged at him, but the paparazzo was already escaping among the crowd of passersby.

"Damn," Jack muttered. "I could probably have grabbed his camera, but that would only make a bigger headline in the scandal sheets. This is bad enough, but it'll at least be relegated to the back pages."

"My father doesn't read those papers, Jack. He won't see

the picture unless someone makes a special effort to point it out to him, and I don't know of anyone who would do such a thing."

They walked toward the spot where she was to meet Josie, Jack still looking worried and upset. "I know of a place where we can meet in the afternoons without having to worry about photographers." She smiled when he raised his eyebrows. "On the top floor of the palazzo there are some rooms that are no longer used. It's the nursery floor, and it's been closed up for years.

Jack laughed. "So tomorrow I'll walk up to the palazzo and announce that I have a rendezvous with you in the attic."

"As soon as my father leaves for the office after lunch, I'll call you. You come to the little door the delivery men use. I'll wait for you there, and we'll go upstairs and make love every afternoon."

Jack stared at her in amazement. "And to think I regarded you as a helpless innocent! Francesca, are you a descendant of Machiavelli?"

"I am a descendant," she said wryly, "of Carlo Nordonia, which is even better."

"Ah, how these hot-blooded Italians love intrigue. Here's your friend," Jack said, nodding at Josie, who was coming toward them. "Call me tomorrow, my darling." He gave her a quick kiss and disappeared in the crowd.

Chapter Eleven

JOSIE, HOME EARLY from her lesson, mounted the stairs to her bedroom. On summer afternoons the palazzo slept. Francesca disappeared while Carlo was at work, and the servants took a siesta. Josie, lonely since Charles left Venice a week ago, lived for her lessons. There was little else for her to do on these hot afternoons when the thick air, reeking of the swampy canal water, covered Venice like a lid. She longed for Nassau's fresh air, carefree pleasures, and uncomplicated friendships.

Francesca, *p'tite soeur*, now seemed lost to her. Although, to all appearances, they remained friends, the old intimacy had been shattered, a victim of Josie's resentment and Francesca's distraction. The two of them no longer talked in whispers late into the night. They chatted, yes, but their secrets stood between them like an invisible wall erected during almost two months in Venice. Francesca spoke only of her love for Jack Westman, her longing to be with him, her determination to run away to Paris with him. She did not tell Josie she had been to bed with him, but Josie had guessed as much from the glow that had surrounded Francesca the last time they met after a singing lesson to walk back to the palazzo together. The contessina was keeping other secrets, too, Josie suspected. There was a new cynicism in the way she spoke of her father. She no longer left the palazzo with Josie each afternoon, declaring with transparent dishonesty that she and Jack loved each other too much to sneak around in back alleys. Another lie, Josie concluded. She had found a better way to meet her lover.

Josie went into her room and stretched out on her bed, wanting to sleep through the hottest hours of the brutal summer afternoon. After fifteen minutes, she admitted to herself that her thoughts would give her no rest. She missed Charles, and that surprised her. She did not love him. She felt no rush of passion when he took her in his arms. There had been no crashing cymbals and sounding trumpets when she lay beneath him in his bed. She had used him, and she suspected he knew that. Used him to rid herself of her virginity and inexperience, to introduce her to musicians who might one day be of help to her, to keep her mind off Jack Westman's blue eyes and easy humor. And yet she missed Charles Cash in the same way she missed Francesca—the old Francesca. Another warm presence had disappeared from her life, and there was suddenly no one left in the world who cared about her except her mother, who was a thousand miles away.

She got off the bed, went to her bureau, and picked up the framed photograph of Marianne Lapoiret. She longed to feel the warmth of her mother's strong arms around her, taste the fresh, simple meals she cooked. And most of all she missed being able to tell her things. "Mama, wait till you hear what Signorina Varchi told me today!" Or, more often these days, "Oh, Mama, I'm so mad at Francesca I could just scream!"

Josie put the picture back in its place and wandered restlessly into the hall, listening for sounds of life in the palazzo. Hearing nothing, she walked to the stairway, thinking that somewhere in this great echoing golden prison there must be a living soul. She started down to the second floor, but then a noise—metal scraping on wood?—drew her attention to the stairway that led to the top floor, the old nursery wing. Francesca had shown it to her soon after they arrived in Venice, but neither of them had been up there since that day. There was no reason to visit the nursery; even the servants went there only on cleaning day. But the sound had come from the fourth floor; of that she was certain.

Silently, slowly, she mounted the staircase and then crept along the hall, holding her breath, wondering if a servant had sneaked up here to do some mischief.

A mural covered the walls. It depicted a jungle in which monkeys hung from emerald-green vines, and toylike giraffes and lions with large, gentle eyes peered from behind the trees. Francesca had spent her earliest years in this childlike paradise.

A few feet down the hall a door stood a few inches ajar, as if it had been opened just enough to admit a cross-breeze. Was that the metallic sound she had heard from the foot of the stairs? Had someone hidden in that room and found the heat too oppressive to endure? She inched her way to the door. The hinged side was toward her, and she would be able to see a part of the room through the crack. She stood still for a moment, listening, expecting to hear a couple of the servants.

But the voice she heard was unmistakably Francesca's. The other voice was a rumbling baritone, thick and husky now but easily recognizable as Jack Westman's.

She slid her cheek along the wall until she could look through the crack in the hinged side of the door. Through the narrow opening she could see only a small strip of the room. A bed, a bare breast, the upper part of a naked male torso, and on the floor a cotton shirt. A man's tanned hand appeared, cupped the white breast and stroked it.

Josie stood there, stunned, as the fragmentary scene unfolded before her. Westman's body seemed to capture sunlight, illuminating Francesca's pale skin as he moved over her. Their murmurs, the movements of their bodies and hands told Josie all she needed or wanted to know of the way they felt about each other. A jolt of sheer physical pain racked her body as a current of emotions ran through her. The guilt she felt as she spied on the lovers nearly sent her running down the stairs, but for a long moment she remained paralyzed in a grip of other feelings—jealousy of Francesca, who had won the man they both loved; envy of her friend, who had found passion with Jack while Josie had found only warmth and tenderness in Charles's bed; horror at the thought of what would happen if Carlo learned of his daughter's affair with Westman; and, most terrifying of all, a vague satisfaction at the power she suddenly held in her hands. Word of this scene, breathed in the appropriate ear, could ruin two, maybe three people's lives.

Josie went cold and at the same instant began to perspire. What kind of a person was she turning into? A month ago such a thought would never have entered her mind. Had Carlo Nordonia's ruthless and manipulative nature begun to rub off on her?

Head spinning, she fled silently down the stairs and into her room, then fell across the bed and burst into tears.

"Vieri, help me with this clothesline." Josie's voice was angry, her manner imperious.

"Do it yourself," Vieri shouted across the courtyard. "What makes you think you can give me orders, you lazy foreigner."

Josie mumbled an expletive and juggled the summer blouses and skirts she had laundered by hand, trying to get them back into the basket without letting them touch the ground. "The clothesline just broke, Vieri. Put down that hose and come over here." She held out one end of the line. "Take this and tie it around the trellis."

Vieri stopped washing down the flagstones and dropped the hose, turning a resentful scowl on Josie. "You eat with the rest of us, but you do no work," he said, his voice unusually quiet, the words enunciated with unnecessary care, as if he had rehearsed them and saved them for the right moment. "You order us around as if you were the mistress of the household. You run off to take lessons in the afternoon while we clean and cook and garden." His voice rose, and his eyes grew hard as he stroked the fire of his pent-up rage. "Understand this, *bastarda*, the circumstances of your birth do not make you better than we are. Not in our eyes, not in the count's eyes."

Josie had frozen, the end of the clothesline still clutched in her hand. She stared at Vieri, unblinking, her eyes dull with shock. *Bastarda*, he had called her. She tried to wrap her mind around the word, hardly hearing the rest of the servant's diatribe. Marianne's husband had not died at sea; she had had no husband at all. Josie was illegitimate. Even the servants knew it, and Vieri apparently thought she knew it, too.

Illegitimate. A bastard. She felt as if Vieri had struck her hard in the stomach. It was just an expression. He didn't mean it.

But something in Vieri's tone of voice caught her attention.

"You ought to know by now that the count will never accept you as his child. He is ashamed of you because you are not white." Vieri hawked and spit on the ground near Josie's feet. "That is what we think of you, Contessina *Bastarda*!" He made a contemptuous gesture with his hand, then turned and disappeared into the palazzo.

Josie fell to her knees, her eyes glazed; her mouth was open, yet she couldn't gulp in enough air. If only the earth would open up and swallow her, plunge her into darkness, smother her, keep her hidden from sight forever.

Simply by being born, she had destroyed her mother, shamed her, forced her to leave her home and live among strangers. And she had always been, would always be, a source of embarrassment for her father.

Her father. Josie's heart began to ache. The mighty Count Nordonia. A man of such high principles. No wonder he had sent her to eat with the servants; she reminded him that he had slept with his Haitian housekeeper. Had he been married to Susannah when he slept with Marianne? No, Josie realized. He had married Susannah later. After he had safely hidden his housekeeper and her baby daughter in Haiti, getting rid of the evidence of his indiscretion. Josie remembered going to Lyford Cay when she was about five. Carlo must have sent for them, must have thought no one would connect him with Marianne's almost-white child.

Her throat constricted as she remembered what Mirella Varchi had said about Carlo's mother: "She had one of the most remarkable voices I've ever heard. Like you, she had a rich, flexible contralto."

Like you. Like you. Like you . . .

Josie had Carlo's mother's voice, her grandmother. Was that her only legacy from the Nordonia family? Or had she also been given her father's cold and unloving nature? She couldn't love Charles. And for Francesca, whom she had once loved, she now felt only resentment for all that the younger woman had stolen from her. Wealth, prestige, legitimacy, a title, a man who actually looked like the prince in a fairy tale. All Francesca's simply for the asking.

Josie covered her face with her hands. "God forgive me," she murmured. "I'm growing to hate my own sister."

"Where is my lighter?" Carlo bellowed to make himself heard through the bathroom door.

"No need to shout," Antonia said, flinging the door open. "I'm out of the shower."

Her lean, boyish body was wrapped in a thick blue towel, but the parts that showed made Carlo wish he were young enough to make love to her again. He ran a hand over her smooth shoulder and along her collarbone, then shook his head. He was too old for this.

"My lighter, *piccola*. Where is it?"

"It probably fell out of your pocket when you took off your clothes. If you can't find it, look in my shoulder bag; there's a pack of matches in one of the compartments." She turned to go back into the bathroom, then whirled around again, her face suddenly pale, one hand thrust out as if to stop him. "Let me find them for you. That bag is stuffed with junk."

But she had recovered her poise too late. Carlo had seen the guilt. "What are you up to, Toni?" He knew she had heard the teasing laughter in his voice, and he wondered why she continued to stare at him with fear in her eyes. Surely she wasn't afraid of him; she knew he lived for the hours they spent together. His pulse began to pound. He had seen that same fear in his daughter's eyes so often. Had he driven his mistress away, too? He opened Antonia's purse and began to take out its contents. "Will I find passionate letters in here from all of your other lovers?"

"Carlo, let me—"

She fell silent when he held up a tattered newspaper clipping.

"What is this, Antonia? It looks as if it came from one of the scandal sheets." He unfolded the clipping, walked to the window to look at it in the light, and found himself staring at a photograph of his daughter and the American movie star.

"My mother cut it out." Antonia's voice was tight with anxiety. "I meant to show it to you, Carlo, but I just didn't have the heart." She went over to him and put an arm around his waist. "Don't upset yourself, *tesoro*. She's only a child, and I'm sure the photograph means nothing. They're simply talking—"

"They are kissing, or starting to kiss." He heard the anger in his voice and felt his breathing quicken. "They are coming out of a hotel."

He walked away from Antonia; she was the least of his problems. His daughter had been lying to him from the start, sneaking away from the palazzo in secrecy, ignoring his directives, his commands. Just as Susannah had done. And Josie Lapoiret had conspired with Francesca to deceive him.

"Call the palazzo," he snapped. "Tell Vieri to pick me up with the motorboat immediately. Ask Emilio and Ruggieri to meet me at this address in fifteen minutes." He scribbled on a piece of paper and thrust it at Antonia, then stalked into the bathroom and slammed the door.

"A gentleman to see Signorina Lapoiret. I put him in the reception room," the maid said, bobbing her head at Mirella Varchi as she backed out of the room.

Josie's brow furrowed. "I'm sorry, signorina. I can't imagine who would interrupt my lesson."

The diva bowed her head. "Go speak to your guest, Josephine. We will continue when you return."

Josie followed the maid out of the room, along a narrow corridor. At a closed door, the maid stopped, rapped lightly, and stuck her head into the room. "Signorina Lapoiret is here, signore."

A male voice rumbled something Josie couldn't hear, and the maid gestured her into a spacious and imposing reception room and closed the door behind her.

Carlo Nordonia turned away from the window and pinned Josie with an icy stare. For a long moment he didn't speak. Josie knew he was simply waiting for the maid to walk out of earshot, but his silence and the coldness in his eyes made a shiver run through her.

Finally he took two steps toward her and stopped. "You will tell me where Francesca is."

Josie swallowed hard and lifted her chin, refusing to flinch under the steady gaze of his hard eyes. "I don't know."

"You lied when you said she accompanied you here, didn't you."

"Yes." Josie held her head high and forced herself to look directly at him. The thought of using Francesca's secret against her now seemed unthinkable. There was cruelty in this man who was their father.

"And you are lying when you say you don't know where she is right now." He advanced toward her slowly, menacingly, and for a moment she was certain he would strike her. "She's not in this house. Of that I am certain. My men have questioned the servants. We have also been to Westman's hotel. She is not there."

He was close to her now; she could see that his hair was wet and she could smell something sweet. Soap. He had just showered. Josie guessed he had been with Antonia; she had listened to the talk of the servants. Did Toni know about Francesca and Jack? Surely, even if she did know, she wouldn't have told Carlo . . .

Carlo didn't move; his eyes never wavered. "I made sure Francesca had little time to spend with you. And still you corrupted her." A tiny muscle under his left eye jumped. "I was too kind to you. I should have forbidden Francesca to bring you to Venice. Where is she?'' Carlo's voice rose almost to a shout as he asked the question once more.

''I don't know.'' Josie heard in her tone an icy hatred that matched the count's.

''You will tell me where she is, Josephine. If you don't, I will end your singing lessons this instant. You will be back in Nassau by tomorrow night.''

Josie felt her composure crumble. She bowed her head, refusing to let him see how much this threat hurt her, but she kept her lips tightly shut. She had much to gain by telling Carlo everything she knew. Doing so would pay Francesca back for her refusal to stand up to her father; it would also free Jack Westman, who might turn to her for comfort when Carlo separated him from Francesca. But Josie's loathing of the count was too deep and too bitter; she would never tell him anything, no matter how much he threatened.

''Still determined to be noble, are you?''

She looked up, surprised. His voice had gentled, and the hard line of his mouth had softened. Thrown off guard, she simply stared at him.

''What are you afraid of, Josie? That I will harm my daughter when I find her?'' He shrugged and looked hurt. ''I am angry, yes, but I am not a monster. I will not punish Francesca. All I want is to separate her from that fortune-hunting American.''

Josie studied his eyes, his voice. His rage seemed to have vanished when he realized she considered him a threat to his own child, but the ice in his eyes had not melted, and the muscle over his cheekbone had jumped again. The count was trying to throw her off-balance. Let him try. He wouldn't get far.

Carlo regarded her sadly. ''However, I must find her before she becomes a subject for gossip. That is imperative, Josie. I cannot allow another scandal to fall on the Nordonia name.''

Scandal? Josie looked at him quizzically, but he apparently thought she knew about this ''scandal'' he had mentioned, or else he was attempting to distract her, make her lose her presence of mind. She looked at him steadily, but said nothing.

''Where is my daughter?''

''I don't know.''

''Josie, if you don't tell me where she is, if you won't help me save her, then you certainly can't expect me to let you stay in my home, pay for your lessons, allow you to associate with my daughter.'' He walked over to the window and stood with the light behind him so that his words came to Josie from a faceless silhouette. ''You will return to Nassau tomorrow; your singing lessons are over.''

A hand seemed to tighten around Josie's heart. She looked at the floor so that Carlo wouldn't see the mist of tears in her eyes.

''As soon as you have left Venice,'' he continued, ''I shall call Marianne. I shall tell her I am sending you home because you have brought shame to me.''

Josie's head snapped up.

''By behaving like a tramp,'' he went on, ''with your American piano player. Sleeping with him in his hotel near the Piazzale Roma. Standing below the outside staircase of my home telling him how much you enjoyed being in his bed. I cannot tolerate such behavior and such talk in a member of my household. I'm sure your mother will be interested to hear that her daughter has a lover.''

Josie had stopped breathing. Carlo had ordered his servants to follow her and even to listen as she said good-bye to Charles in the courtyard. He would make their friendship into something dirty and cheap when he told the story to Marianne.

She shook her head. This would kill her mother, and Carlo knew it.

''In the nursery.'' The words sounded strangled as they emerged from her throat.

Carlo's eyebrows shot up. ''At the palazzo?'' His voice registered disbelief.

Josie nodded, beaten, loathing herself more with each moment that passed. She stood trembling in the center of the huge room until long after Carlo had slammed out of the house. She had resented and even hated Francesca. That she admitted. But to betray her to a man such as this. Josie Lapoiret, she feared, truly *was* Carlo Nordonia's bastard.

Francesca quickly slipped out of her clothes and climbed into the bed, pulling the crisp sheet up to her waist. She watched as Jack kicked off his loafers and shed his jacket and shirt.

''How did the shooting go yesterday afternoon?'' she asked.

Jack sat on the edge of the bed and pulled off his socks.

"Okay. Lots of standing around, waiting, but eventually they got the shots they wanted."

He shed the rest of his clothes, but still he sat on the bed, his bare back to Francesca.

"I spent most of the afternoon wishing I were here with you." He lay back and took her in his arms. "By the time we finished, it was too late to come or even to call." He kissed her, long and lovingly, then held her close against him, not moving.

Francesca caught his head in her hands and forced it up so that she could see his face. "Something's wrong, Jack. What is it?"

He tried to make light of it. "I missed you. Thought about you all afternoon." He managed a smile, but his eyes were worried. "You raise merry hell with my concentration, Francesca."

He began to stroke her slowly, from her breastbone down over her abdomen, until her body strained with an unbearable pleasure. Before he bent his head to her breast, she caught once more a glimpse of the unhappiness in his eyes.

They made love slowly, tenderly, then lay together talking, whispering, until the shadows in the room began to darken and lengthen. Jack got up heavily and pulled on his Levi's, then lay on top of the sheet, his head propped up on his hand.

"Jack, please tell me why you're so blue today."

"It's not just today, Francesca. It's all the time, every day. Sometimes I can't see you because I have to work. Then, when we can be together, we have to sneak around." With one finger, he absently traced the planes of her face. "I want to be with you all the time. I want to take you places, be seen with you, take you home openly, and spend the night with you." He looked at her silently for a moment before he spoke again. "We have to make a decision, Francesca."

"We already have. We're going to be together."

"When?"

"Soon, Jack, when your work is finished. We'll go to Paris."

"You'll have to tell your father where you're going. Why not tell him now, prepare him for what's about to happen?"

Francesca shook her head. "I'll just go away with you. I'll leave him a letter, but I won't tell him anything in person. If I tried to, he'd find a way to stop me. He has three strong, loyal servants: Emilio, Vieri, and Ruggieri. They could make sure I stayed in the palazzo." She shrugged hopelessly. "They could even put me on a plane and send me off somewhere where you'd never find me."

Shock and then horror flicked across Jack's face. "He would do something like that to his own daughter?"

"Jack, you're everything he despises. An American, a celebrity, an actor. He thinks you're after me for my fortune and my title."

Jack sat up and put on his shoes and socks. "Get dressed, Francesca. You're coming with me." He took her hand and pulled her up to a sitting position, then sat next to her, his arms around her. He cupped her breast in his hand and covered her mouth with his.

Then the door flew open, hitting the wall with a startling crash, and the nightmare began.

Carlo stood in the doorway, towering over them, his wild eyes fixed on Jack's hand.

Jack pulled the sheet up to cover Francesca, then stood to face her father, trying to shield her with his body.

"Get out of my house, *maiale*."

"Gladly, but Francesca comes with me."

"Never."

Jack snatched Francesca's clothes from the back of a chair and handed them to her. Under the sheet, she scrambled into them while Jack tried to draw Carlo's anger away from her. "You call yourself her father!" he shouted. "You act like an executioner. She's terrified of you, can't you see that? What kind of man are you, Nordonia?"

Francesca, disheveled but decent, stood up and ran to Jack's side. He pushed her behind him. "Get out of my way," he said to Carlo. "I'm taking your daughter with me. She's not safe with you."

Outraged, Carlo swung his arm, but Jack caught his wrist before the palm of the count's hand reached his face. He twisted, swinging his other fist, just as three men burst into the room. They seized Jack's arms and wrestled him through the door. Francesca tried to follow, but Carlo sent her tumbling onto the bed with a fierce slap across the face.

Jack struggled and shouted, but the servants forced him out of the room. "Francesca," he called from the hallway.

When he stopped shouting abruptly, Francesca struggled to her feet. Had they gagged him, knocked him unconscious? "Jack!" she screamed, racing for the door.

Carlo, anger blazing from his eyes, grabbed her shoulders and shook her. "*Puttana!*" he shouted.

"I love him. I'm going to marry him."

"That filth. He has ruined you."

He flung her hard onto the bed and walked out of the room. The door slammed behind him.

Carlo allowed himself one night to lick his wounds; in the morning he set a new course. He had no intention of letting his daughter's triumphant debut into society go to waste. The season was not over yet. The ball was still the talk of Venice and hopefully Francesca and Jack's publicity had not been taken too seriously. He would pull Francesca up by the scruff of her neck if he had to, to make her behave like a lady.

He finished issuing his invitations for the cruise of the Greek Islands in record time, and luckily the Mdvani boy was still calling on Francesca. He had not given up in spite of Francesca's unresponsiveness. He would come on the cruise with another young couple, the girl a little older and not too pretty. Hopefully she would serve to replace Josie if Francesca needed a shoulder to cry on. His cousin Caterina and two other friends of his own would also be there. They would be off to new and beautiful vistas before Francesca had a chance to brood.

But brood she did soon after the cruise began, staring out to sea and in general behaving impossibly. In the privacy of his cabin, Carlo despaired. He had determined to be cheerful and pleasant no matter what, but Francesca was turning out to be as obstinate as her mother. Still, he refused to be discouraged. He would find a more entertaining group of young people in Sardinia, the next port, and they would have a party and he would take lots of pictures. He'd always been a photography buff, but now he'd put it to good use. He looked over his latest batch of Polaroids and found just what he needed: a picture of Francesca with a big smile looking lovingly up at the Mdvani boy, or so it seemed. In actual fact she had been looking just past his profile at Hush Puppy peeking out of the porthole. Carlo took out the scissors and carefully cut out the basset hound. The result was as misleading as a sentence out of context.

Carlo slipped the picture in an envelope and addressed it to Toni in Venice. He had convinced her that this deception was all for Francesca's own good and she had finally cooperated in contacting the press for him. The result was that the newspapers printed pictures of Francesca aboard the yacht, smiling and sunburned, her hair blowing in the wind, chatting with one or another of Carlo's handsome young friends. All this would not be wasted on Westman, who, he hoped, would be properly discouraged.

Josie waited until almost three o'clock in the morning before she crept out of her room and into Carlo's study. There was no point in stirring up the suspicions of the servants; she had antagonized them enough since the count left on the cruise.

In the dimly lit hallway, Josie paused and listened. No one was stirring. Swiftly she made her way to Carlo's study, the soft folds of the black lace peignoir swirling about her slender legs. She let herself into the book-lined room and stood still until her eyes adjusted to the darkness. When she was able to make out the shapes of the larger pieces of furniture, she inched her way over to the count's desk and flicked on a small brass lamp with a green glass shade. She eased open the French doors that led to the balcony and put on a record of Callas singing *Tosca*, careful to keep the volume down. It was a starless night without a breath of air. Periodically the music would be interrupted by static, as thunder rumbled in the distance. Josie tipped back Carlo's big leather armchair and squinted at the light through the brandy in her snifter. Carlo's pens stood in a brass rack on top of the desk; she tried several before settling on the one with the thinnest, most delicate point. Then she took a piece of heavy vellum stationery embossed with the Nordonia crest and, very carefully copying Francesca's schoolgirl handwriting, she wrote a revised version of the letter to Jack lying beside her on the desk.

The tip of her tongue peeped out the corner of her mouth as she concentrated on her task, making each letter fat and schoolgirlish, choosing just the words and phrases Francesca would have used. *"I am sorry to hurt you, Jack,"* she began. *"Our time together meant so much to me; I will never forget you."*

Josie held the paper up and squinted at the handwriting. It was perfect. Exactly like Francesca's. She laid the paper down and continued, remembering to cross out a word here and there, as Francesca always did; and to misspell one or two, not long ones though—Francesca was careful with those—just the short, easy ones she didn't bother to think about.

". . . and so I cannot see you again under any circumstances. Please forgive me. Francesca."

"There!" The note of final and utter rejection was completed. As the ink dried, Josie studied a newspaper picture of Francesca and Franco Mdvani looking tan and happy. Strange, Francesca really did look happy. Maybe Josie was doing her a favor. Would it be pushing it to happen to be carrying the clipping when she delivered the letter? Perhaps Jack had missed it. Josie picked a cigar from the humidor and lit it with a grin. Marianne had smoked cigars in private. Perhaps she learned the habit from Carlo. She put the letter in an envelope and carefully printed Jack's name on it; then she held Francesca's original letter to the end of her cigar and, setting it on fire, watched as it disintegrated in the ashtray.

Josie borrowed one of Francesca's dresses, an expensive gold Missoni knit, for the meeting. On Francesca it silhouetted her slimness but Josie filled it out like a voluptuous Italian girl. The dress was long, below the knee; it seemed elegant despite the way it clung to her hips and breast. She braided strands of gold ribbon into her hair and carefully made up her eyes with gold and green shadow. It was a hot afternoon, but Vieri, seeing her, forgot his usual resentment and gladly agreed to take her by gondola to Harry's Bar. She knew she looked beautiful in her borrowed feathers. Even the gondoliers whistled at her.

When she arrived at Harry's Bar, she saw Jack sitting with another man. They both rose when she strolled in. The stranger's face lit up with admiration, but Jack's only showed relief.

"Josie, this is Arkansas Whalen," Jack said. "Josie is Francesca's best friend."

"Can I order you *un'ombra*, as the Venetians call a glass of wine," Arkansas asked with a charming smile.

"Yes, thank you."

Josie handed Jack the envelope, and, turning her chair to Whalen, pretended to give him all her attention; but out of the corner of her eye she watched Jack tensely. He opened the letter and began to read eagerly—but halfway through he muttered disgustedly, "This doesn't sound like Francesca."

Jack rose, his face a crimson mask of pain and fury, and with one gesture swept the table clean, knocking his chair backwards. As Jack strode out of the bar, Whalen got up, too, stammering excuses and throwing some money on the table as he blundered after Jack like a lame dog.

Josie finished her drink, shaken that the encounter hadn't gone quite the way she planned it. Jack had reacted with rage, not sadness; and worse, hadn't turned to her for friendship and comfort. In driving him away from Francesca, she realized she might have lost him, too.

But maybe not forever. He would mourn his lost contessina for a while, but he would recover. And maybe he would remember her.

As she rose to leave she spotted the letter lying under the table in a puddle of spilled drinks. The handwriting was already an indecipherable blur.

In the meantime, Carlo did his best to endure the cruise. It wasn't really his type of sailing, sleeping on Pratesi sheets and bathing in carpeted bathrooms with Porthault towels. Susannah had never cared for "Gucci Pucci baloney" as she'd called it, but she knew quality. He had bought the yacht to distract her, give her a new project, but time had run out and she had gotten no further with the yacht than ordering the linens. She had also hung some of Sybilla's paintings. He had gotten rid of those.

Now they were anchored off Patmos on a particularly hot day when the entire party decided to go ashore for a picnic lunch. When they returned Hush Puppy was nowhere to be found at first, and then, with a cry, Francesca saw the dog lying in the little bit of shade she had found after having been somehow locked out of the cabins by the crew. Hush Puppy's old heart had finally stopped. Francesca's weeping was too much for Carlo. He knew she cried for more than just the beast. At sundown he took Francesca and a member of the crew with him to shore. Hush Puppy, wrapped in a cashmere sweater of Francesca's and put in a handsome wooden box bought from a Greek fisherman, was borne up a hill and buried under a field of brilliant red poppies. Francesca stood next to her father as he lowered the little coffin himself into a deep grave the crewman had dug. As they walked back down the hill, Francesca saw her father pinch tears away from where they trickled down the sides of his nose, and for the first time in weeks, she voluntarily touched him, putting her arm around him. He squeezed her shoulder and laughed wryly. Francesca choked back her own tears and hugged her father around the waist.

But Carlo's sentimentality soured and turned to impatience. Bored with the trip, he abruptly ordered the yacht back to Venice. His mission was partly accomplished; Francesca had shown him some warmth. It would only be a question of time before he won her back entirely.

Francesca woke the next morning to the news that they were returning to Venice at full speed. For the first time in days she ate breakfast with an appetite as voracious as her desire to get home.

Venice in August was like a beauty past her prime, weighed down by her own elaborate jewels. The canals stank in the heat and the streets and piazzas were glutted with tourists. Francesca's knees shook as she practiced every bit of self-control not to run up the marble staircase ahead of her father. The privacy of her room and the telephone there beckoned like a powerful magnet. She had been in an agony of suspense since she had gotten off the yacht, and for three weeks had not been allowed to telephone alone. Her conversations with Josie in her father's presence from the boat had been infuriating. Josie seemed to have lost all her powers of imagination and given her absolutely no significant information about Jack. She probably thought the phone was tapped.

Francesca left her father on the second floor and hurled herself up the last flight of stairs and into her room. As she sat down to phone, there was a knock at the door. Emilio entered with her bags and she was forced to be civil for another eternity. She was dialing Jack's number with a trembling finger when her eyes fell on the pile of newspaper clippings lying on the table by the phone. The first caption stopped her cold. The only paper they had gotten on board the yacht was the Paris *Herald*. Even that dignified publication carried the news of Nadia's suicide attempt. There had been a picture of Jack carrying flowers to her hospital bed, which was understandable. But somehow these pictures were different.

Francesca stared at them, trying to discover what had attracted Jack. Nadia had an earthy Mediterranean beauty, with enormous, luminous eyes and glossy black hair that fell in waves over her full bosom. There were shots of them in front of Jack's hotel and sitting at an outdoor café, Nadia looking plump in a ludicrously short miniskirt. She's too old to get away with that, Francesca thought, but then admitted the truth. Nadia was petite and voluptuous, with delicate legs, and she could get away with anything, even a phony suicide attempt. The last clipping was dated only the day before yesterday—Jack and Nadia had announced their engagement; they would be married in Paris.

"You're back!" Josie stood in the doorway.

"Have you seen these?" Francesca turned to her accusingly.

"Yes."

"Why didn't you tell me, for God's sake?" Francesca almost screamed.

"I didn't want to hurt you."

"So you let me sit like an idiot, pining away for three weeks. Did you give him my letter?"

"Of course."

"Well, what did he say?" Francesca could have shaken Josie. Her placidity was exasperating.

"He just put it in his pocket. He said he was leaving town the end of this month." Josie shrugged and shuffled her feet.

"Didn't he give you a message, a letter, anything for me?" Francesca tried to make Josie look up. Her attitude reminded her of an ignorant servant Marianne had fired for stealing something worthless.

"You're the one who told my father where to find Jack and me, didn't you? How did you know about the nursery? Did you spy on us, Josie? I've known all along that you were attracted to Jack; I saw the way you looked at him. But I called my father a liar when he said you betrayed me. I simply couldn't believe you would do such a thing."

Josie's face grew hot with shame and anger. "He forced me to. You must know that."

"Nothing," Francesca said, her voice trembling now, "nothing could have made me do such a thing to you."

"You would have done it in a minute," Josie snapped. "You'll do anything your father asks you to do, Francesca, because you're weak, and you're a fool. You let him treat me like a servant, didn't you? Because you were too spineless to stand up to him. You didn't care what happened to me. You thought only of yourself and your love for Jack. Even my singing lessons came about because you saw them as a way to get out of the palazzo to meet him." Josie felt no shame at all now, only the blazing anger that had been building in her since that first day in Venice.

"Why did you meet Jack in the palazzo, under your father's nose? That was stupid, Francesca; it was only a matter of time before you were caught."

"That's beside the point. You betrayed me." Francesca stopped Josie as she started to march from the room. "I've got to see him. Is he still at the same hotel?"

"It says right there," Josie said derisively, pointing at a newspaper picture of Nadia and Jack leaving their hotel for the film festival.

Francesca turned back to the desk and quickly wrote a note. She had to see him. She would not believe the evidence in front of her. Licking the envelope, she closed her note and started to rush past Josie, her eyes blazing out at her with such ferocity Josie did not dare utter another word. "I'll never trust you again," Francesca said.

Josie's mind raced frantically. She hadn't expected Francesca back for another week. What if Jack hadn't left and told her about the letter? Perhaps Francesca wouldn't believe him? At least he didn't have it anymore to show to her.

Suddenly Josie felt very calm. Whatever happened, she and Francesca would never be friends again—so what difference did it make? Perhaps she would even tell her they were sisters. Why should she bear the burden of that secret alone? She decided she would only tell her if Francesca had found out about the letter when she returned. Resigned to let fate decide the course of her life, Josie sat down by the window to wait.

Francesca rushed through the streets like a madwoman, her heart pounding, the sweat pouring into her eyes. It was high noon and the bells of San Marco were booming as she crossed the square through the milling tourists and beating of pigeons' wings as they rose at the sound. She knocked a woman's camera out of her hand. "Sorry, sorry," she muttered without stopping to pick it up.

As she arrived in front of the hotel she was stopped. In a

crowd of photographers, she pushed her way rudely to the front. Jack was leading Nadia into a motorboat piled high with luggage. He kissed her hand and laughed for the cameras as the motor revved. Francesca stood rooted to the spot, the envelope in her outstretched hand. As Arkansas climbed in after them he turned and, recognizing Francesca, gave a smirk and shrugged his shoulders as if to say, "That's life." The boat jerked forward. Jack half turned to say something to Arkansas, but the other man pushed him back down in his seat.

Francesca felt as if her throat were going to burst. She wanted to sink to the ground right there on the hard stones and howl. Instead she turned and very deliberately and slowly walked toward the gondola station, and waited mutely till one was free.

"Palazzo Nordonia," she said to the gondolier, willfully forming an impenetrable shell around herself.

"*Sì*, signorina."

As they passed the church where she had first seen Jack, she gave a savage yank to the chain holding his ring from around her neck and threw it into the water along with the letter, watching as the envelope grew smaller and smaller, fading in the distant water.

"Miss . . . miss . . ." Francesca woke with a start as the stewardess pitched forward almost into her lap. "Fasten your seat belt, please. We are having some turbulence."

With that the plane gave a particularly nasty lurch as the stewardess continued down the aisle to attend to other passengers. Francesca sat upright and stared out at the storm. She exulted at every flash of lightning, at every pitch and drop of the plane, willing it to do its worst. Dying would suit her just fine, she thought defiantly. But she hadn't finished the thought when the air was suddenly forced out of her lungs as the plane was sucked straight down. Down it dropped and continued until a moan rose up from the passengers and Francesca's entire being was flooded with terror. When the plane finally leveled off she was shaking.

She opened her bag and took out the little vial of her mother's perfume she had slipped into her purse just before leaving the palazzo for the airport. Staring into the mirror over her mother's dressing table, she had had the strange sensation that her mother would understand the anguish she was feeling over Jack and remembered courage seeping into her. She had wondered when she would see her mother's room again—and realized it would probably not be until after her father's death.

Carlo had not taken her to the plane; instead he had gone to his office, wishing her good-bye in an almost offhand manner, a manner that told her she just wasn't important enough for him to waste any more of his time. Everything was done quickly. Carlo had decreed it better that Josie leave for Nassau earlier in the week and for once both girls were quick to agree.

Suddenly the plane began to buck and shake again and Francesca clutched the little perfume bottle like a rosary, praying fervently to be allowed to live. As if God had only been waiting for her admission that life was still precious to her, the storm ended as quickly as it had begun, and murmurs of surprise and laughter filled the cabin.

Francesca took off her seat belt and stretched out on the empty seat next to her, pulling the blanket close. With the scent of her mother's comforting perfume still in her nostrils, she gave a sob of relief and gratitude and fell into a deep sleep.

PART TWO

Lyford Cay, Commonwealth of the Bahamas 1968–1973

Chapter Twelve

A FLAT STRETCH of highway linked Lyford Cay with the rest of the island of New Providence. Better known simply as Nassau, the cay had once been a grazing ground for cattle; the grassy, rolling earth was rich and verdant. But much of the area was now an exclusive planned community. Screens of tropical vegetation kept the lavish resort homes so well hidden that it was almost impossible to discern some of the driveways that led to the houses behind the basket weave of palms.

The uninhabited Nordonia mansion rarely aroused the curiosity of the cay's residents, in part because few who owned houses and enjoyed club privileges spent more than a few months of every year there. They came for the golf, for the winter social season, and occasionally for a week of relaxation, then left for noisier, livelier spots or to resume their responsibilities. Their houses were then closed, the windows shuttered, the furniture covered with sheets, like the house that Carlo Nordonia had built for his wife.

Only one neighbor paid much attention to the condition of the Nordonia estate. From the top floor of the Hillford mansion, Lady Jane could see the house, with its fine chimneys and its broad veranda facing the sea. Through her binoculars she could trace the growth of the moss and ivy over the north side of the house and watch the progress of the grass. She could just make out any activity that took place in the driveway that circled back to the smaller beach house, which was partly screened from her view by dark and secretive cypresses. The mansion's emptiness did not dismay her. She had plenty of time; she could wait. Night after night she checked the view from her daughter's bedroom window, as she knew Sybilla must have done when she was alive. The sea lay beyond the Nordonia house, an enormous chasm held in by the rim of shore.

During the last week of September, Lady Jane noted the arrival of a visitor to the beach house, but the main house remained as deserted as ever. In its hollow stillness it seemed to have suffered a mortal loss like the one Lady Jane had been dealt.

"Lord, how I've missed you, Josie!" Marianne hugged her daughter once more.

It was hurricane season, and the sky had turned to the pewter color of the sea, but the heat had not let up. Inside, the house was cool. Its pale green and beige walls smelled of pine. Josie found it cozy and welcoming after the stony grandeur of the palazzo. Marianne had grown thinner, she noticed, but her smile was warm and brilliant. Her face was all eyes, large and amber like Josie's. They were rimmed now with black circles.

"What's wrong, Mama?" Josie cried in alarm.

"Just tired, overtired, child, trying to keep this house in shape all by myself."

Josie walked outside, pulling Marianne behind her. The garden in the back was bright with gaudy tropical flowers. The queer change in the weather turned the grass an even darker green, almost blue. In the distance the palm trees were roiling in the wind, their tops spinning silver hoops. She drank in the clean smell of the tropical forest. The winds of the coming storm were bracing, not like the hurricanes of emotion by which she had been buffeted. Josie felt strength flow into her from the deep black loam and the fragrant air.

Marianne smoothed a hand through Josie's soft, dark hair. She was troubled at the change in her daughter. The musical laugh Josie had once given so freely to the world was silent now. In Venice she had become cynical.

"Your letters were so cheerful, so full of your singing lessons," Marianne said. "But there's a sadness in your eyes that wasn't there before. You were trying to keep me from worrying about you, Josephine." She walked Josie to a garden bench and sat down, pulling her daughter down beside her. "You've come home earlier than I expected, and you've come without Francesca. Don't ask me to believe you left Mirella Varchi because you wanted to."

Josie turned away, but Marianne touched her face and

forced her to turn back. "Did the count treat you badly, Josie?"

"He treated me like Francesca's maid. He made me eat with the servants. He never spoke to me or even looked at me."

Marianne remained silent, absorbing her daughter's pain.

"I know he's my father, Mama."

Marianne grew very still. "Who told you that?"

"One of the servants. They all knew. They called me *bastarda* behind my back, sometimes even to my face."

"You weren't rude to Carlo?" Marianne's voice was sharp.

"Oh, Mama, of course not. I seldom saw him. If that's all you care about, protecting his feelings, then I have nothing more to say."

"Look around you, child," Marianne said gently. "Look at the way we live. A beautiful home, everything we need. A private school, pretty clothes, the white dentist, the best doctor in Nassau whenever you were ill. A trip to Venice. Voice lessons with a famous diva!"

Josie was silent.

"I left school when I was fifteen and came to this island from Haiti," Marianne reminded her. "I cleaned and worked as a chambermaid in a hotel downtown before Carlo hired me. I was so grateful for the chance to work in a fine house for a kind man. And I've never changed my mind about that man. But, Josie, you can't remember any other life. I don't blame you for your anger, child, but a lot of other men would have fired me when I got pregnant, and then think of the life you would have had."

"Why didn't you tell me the truth, Mama?"

"I never wanted anyone to know the truth. My grandmother and my father died without ever knowing I wasn't married when you were born. That was such a happy day in my life, Josie, but I was so frightened they would find out! In Haiti the worst crime a person can commit is to be born a bastard. It's like original sin; its stain can never be washed away. Illegitimate children are treated as outcasts."

"So you lied to me."

"I lied to everyone. How could I have taken you back there for visits if I'd told the truth? Don't blame Carlo, darling. He protected us both. I'm sure he's never told anyone. God knows how the servants found out."

Josie's silence cut through her heart.

"Does Francesca know?"

"No."

"But the two of you are best friends; you always tell her everything."

"Not anymore, Mama. I'm her sister now, not her friend."

Marianne led Josie into the house when the rain began to fall, hard and silver, borne toward the cay on a sheet of wind.

"I'm going to unpack, Mama. I'm very tired."

Marianne stared blindly out the window long after Josie had left the room. How could she tell her troubled daughter the terrible new truth she now kept curtained away in her heart? She closed her eyes and whispered a desperate prayer: "Give me enough time to put the love back in her heart and wash away the bitterness. Please, dear God, just a little more time."

From the small window on the top floor of her house, Lady Jane watched the young woman with the golden-red hair. She had appeared three days ago.

This was Susannah's daughter. Of that, Lady Jane was certain. Thirteen years of being shut up in her husband's drafty English country house had not dulled either her senses or her memory. This girl was taller and slimmer than Susannah, but she had the same bright hair, the same proud carriage, the same passion for flowers.

Lady Jane put down her binoculars and smiled, infinitely pleased with the way things were working out. Francesca Nordonia could not have chosen a more perfect time to return from Venice, Lady Jane realized. She herself had been back only two months. It had taken a long time after her husband's death to talk her way out of the virtual imprisonment in which he had kept her all these years. But she had managed in the end to convince Cyril's household staff that she was as sane as a grieving widow could be expected to be; of course she was—her husband had been the lunatic—and they had let her come back to this haunted island, this evil place where it had all begun.

Lady Jane wondered vaguely where the black woman and the young girl had gone. Well, it didn't matter. This was the woman she was interested in.

* * *

It was nearly nine o'clock when Francesca left the beach house. The weather was cool after a dawn shower, and the gardens looked refreshed, but even the blaze of tropical flowers and her own continuous activity hadn't palliated the loneliness and despair that clung to her like a shroud.

She made her way to a garden bench near the place where her mother's rose garden had flourished years ago. She remembered Susannah in a wide-brimmed straw hat, down on her knees pruning and weeding contentedly. The garden had been dug up and seeded with grass after her death; only the stone bench overlooking the sea remained.

The day before, desperate for a project that would take her mind away from her memories of Jack and her dread of the future, she had sought out Joe Munroe, the old gardener, and asked his help in restoring Susannah's rose bed. Francesca smiled, remembering his excitement. He had hurried into the long-abandoned greenhouse and returned with the faded and yellowed diagrams her mother had made before laying out the original garden. Together he and Francesca had measured and dug until the shadows lengthened and weariness drove them indoors. Working the rich, friable earth through her fingers, she had begun to feel stronger and more at home, safe from the treachery of Venice.

She got up from the bench when she spotted Joe coming toward her carrying a large plant that bore a beautiful, five-petaled white blossom. Francesca reached up for it, delighted, recognizing it instantly.

"My father gave me the most beautiful pearl necklace, Joe; the pendant looks just like this flower. Could this have been the model?"

"Could be. This was your mother's favorite. A hundred years ago it covered the island; it grew everywhere like a wildflower, a weed. But you seldom see it anymore."

She bent her head to inhale its fragrance, and was carried back, back through the years to the night when Susannah had bent to kiss her good night and Francesca had smelled the flowers in her hair. This was the scent Susannah had made into a perfume and that Francesca had brought back from Venice: "Lyford Rose."

When she looked up, Joe was smiling at her. "What is it called, Joe? Is this Lyford Rose?"

"That's what Miss Susannah called it. I always thought it was such a pretty name." He pointed at a patch of earth in the center of the rose garden. "Why don't you plant this right here where your mother had it? Then you take a rest while I lay out a few more of these beds. You look tired today."

Francesca planted the Lyford Rose in the newly turned earth, feeling her mother's presence each time she inhaled the fragrance. She patted the earth firmly over the plant's roots and sat back to look at it. Already Susannah's garden was springing to life beneath her fingers.

The next morning, walking on the distant edges of the grounds, Francesca felt the blood rush from her head. She reached out to grasp the branch of a tree, but the faintness overwhelmed her and she fell to the ground. Her mind, weightless, spun away into darkness. She felt the damp grass in her nostrils. A strange servant was pulling up her torso, helping her to her feet.

"What happened?"

"You fainted, miss. You just tumbled to the ground."

"Thank you for helping me." Francesca tried to stand alone now. She still felt dizzy and weak. "But who are you? You don't work for my father."

"No, miss," the young mulatto servant said. "I work for Lady Jane Hillford. She sent me to get you." The girl pointed in the direction of the Hillford estate. Beyond a hedge, on a slight rise, the terrace of Lady Jane's house was just visible.

Francesca had never met Lady Hillford and knew none of the other residents of the area who had once been her mother's friends and who might visit the palazzo in season. She had a few playmates from school, but they were daughters of Nassau's middle class, and as unfamiliar with the Lyford Cay property owners as was Francesca.

The servant had braced her back with an arm and started to walk her through the hedge toward the Hillford estate.

"Where are you taking me?" Francesca asked.

"Lady Jane said to bring you. She'll help you."

"I don't need help."

"Please, miss," said the servant as Francesca began to wobble, another wave of dizziness and nausea nearly overwhelming her again.

Crossing the Hillford lawn took an eternity, but Francesca was grateful for the help now. It would have been much farther back to the beach house, and she realized she could never have made it alone. She needed desperately to lie down.

A heavyset, short woman with gray hair and intelligent eyes came running to meet them. Like Francesca she was dressed in her gardening clothes. She braced Francesca on the other side, and the servant and the older woman half carried the girl up to the terrace.

"Lie down here," the woman said, pulling forward a chaise longue. Francesca lay back and the darkness swam over her again. When she opened her eyes, the woman was standing over her with a glass of tomato juice.

"You look dreadfully pale. I must call a doctor."

"No, I'm fine, really. I don't understand what's come over me lately." She struggled to rise. "Thank you for helping me."

"No, no, lie back. I'm Lady Jane Hillford." She held out a hand.

"I'm Francesca Nordonia. I'm sorry to meet you this way, but thank you so much for helping me."

Francesca liked the woman enormously. There was a frank honesty in the natural strong gray color of her hair, and in her expression, at once shrewd and kind. She seemed capable and warm, and Francesca in her loneliness was drawn to her.

"I'm sure I'm well enough to go back home," Francesca said as she struggled to her feet.

"Nonsense. I'll send you back home in my car." Francesca knew from her tone of voice that there was no point in arguing. "You must be Susannah Nordonia's daughter," Lady Jane said with great kindness. "I knew your mother well. How you've grown to resemble her! I remember you as a little girl, playing on the lawn."

"You knew my mother?"

"Oh, of course. We all did. She was the center of everything. You must be now, let's see, nineteen or twenty?"

"Eighteen."

"Eighteen! But what a lady you've become, under our very noses. I must introduce you to some of Susannah's other friends one day."

"Thank you," Francesca said shyly, taking a sip of the tomato juice.

"How are you feeling? Better?"

"Yes, much. The dizziness must come from working in the garden. Every morning while I weed I feel a little ill, as if some plant were poisoning me. Do you suppose that's possible?"

Lady Jane sat down opposite the girl and folded her arms across her chest. "Yes, I suppose so. Tell me, how do you feel ill?"

"Dizzy. Nausea."

"And has it been going on long?"

"Just since I've been working in the garden. Two weeks."

"That's it then." Lady Jane rose decisively. "I won't bother with the doctor. You must let someone else do your weeding for you. It sounds like an allergy, and if you stay away from the plants it will probably pass. But dear, I don't think you're eating properly. You're terribly thin and there are circles under your eyes. Can I offer you breakfast?"

"Oh, no, no. It's very kind of you." Francesca realized how hungry she was for human companionship, and especially for mothering.

"Oh, it's no trouble. I'll bet you haven't eaten this morning."

Francesca shook her head guiltily.

"The count isn't here, is he? Is there anyone to look after you?"

"The housekeeper and her daughter had to visit their family in Haiti."

"Ah, so you *are* alone. Well, that settles it. Now, how would you like your eggs?"

A table was set on the terrace. Rain had rinsed the air and the earth clean, and the sky over their heads turned a pale turquoise in the morning sunlight. The vista of Lady Jane's roses and bougainvillea parading down to the ocean inspired Francesca with the happiness that had once been her habitual feeling in Nassau.

"Your garden is breathtaking, Lady Hillford," Francesca said.

The woman returned her smile. "Now—you must call me Lady Jane, dear, or you'll make me feel even more ancient than I am. It's not the proper form, of course, but everyone else does."

Gently Lady Jane began to probe Francesca, and in the space of a convivial meal managed to learn most of what there was to know about Francesca's life in Nassau and her visit to Venice. Francesca hid only the existence of her lover.

After she sent Francesca home, Lady Jane realized it had grown too hot to finish her gardening—but she was too restless to sit indoors. Meeting Susannah's daughter had stirred up buried memories, and they seethed within her. She paced the house nervously.

At this hour, the quiet was sepulchral. She sank into a deep flowered-chintz couch and nervously lit a cigarette. The habit annoyed her. In a moment she would ring for the maid to come and take the filthy ashtray away. Then she'd dirty another.

Suddenly she heard a heavy step on the stair. A man took the last four steps in a single bound.

"Speak of the devil," Jane said dryly, even before he came into view. "I was just thinking of you."

"Kindly, I hope," said a voice with a cheerful, Anglo-Irish accent. "Of course I know better."

"You're up early, Michael."

The young man walked into the room shirtless and barefoot. Lady Jane was enough of a sensualist to enjoy the spectacle of his heavily muscled torso and flat stomach, but his casual manner annoyed her as well.

"It's too much to ask you to dress before noon, I suppose. Really, Michael, it isn't decent. This isn't a ship; it's my home."

Michael kissed her forehead. "Oh, Auntie, I haven't seen a woman in a week." Then he was off to the kitchen to round up some coffee.

Jane laughed in spite of herself. Her nephew, Michael, was the son of Lord Hillford's younger brother, who had married a well-bred Irish woman and settled on a small estate in Ireland. Without a title or inheritance, Michael was forced to work for a living, and work was something for which he had no natural gift. His onc love was the sea, and he had dropped out of Trinity to serve in the Royal Navy for several years. He had acquired discipline and polish, but he still couldn't stick with a civilian job. He wanted to be nothing more than a sailor, but he had been born in the wrong century and the wrong class.

Having learned that Michael had gone off to the Bahamas, Lady Jane had looked him up soon after her return to the islands. She had found him hiring himself out by the week or the day as a captain to vacationing tourists who rented boats. In port he had developed a taste for whiskey. He was almost thirty, but he still lived like a college student on spring vacation, with too much pent-up energy, fast on the water, drunk in the bars, and burning through money as soon as he got it.

Once Lady Jane got over the initial shock of seeing him on the dock dressed in his sailor clothes, she saw nothing extraordinary in it. Where would her late husband have been without his title? At least Michael could tie a score of knots and judge the wind. And he was thoroughly charming—a trait he had certainly not inherited from the Hillford side of his family.

Lady Hillford had brought him home with her, and he had been living in her mansion off and on ever since. He often shocked her, but he paid for his keep by escorting her to social functions at the club. With his dancing eyes and strong chin, he always made a favorable impression. Something about his Irish boldness and roughness excited women, and Lady Jane found herself envied. It wasn't a bad bargain they had struck. But now Lady Jane's kindness to her nephew was about to pay off.

Jane smiled to herself. Her ne'er-do-well nephew wouldn't be able to resist a girl as beautiful as Francesca Nordonia. He was sure to fall in love with her. And if Lady Jane had read the signs right, the ravishing contessina had immediate need of a husband.

Again she marveled at the exquisite timing, the elegant strokes of luck that had combined to make her task so much simpler than she had expected it to be. She would have Susannah's daughter not only next door but in the bosom of her own family. If all went as she planned it, she would have the pleasure of watching her dashing nephew gaily deplete the Nordonia fortune and, when he grew tired of Francesca, which could be expected to happen within a year, destroy her life and her reputation with his proclivity for alcohol and island women. Child's play, that's what it would be.

"Michael, my dear," she called, "bring your coffee in here and sit with me awhile."

Michael appeared, still shirtless and unkempt. He held a cup of coffee in one hand, and in the other a lit cigarette and the morning paper.

"You rang, darling Aunt?"

"Careful you don't start a fire. You're dripping ash on my rug."

Michael gave her an impassive stare. "What use are carpets if you can't flick an ash or two on them?"

"Here, take this ashtray. Michael, there's someone very special I'd like you to meet. She's a lovely girl, quite beautiful, and she's here all alone."

"Fixing me up again! I hope she's not one of these stuffy Lyford Cay debutantes who squeal if you touch them and expect you to buy them fifty-dollar dinners."

"No, Michael, she's not that sort—"

"Boring."

"She *is* rich, however. You know you can't go on living this way forever."

"You mean off your generosity? Why, Auntie, I'm offended." He gave her a dazzling smile. "I'll leave tomorrow."

"That's not what I meant, and you know it. I meant you can't make your living as a sailor forever. I certainly don't want you to leave. You know I'm fond of you."

"Well, give us some gas money, then. I want to go into town this afternoon."

She dropped the subject. "Will you be back for dinner?"

"Might be. Don't hold me to it."

"Call and let me know by four." But he was already out of earshot.

The dinner had been excellent, and Francesca had eaten twice as much as usual, even accepting a second helping of strawberry mousse. Lady Jane apologized for her "wretched nephew" who had not shown up, and led her into the drawing room. Glad as she was to have some company at last, Lady Jane's cheerfulness began to ring slightly false on Francesca's ear. She was now plying her with coffee and another story about her English childhood. Francesca listened, her eyes wandering around the oddly uncomfortable room. Lady Jane's home, Francesca decided, reflected a kind of rootless despair, as if it had been transplanted from England with no thought for its suitability to its new surroundings. It had been decorated in a style meant to be informal, comfortable, unpretentious. But something must have gone wrong over the years. The drawing room was too prim, too neat, as if Lady Jane had tidied and straightened until there was no trace of the casual clutter that made most country homes so charming. There were no affectionate displays of sterling-framed family photographs, no needlepoint hoops or stacks of well-thumbed books. It looked to Francesca like a house in which no one had ever loved anyone else.

"Ah, here he is at last, the dreadful man." Lady Jane put down her cup at the sound of footsteps in the hall.

"Francesca, may I present Michael Hillford, my nephew from Ireland. Michael, this is Francesca Nordonia, our next-door neighbor. You will remember my speaking of her father, Count Nordonia."

Michael reached out a strong arm to Francesca, whose hand was lost in his warm, confident grip. She nodded pleasantly and pulled her hand away. Francesca Nordonia had had quite enough of handsome men.

"I have eaten, Aunt Jane, but I'll join you in dessert." Michael slipped into Lady Jane's game quickly and easily. He excelled at creating a favorable first impression; maintaining it was the difficulty. He didn't know why this slip of a girl was so important to his aunt; he had no use for her socialite friends at Lyford Cay Club, and didn't trust her taste. But this shy girl was marvelous.

At first Francesca drew back from Michael's exuberant smile. But the sheer force of his personality made her turn toward him. She saw he was attractive, with high coloring and bemused hazel eyes. She began to relax. He looked at her in exactly the way he looked at his aged, wrinkled aunt and there was nothing but high spirits in his voice.

"I'll just be a moment, Michael. I've got to make a call. Excuse me, won't you?" Lady Jane, who was quite pleased with herself, disappeared.

There was a moment of total quiet; only the clank of dishes could be heard in the kitchen. Michael looked at Francesca and started to laugh quietly, and then harder and harder. The more confused Francesca looked, the harder he laughed. He pointed wordlessly at the ceiling, slapped his thigh, and laughed soundlessly. Francesca got it. He was indicating his aunt upstairs, Lady Jane. Finally he stopped and wiped his eyes with a handkerchief.

"Oh, dear old Auntie, subtle, isn't she? Matchmaker, matchmaker." He waggled his finger accusingly at the ceiling. It occurred to Francesca he'd been drinking. Seeing her discomfiture, he sprang up and pulled her out of the chair.

"Come, child, I shall escort you home. It's too beautiful a night to sit in this mausoleum." Sober and avuncular, he put her hand through his arm as they started across the grass. "Auntie told me you live next door. Strange, I haven't seen you around . . . but I'm mostly out to sea." He went on before she could answer. "And you've been away I hear . . ."

"Yes . . . visiting my father . . . in Venice."

"Venice—great sailors, the Venetians. Do you like to sail? Have you sailed much around here?"

"No, just a few times on my father's sailboat."

"Then you must let me take you." His enthusiasm was infectious. She laughed a little at the offer. "I'll come for you tomorrow morning, bright and early. And you can tell me about Venice."

Michael knew the stars, and he traced the constellations for her as they crossed the great lawn of the Nordonia estate.

He stopped as they approached the house, sweeping his arm about to include both the house and the view it overlooked. "Extraordinary home. Nothing in the islands to compare with it. Looks as if it grew here. Extraordinary!"

"I lived in it when I was a little girl," Francesca said, warmed by his admiration for the house. "It's been closed for almost thirteen years, except at Christmas when my father visits, but our housekeeper takes good care of the rooms and the gardener keeps the grounds beautiful. I've taken to going inside every day to pay a visit. When I walk through the rooms, sometimes I remember things—little things—about my childhood and my parents." She stopped, embarrassed to have told him so much.

Delighted, Michael followed her into the front hallway and let her lead him to the huge central room flooded with moonlight.

"This house is haunted," he said matter-of-factly. "In Ireland there are lots of old houses where the spirits cling to the homes they loved. They won't let go. The air is troubled here, I can sense it."

"Nonsense. Something did go wrong, but not here. My mother went to Venice for a visit, and she died there. That's when I moved into the beach house."

Michael was touching the walls and testing the vibrations in the air. In the dark she suddenly had a clear vision of how Irish he was. Perhaps for generations men in Ireland had tapped the walls like this, listening to the other, spirit world that existed in old houses. Although he loomed large in the small entryway, his movements were delicate as gossamer. She thought he might be half spirit himself.

"I sense a disturbance, an ill will." His voice was authoritative, final. "Put on the light, will you?"

The hallway chandelier lit up in a glorious burst of crystal. Its glass prisms hung like wind chimes above their heads. The rooms that gave off the hallway were dark, their furnishings shrouded in sheets, but the light had dispelled Michael's ghosts.

"See? No one here." Francesca led him from room to room, pulling the dust covers off the comfortable furniture. Susannah's taste seemed contemporary, as if she had anticipated the wit and freedom of the decade that followed her death.

Michael paused to examine a photograph. "Is this you? What a beautiful child."

Francesca laughed and led him through the house and out the front door. They walked through the grass slowly, a cool breeze rippling around them. When he left her at the door of the beach house, she realized that some of the sadness had been lifted from her shoulders. He was a marvelous tonic for her depression. She hadn't thought about Jack for two whole hours, and Michael had pinpointed her own problem when he talked about the presence in her mother's house. She was overwhelmed with loneliness. Perhaps that was the ghost whose presence he sensed: her unhappiness. Yes, she would be glad to go sailing with him tomorrow.

She thought Michael might be a lucky omen, like a starfish thrown up on the beach. The sea had many cures.

A week later the time, which she had worried so about filling, now sped by. By noon, Francesca finally felt well enough to get out of bed. The waves of nausea had passed, at least, and she had persuaded herself to ignore the soft voice of malaise that told her to stay in bed all day. For a long time she stood naked before the full-length mirror examining her thin body. Was there a thickening at the waist, a new fullness about the breasts? Or was it only her imagination? She had missed her period in September, and the October one was nearly a week late. She had no doubt that she was carrying Jack's child.

She pressed a hand to her abdomen. How could so much passion have ended any other way? It was as if their physical attraction had been so powerful that it had set in motion its own means of perpetuating itself. A new life was growing inside her, insuring that the reality of her love for Jack would be with her forever. It was time to put aside her bitterness toward her lover's faithlessness and make plans for the future.

"Francesca! Are you up and about, lazy creature?"

Michael's voice outside in the garden. Again. She pulled on a robe and went to the window, glad to see his friendly smile. "Not *again*, Michael! Why are you so determined to make a sailor out of me?"

He held up a picnic basket. "You made the lunch yesterday and the day before. Today it was my turn. Ham sandwiches, potato salad, wine, and a tremendous papaya. Hurry."

"Be right out." She dressed hurriedly, grateful for the distraction Michael provided.

Unlike Jack Westman, Michael did not overwhelm her with passion. Although she suspected he had had much experience with women, Michael had kept his distance from her, treating her like a good friend all week long. They had touched often while sailing together—his arm thrown lightly around her shoulders, a light kiss dropped on her forehead, an exuberant hug at the end of a pleasant day—but never had she worried that he would press her for a deeper intimacy. She enjoyed his touch; he was comfortable, reassuring. She trusted herself with him, and she genuinely liked him.

She hurried out to meet him. He led her to his small sailboat, and they spent the afternoon drifting slowly over an almost windless sea, sipping wine while Michael told stories of his childhood. Francesca laughed almost constantly, enjoying his gift for straight-faced humor.

"We'd better head for shore," he said after a short silence.

Francesca realized with astonishment that the sun hung low over the horizon and purple shadows thickened the island. She had barely given a thought to her problems since that morning when she'd first heard Michael's voice calling her out of the beach house.

Contentedly she watched the surface of the sea turn red as they reached the shore. By the time they had moored the sailboat and unloaded their gear, darkness had fallen, warm and thick all around them.

Late that same night they left the blare and heat of the

Nassau nightclub where they had gone dancing, and took what was left of the champagne with them in the open car to the beach. At the cabana they turned on the radio and continued their wild gyrations under the moon. Francesca knew she had never drunk so much in her life but at last the tension that had gripped her for weeks was eased.

The music slowed and Michael drew Francesca close. He kissed her gently as they danced and then more and more deeply. Near the water Francesca whispered, "Let's go in," and without a thought slipped out of her dress. In the sea she dived immediately under the surface as was her habit and swam with long strokes, her eyes open, into deeper water. Michael's form swam next to her in the dark silence. She smiled to herself, imagining the intimacy of sea creatures, whales and porpoises. They surfaced together out of breath, laughing quietly. Michael turned on his back and then swam slowly into shallower water. Michael found his footing; he was not much taller than she. As he was holding her close and kissing her, she felt his hardness press against her. Though some last shred of modesty had caused her to leave on her underpants, he pulled them off leg by leg. Francesca giggled, imagining the poor fisherman who was going to pull them up on his line. Remembering the Adriatic, she looked up at the stars. The sky was so completely different here, a mild indigo filled with sweet winds. Soon she felt lost in Michael's large strong hands, and as he entered her, she bit her lip to keep from calling out Jack's name until she came and the last of her misery seemed to flow out of her. When Michael carried her up the beach she kissed him, with a clear mind and for himself alone.

She had left behind her prim and proper self under this full moon and become the creature she had only been able to imagine herself in daydreams about Jack. Any lack of inhibition had been sheer bravado. In reality she had been too shy in their intimacy to ever take the initiative. She was the recipient of his love but to him she was only able to bestow the most modest of caresses. Ironically with Michael, whom she did not love, she had discovered a new abandon that allowed her to wind her legs around him and thrust against him, her breasts cool above the warm water . . . moaning and laughing aloud with pleasure under the wide night sky. She felt no embarrassment; instead, she relished her newfound sensuality.

* * *

The soft rain fell like mist on Francesca's face as she left the doctor's office and walked through the streets of Nassau. Why wasn't she upset? she asked herself. In the waiting room she had felt the curious stares of the black women. They had known immediately why she was there in the office of a native obstetrician "over the hill." And yet she felt only a sheer elation as she walked in the warm breeze.

That morning, Francesca had awakened in Michael's arms, calm and protected, but shortly after he left, she had felt the familiar convulsions in her stomach. Then, after the waves of nausea had passed, she had been filled with another kind of sickness, a dread and terrible fear of what lay ahead. She had stood once more in front of the mirror and had known that this time the thickness in her abdomen was not her imagination.

The night before, Michael had begun to wean her away from her constant daydreams about Jack, but her body, in its deep and silent depths, was filled with him.

Panic had sent her running to the doctor, but now that her own suspicions had been confirmed, her panic had been replaced by serenity. She had lost Jack forever, but deep in its recesses, her body held a tiny gift from him. In his child their love would go on despite Jack's desertion. She could believe in herself again, trust her instincts. She could love herself and the child Jack had created inside her.

As the car purred along the cay, the low-lying clouds broke and light poured onto the sea. Her mind was working rapidly; at last she was able to put aside her despair and face the practical problems that lay before her. Whom could she ask for help? Marianne was in Haiti, and Josie might as well have vanished from Francesca's life. She had only gotten one postcard saying they had been delayed by illness. There was no phone. She didn't even have an address.

Could she bear the child in Nassau and later claim it was adopted? She discarded the idea. Her father would know the truth, and so would everyone else. She would have to tell him. The child was more important than the Nordonia pride. Carlo could stare down the scandal, if he chose to . . . but would he do that for Jack Westman's baby? Or would he try to insist that she have this child in secret and give it up for adoption?

Her mind seemed unable to grapple the wall of problems that hemmed her in. There was only one person she could ask for help, and by telling him the truth, she would drive him away. He was too proud to marry a woman who was carrying another man's child, of that she was certain. Still, she knew he would remain her friend; he was too decent to turn his back on her. She would tell Michael Hillford the whole story, and throw herself on his mercy.

As she pulled into the drive, she saw a familiar shape striding across the grounds, headed for the beach house. It was Michael, come to talk or to invite her out sailing. Today was the first day they had not spent together since she met him at dinner more than a week ago. He waved as he approached her.

"Looking for someone?"

"Yes, as a matter of fact. Francesca, I've come to ask you to dinner. My aunt is sparing no expense. I hope you're not busy."

"I have no plans. You know me, Michael. Completely at loose ends." How long would it be, she wondered, before people like Lady Jane noticed her pregnancy and began to gossip? She started across the lawn toward the house. He fell in beside her. They walked in silence and she thought how different it was from walking next to Jack, whose extra height and protective attitude had always made her feel fragile and vulnerable. Michael, on the other hand, strode next to her on her own level and, though he certainly seemed independent and strong, there was something about him that made her feel he was the one who needed protection.

"You're unusually quiet today, miss," he said, breaking into her thoughts.

"Am I generally such a chatterbox?" she asked, watching him out of the corner of her eye.

When he didn't answer immediately she laughed. "Oh, well, it's only because I can never get a word in edgewise with all the blarney I've been forced to listen to all week." Her imitation of his accent was so terrible it broke them both up.

Michael threw himself down on the grass in front of her house. "Don't go in yet, girl, I've missed you. Where were you all morning anyway?"

Francesca stretched out next to him. She felt him studying

her profile and closed her eyes, putting her face up to the sun. "I'm thinking of doing some traveling," she said evenly.

"What, and leave me all alone here?" Michael sounded shocked. "I'm at loose ends, too, you know," he said, collecting his thoughts. "Unless, of course, we go away together."

"Now, there's a thought. Where would we go?"

"I'd take you to Ireland and introduce you to my father. Dear old da. He'd love a pretty girl like you. I'd show you the trout stream and the woods near the place where I grew up. Nassau is almost as beautiful, but not quite."

"What are you doing here, then?"

"The weather's better for sailing, and I hope to make a go at setting up my own business here. Luxury charter boats. I told you about that, remember? Couldn't do that at home. The Irish have to leave the auld sod to make a living; they go back to be buried. Say you'll come with me!"

"Oh, Michael, I don't know. When would this trip take place?"

"Next week, I suppose. I'll call the airlines."

"And we'll just fly off."

"Just like that. Of course, we'll get married first. How about this weekend?"

The suggestion startled her. For an instant, she toyed with the possibilities it offered her. Then she realized he must be joking, as usual. She kept her tone light. "I can't get married this weekend, Michael. I promised I'd go to the church bazaar, and there's so much work in the garden. Can you wait?"

"No," he said.

"Then you'll have to marry someone else."

"And take a stranger to Ireland? Now what would I want to be doing that for, when you're the one my heart is set on?" he said lightly.

"Still, I can't marry you just now, Michael." She ignored his suddenly serious expression.

He reached out and gripped her hands and held her before him, forcing her to look into his face. His square jaw clenched with determination, and his hazel eyes were heavy with sadness. She saw that he was afraid to push his case. If he went any further she would have to say no, and then their friendship would end. Already an awkwardness had seized her, so that her smile was a lie. She knew what she ought to say: that someone else would find him so easy to love, that she was not worthy of him, that she was carrying another man's child. But instead, glib words slipped out of her mouth. "Look, I'd love to come to dinner, Michael. Tell Lady Jane for me, will you? Later on, we'll talk some more about going to Ireland."

He seized her and kissed her, fiercely at first, then more gently. She enjoyed his kisses. They spoke of friendship as well as passion, and she was grateful to be loved. In Michael's arms she felt safe from the kind of pain Jack had inflicted on her. Michael wouldn't fall into another woman's arms at the first sign of trouble.

She watched him stride over the grounds to the Hillford house, then turned and went inside to brew some tea. She knew that she would not tell him the truth as she had resolved to do. Her choices lay before her—to bear the child alone and raise it without a father, to throw herself on her own father's mercy, or to keep silent about her pregnancy and marry Michael.

For a long time, she sat in the cozy kitchen drinking tea and looking out at the blossoms in Marianne's garden. It would pain her to deceive Michael; he would despise her if he knew she had loved, still loved, another man. But her child must have a father to protect him and give him a name.

A breeze swept through the room, and Francesca rose to close the window. Outside, the sun turned the sea into a mirror of gold that broke into shards in the gentle surf near the shore. Palm trees swung in the wind that had begun to blow over the island in hearty gusts from the sea. Her hand rested for a moment on her thickening abdomen. Deep inside her a tiny heart was beating, and a new life was growing. She would protect that life with whatever means she was offered.

In the Palazzo Nordonia, Antonia was already asleep. Her slender body cuddled against Carlo, her breath fanning his chest. Moving slowly, careful not to awaken her, Carlo eased himself out of the bed and pulled on his robe. In the moonlight that streamed through the open balcony doors, he could see the letter lying open on a table. He picked it up and held it in his hands. The words were etched on his memory; he felt no need to turn on the light and read them again.

"Please wish me happiness, Papa, and forgive me for not wanting to return to Venice. Michael and I don't want a big wedding, just a simple church ceremony here on the island. We've already made our plans. We'll be married next Saturday."

Next Saturday. The words hurt him. Francesca's letter had reached him that morning, and "next Saturday" was tomorrow. Had she purposely withheld the news of her wedding until the last minute so that he would not be able to get there in time to attend it? Had he finally destroyed every vestige of her love for him?

He put down the letter and walked out on the balcony to stare at the dark water below him. He did not deceive himself with fairy tales about the beautiful princess who had at last met and married the handsome prince. He had seen Francesca and her American lover together in bed in the little room upstairs, and he knew—was almost certain—why his daughter had rushed into marriage with a man she had known for only a few weeks. The glittering lights of Venice burned before his eyes.

If only he could have made her understand why he kept such a close watch over her. If only he could have told her his fear: that this would happen, that she would leave him, as her mother had left him, that she would bring another scandal down on his head, and on her own. But he couldn't tell her—God help him, he certainly couldn't tell her about Susannah—and in his silence he had driven her away, perhaps forever.

"I wish you could be here, Papa," she had said in the letter. Carlo smiled sardonically. Polite lies. He had taught her to tell them.

1955

"YOU SPEND MORE time with your friend Sybilla than you do with me," he had complained one night after Susannah and her young English friend had spent the entire day riding their horses hell-bent for leather over the green hills of the island.

Susannah had been contrite, sitting naked before her dressing table brushing her dark red hair, promising to pay more attention to him, spend less time with Sybilla, whom he simply could not like.

"She's embarrassing," he said. "She'll end up one of those eccentric women who smoke cigars and live with a female companion and forty pet cats. Like Gertrude Stein."

"Really, Carlo. Much as I admire Gertrude Stein, that's very insulting to Sybilla. She's an attractive girl. And her taste is so cultivated—"

"Good God! She's even got you talking like her. I suppose you sit around talking about Francis Bacon and *angst* and, let me see, Schopenhauer—wasn't it Schopenhauer she lectured us on last evening?"

"How could you forget? It was a fascinating explanation of the violence of the twentieth century. It's an important theme in contemporary art."

Carlo hung his head in mock shame. "How can I have forgotten the most boring dinner I ever sat through?"

"You're impossible, Carlo. Why are you so jealous of that girl?"

"I'm not jealous, darling," he said, strolling over to the bed. His wife's arm moved rhythmically, the soft red hair falling in waves over her shoulders. "But couldn't you befriend someone slightly less arty?"

Thoroughly annoyed, with his own silly jealousy as well as with Susannah's odd choice of companions, he had tried to disguise his anger with humor.

"I never thought I'd be nostalgic for Bunny Biddle and those DuPont cousins. But at least they didn't pontificate about Artaud."

"Sybilla is young, Carlo, but she's serious and talented. She's set her sights on the top. She means to be a major woman artist, like Cassatt. I admire her. How can you be so critical? Sybilla has nothing but her own talent and bravery."

"Nothing?" said Carlo. "She's got you."

Susannah's startled eyes met his across the bed cover. Their bravado was suddenly gone. She looked like a child who had wandered off into the forest at night. He refused to believe his own stumbling discovery. But as she sat there frozen, her silence explained everything—the long absences, her curious passivity in bed, the strained, guilty effort to please him in so many other ways. He saw his alarm mirrored in her eyes, and wondered how many other people had guessed the nature of the women's friendship. Her arm began to move again, and hair fell in a veil across her face.

"I've hurt you, I've neglected you, darling." Her voice was dark southern honey. "If you feel that strongly about Sybilla, I won't have her around. I enjoy her, I can talk to her, but I forget sometimes how uncontrollable she is, how self-centered. I didn't mean to upset you so much. Don't brood, darling."

When she stood and walked into his arms, Carlo wanted to believe her. Her hands moving over him, her mouth on his neck told him beautiful lies.

Carlo had been leaning against the bay windows in the glassed porch of the Lyford Cay Club when he realized that he couldn't go on pretending anymore.

Far out on the horizon the indigo sea glittered with the small lights of yachts. On one end of the glassed veranda Lady Jane and the author, Converse Archer, held court for their intimate circle of Lyford Cay members, wealthy Europeans and Americans who came here every winter to play golf.

The occasion was a celebration in honor of Archer, who had recently published a new novel. Archer was an American, a Southerner like Susannah, and an avowed homosexual whose novel dealt frankly with his persecution in the brutally repressive South. He came from a working-class background, and he had transcended it with prodigal energy and intelligence. Magazine editors in New York were impressed by his flamboyantly gracious manners and precocious talent. He recreated himself as a southern dandy, assumed the airs of a pre–Civil War gentleman, and wore white suits exclusively. He made wonderful copy, as did the idiosyncratic people he courted.

Among the guests at this party, Susannah and Sybilla, both tanned and slim in black, stood out. They seemed exceptional, far too vital for this crowd. Their self-confidence and their matched happiness shut the others out. Carlo turned away from the window in time to see Sybilla stroke her hand along the tender inside of Susannah's arm. He could almost feel the electricity of that caress thrill through every man in the room with a secret jolt so exquisite that the rhythm of conversation broke.

Then the moment passed, glasses were lifted, conversations were resumed, and Carlo realized that the silence had fallen not because people were surprised but because they were embarrassed. They had noticed the intimacy between the two women before, perhaps commented on it in private, behind his back, of course, out of consideration for his feelings. But they knew, they all knew. Only he had been blind to his wife's physical intimacy with Sybilla Hillford.

Sybilla bent to kiss her cheek. "Why so serious, darling?" she asked. Those around them looked uncomfortably away. The intimate, cloying tone of the young woman's voice disturbed them all. Noticing their attention, Sybilla whispered loud enough for the room to hear, in an affected southern accent drenched with tenderness, "We've just got to get you away from here, darlin'. Poor thing, how can you stand it?"

No one looked at Carlo. Susannah withdrew her hand and had the grace to be embarrassed. Converse found it a provocative opening. "What's all this whispering about, girls?" He wagged a finger in Susannah's face. He'd been longing to talk to her all night. "Let's behave in front of company. What are all these secret plans you're making?"

Susannah flung her head back to get the light out of her eyes. Carlo thought she looked ill, peaked, as if she were about to faint. He knew before she started to speak what she was about to say: that she was on the verge of leaving again.

"I thought I'd take Sybilla to Venice tomorrow. She's never been."

The room hushed at this announcement, and Carlo felt all eyes on him. His suspicions were confirmed; they did know, had long known, and now they were waiting to see what he would do. Only Sybilla stared directly at him. He was speechless, watching helplessly while the moment to act passed. He had only to say, "What a good idea, we'll all go," to dispel the tension in the room, but his lips remained taut and drawn on the first syllable.

"How wonderful for you girls," Converse rushed in to fill the silence. "I'm giving a party next week at the Gritti Palace. You're coming, of course. Sybilla, I'll show you a side of Venice that even Susannah doesn't know about. Such divine decadence." His fingers flapped in the air.

Converse sickened Carlo. He was a short man with a large head, like a dwarf, and a string of a mouth that threaded into a bow as he smiled, boasting of the extravagance of his party. Carlo rose to go home.

He carried his empty glass to the bar and looked back for Susannah, but in a split second she had disappeared. He walked out to the moonlit terrace to get some air and found her there. She was leaning against the railing, her back to him. When Carlo's footsteps sounded on the slate, she turned eagerly, and he realized she'd been waiting for someone else.

Her face fell. "It's you."

"That was quite a scene between you and Sybilla."

She looked down at the sea. "You're imagining things. You've never been fair to her." She said the words automatically. He sensed a desperation packed behind them, and the face that rose to meet his was despondent. But he was too angry to care about her moodiness; he had suffered too much from it already.

"She's a scandal."

"She's only a kid. Leave her alone, Carlo."

" 'Kid.' How American. You're taking her with you?"

"Yes." She pulled a cape over her shoulders.

"But you agreed. Not in our home."

"You and Francesca won't be there—besides, it's a social event, the party in the Gritti Palace, and Sybilla has her heart set on it." She met his eye only for a moment, then fled back to the veranda. Carlo was alone with the silver-lit water.

But he and Susannah had had an audience. Lady Jane Hillford had been sitting in a lawn chair behind them, in the shadow of the building. Now she rose and came slowly toward the count. The light played on her short, silver hair. In her forties then, she was stylishly and neatly dressed in a rose dress, a heavy, carved jade necklace on her breast. It was difficult for Carlo to associate this capable, practical woman with the aesthete who had somehow issued from her loins.

"Lady Jane," he said pleasantly, as if nothing had happened.

Lady Jane would have none of his small talk. "You agree, of course, that you can't let them go. You must see the need for it. You've got to stop her."

"Stop her? Stop Susannah?"

"Don't act so incredulous, Carlo. You know as well as I do what's going on. Don't tell me you're the last to know, you're far too smart for that. Susannah is destroying my daughter's life, she's corrupting her, it's positively evil—"

Lady Jane was speaking so vehemently that Carlo was afraid the others, indoors, would hear her. He wanted to clap a hand over her mouth.

"Susannah?" he whispered. "It's Sybilla who's mad. It's Sybilla who is dragging them away. I've had to forbid her to set foot in my house."

"Surely you're not that naive, Carlo, about your wife and what she's done? She's several years older than Sybilla and there was nothing wrong with my daughter when they met."

"She's three years older, and, Lady Jane, I hardly need to mention what your daughter's reputation is."

"Stop them. I demand that you stop them." She turned in a huff and strode back into the party.

He stared after her in dismay. It was a preposterous, shameful argument. How had he gotten snared in it? Lady Jane might be blind about who was to blame, but she was dead right about what must be done. Was he defending whatever shreds were left of Susannah's honor, and by implication, his own, to Sybilla's mother because he was too weak to actually make Susannah do the right thing? He stared out to sea, his hands lying useless on the railing. Even the winking stars seemed to ridicule him.

When Carlo returned to collect Susannah and take her home, the veranda was oddly empty. Converse Archer still dominated the conversation at the bar, but the only audience he cared about was gone: Susannah had already departed. Carlo walked past them swiftly out of the club.

In the parking lot under the glow of one of the club's spotlights, Sybilla was smoking a cigarette and lounging against the door of her Mercedes. The girl was all spine, and she had learned early to throw herself into poses. The light danced off her helmet of short dark hair; her long fingers flashed through the air as she lifted the cigarette to her mouth. Carlo was suddenly furious. He felt that he could strangle the girl. Killing her would be as easy as drowning a cat.

"*Ciao*, Carlo," Sybilla said, throwing down her cigarette. Her voice was cool.

"Where is Susannah?"

"Not with me. Gone home to pack." Her large eyes looked at him knowingly, divining his banked anger. She had a trick of lowering the range of her voice and making it emanate from under those thin ribs, like a pleased cat purring at his frustration. The sound of that voice implying some intimacy with his own secrets had the usual effect of triggering his disgust.

He knew what must be done. The thought formed clearly and coolly in his mind. Facing Sybilla, he said firmly, "Good-bye." He was determined that he would never set eyes on her again.

The suitcases were out on the double bed in the bedroom, sports clothes and a silver ball gown thrown over them. The pale beige room, usually so serene, was chaotic. Belongings were scattered everywhere.

Susannah was sitting before her mirror in a satin slip, removing makeup from her face. Her eyes, glistening from the cold cream, met him as Carlo stepped through the door to assess the disarray in the room. She looked guiltily away and pulled the pins out of her red hair. It streamed down her back.

"You look ill, Susannah," he said quietly.

"I'm not feeling well," she admitted in a small voice, not looking up.

"I'll call a doctor."

"No, you mustn't. I just need sleep. I need to get away."

"That's what I wanted to talk to you about."

"Oh, Carlo, I know what you're going to say. Don't, please." She put her face in her hands.

Although she was distraught, something wouldn't allow him to go to her.

"You know what you must do," he said icily.

"I know it, and Sybilla knows it. I told her it's got to end. It's tearing me apart. Do you think I want to go on this way?"

"I don't know anymore what you want." He saw the contours of Susannah's body beneath her silk slip and it struck him that Sybilla must have watched his wife this way, with a similar desire.

"But I know one thing—if you go to Venice, don't come back."

"What?" She turned to face him now, alarm in her eyes. The flush of blood turned her teary eyes to emerald. Her mouth was swollen.

Carlo steeled himself, but it was easier than he thought to tell her. All he had to do was to keep the image of Sybilla before his eyes. "You heard what I said."

She half rose. The strong muscles in her arms were taut. "I can't just sever things overnight. It must be done the right way. You have to understand—"

"This is the right way, Susannah. You have to decide now."

"Why?" she asked defiantly.

"Because of the *disgrace*. Everyone was scandalized tonight. There must be no more parties, no more rumors. If you can't save yourself and spare me, at least think of your daughter."

"And if I do leave?"

"You leave for good."

"If I leave you then I must take Francesca."

He was silent. And she soon realized what that silence meant.

"You wouldn't dare hold her hostage, Carlo. You wouldn't hurt her."

"What kind of life would she be exposed to with you?"

She turned back to her mirror and, after struggling to contain the grief, said quietly, "It's not just Francesca. I love you, too. It's impossible for me to lose my daughter, but I also don't want to leave you. Why are you forcing me?"

He stared at her impassively.

"Oh, I have lost you," she cried. "Do you have to take her from me, too? Are you telling me I'll never see her again?"

He walked to the door and said in a low voice, "I can't have this depravity in my family or in my house. Or in my daughter's life."

Then she stood in front of him, tugging at his arms. Though he stood rigidly, she began pulling him toward her, making him feel the tears on her face, her chest. "Give me this last week with Sybilla to break it off. Then she'll go away for good and I'll give you the rest of my life. Francesca deserves that, and so do you and I. I promise I'll never dishonor you again—"

He shook her off and straightened. Her face was wild and confused. He couldn't stand to see her beg. "When you come back to me, we'll start fresh. I can't have these compromises, this lying."

"Just a week in Venice. Then I'll be back forever." Her strong hands held his arms. They were sun-freckled, and reminded him of the way she drove her horses, the way she always strove hell-bound for whatever she wanted. He knew he could not stop himself from relenting. "Believe me, it's what I want, to end the strain of this, to love you completely."

She began to pack, trying to hide her tears, and he realized then how rarely he had seen her cry.

In the early morning Sybilla's Mercedes crunched along the gravel of the drive. Lady Jane's manservant leaped out to load Susannah's Vuitton luggage aboard. Converse Archer helped Sybilla out of the backseat. This morning he wore sunglasses and his usual immaculate white jacket. Carlo was not impressed. He thought it made him look like a waiter.

"Susannah! So few bags. You're not coming just for the night, are you?" Archer called.

Susannah strode across the wide veranda of the mansion. "Everything I need is in Venice already. This is where I visit, but Venice is where I live." There was no trace of last night's quarrel or strain in her gay voice. She bent down to kiss Carlo good-bye, and he saw the pain in her face.

"Trust me," she whispered. "I know I've hurt you, but trust me."

Sybilla strolled around the side of the house where five-year-old Francesca was playing with the housekeeper and her daughter. "Who's this? Have we met before?" Sybilla said brightly, as she bent down and lifted Francesca into the air.

"I know you," the little girl squealed. "You're Sybbie."

Marianne Lapoiret stood to the side, wiping her hands on her apron.

As Sybilla swung Francesca high aloft, the child watched the luggage being piled into the trunk of the Mercedes. Her mother strode toward her in a neat navy and white suit.

"Mama," she cried, reaching her hands out to the woman.

As Susannah took her in her arms and hugged her tightly, Carlo took a sip of his bourbon and watched intently from the veranda. The little girl had seen her mother leave too often.

He hoped Susannah was making promises to the girl that this time she would keep.

As if sensing his mood, Converse and Sybilla avoided the house. Susannah came up to the screen door. "Thank you for trusting me," she said.

He turned his head, and when the motor began to purr, he went indoors. From a window he saw Francesca and Josie far out on the lawn following the car down the driveway. They were laughing together and skimming the grass with wide-spread arms, mimicking little airplanes carrying Susannah and Sybilla across the sea to Venice.

The second day Susannah was gone Carlo had become too drunk by dinnertime to care if he ever moved from his deck chair at the edge of the beach. The water was luminous as the moon rose. The palms rustled behind him. As he looked up at the night sky a servant came with a tray and candles and set them on a low table at his side. But later, when the tray was brought back untouched to the kitchen, Marianne made some strong coffee and brought it out to Carlo herself. She poured it and placed the cup in his hands, so he could not ignore it. After the first swallow he raised his eyes to her and gave a small smile of gratitude.

She sat in the sand next to his chair and chewed on a long piece of grass. They had not been alone together like this since his marriage, yet their silence was one of complete understanding. Instinctively Marianne knew when he needed her and in what capacity. They had been lovers since they were little more than children when Marianne had worked in Carlo's parents' house on Hog Island. Although Marianne had introduced him to love and then left him totally free to follow the prescribed course of his life, for her there was only Carlo. But she knew she could never be more than she was. His child, his animals, his possessions, his wife even, were hers to care for—nothing more. This was her unquestioned role, her destiny, and she protected it by being the soul of discretion.

Carlo poured the second cup himself and drank it slowly. A breeze carried her scent to him of jasmine and freshly ironed linen that was at once comforting and exciting, bringing back memories he had put aside for so long. He did not have to turn his head to know exactly how her soft features looked in the candlelight. She was staring out at the water, her long hands playing with the straw. And then he thought of her breasts and to his own surprise he was aroused. Out of consideration to Susannah he had suppressed all physical desire for months, but now he reached out and cupped Marianne's chin in his hand and turned her to face him, searching her dark eyes. He found the response he had not dared to hope for.

Gently he pulled her to him and as her mouth opened under his and he felt the tip of her tongue, a jolt went through him. Suddenly he was almost sober again, and as excited as a sixteen-year-old. He let out a laugh and got up from the chair, pulling her to him. They walked quickly to the cabana, their arms entwined, and as soon as they entered, Marianne took off her apron and unpinned her hair. Carlo quickly undressed and lay on the couch, his arms reaching out to her.

"Ma jolie, ma belle . . ." he murmured, smiling as she came close to him, realizing again how extraordinarily beautiful she was. He unbuttoned her dress and buried his face in the deep hollow between her breasts as the curtain of her soft glistening hair fell around them. Marianne slid on top of him, responding to his touch like quicksilver, and for the first time it occurred to him that it might not be his fault that Susannah was the only woman he had failed with.

It was clear that Marianne and Carlo knew each other's rhythms.

But this time his passion took him out of control, and he quickly came, groaning with the pleasure of the release that seemed to go on and on. Out of breath, he whispered, "I'm sorry . . . I was—"

She lovingly touched his mouth with her fingers, and said softly, "Don't. We have all night." With her head on his shoulder they fell asleep.

Suddenly Marianne awoke. Something was wrong. What had wakened her? Tensely she listened. Yes, it was the phone ringing in the big house. Usually one couldn't hear it from here unless the wind . . . She rose quickly and plugged in the extension; the static told her it was long distance. She wrapped a towel around her as if the instrument had eyes and carried the phone to Carlo. He had awakened and immediately caught her sense of urgency.

"Yes, yes, this is he," he mumbled, but soon broke into Italian. She became more alarmed as she watched his face. When he hung up he was shaking. He reached for his cigarettes. "There's been an accident."

"Susannah?"

"Sybilla," he answered. "She's dead."

A BOAT PASSED quietly along the canal beneath the balcony. Carlo swallowed the last of the brandy and forced his thoughts back to the present. No need to dwell on what might have been, he told himself. He *hadn't* done things differently, and he *had* lost Susannah. And now he had lost his daughter as well.

He remembered the one line in Francesca's letter that had upset him more than all the others combined. The man she was marrying, Michael Hillford, was the nephew of Lady Jane. "And Michael's aunt," Francesca had written, "seems absolutely delighted with our marriage plans."

Chapter Thirteen

JOSIE LED THE old woman up the hill past shacks of concrete and tin and twisted and barbed wire. Thin black pigs, half-wild, snorted in the grassless yards. The flies were thicker there and the heat more oppressive. The woman paused for breath, and Josie waited beside her. Augustine was elderly, but not frail. Her pure white hair was plaited into two braids that circled her head. She carried a pouch filled with herbs she had gathered at the edge of the forest, believing they would cure her daughter, Marianne. Augustine's healing powers were legendary. She had brought people back from the brink of death with her potions and her chants. But despite her incense and candles, herbs and roots, prayers and incantations, Marianne grew worse with every day that passed.

Augustine come from one of the oldest and proudest families in Haiti. Her husband had been forced into exile after he was caught plotting an abortive coup against the island's dictator. Once Josie had asked Augustine why she had never joined her husband in Chile or her exiled brothers in America, and the old woman had spat onto the sizzling hot concrete path.

Augustine had swept her arm like a monarch in an arch over the pathetic shacks. "My husband could not afford ship's passage for me, and my people needed me here for obeah, for my healing arts, my magic. Marianne was different. She always wanted to leave."

"Why?"

"She thought she could earn enough money in Nassau to join her father in Chile. Instead, one day she came back home with you in her arms."

Josie wondered how much Augustine knew about her birth. Marianne had said there was only one sin in Haiti as unforgivable as political dissent: illegitimacy. No matter what he might accomplish in life, a bastard could never overcome the social stigma of illegitimate birth. The Lapoiret family was proud of its ancestry, but Josie herself, half-white and fatherless, was a disgrace. Josie felt compassion for her mother, now that she had seen the hellish life that she had escaped.

Josie had wanted to turn around and leave Haiti the moment they arrived. She found the sight of so much misery physically painful, and after the splendor of Venice, it seemed unreal. But Marianne was dying and would not leave her childhood home. It did no good to point out to her the primitive and inadequate medical care on the island. Marianne had accepted her illness as fate; all she wanted was an escape from pain.

Augustine, who sniffed around the doctors like a suspicious dog, was pleased when Marianne sent them away. As one of the most powerful practitioners of obeah on the island, she had her own reputation to protect. She wanted the house rid of the men she viewed as charlatans. But in spite of her efforts, Marianne lost weight rapidly, and her eyes began to roll back with pain. She hardly seemed aware of Augustine's rites. The old woman would shake a censer over her like a priest but the only thing that seemed to dull the pain was the morphine the doctors had prescribed when they admitted that the disease had spread too far to be stopped.

Josie and Augustine shuffled on through the sun, up the steep incline to the wood-and-stone house that was shielded from the path by a screen of bougainvillea. Augustine's house was a fraction of the size of the beach house on the Nordonia estate, but solid and respectable in comparison to the other houses in the neighborhood it dominated. A group of villagers, who had gathered on the path outside the door, respectfully moved aside for Augustine. Josie noticed the way they averted their eyes as if in fear. She had seen most of them in the house at one time or another, eyes downcast, offering presents in payment for a charm or a curse. Much to Josie's embarrassment, Augustine had introduced them to her as if she were not Marianne's daughter who had been given a white, upper-class, convent education, but Augustine's own creation, conjured up from charms spoken over batwings and rose petals. The deception frightened Josie. But then, all of Haiti was a nightmare in broad daylight. Augustine had perpetuated the lie about Josie's father having died at sea and had seized on her like a rare, valuable doll that could work the final voodoo charm, and shore up her family's pride.

Josie helped the old woman into the house. The living room was shuttered and cool. Marianne lay on the couch half-conscious, moaning softly. Augustine hurried out to her odd, shedlike kitchen to mix the herbs into potions.

Marianne opened her eyes. "Josie? The Blessed Virgin has appeared to me," she said suddenly. "She gave me a warning. I must tell you."

Josie bent over to make out the slurred words. Her mother hallucinated now, sometimes with pain, sometimes with drugs.

"Promise me that when this is over you'll go back to Nassau."

"Of course, Mama."

"Augustine wants you to stay and learn her magic. I was supposed to learn it, but I ran away. Don't let her take you."

She became incoherent. Then Augustine was there, kneeling beside the couch, one hand on her daughter's brow, the other on Marianne's knee. It was the pose of a pietà. It often struck Josie that Augustine's rites were a crude parody of the Catholic religion.

Marianne reached for Josie's hand and muttered, "Call Carlo."

Josie held her mother's hand tightly. "I called him, Mama. He's on his way." She hated herself for the lie, but thought even a false promise was better than nothing. "It will be hard for him to get here from the airport. You know this village is almost inaccessible from the city."

"He'll come," Marianne murmured, then drifted again into semiconsciousness.

Josie gripped the hand tighter, as if to keep her mother's life from escaping. She had felt so helpless for so long that when Marianne first asked for Carlo, she'd been happy to be able to do something for her. She had to run to the post office in the village, which had the nearest telephone. She had called the palazzo and been told he was in Lyford Cay. When she got through to Lyford Cay she was told he hadn't been there in nearly two years. She had been frantic until she realized that no matter where he was he would not come to Haiti to bid good-bye to his colored housekeeper. It was best to forget him and send her mother to her death with a well-meant lie.

She closed her eyes and felt another layer of bitterness coil itself around her heart, creating a thick callus around her emotions, burying them deeper, protecting them from the blows life kept dealing her.

For nearly a week, she remained at her mother's bedside almost constantly, holding Marianne's hand, talking softly to her during her brief periods of consciousness. And it was through that hand that Josie felt the first death spasm as it ran through her mother's body. Helpless, she felt the second paroxysm and then the third, watching the life beaten out of the only person who had ever cared for her. She buried her head in her hands and sobbed silently until Augustine dragged her away.

In the depressing little church, the choir sang as if their voices could undo the pain in Josie's heart. The priest, solemn and beautiful in his black chasuble, celebrated the requiem mass in Latin; the changes of the Ecumenical Council had not yet reached this Haitian village. The prayers meant nothing to Josie's mind, but the ritual was snug and familiar. Around her, women were sobbing, but Josie had no tears left.

Before the funeral service, Josie had walked to the post office again to call Francesca, thinking she owed her that much. A woman whose voice she didn't recognize had answered the phone at the beach house. Francesca, she had said, had gone abroad on her wedding trip.

The news had struck Josie like the final, crippling blow. The golden-haired sister had been reunited with her prince and would live happily ever after. Francesca had been born to be loved by everyone. Josephine, it seemed, had been born for no reason at all.

As she listened to the Latin prayers she tried to understand what Marianne's unnecessary death meant. Although she had lived like the mistress of a grand estate, she had died like any native Haitian, without proper medical care or even a hospital stay. But at least there's no more pain, Josie thought. At least her mother was beyond harm. She saw harm all around herself now. Josie had little money and now that her mother no longer worked for Carlo, she had no home. Francesca owed her nothing; they were no longer friends. She thought back to the voice lessons in Venice and the shouts of praise from the audience for whom she'd sung at the ball, and wondered how so much promise could have turned to ashes—

Lucas, she suddenly thought. Perhaps if she could get back to Nassau, Lucas would take her in until she found some way to survive on her own.

Augustine's hand on her elbow brought her back to the funeral service, which was just ending. She rose and followed her grandmother back to the house for a supper of fish, fruit, and wine.

When she could, Josie crept into her room and took what money she and her mother had out of their suitcases. She wrapped it in one of her mother's linen handkerchiefs and slipped it into her pocket. Josie had the eerie feeling Augustine could see everything she did. The old woman often bragged of performing great tricks of clairvoyance.

Casually she walked back among the mourners, nodding to them and accepting their condolences until she felt her grandmother's hand on her shoulder.

"We must talk, *ma petite*." The old woman's voice was soft but firm. "Come into the kitchen."

She led Josie away from the other mourners and sat her down at a table. "I've watched you, Josephine," she said. "You are filled with anger. It eats away at you; it paralyzes you the way a spider stuns its enemies and leaves them to rot. I am right?"

Josie watched her and said nothing.

"I will give you something that will help you. A very simple charm. I want you to say it after me."

Josie was fascinated by the half-French, half-African rhyme her grandmother taught her. She repeated it over and over until she knew it by heart. Then Augustine made a little cross of ashes on her forehead in a voodoo mockery of the Ash Wednesday ritual.

"When you use the charm, light a candle. Your troubles will pass from you to those who trouble you. It is very beautiful, very fair."

Suddenly Josie understood why so many Haitians, who went to mass and confession every week, still made their way to Augustine's door. They came for something the priests couldn't offer: justice. *"Très juste,"* Augustine had said.

She followed her grandmother back into the room where the guests awaited and moved among them, accepting their sympathy. She intended to slip out of the house and escape to the airport at the first possible moment, but she had a terrible fear of the old woman's powers. Even if she made it to the safety of the airport, Augustine could say one of her chants and the nose of the plane would point toward the blue of the ocean, or the landing gear would buckle upon landing and the plane would go up in a fiery explosion. She knew Augustine had divined her intention to run away. The old woman probably already knew the exact minute Josie would break for the door. But since the worst was fated to happen, now or later, Josie made up her mind to try to get away. She left everything behind and simply walked out of the house, past her grandmother and the other mourners, without even saying good-bye.

"I've got to get some air," she murmured to the strangers on the rickety porch.

The guests parted for her as if she deserved special treatment. After all, it was her mother they had just buried. She felt as if she were walking to her own death, scarcely daring to breathe all the way to the airport.

Hours later, when she was safely on the plane and it lifted high in the air over the glittering sea, she still expected Augustine's incantation to stop her heart. But nothing happened. She arrived safely in Nassau, drew in a deep breath of the island's sweet air, and shoved her grandmother's incantations and curses into the back of her mind. She hoped Francesca was still away and she would not run into her, but she didn't really care.

She took a taxi to the beach house, and went first into the room that had been hers all her life. She emptied her desk and packed all of her clothes neatly into suitcases. She stripped the bed, putting the linens into a hamper in the bathroom. Then she took down the curtains, folded them, and stored them on a high shelf in a hallway closet. When she was finished, she stood in the doorway and surveyed the room. She had forgotten the pictures. Methodically she went around the room clockwise, removing from the walls the photographs and posters she had tacked up to brighten the room. She wadded them up and burned them in the living room fireplace. When she checked the room for the last time, she was satisfied that nothing remained to remind anyone that she had ever lived there on the charity of Carlo Nordonia.

She had decided to keep her mother's coral necklace and missal, the blue silk blouse Marianne had loved so much, and the bright parasol Josie had bought for her with the first money she had ever earned. Every time she looked at it she remembered her mother's proud walk, the soft curves of her face shaded in its golden light. The rest of Marianne's clothes and belongings she wrapped in heavy brown paper and addressed to Augustine in Haiti. She would mail them from Nassau the next day; the old woman would treasure them.

Among Marianne's papers she found the name of a lawyer. She would visit him tomorrow and ask him to attend to the obituary for the local paper. He would also take care of the will Marianne had mentioned before she went home to die, though Josie knew she'd had no money to leave to anyone.

When she left her mother's room, it was as barren as her own. The Nordonias would get no mementos of Marianne Lapoiret.

She went to the telephone and summoned a taxi, then printed a brief note on a piece of white paper: "Marianne Lapoiret died of cancer in Haiti." She added the date of her mother's death, signed her name beneath it, and propped the note on the counter in the cheerful kitchen where Marianne Lapoiret had spent most of her time.

The taxi driver helped her load the suitcases and packages into the cab. Without looking back at the house, she climbed into the rear seat and gave him Lucas Caswell's address in Nassau.

Josie was only halfway through the first song when she felt the audience fall silent. The attentive hush sent a rush of excitement through her, and she leaned hard into the melody. The silence endured. In the darkness beyond the spotlight, the glasses had stopped clinking, the coughing had ended, even the waiters had fallen still and were standing along the walls near the tiny stage.

Behind her, Lucas whispered, "Got 'em, baby. I'm taking you right into the next one." As her voice clung to the last note, Lucas modulated to a new key and led her out of the blues song and into a jumping novelty tune he had written before she left for Venice.

She heard the audience's pleasure—a sort of prolonged "Oh" that preceded a rustling movement among them, as if they'd pushed back their chairs to listen just as intently but in a different way. She played with the blatantly bawdy lyrics, flirting with the crowd, inviting their laughter and an occasional whistle. Lucas joined her on the choruses, his slightly gravelly voice adding comic effects as well as innuendo, and together they charmed the audience into begging for more.

When the set was over, the crowd didn't want to let them go, and Lucas led her through three extra choruses; then they bowed their way off the stage, Josie throwing bold kisses to the audience, Lucas pretending to scold her for flirting. The laughter and applause followed them from the room, and Josie felt as if she had come home, in more ways than one.

Lucas, high with excitement, hurried her along the narrow corridor to the cubicles they used as dressing rooms. "You have got *some* magic, Josie. Without you I'm terrific, but with you I'm dynamite. Get in there and rest your voice. I'll bring you something to drink."

Josie shut herself in the room and looked at her reflection in the mirror. Her amber eyes were shining and her tawny skin glowed with excitement. The old lighthearted exuberance had been tempered by a new strength and confidence, and she made a promise to her reflection. "You are going to be a star, Josephine Lapoiret. You're going to be bigger than Billie Holiday and Lena Horne and Josephine Baker all rolled together."

She eyed her outfit, pleased at its eccentric beauty. Lucas had been right about the dress, she admitted to herself. She had wanted to wear the red gown she'd worn to Francesca's ball, but this was more suitable for the small Nassau club. She whirled around in front of the mirror, and a light laugh bubbled up in her throat. The silly costume wasn't even a dress, just several dozen chiffon scarves in blinding reds, oranges, and pinks, one corner of each sewn to a red bikini. She whirled again and felt the silken streamers fly out and then wrap themselves around her trim body before shimmering into place again. Boy, was Lucas right! Huge gold loops dangled from her earlobes and jangled on her wrists; the heels of her gold sandals were so high they kept her at eye level with Lucas and his backup men; and her wavy hair bounced over her eyes and around her neck when she moved her head.

"You're exotic," she told herself aloud. "And you're cute, and you are going to make it big. *Huge*!"

Lucas rapped on the door, then kicked it open and handed her a glass of lemonade. "Drink this. Slowly, now. You were great, you know that?"

"So were you. Thanks for sharing the gig with me."

"Still sorry you agreed to work tonight without pay?"

"Yes." She made a face at him. "Skinflint."

"Hey, you're living rent free in my castle."

"Some castle. Peeling paint, broken steps, loose floorboards. And until I went to work on my bedroom, it consisted of four dirty walls, six resident tree roaches, and a mattress on the floor. Ugh." She waggled a finger at him. "From now on you pay me, Lucas. I'm good. You said so yourself."

"I'll talk to the owner. Maybe he'll pay you." He opened the door and started to leave. "Speaking of pay, I've got to spread some cash among my backup men. Why don't you close your eyes and get some rest? Twenty minutes to the next set."

Josie stretched out carefully on a battered sofa that stood along one wall. She closed her eyes, but she was much too excited to sleep. Lucas, at least, had turned out to be a loyal friend. He had become quite a success, and worked almost constantly at the Bay Street hotels. This was his second gig in a club that catered to rich Nassau residents and wealthy tourists. He had made more money in the past month than most island natives earn in a year, and it went through his fingers like water through a sieve.

She smiled, thinking of the run-down house he had bought, right on the edge of the black district—"over the hill," as it was called. She had spent the last two weeks scraping, cleaning, and painting with a kind of fury, as if she were scrubbing out her soul and chasing the demons from her mind. She squandered her passion in sandpapering and polishing, wearing herself out so that she could fall into a dreamless sleep at the end of the day, untormented by the nightmares of the past month.

She had almost finished the work; the house was sparkling clean and respectable looking, though it needed more painting. Grateful for her efforts, Lucas had offered her a chance to sing with his combo for one night. He had also told her she could stay in the spare room as long as she wanted to, and had asked nothing in return. So far, at least.

What would she do when he decided to share her bed? She had no idea; she'd worry about that when and if it happened. Now she was content to know that she had a place to stay for a while, and maybe even a job, if Lucas could talk the owner of the club into paying her.

She opened her eyes and stared at the ceiling. If she squinted hard, she could see sunshine up ahead somewhere.

A roof, a job, one friend, and best of all, the knowledge that Francesca had not married Jack Westman. Lucas had straightened her out about that; he'd seen the wedding announcement in the local newspaper. That meant Jack was still free. His marriage to Nadia Baldini didn't worry Josie one bit. He'd married her on the rebound; the divorce wouldn't be long in coming. Anyway, Josie had decided it was time to go out and get her hands on some of the happiness she deserved.

She stood up and checked her costume in the mirror. As soon as she earned enough money, she would fly to Europe and find Charles; he worked mostly in Venice, Paris, and Rome, and the network of American musicians in those cities was small enough so that she'd be able to locate him fairly quickly. With a couple of Bahamian nightclub credits under her belt, she could ask him to help her find work in Europe. Jack Westman spent almost all of his time there now, in Paris mostly. Josie smiled at the thought of him. He would be even easier to locate than Charles.

Lucas stuck his head into the room. "Hey, Josie, your friend's out front. Must've just got back from her honeymoon."

Josie stared. "Francesca? She came to hear me sing?"

"Not unless you told her you were going to be here. Did you?"

Josie shook her head. "I haven't seen her in months."

"Then how would she know you were here? Your name's not on the bill; you weren't scheduled until an hour before the first set. Must be coincidence." He studied her quizzically. "What's the matter with you, Josie? You look sick. She's still your friend, isn't she?"

"No, Lucas. We're not friends anymore."

He let out an exaggerated groan. "Fine time to have a fight. Ruben says she arrived with a guy who looks like a movie star. What's the matter with you? You could use a rich friend like that."

She nodded numbly and followed him out for the next set. Lucas went onstage ahead of her and did three calypso numbers with his backup men, warming up the audience. She heard him announce her name and walked proudly onto the stage.

Josie swung into her first number confidently, but she couldn't stop her eyes from searching the room for Francesca. And then she spotted her, and as if she were looking through a telephoto lens, Francesca's face sprang into focus. Her eyes, larger than life, stared into hers. She listened with horror as the self-confidence drained out of her voice. Suddenly it sounded hollow, disembodied. Frightened, she pushed for control and heard herself like a shrill bird screeching desperately. She signaled to Lucas to cut her portion of the set short and left the stage. She had to get out of there. The last thing she wanted was to see Francesca. She quickly grabbed her purse out of the makeshift dressing room and ran out the back door. But Francesca had outwitted her and was already waiting.

"Josie," she began.

"Leave me alone, Francesca."

Francesca backed off a step. Any thought she might have had of reconciling their differences left Francesca's mind in that instant.

"All right," she said, her voice cold, "I don't want to have anything to do with you either, but I have to know about Marianne . . . where is she?"

Josie just stared at her.

"She couldn't be here . . . she would have called me. Is she still in Haiti?" Francesca persisted.

"Yes, she is still in Haiti," Josie answered bitterly, and turned and ran out of the alley. If she told Francesca that Marianne was dead, Francesca would cry and, as much as she hated her, she knew at the sight of Francesca's tears for Marianne, she would weaken. She wanted no part of the new bond their mutual sorrow might create.

Francesca walked around to the front of the building where Michael was waiting and got into the Mercedes convertible. Michael, seeing her expression, gave her a hug before he turned on the ignition. A few doors away Josie watched in the shadows as they drove away. Then she began to walk slowly in the direction of the sea. So that was the man that had replaced Jack Westman in Francesca's heart. She had triumphed over Josie's feeble designs after all. Was there nothing that could hurt her? Josie suddenly saw how shabby her own life was in comparison with her half sister's: What could *she* boast of? An old ruined house patched together with a new coat of paint, her struggling native friends, each one poorer than the next, her so-called singing career singing backup for a native band most people in Nassau had never heard of?

The water shone like a silver shield in the moonlight. It

was so calm that Josie longed to walk into it and lie under its roof. To have it wash her pure as one of those white stones by the road. But instead of merging with the water she talked to it. She began to murmur slowly, rhythmically, enunciating each African syllable, carried along by the force of her despair until the last words of the obeah curse that would bring down her sister had drifted off on the night wind. Now I am lost, she thought. I even speak with my grandmother's tongue. But later in her freshly painted bedroom in Lucas's house she lit a candle to seal the curse. She wanted Francesca's life and for Francesca to have hers.

As Carlo's chauffeured car carried him from the airport to the big house, he was filled with mixed emotions that he himself did not understand fully. He had waited until Francesca and Michael had returned from their honeymoon in Ireland and then chosen to pay them a visit like this, unannounced. What did he expect to find by catching his new son-in-law unawares, so to speak? From what he had been able to find out, Michael, though penniless, was hardly the fortune-hunting type. He had a reputation as an honest and good sailor, notorious for his lack of ambition and love of a good time.

As they wound up the drive and the graceful mansion came into view, Carlo was glad he had told Francesca to move in. He would carry the expense somehow until her groom could establish his chartering business. Still, he thought, as he saw the handsome Mercedes sitting outside, he could have given them a less extravagant wedding present. The money was running out. That was a fact that could no longer be avoided. After this visit he would have to go back to Italy and take some drastic steps or he would lose the palazzo. But for the next few days his plan of action was business as usual.

A servant he didn't recognize opened the door for him and told him Francesca and Michael had gone to Lady Jane's for lunch. When he asked for Marianne the woman admitted she was new and didn't know of any Marianne. With a strange feeling of foreboding, Carlo left her his luggage and his jacket and started across the lawn in his shirt sleeves. Marianne was sure to be at the beach house. He would take this opportunity to have a talk with her; she would be sure to give him all the facts he needed to know. It was Lady Jane who was his main concern; she had been a lunatic even before

Sybilla's death. He'd heard the old man had shut her up in their house in England and seen that she never left the grounds. There'd been thirteen years of relative peace, but now Lord Hillford was dead and Jane had come back to the Bahamas and attached herself to Francesca. Carlo had to get his daughter away from her.

The beach house was empty. Carlo stood in the middle of the cheerful living room and wondered where Marianne Lapoiret and Josephine could be at this time of day. Thirsty from his long drive from the airport, he wandered into the kitchen.

The first thing he saw was the note Josie had left on the counter: "Marianne Lapoiret died of cancer in Haiti."

His head began to ache as he stared at the printing, absorbing the date, only. He'd been inspecting his vineyards at the time and would have been hard to reach. Still, cancer was never sudden. Why hadn't she asked him for help? He would have seen to her care, found her the best doctors, the best hospitals in Europe. Instead, she'd gone to Haiti to that witch doctor of a mother she'd told him about. He looked at Josie's signature and felt the sharp pain in his head increase unbearably. Did she hate him so much that she wouldn't ask for his help or even let him know her mother had died?

Clutching the note in his hand, he stumbled to a chair and sat down, holding his aching head in both hands.

"Papa?" He heard Francesca step up to the door of the beach house. "Papa, are you there?"

Carlo gripped the edge of the kitchen table and tried to answer her. When he heard her open the door and walk toward the kitchen, he willed himself to ignore the headache.

"Joe told me you'd arrived, Papa." Francesca was smiling, but her voice was cool. "What a pleasant surprise."

Polite lies, Carlo thought.

His daughter's appearance stunned him. She stood in the doorway to the kitchen with the sun behind her making a halo of her red-gold hair. Her face had a new radiance, and she held her chin higher. All traces of timidity were gone, replaced by a regal serenity that had nothing at all to do with beauty, though she was beautiful now, even lovelier than her mother. She wore a simple dress of sea green; the soft fabric shifted and rippled around her long legs when she moved. Carlo held his breath.

"Papa, you don't look well. Is anything wrong?"

He held out the note and watched her face while she read

it. Her expression told him she hadn't known until this moment that Marianne was dead. "I saw Josie last night. She didn't tell me. Nobody here knew she'd even come back," Francesca said wonderingly, staring at the note.

Too stunned to cry, Francesca stumbled along the hallway to Marianne's room, as if in search of proof that the note was a lie. When she returned, her face was gray with shock. "The rooms have been stripped bare, Papa. Both Marianne's and Josie's. Everything is gone, down to the last scrap of paper from the desks and the pictures that were hanging on the walls."

She was staring at him; even her blue-green eyes seemed to have paled. "If I'd known she was dying, I would have gone to Haiti. I'd have stayed with Marianne every minute, you know I would have. She was like a mother to me."

"Perhaps that's why she didn't let you know, Francesca, so as not to allow the sadness of her death to hang over your wedding."

She shook her head. "Marianne couldn't have known about that. She had left when I arrived in Lyford Cay. So had Josie. But their clothes and personal things were in their rooms." She looked bewildered. "What does this mean, Papa?"

Carlo sighed. The pain in his head had subsided. "I think it means simply that it's too late for us to make amends. I suspect that this is Josie's way of saying she wants nothing more to do with us." He looked into Francesca's eyes and wondered how close she was to wanting him out of her life as well. Very close, he decided. He would have to proceed with care and tact. The deceitful tactics he'd used in Venice had been a disastrous mistake. Still, one way or another he had to see to her comfort and get her away from Lady Jane.

"Why didn't Josie let me know Marianne was so sick? Why, Papa?" Francesca was sobbing. He tried to take her in his arms.

"Probably it was too late."

Feeling her anguish, timidly he stroked her hair and wondered if Marianne had told Josie he was her father before she died. He doubted it. At least Josie didn't seem eager to share the information with Francesca if she had. Still it was another thing to worry about.

"I must do something for Josie," he muttered under his breath.

"Why?" Francesca pulled away from him angrily. "I hate her."

"It's the right thing to do, Francesca. Life will not be easy for her now. Marianne couldn't have left any money. She never accepted anything except the minimal salary."

Francesca pulled her sleeve roughly across her eyes. "Come to the big house, Papa. I'll get a room ready for you. You look tired."

But there was no real concern in Francesca's voice and Carlo realized she would miss Marianne far more than she would ever miss him.

"No, I would prefer to stay here," he said quietly.

"If you're sure, then I'll send the maid with your bags. I'll see you later." With that Francesca ran out the door. He heard her sobbing as she ran across the grass, sobbing for Marianne as she had so often as a child. He was glad to be alone in this house. Memories of Marianne were strong here and less painful than the memories the mansion would hurl at him in the dark of the night.

Francesca caught the whiff of brandy on him when her father arrived for dinner that evening. After the first course, Carlo called for a second bottle of wine to be opened and Francesca excused herself. Though he made perfect sense, enunciating precisely, Francesca did not want to watch her father getting deliberately drunk. Obviously this was his personal way of mourning Marianne, but it wasn't hers.

Michael leaned across the table and looked Carlo Nordonia in the eyes. "Again, sir, I thank you for the offer, but I have the notion to start small and watch my charter business grow gradually over the years. I've had a good lot of experience with tourists and with boats. I know where the need is and how to provide it, and I have quite enough capital of my own to get started." He smiled and tried to keep the sarcasm out of his voice. "You've no need to worry, Count Nordonia. I'll see to it that your daughter lives well."

Carlo nodded. He knew when he was beaten, and this devil of an Irishman had beaten him roundly. Francesca had left the table an hour ago, and in that time her young husband had not given an inch. He wanted no part of his father-in-law's generosity. Carlo was nearly worn out with arguing and he had to give Hillford credit. The man obviously loved Francesca; he had charm and he exuded a kind of rough-edged integrity. "You will come to me for help if you run into a disaster, won't you? Please understand that I'm not offering you charity. I would like to help you, if you'll let me."

Michael smiled, apparently as aware of his victory as his father-in-law was. "Aye, Carlo—may I call you Carlo?—if a hurricane destroys my fleet, you'll hear from me. Count on it."

Carlo was relieved. Now he would have time to recoup some of his losses. Lucky Michael was such an independent rascal. If he had asked for help it would have been a damned inconvenient time to give it to him. Carlo waved his hands for the last of the plates to be taken away.

"You've got a good cook. Francesca runs this house well." He leaned back in his chair and caught Michael studying him. He chuckled. "More wine, my boy?"

"Why not?"

The man could hold his liquor, too. He filled Michael's glass and poured some for himself. The candles burned low and the house was quiet, but it was not an uncomfortable silence. He liked this man Francesca had chosen in haste. Leaning over, he clapped Michael on the shoulder.

"Business is a bore. Let's talk about the sea. I haven't sailed around here in years."

When Francesca woke late in the night she heard them still laughing. Well, she thought cynically, Marianne's death had served a purpose after all. Sober, Carlo and his new son-in-law would never have become such fast friends.

When she came downstairs the next morning her father was already up. Clean shaven, his clothes impeccable, he was seated by the window having coffee and reading the paper. The smell of the familiar Gauloises cigarettes filled the air and she felt a little lurch of her old affection for him in spite of herself.

"Ah, *piccola*." He rose and kissed her. "How about a walk? The air is fresh. It's a new day. No more tears; Marianne would not approve."

"That's true." Typically, there was no sign of the night's excesses about his behavior. She followed him out the French doors into the garden.

He kept on chatting pleasantly as Francesca led him out of the house and toward the sea. He needed to know for certain why his daughter had married in such a hurry. If his suspicions were unfounded, he would spend another few days here and then leave his daughter alone with her new husband. But if he was right about her reason for marrying Hillford, he would have to make some complicated arrangements, and he wanted to discuss them with his daughter. He was determined to handle the situation calmly; hc must not allow the rage to swallow him up again.

When he and Francesca reached the hill where the restored rose garden sent its perfume out on thc breeze, he stopped and turned to face her.

Francesca rushed into speech, carefully choosing a topic that had nothing to do with marriage. ''How is Antonia, Papa?''

''She is fine, just fine.'' He had not come all the way to the Bahamas to talk about his mistress. ''I was hurt when you didn't invite me to your wedding, *cara*.''

''I'm sorry, Papa, but there wasn't time. We decided to marry on the spur of the moment. It was over and done with a week after Michael proposed. The wedding was pretty, but very small. Just Lady Jane and a few of her friends.''

''Yes,'' Carlo said slowly, ''you mentioned Lady Jane in your letter. How much did she have to do with this?''

''She introduced me to Michael, that's all.'' Francesca quickly related the story of Lady Jane's invitation to tea, the dinner that had ended in her introduction to Michael, the afternoons of sailing, and their decision to marry.

''Francesca, my dear.'' Carlo took her hands and was pleased when she didn't pull away. ''You have my blessing and my best wishes.''

''Thank you, Papa.''

''But I have a question or two. Will you indulge a worried father with some answers?'' He waited for her nod and then said, ''You're very young, Francesca, and you do have a way of changing your mind. Not long ago you were head over heels in love with another man and—''

''Jack is married to someone else, Papa.'' Francesca pulled her hands away from his and turned to face the sea.

''Yes, he married Nadia Baldini. I heard about that. But that has little to do with your marriage to Michael, my dear.''

''It has everything to do with my marriage. I loved Jack. I would have married him if you hadn't driven him away.'' Resentment filled her voice.

Again Carlo wished he had rid his household of Westman

by more subtle means. He kept his voice gentle. "I drove him away, yes, but I didn't send him directly to Nadia Baldini. You know that."

Francesca was looking down as if studying the ground at her feet. "I know. He turned to another woman the minute he saw that I would cause trouble for him, maybe even bad publicity that could ruin his image." Her voice reflected the pain that this insight had cost her. "I now know he's shallow and faithless, Papa. But I loved him and I know he loved me. We would have been happy together if you hadn't interfered."

Carlo could hear his own breathing in the silence that followed. "And what has all this to do with Michael Hillford?"

"I wanted to be married."

"But you're still just a girl. You should be dancing, meeting people. You should have a chance to be carefree and free of responsibilities before you chain yourself to one man. Why such a hurry, *cara*?"

The silence this time was more than uncomfortable; it was charged with possibilities. It lasted so long that Carlo finally broke it, determined to torment himself with the certain knowledge that the American had planted his seed in the Nordonia line.

"Not to spite me, surely. You chose a fine man from a good family, a man I couldn't possibly object to." He watched the sun spill over her shining hair. "Forgive me, Francesca, but I cannot believe you married this man out of the same kind of passion you professed to feel for Westman. One doesn't move in and out of that sort of infatuation in the space of a few weeks."

"Leave me alone, Papa. You've asked enough questions."

She wrapped her arms tightly around her waist in a gesture so natural and so protective that it confirmed Carlo's suspicions as surely as if she'd offered a confession. He willed himself not to let his emotions respond, not to think about the scene in the bedroom on the nursery floor, not to give in to the fury. But the rage seemed to have a life of its own. It rose up on him like a physical presence, clogging his throat and making his hands tremble. His head began to ache again, this time with a vengeance, and when he spoke, his voice sounded hoarse and strained.

"You married Michael Hillford because you needed to provide a father for Westman's bastard." A spasm of pain swept across her face. "Behind my back and in my home, you took him as your lover."

"You hypocrite!" Francesca's voice shook with rage. "Do you think I don't know about you and your *research assistant*? Do you have more freedom than I because you're my father? Does Antonia have a clearer right to a lover than I do?"

"You are my only child, Francesca. You have a responsibility to marry well, produce an heir, and provide an example for others."

"Provide an example! I took my cue from you, Papa. You slept with Antonia in secret; I saw no reason not to do the same thing with Jack. I *have* married well, and I *am* going to produce an heir. You should be proud of me, Papa. I'm a true Nordonia!"

"You're an Ingraham through and through, like your mother. You think of nothing but living out your erotic fantasies—"

"Stop trying to blame my mother for my sins. If I'm no longer your silent and submissive little girl, look to yourself for the reasons why. What I am I owe to you."

She turned and strode toward the mansion, leaving Carlo alone in the garden. Thoroughly shaken, he stumbled toward the beach house, slammed into the living room, and collapsed in a chair, holding his head between his hands.

Was there to be no end to the disgrace? The stain on the Nordonia name grew dark and indelible enough after the news of Susannah's sexual exploits began to spread. It had been smeared wider and deeper after Sybilla had died in Venice. "An aneurism," he had told the press. How many government officials had he bribed in the aftermath of that tragic incident? How many policemen? How many times had he told the lie to his friends and acquaintances? And most of them had shaken their heads, clucked sympathetically, and then, he was sure, gone off to exchange whispered conjectures about what had really happened.

Now the seed of disgrace had been passed along, planted, fertilized, and nurtured. It had come to fruition in the daughter whose affair with the American had been common knowledge among the readers of the scandal sheets. He suspected that everyone in Venice had known what she was up to. Everyone except her father. And now someone—he was sure it was Lady Hillford—had sent announcements of Francesca's marriage to all of the major newspapers in Europe and North

America. He could imagine the ripple of self-satisfied laughter that would sweep over Italy when the pristine Contessa Nordonia gave birth to a child six months, perhaps only five months, after her marriage! Lady Jane, of course, would see to it that the date of birth was widely published. Not a soul in Italy would doubt the paternity of this infant. Carlo would have to grease the palms of the Nassau officials who kept the birth records, and he would have to stop Lady Jane immediately.

Damn Jane Hillford. The woman was as insane as she had been the night he called her from Venice thirteen years ago. She had told him then that she would never stop until she had taken from him as much as he had taken from her. A life for a life. A daughter for a daughter.

As he remembered the threat, Carlo's anger began to ebb. It was replaced by a cold fear that crept over him like silent death and then was transformed into a sweaty, heart-thumping panic as he realized that Jane Hillford was mad enough to carry out her threat. Carlo hauled himself to his feet, swaying slightly as he moved along the hallway. He shouldn't have allowed Francesca to stalk away from him; it was dangerous for her to walk across the grounds alone. He needed to warn her, warn Michael, send Lady Jane away from Lyford Cay. He had no time to lose.

Carlo staggered to the door—God, how his head ached! —and made his way toward the mansion. He was nearly there when darkness came over him. He called out Francesca's name before he fell to the ground.

Three weeks had gone by since Carlo's stroke. He was now able to breathe without life-support equipment, and he occasionally regained consciousness for a few minutes, but he could not move or speak. With good care and a strong will, the doctors said, Carlo Nordonia would recover partial use of his body. Dr. Edward Patiné, the brilliant plastic surgeon who had built the clinic, had become interested in the case. He spent as much time with the count as he could spare from his own patients, and he had been extremely kind to Francesca. She had first caught his attention in the solarium where she would go every day between vigils at her father's bedside. He had been impressed with the cheerfulness she seemed to pass on to the other patients and he asked her to visit the children's ward where his own patients, mostly burn victims, especially needed comfort and companionship. She had been glad to have something useful to do while she waited for a sign of improvement in her father's condition.

One afternoon he found her staring down at Carlo's inert form. "Talk to him," he told her.

"Will he hear me?"

Edward Patiné shrugged. "I don't know, but it certainly can't hurt, can it? He definitely won't hear you if you just sit there looking sad and guilty."

"Guilty?" She was startled by his use of the word, and Patiné put one hand on the top of her head, as if he were comforting a child, although he was not much more than thirty himself.

"Yes, Francesca, guilty. Like every other child of every other parent who has ever suffered a stroke." He lowered himself into the other visitor's chair next to Carlo's bed. "When something like this happens, we all look back at things we've done or said, and we say to ourselves, 'If only I'd been able to control my temper,' or, 'If only I'd done as he wished, this would never have happened.' But, of course, we're always wrong. Always, Francesca. No matter how important we think we are, we haven't the power to cause something like this to happen."

Francesca looked into his warm gray eyes and realized he was telling her the truth, not just trying to make her feel less guilty. "Of course, you're right, but you see, Doctor, the day this happened I had—"

He held up a hand to silence her. "You don't need to address me as Doctor; my name is Edward. And you don't have to tell me about this unspeakable thing you believe you did. Whatever it was—and I doubt it was as bad as you think—it did not cause your father's illness. You are not to blame, Francesca. I've seen the medical records from the doctors in Venice. Your father has had high blood pressure for years. This would have happened even if you had been a perfect daughter. Do you understand that, Francesca?"

She hung her head, wanting to accept his comforting explanation but not quite able to forgive herself for having lost her temper at her father.

Edward Patiné leaned over and took both of her hands between his. "Forgive yourself, Francesca. This is no time for you to be flogging yourself. Your baby needs a happy mother."

Francesca's head flew up, and she stared at him. No one except her father knew that she was pregnant.

Edward laughed. "I am a physician, remember? I notice such things, and I congratulate you and your handsome husband."

He rose and left the room to continue his afternoon rounds, leaving Francesca to stare down at her unconscious father. He looked so vulnerable in the stark white hospital bed, his cheeks concave, his face deeply lined. Without his vital expressions and the powerful gaze of the dark eyes, he looked as if he had turned in on himself, as if he were dreaming of death.

"I'm sorry, Papa." She leaned over his inert body and whispered intently as if willing him to hear her. "I lost my temper. I shouldn't have said such terrible things." She took his lifeless hand and held it tightly. "We can get along, you and I. From now on, I promise to try harder. Get well, Papa, please. Please."

As she held his hand, her father's long fingers tensed for a moment, as if trying to encircle hers. Then, almost immediately, his hand relaxed; the movement had been so slight and so ephemeral that at first she didn't dare believe she had felt it. She held her breath, but it didn't happen again. "Papa, you squeezed my hand. You can hear me. You *are* going to get well, I know you are."

Carlo's skin seemed to have come loose from his bones. His face, even in repose, was ravaged and exhausted, as if while he lay inert some terrible war were going on underneath the slack skin.

Francesca bent over him and heard his faint breath. In a second he began to breathe more heavily, as if the effort to move his hand seemed to have taken all his strength.

She left the hospital with a light step. For the first time in days she paused to notice the glorious weather and the beautifully kept grounds. The air was filled with the lush heavy scent of the towering angels' trumpets that banked the drive. The large, snowy blossoms hid the clinic from the road and forced their beauty on her, insistent as hope. Her father's hand had moved willfully; he had reached out toward her. She smiled as she maneuvered her car onto the highway. She was late getting home and found Michael in the kitchen.

He wore an apron and was stirring a steaming pot with a wooden spoon. There was a delectable smell of mingled cheese and sherry. On a cutting board were slices of apple and a handful of walnuts.

Francesca stood on her tiptoes to give him a wifely kiss on the cheek. "So you've gotten dinner underway! We'll eat tonight after all. What are you making?"

She meant to pull away from him, but he held her fast, rubbing his cheek in her hair.

Francesca suppressed a twinge of dread. In almost every way Michael was too vital and demanding, like an enormous, overgrown child. Sometimes she felt that he would crush her with his love. Still, it was not his fault. When Michael gave her a bear hug and a long, hard kiss, as he did now, Jack's unwanted face rose up before her eyes. Jack had been a better lover. He was more sophisticated and gentle, endlessly affectionate. But many women would have preferred Michael's roughness, his headstrong kisses and strong embraces. What he lacked in subtlety and skill, he more than made up for in passion. His lovemaking deserved to be returned and she hated her body's stubborn allegiance to Jack. The pretense of love exhausted her, and her guilt made her want to flee his arms, his bed. The worst part of it was that although her resistance tormented her, it stimulated Michael. She was his wife, but still a challenge. Forcing her mind away from such thoughts, she wriggled out of Michael's arms, claiming to be starved half to death.

"Conch soup and Welsh rarebit coming up," he announced. "Allow me to serve you."

As they ate, she told him about her father's attempt to squeeze her hand, and warmed to his pleasure at the good news.

But thin lines of worry appeared between his eyes when he spoke of the trouble he was having finding customers for his charter service, and Francesca murmured words of encouragement.

"Here I am going on and on about myself. Forgive me, Francesca. You'd think I was the only man in the world with business problems. You're looking so sad it tugs at my heart. What's the matter?"

"Nothing."

"Tell me, and then I'll tell you what I've made for dessert."

"Michael, nothing happened, and nothing's the matter. I've felt a little queasy lately, that's all."

"You're not ill?" He drew back to examine her face.

"No." His eyes were full of trust. It wasn't fair to make him worry for her sake. Perhaps now was the time to tell him.

"Is it your father?"

"No, Michael. I think I may be pregnant."

Michael grasped her shoulders, gave her a startled look, and threw his head back in an exuberant laugh. He pulled her to her feet and danced her around the room. "A child! An heir! My old da will bust his braces when he hears. What a wonderful wife you are, Francesca!" He stopped dancing suddenly and led her to a chair. "We must have created this baby that first night we made love on the beach. Oh, Francesca, this is the best news you could possibly have given me."

That night, as Michael slept soundly, Francesca began to ponder names for the baby. She knew almost nothing about real happiness. There had been little of it in her life, and just as little love. She felt she had not been truly happy since her mother died. Jack had made her forget the past, but in the end his love was the cruelest of all, for when he abandoned her, she had felt as helpless as when she was six years old. She could not trick herself into forgetting him; her body would not let her. Nor would she ever be able to love Michael the way he deserved. And yet now she was happy, and steady in her happiness. Jack's love might have been exhilarating, but it could not sustain her, nor her child. She would become a mother like her mother. That would give her true joy at last. If the baby was a girl, she would name her Susannah.

Chapter Fourteen

CARLO'S PERIODS OF consciousness increased in length and frequency, but his recovery was slow. It seemed to Francesca that he came alive as the child within her formed, imperceptibly but steadily. Each day she told him again that she was sorry she'd upset him. His fingers squeezed a message of understanding, and her heart lightened with relief. Now he spent less time sleeping, but when he looked at her, his expression was blank. Sitting beside his bed, she gave him news of the palazzo from Emilio, or talked to him about Michael's new business venture. She wasn't sure how much of it Carlo understood.

Now that the island's busy tourist season was upon them, Michael was immersed in establishing his fledgling company's reputation. It was difficult, and advertising had proven to be expensive but necessary in order to lure tourists off the beaten track. Lady Jane, who could have easily helped them by steering some of her well-connected friends their way, had been avoiding them ever since Carlo's arrival. This struck Francesca as strange. The woman had fluttered around her like a mother hen until her father appeared on the scene. Surely Lady Jane was lonely, batting around her perfect, lifeless house or spending all morning on her knees digging in a garden that no one ever came by to admire.

Any mention of Lady Jane had an odd effect on her father. His long, weak torso seemed to strain whenever he heard her name.

Her father's fingers jerked slightly, and his mouth began moving in nervous twitches, and she realized he was making his first real attempt at speech.

His hand clutched hers and seemed to be trying to pull her down toward his mouth. She bent closer, trying to hear his words, but it was no use. He couldn't produce coherent sounds.

Francesca fished a pencil out of her bag and pressed it into her father's fingers. She held a slip of paper under his hand. "Can you write down what you want to say, Papa?"

Carlo's hand moved slowly in a sort of squiggle. His eyes closed, and the pencil fell to the floor. When Francesca looked down at the paper, she saw that he had managed to scrawl a faint and spindly capital "J."

When she was sure Carlo was asleep, she found Edward Patiné and showed him the slip of paper.

"Your father was probably trying to tell you something about this Lady Jane you were talking to him about. Something he thinks is important." He handed her the slip of paper. "Best to let it go for now. He must have felt very strongly about whatever he wanted to say. It might be better not to mention this woman again until he recovers some of his power of speech. We don't want to get him excited about anything right now."

She nodded, noticing again the serenity of his gray eyes.

"Come, then," he said. "I said I have another beautiful woman hidden away down this corridor. She needed some fixing up, so I repaired her. Now she's well, but she needs cheering up."

He rapped smartly on a heavy door, waited for permission to enter, swung the door open with a flourish, and ushered Francesca into a private room. A handsome woman who seemed to be in her forties lay on the bed, her head and shoulders propped up on a mountain of pillows. Edward swept his free arm toward the woman and launched himself into speech.

"This, *ma chère* Apollonie," he said to the woman, "is the world-famous Dr. Francesca Nordonia Hillford. She is a cheerful countess from Italy."

He gazed solemnly into the patient's eyes. "And this," he said to Francesca, "is Apollonie de Tions. She is a gloomy duchess from France. Come closer. I won't let her bite you."

Ignoring the woman's dismissive wave of the hand, he led Francesca over to the bed, keeping his arm around her as if to protect her from potential harm. "Apollonie is a plastic surgeon's nightmare." He reached out his free hand and lightly traced the downturned corners of the woman's mouth with an index finger. "Do you see this? The medical term for it is grumposis. In everyday language it is called long face." He let go of Francesca and folded his arms over his chest.

"Unfortunately, it's inoperable. Not a thing I can do for this woman. That's why I called you in on this case, Dr. Hillford."

He bent over and patted Apollonie's hand. "Take heart, Gloomy Duchess. A cure is at hand."

"You are impertinent," the woman said, allowing the corners of her mouth to tilt ever so slightly upward. "And expensive," she added. She glanced up at Francesca, then back at Edward. "And a disgraceful flirt."

"Yes," he admitted.

Francesca laughed. Apollonie gave a soft chuckle.

"Get along with you, Edward. Francesca and I shall have some tea if you'll light a fire under those lazy nurses of yours."

"You see how fierce she is, Francesca," Edward warned. "Be on your guard. Take no chances. Flee at the first sign of violence." He bent over and kissed Apollonie's forehead. "You two have something in common, my dear. Francesca has a garden so beautiful that it has become the talk of Lyford Cay." He looked at Francesca. "And Apollonie is perhaps the best-known botanist in all of Europe." He waggled a finger in the duchess's face. "I'll leave you alone, but I warn you, Apollonie, no gloom and doom. Francesca doesn't need to hear about your latest faithless lover."

He left the two women together. Francesca sat down next to the bed. "Perhaps you could give me some advice about my garden?"

"I'm full of advice and I love to give it. Here I am in Nassau, and I haven't had a chance to do one bit of field work. But I love tropical vegetation. Perhaps I'll stay here a while longer to recuperate."

"If you do, you must come and visit me. I live nearby."

Slowly Francesca drew the woman into a discussion about the intricacies of gardening on the island. Apollonie seemed to forget herself, and her voice grew vivacious as she warmed to her subject. As she talked about her visits to the island years before, she soon realized that she had met Francesca's parents. "I didn't keep up with the social whirl. I was too busy trying to establish my reputation as a scientist. But I remember your mother. Who wouldn't? She was a great beauty, charming, yet candid in her American way. The papers in Paris were full of her photographs whenever she came to the Continent. I remember hearing some story about her, oh, it must have been nearly fifteen years ago . . ." Her voice drifted off.

"What story?" Francesca pressed her.

"I just don't seem to remember *any*thing anymore. Well, you must have been just a child when that happened, so it doesn't matter anyway." She waved a hand vaguely, leaving Francesca to untangle her logic. "What brings you to Edward's clinic?"

"My father is in the hospital wing. He had a stroke, but he seems to be recovering."

"Oh, dear. Poor, poor thing. When he feels better, I must visit him." Before Francesca's eyes, the woman fell into a sea of gloom. "He'll see how terribly I've aged over the years . . ."

"Nonsense. You're gorgeous, and you know it." Francesca made her voice brisk. "Stop fishing for compliments, Apollonie."

The duchess laughed and hit the bed with her fist. "I *hate* this place. No one lets me wallow in self-pity for even a moment. Whenever I feel like having a good cry, someone comes in here and cheers me up. I just hate it!"

Francesca laughed. "My father's been sick for so long, Apollonie. I could use some cheering up myself." She waved a hand to encompass most of the world. "Pick a topic, and we'll chat about it. A *cheerful* topic."

Apollonie suddenly sat up straight, then leaned toward Francesca confidentially. "We could talk about men."

"All right."

But at the expression on Francesca's face, Edward's "Gloomy Duchess" went off into a peal of laughter. "Oh. My dear!"

An hour later Francesca was still listening to Apollonie talk with great humor about the men in her life.

"An acrobat!" Francesca exclaimed.

"He was very handsome, dear. I can't remember a word he ever said, but, oh, such a body!"

Francesca pulled her chair closer to the bed, as if by physical proximity she would absorb Apollonie's talent for recovering from a broken heart. She told her new friend as little as possible. She raved about Michael and obliquely mentioned a brief affair with an American in Venice, unwilling to send Apollonie into a fit of despair by telling her the truth about Jack.

The duchess had not been fooled. She had murmured, "Yes, well, I suppose . . ."

Soon afterward, Francesca returned to her father's room for a brief visit and found him in a deep sleep. She kissed his forehead and went home, filled with a deep contentment at having made a new friend.

Carlo spent the winter in Nassau. He hovered near consciousness, in limbo close to life. At times he seemed lucid, but then an acute pain darkened his eyes, and Francesca feared that he no longer wanted to live. Was it fair, she wondered, to keep him trapped in his body? There was no way of knowing, for he never recovered his speech. She asked Edward to allow her to care for Carlo at home, but the doctor refused. Recovery periods were often long for stroke victims, he explained. Carlo had survived the stroke, but in his weakened condition he might succumb to a secondary disease. That was the real danger.

Francesca longed to share her happiness with her father. In her pregnancy she felt herself reborn. She sensed she was invulnerable now; some god, some angel had drawn an invisible shield in the air around her that no harm could penetrate. Incandescent, robust instead of frail, she relished every sign of life within her.

At first Michael also thrived. A businessman now, he missed his languorous days sailing over the archipelago's turquoise waters, but he seemed shrewdly invigorated as he set about pleasing customers and managing his two-man staff. His new company actually turned a small profit in January, and Michael seemed to visibly grow before Francesca's eyes. But when the tourists ebbed away as the busy season passed, the profit was quickly eaten up by the expenses of office rent and boat repair. Michael needed to buy at least two more boats to earn enough profit, or the company would go out of business. He decided at last to approach his aunt for help. Perhaps she could interest one of her wealthy friends in his business. With investors, he would soon make the fledgling company profitable on a solid, year-round basis. But they were cautious about asking the older woman for help. Lady Jane had dropped Francesca. She was coldly polite to her in the street when they passed in town.

At the height of the cay's social season, Lady Jane called Michael and asked him to escort her to a function at the

Lyford Cay Club. Michael put her off gently, saying that he could not leave Francesca.

"Oh, Francesca is an angel, she won't mind," Lady Jane said imperiously.

"I'd never leave her alone in her condition," Michael told her firmly. When he got the woman off the phone, he turned to Francesca with a groan. "I think my aunt has lost her senses. She sounds like she's taken up drinking."

Michael was a changed man since he'd freed himself of his dependency on Lady Jane. He rarely drank now, and avoided his old haunts on Bay Street.

"You should go, she's so lonely," said Francesca. "I'll be all right, there's nothing to worry about." Francesca felt Lady Jane was far too isolated; her society friends could not take the place of family, and although she understood Michael's insistence on being his own man, she dreaded this estrangement from their former benefactor. The day would come, she feared, when Michael would have no other recourse than to use his aunt's contacts to save his business.

The day she dreaded arrived. He came home from work early and announced he was going to go and see his aunt. After he took a shower, Francesca helped him put on his suit and gave him a kiss good-bye. He marched off looking scrubbed and earnest as a six-year-old boy bound for church.

After Michael left, Francesca settled in her favorite chair and pulled out an old album of photographs. There she was as a round-faced, beaming child held in her mother's arms. The sight of her father, so handsome in his youth, was painful, now that he was feeble and helpless. Then in her adolescence, her suntanned face as dark as Josie's, as they stood with their arms around each other in one series of pictures taken when she was about fourteen, she posed glamorously, one bare leg drawn up high, in a pair of shorts. Josie was the photographer, and posed herself in the next series of snapshots, mugging in a low-cut dress of Marianne's that was far too big for her. There were snapshots of Christmas parties and Easter egg hunts, birthdays, graduations, picnics, boat trips . . .

Tears blurred her eyes at the thought of what had become of them. Marianne had gone away to die among her own people in Haiti. Josie and she were now worlds apart and would probably remain so forever.

Her mind swept back to that night last fall when she had felt herself grow cold with fury at the sight of Josie striding out onto the stage with the colored scarves streaming out behind her. She had been able to think of nothing but her father's words in Venice: "You can thank your friend Josephine for telling me about your meetings with that American."

As she looked once again at the photographs of Josie and herself, smiling, happy, Josie's words came back to her: "He forced me to; you must know that."

Had her father forced Josie to reveal their hiding place? She shook her head. What did it matter now? He would have found it eventually, and her affair with Jack would have ended the same way.

At last she opened the envelope tucked into the pocket in the back of the album. She stared into Jack Westman's blue eyes, ran her finger over his tanned face as if she might be able to feel the texture of his skin. Again she remembered the clean smell of his cotton shirts when she pressed her face against his chest. And she could hear that particular note in his voice as he spoke her name.

She looked up from the photographs, willing herself to walk across the room and toss them into the fireplace, watch them crumble into ashes with the memories she carried in her heart.

But she couldn't make herself destroy his picture any more than she could force herself to erase his image from the inside of her head.

She put the photographs back in the envelope, closed the album, and slipped it back into its place on the top shelf of the bookcase. An hour passed; then another. Surely that was a good sign. Lady Jane must be serving him supper. A third hour ticked past while Francesca sewed a yellow baby blanket with ribbon trim. She began to worry. She climbed to the top floor of the mansion and looked out at the gables of Lady Jane's house. The estate was stony in the moonlight. Three of its windows were lit. The dark house was like a ship looming out of the night; behind it the sea, a sheet of silver glass. Francesca's hand fell instinctively in a protective gesture over her stomach. Perhaps it had been a mistake to send Michael alone to ask the favor. It was such a small thing that they wanted, merely references for the woman's social set. Yet now Francesca felt sure that Lady Jane had been waiting for just such a visit.

Francesca waited up for Michael until almost midnight and was heading for their bedroom when she heard his footsteps at the door. Stumbling footsteps, she noticed. Michael had been drinking.

Francesca sighed and made her way to the door to let him in. He was leaning against the outside wall of the house, humming quietly. When he saw her, he held up his key and scowled.

"This key doesn't work, Francesca."

She pulled him inside and kicked the door shut. "Of course it doesn't work. It's the key to the beach house. You wouldn't have mistaken it if you'd stayed away from the Old Bushmills as you promised."

"Just a wee drink or two to please my dear aunt. Nothing to worry about, my love; I'll be on the wagon as usual tomorrow. Now come along and put me to bed. I can't make it without you." Michael put his arm around her. She steadied him and led him toward the bedroom.

"Did she say she'd help you, at least?"

"Yes, she promised the clients would be lined up outside my door in the morning."

Francesca began to feel guilty for her earlier doubts about the woman. "I just wish she hadn't done this to you. However will you be able to work in the morning?"

"I'll be up making breakfast while you're still asleep."

It was a promise Michael wasn't able to keep. At nine Francesca woke him and nursed him with aspirin and coffee and sent him off late to work. He was mortified by his own behavior the night before. But it hardly seemed to matter what time he arrived at his office. Lady Jane's friends never knocked on his door. The telephone stopped ringing altogether. Now not only Lady Jane avoided them, but all her friends did as well.

It didn't hurt Francesca. She was beyond harm now as she prepared for the baby. She spent more and more time at home, furnishing a room overlooking the sea as a nursery. When she felt the child turn within her, she thought, with guilty pleasure, that it was Jack's. It was almost as if Westman were coming back to her. Not even Michael's gradual despair could spoil her happiness.

Chapter Fifteen

SPRING CAME EARLY, tugging at the unborn child. Lady Jane watched the stages of Francesca's pregnancy from across the hedges. Lady Jane had lost the will to entertain, and was almost relieved that the winter residents of Lyford Cay had closed up their houses and flown away. Somehow the island now seemed poisoned for her. She spied Francesca strolling across the grounds, sniffing the flowering trees and picking the ripening fruit. The young woman had acquired a slow, matronly walk, but she moved as if she had been blessed with the child of God. Lady Jane knew she had only herself to blame for Francesca's happiness. She had thrown her at her degenerate nephew like a helpless lure. But instead of destroying her with his dissolute behavior, Michael had reformed. Now he even bored Lady Jane. Oh, it had been easy as ever to get him drunk on Bushmills now and then, but even when he was disgusted with himself, he had nothing but praise for Francesca, and boasted about the child that Francesca had obviously led him to believe was his.

Michael had told Lady Jane that Carlo seemed to be recovering his mental alertness. Although he might never regain his speech, one day he might at least be able to come home from the hospital. Then, Michael exclaimed, his family would be complete. He would have a wife, a baby, and a father of far more substance than his own. It galled Lady Jane that instead of destroying Francesca, she had redeemed Michael. But it would not last, this happiness; Lady Jane would see to that when the time was right.

It was not fair, Lady Jane mused as she knelt in the rich topsoil of her rose garden, that Count Nordonia's family should thrive while hers came to a barren end. Had it not been for Carlo's wife, Sybilla would be alive today, with a husband and children of her own. Instead, Francesca had emerged unscathed from the ashes of her family and was carrying on just as her mother had done, loving whom she chose, deceiving those closest to her.

The sun wheeled high in the sky and the garden fell silent as the birds hid from the noon heat. Lady Jane could not free her thoughts from Francesca, who was walking about like Susannah reincarnated. Selfish and dishonest and unclean. Yet Francesca was happy, as if her immorality had been sanctioned on high. And now Lady Jane had lost Michael, too, to the Nordonias.

She rose and brushed the dirt from her knees. Such a pretty garden with no one to see it, she thought. With each year, as she pruned and tugged the trees and bushes to flower, Lady Jane's loneliness grew more and more intolerable. Carlo had a daughter to console him but there would be no one to care for Lady Jane in her old age.

It was too late to water the garden; the sun would scorch the leaves. Lady Jane went indoors. She made herself a Tom Collins. The chimes of the clock seemed to exaggerate the stillness of the house. She could only afford the maid a few times a week. In her bedroom she changed from her work clothes to a cool, silk dress with a high neckline. She thought of the early years, when she had been Lyford Cay's premier hostess during the social season. That was before Susannah arrived and eclipsed Lady Jane with her beauty and charm, before Susannah seduced Sybilla and took her away to Venice.

Lady Jane leaned forward to examine her appearance in the mirror. No makeup could mask the toll the years had taken on her face. Her features had become lopsided; one eye sank with bitterness. And the mouth, a cynical line, was taut with the silence it had kept. Her face was an accusation, and she would confront Carlo Nordonia without shame in her ruined vanity. His wife had done this to her.

Lady Jane put on a wide-brimmed straw hat and sunglasses, and walked outside with long, determined strides. She drove the short distance to the clinic and found Carlo's room as if she had been there many times, and indeed she *had* traveled this psychic distance dozens of times—every night since she learned that her enemy was here on the cay, and mortally ill and within easy reach.

A nurse moved around the room, straightening the flowers. Lady Jane's vision had begun to blur, as if her anger had thrown up a translucent screen between her and reality, softening the edges of the world. But she could make out the prone form of Carlo Nordonia, lying on the bed like a statue on top of a tomb. The nurse stood between her and her enemy, between the need for action and the fact. Lady Jane invested her fear in that white-clad figure and then, claiming an icy control of her voice, dismissed the woman from the room. Lady Jane's own fear went out the door with the nurse. Nothing, no weakness of the will, no outsider, would now impede the perfect symmetry of her justice.

"Carlo, how sorry I am to have to visit you here," Lady Jane said to the still man, not sure that he was awake.

He moved. His dark eyes turned toward her, the only points of life in his gaunt, sheeted body. Lady Jane took courage from his weakness. She was immensely gratified to discover Carlo so diminished by age and illness; her heart took comfort from the signs of suffering and despair that marked his face, and she saw that she had already begun to exact her revenge from the Nordonia family. The count was in no condition to report anything she did or said. She could at last begin to put into action the plan that had formed in her mind on the day she first saw Francesca working in her mother's garden.

She sat silently at Carlo's bedside for a moment, enjoying the unhidden fear that had crept into his eyes. It was clear that he knew who she was; surely he would understand what she was about to tell him.

"My husband kept me silent all these years, you know. He locked me up and told people I was unwell." She laughed harshly. "Cyril was such a coward. Oh, he *said* he kept me quiet because Sybilla and I had both suffered enough, and it was time to let the past go. But I knew the real reason he locked me up—he was afraid of what the scandal might do to his precious family name. Like you, Carlo, hmm?"

She sat in silence for a while, watching the terror glint in Carlo's eyes. "Cyril made everything very convenient for you, didn't he? His cowardice allowed your wife to go unpunished. Ah, yes, he was so much like you. Lord Hillford and Count Nordonia, two weak men cut from the same fabric, caring more for their family name than for justice!"

Lady Jane leaned forward and whispered in Carlo's ear. "But *I* care for justice, sir. *I care*! And I shall see justice done."

Satisfied with the effect her speech had had on the count, she leaned back in the chair, settling in for a long visit. "My, how lucky you are, Carlo, to have a daughter to bring you all of this.'' She waved her hand to indicate the room, which was filled with flowers from the gardens of the Nordonia estate. ''Her concern for you in these difficult days must have made it easy for you to forgive her for falling in love with the American actor.''

She laughed softly at the twinge of pain that passed over Carlo Nordonia's dark eyes. It was such a pleasure to see him lying there helpless, immobile.

''She's like her mother after all, this daughter of yours. How that must please you, Carlo.''

Carlo's hand moved spasmodically, and he made a sound in his throat, as if he were trying to speak.

Lady Jane bent over the bed and spoke softly, her voice hoarse with hatred. ''Your wife killed my daughter, Nordonia, and Francesca is going to pay for it.'' As if from a distance, she heard her own mad laughter fill the room and echo off the walls.

In response to her final words, the count's head freed itself from the pillow, and he made a loud gagging noise, as if something were caught in his throat. A spasm shook his body, and left it trembling.

''Oh, my God, what have you done?''

Lady Jane whirled around at the voice.

Francesca stood in the doorway, her eyes wild with shock. ''How dare you upset him? Can't you see the condition he's in?''

Francesca flew into the hall screaming for someone to help her father. As nurses rushed into the room, Francesca was bustled out. She stood pinned outside the door until Edward arrived minutes later. He gave her arm a squeeze as he passed her. Far down the hall she saw Lady Jane. She ran toward her, skidding on the slippery floors. Lady Jane was standing with her back to her. She had taken out a compact and was dabbing at her face with a handkerchief.

''What did you say to my father to upset him so?'' Francesca demanded.

Lady Jane whirled around and snapped the compact shut. Her voice was hoarse and low. ''I've waited all these years to avenge Sybilla's death. All these years my husband kept me shut up to avoid a scandal—the disgrace. How convenient for Carlo that was! And your mother died before she could be punished for what she did to Sybilla. Now you will pay in her place. It's only right. Susannah's sickness runs in this child's veins that you carry so proudly. Michael should be relieved to learn it's not his. Not his, is it, Francesca?'' Lady Jane gloated and then, turning, started swiftly for the doors. Francesca grabbed her arm just as she was reaching for the handle.

''What did my mother do? What are you talking about?''

Lady Jane pulled away roughly and opened the door. ''You deserve everything you're going to get!'' she shouted over her shoulder as she strode across the gravel to her car.

Francesca stood rooted to the spot. She wanted to follow but she had to stay there until her father was out of danger. As she started back up the corridor, she realized her legs were shaking. She felt as if she were going to be ill.

All the way home Lady Jane's exhilaration lasted. She had wounded Carlo at last, perhaps mortally. How good it had been to see him helpless like that, suffering. But as she walked from the car to her front door the wind caught her, maddeningly sweeping her skirt up over her head. Infuriated, she tried to hold it down as she fought her way toward the door. It flew open under her hand and she was pushed violently inside the house, as if the wind had a mind of its own. As she struggled to push it shut again a palm branch flew by and caught her like a whip across the throat. She stood inside the dark hall, listening to her heart pound from exertion. The wind whined angrily, shaking the windows. A lightning bolt cracked in her ear, so close she thought the house had been hit.

It seemed to her that outside the storm was unleashing itself against her personally. For an instant she recognized the evil thing she had done but then she traced the stinging laceration across her throat and her fingers, remembered lifting the sheet that covered her daughter's face, a face not beautiful in death, without the dancing intelligent fire of her eyes, the mocking smile that curled her thin mouth. Already the slightly feline bone structure gave a menacing cast to the skin, and the long slender body had a dull yellow luster like wax. In the dark room it gave off a steady cool light like a night-blooming flower. There was a faint smell of rotting leaves. Holding her daughter in her arms, she had cried as if her lament could waken the dead.

Now she heard the same inconsolable cry heave in her breast. Lady Jane staggered to a couch, and, cut in two by her anguish, she curled up as sobs shook her body.

* * *

Francesca wandered aimlessly into the solarium. It was deserted at this hour. The pale yellow wallpaper and white wicker furniture reminded her of a dollhouse. What monstrous thing threatened her child? Jane had mentioned illness. What could her mother possibly have done that deserved such hideous revenge? If only her father would recover his speech and explain away this miserable lie. She must vindicate her mother, whose lost love meant everything to her. Lady Jane had tried the cruelest trick of all. She'd tried to rob Francesca of faith, and threatened her unborn child.

She lost track of time. After what seemed like hours, a nurse came for her.

"Your father is sleeping now," she said. "There is nothing more to be done. You can go home."

"Is he going to be all right?"

"The doctors are taking good care of him. We're monitoring him." There was a note of disapproval in the nurse's voice.

Francesca put on her coat and stumbled past the nurse and out the door. Tears stung her eyes. As she swung the car out on the road, heavy drops of rain began to splatter against the windshield. The wind caught the tops of the mighty palm trees and rattled them like frail reeds. A low moan issued from Francesca's lips; she realized she was in pain. But it passed, and she pressed her foot down on the accelerator. She arrived home only a minute later, but the wind was so strong that the sea seemed about to engulf the island. She could barely see the front door through the sheets of rain. She drove into the garage, then let herself into the house. She was almost relieved to find that Michael wasn't home.

She climbed heavily upstairs. She was exhausted and wanted to sleep. As she undressed, aware of the high curve of her stomach, her mind anxiously cast up images of her mother. Then she slipped under the covers and tried to still her thoughts. The storm rattled the windows, and her mind gave way to exhaustion. Her sleep was fitful, tormented by dreams in which a young, laughing woman was plunging a knife into her stomach. She woke to her own scream of pain, and to the bitter memory of having seen the same young woman in a photograph. That was why the dream was colorless, the woman a lifeless image in black and white. But the memory paled as the pain continued to throb through Francesca's body and she realized that her labor had begun.

The light came on beside the bed, and she heard Michael's comforting voice. How long ago had he come home? She had no clear idea what time it was.

"You all right, love?" Michael pushed himself up on one elbow and looked down at her. "The storm giving you nightmares?"

She sucked in her breath as another contraction seized her. "The—the baby's coming, Michael. I need to get to the hospital."

Michael laid a cool hand on her forehead. "You're covered with sweat, Francesca. Are you sure you're not just having a fright, what with the storm and all? It's too soon for the baby, love, by a couple of months at least."

She cried out as another spasm hit her, and she took hold of his hand and squeezed. "Hospital, Michael. I've got to get there."

He leaped out of bed, his face suddenly pale, and snatched up the telephone, tapping the receiver button desperately. "No dial tone—damn! The lines must be down." He scrambled into his clothes and held out her robe. "Can you put this on, Francesca? I'll bring the car around to the door. Then I'll come back up here and carry you downstairs." He leaned over and pressed a quick kiss on her lips. "Don't be frightened, sweetheart. I'm scared enough for both of us, but I'm excited, too. This baby knows how much we want it, so it's decided to come a bit early!" He shouted the last of it on his way down the stairs.

Francesca struggled up to the edge of the bed and tugged on her robe. She had packed her suitcase weeks ago; it stood by the bedroom door. Michael returned as she was trying to get into a raincoat.

"I can't take you out in this storm. It's too dangerous. Can you wait here alone while I get a doctor?"

"Oh, Michael, hurry. I'll be fine if you hurry."

Then he was gone again. She could hear nothing but the drum and shriek of the storm. The pangs came quickly now. The pain was a kind of refinement. She felt her body yield to the violence of the storm, its bones bending; the storm would hollow her out and release the life within her.

Michael was gone for so long he began to fade out of her consciousness. The storm rang in her ears, the ocean's crescendo, and she groaned under its violence. It was just as well she was alone, she thought. The furious thing that was happening to her had wrenched her out of her body, beyond help. But then there was a hand on her forehead, wiping away the sweat.

"It's me, Edward."

She looked up. Through the wall of pain she saw two men standing. Rain dripped from their mackintoshes.

"Sorry I was gone so long, darling." Michael's voice was tight with worry. "But I brought you the best doctor I could find."

"The *only* doctor you could find," Edward teased.

He smiled into Francesca's eyes, and she felt an infusion of confidence. Everything was going to be all right.

"I know what you're thinking, Francesca." Edward gave her hand a gentle squeeze. "You're thinking, 'Good God, I need a safe delivery, not a nose job.' But I assure you I've done this sort of thing before."

Francesca laughed, and then a contraction seized her, turning the laugh into a cry of pain.

Edward palpated her abdomen with strong, sure hands. "That's good, Francesca. Keep pushing. It won't be long now. Bear down, can you?"

The pain became a presence in the room, and she gave herself up to it, letting it control her thoughts and erase from her mind the hideous truths of the real world.

With a shriek the storm rushed over her and her body lay exhausted, as if it had been turned inside out.

"What's wrong?" she cried, seeing the panic on Edward's face.

He lifted up the tiny child marbled with blood. Edward slapped it on its small bottom. For a terrible moment the child was silent, its face wrinkled in pain. Then a squall broke out of its mouth. Through her tears of exhaustion, Francesca watched the infant curiously, thinking it looked like a baby bird screeching for food. The three adults burst into laughter.

Edward laid the baby on Francesca's breast. It looked like no one she had ever met. Yet it seemed to know her quite well; its tiny lips nuzzled her and its blue-veined eyelids closed over the blind eyes. Michael hovered over her. She turned lightly toward him, as he reached out to touch the child.

"Your son," she said. "I want to name him Michael Christopher Hillford."

With an enormous look of relief, Michael went downstairs

to get glasses for a celebratory drink. He and Edward drank a toast while Francesca marveled at her small boy.

Edward's hand on her forehead was cool and comforting. "As soon as the storm is over, we're going to take you to the hospital and fuss over you and the baby for a day or two."

She looked up at him, searching for signs, but his eyes were smiling.

"The hospital?" Michael's brow had furrowed. "Is something wrong?"

Edward shook his head. "Everything is fine, but I'll feel better if we keep them both under observation for a few days."

Michael summoned up a smile. "You're probably right, Edward." He squeezed Francesca's hand. "And don't look so worried. I'll visit your father for you. I'll read the newspapers to him."

Francesca suddenly looked frantic. "Dear God, my father! I haven't given him a moment's thought—"

"He's in good hands, Francesca." Edward spoke reassuringly, but he did not smile. "He was sleeping soundly when I last saw him."

Francesca closed her eyes. "Sleeping, Edward? Or unconscious?"

Edward remained silent.

"He had another stroke, didn't he?" Francesca's voice was urgent. "Lady Jane said something that made him have another stroke!"

Edward reached into his bag. "Francesca, I want you to rest. Your father is getting the best care available. Right now you have to think of yourself and the baby. Michael and I will stay right here."

She was vaguely aware of the prick of a needle and the warmth of Michael's hand as he brushed the tears from her face. Edward smiled. Francesca was asleep, the child curled on her breast.

Chapter Sixteen

MICHAEL STOOD AT the window of the hospital nursery, looking at his namesake. The infants were kept in a glassed room full of gleaming, elaborate equipment that he hoped his son would never need. Inside, a nurse held up the boy wrapped in a white blanket. His face was red and waxy, and his eyes, when he squeezed them open, a dark, fierce blue.

"Quite a family resemblance," said a dry voice beside him as Michael tapped a large finger on the glass, trying to get the child's attention.

"What?" He whirled around.

Jane stood beside him. Her severely cut hairstyle gave her an artificial look. The gray hair was almost metallic, as if it were covered with a film of silver paint.

Michael had heard from Edward how his aunt had upset Carlo the day before, but had decided that this was not the time to mention it. "And what do you think of my fine, noisy son, Aunt Jane? A strapping lad, wouldn't you say?"

"You are to be congratulated, Michael," she said smoothly. "He's a fine child. I trust your wife is well?"

Michael nodded his thanks and rocked back on his heels. "Oh, Francesca is fine, thank you, and very proud of Christopher, of course."

"Christopher?" Lady Jane looked at him curiously. "I thought he was to be Michael Junior."

"The last thing we need is two Michaels in the same house, Aunt. He shall be called by his middle name, and it must be Christopher, not Chris. Spread the word."

"Of course, dear." Leaning closer to the window, Lady Jane murmured casually, as if to herself, "Michael, I thought the baby was premature."

"Aye, by two and a half months. Scared us good and

proper he did, but the doctors say he's a fine healthy specimen nonetheless."

"But look at the size of him, dear!" She turned to Michael with an innocent smile. "Why, if this child had gone full term, he would have been a giant!" Seeing a satisfactory degree of surprise in Michael's face, she again directed her attention to the infant. "I just can't get over the size of him. It's simply amazing." When Michael remained silent, still smiling proudly, she grew thoughtful. "You and Francesca have been married—let me see, now—how long?"

Michael was fully aware that she was up to some mischief. "You know perfectly well how long. You were a guest at our wedding."

Ignoring his cynical tone, she counted on her fingers, "Five, six . . . not quite seven. You're right; he's two and a half months early." She put one finger up to her cheek and cocked her head coyly. "But, my dear, you and Francesca met each other only two weeks or so before you were married."

"Enough, Aunt Jane!" Michael felt the rage trying to take over his senses. He knew that nothing would please Lady Jane any more than for him to lose his temper, and he was fully aware that his aunt, for some obscure reason of her own, had been trying for some time to cause trouble between him and his wife. He felt firm control over the tone and volume of his voice. "You'd best take yourself home. Whatever's eating at you is no concern of mine."

"So you've let that woman burden you with another man's child, have you? You have no pride, Michael."

Michael glared at her as she walked away. The old devil was right, of course. The baby could be no more than six and a half months, and yet his weight was only very slightly below that of a normal full-term infant.

On the third morning after Christopher's birth, Michael was so weak he could barely walk. He ate steak and eggs for breakfast, then drove to the hospital to fetch his wife and baby. He had not visited Francesca again during her two days in the hospital. He'd spent his nights in the bars on Bay Street and his days sleeping on a couch in the den of the mansion. He would waken late in the afternoon, shower, dress, and head for Bay Street once again to drink. He would sit in bitter silence and think about himself and Francesca and the child who was not his, and about his aunt's claim that he had no pride.

The accusation ate away at him because it was true. His love for Francesca astonished him; he hadn't known he was capable of caring so deeply for a woman. And he wanted the child. He had felt it growing inside her, had thought about it every day for months, looking forward to the time when he and the child would sail together. In that way, at least, this child was his, and he would not give it up for the sake of the useless, even dangerous quality his aunt called "pride."

One thing he was sure of: Francesca had not been unfaithful since she met him. He clung desperately to that truth, and because he knew his wife, he felt certain that she would never be unfaithful to him again. He parked the car near the entrance of the hospital and walked through the door and along the cool corridors to escort Francesca and his son home.

Francesca was sitting in a chair nursing the baby when he reached her room. "Michael, I've been worried about you! Where have you been?"

He sat down, determined to tell her at least half of the truth. "I have been on the last great toot of my life, and I made it a grand one, my dear. I drank every drop of scotch in the city of Nassau, and then I started in on the good Irish grog. I finished off the bender by passing out in the living room, my darling, and when I finally woke up half an hour ago, I had the whole Bavarian dwarf band marching round the room. It was a sight to see, I tell you."

At her accusing look, he held up both hands, palms out. "Never again, my love. I'm a family man now, with a son to worry about."

She held up her face for his kiss. "Don't exaggerate, Michael. You'll never be a real drunk, but neither will you give up the Bushmills for the rest of your life. Here, take your son, and don't breathe whiskey fumes in his face."

Michael's heart twisted around as he looked at the baby. *His* son, he had decided, no matter what his meddlesome aunt might say. Count on her fingers, she might, the old bat, but that was a measure of biology, not love. "Ah, such a handsome lad, just like me, wouldn't you agree, Francesca?"

"Yes, Michael. Just as handsome as you. Also just as noisy. The only time he's quiet is when he's asleep."

"As it should be, my dear. We don't want any timid souls in this family."

Francesca reached up to touch his arm. "Let's take our son home, Michael."

Francesca's first days at home, nursing and playing with the baby and working in the garden while he slept, were serene and joyous. Christopher's eyes were a blue so pure they pierced her with memories of Jack Westman. Francesca found him totally absorbing. Yet the child could not completely distract her from the memory of what Lady Jane had said about her mother.

Instead of seeking Jane out and demanding an explanation, she convinced herself that Lady Jane's ravings were that of a madwoman; to seek her out for an explanation would simply invite more lies. Only her father could tell her the truth.

Francesca buried Jane's accusation inside her, trying to deny its validity, only to feel the monstrous weight of her mother's past pressing on her. Not even the baby's first innocent smiles could lighten her heart for long.

She was sitting in a patch of sunlight one morning, the baby sleeping contentedly in the crib Michael had built for him, when the Mercedes pulled into the driveway and stopped near the house. Francesca watched Michael climb out of the car and stride toward her, his eyes grim.

"Michael! What brings you home in the middle of the morning?" she asked, getting up to kiss him as he joined her on the wide porch.

He took her hands and led her back to her chair. "Please sit down, Francesca."

Something in his tone of voice took away all of the happiness Francesca had felt at the sight of him. "There's trouble, Michael. What is it?"

He pulled up a chair and sat opposite her, holding both her hands tightly. "Edward just called me at the office, Francesca. Your father died an hour ago."

Francesca felt her heart contract painfully. "I should have been there," she said dully.

"He wouldn't have known it if you had been there, darling. He slipped into unconsciousness during the night. Edward said he simply stopped breathing."

Francesca said nothing. She wondered how much of her despair came from the knowledge that now her father would never be able to tell her the truth. The wound Lady Jane had dealt her would remain open and festering until she alone found the answers.

"You did everything you could, Francesca. So did the doctors."

Leaning against his broad chest, Francesca welcomed his comforting presence. "He never saw his grandson," she murmured.

"Francesca, my love, he was too sick to understand that he had a grandson. It's hard, I know, for you to lose your father, but from the little time I spent with him the night he arrived here, I got a strong impression that he wouldn't have wanted to linger on and on, helpless as he was."

Michael gently pulled her over to Christopher's crib. "Here's the man who needs you now, lass. A life lost, and a new life gained." He spread one of his enormous hands out over the tiny infant's back. "Carlo would have admitted that this was a fair exchange."

Francesca looked down at the baby just as he opened his sky-blue eyes and began to fuss. She reached out to run a finger over his soft, rounded cheek. "I'll have to make the funeral arrangements, Michael. Will you help me?"

He nodded, then put both hands on her shoulders. "Something needs to be said, Francesca. My aunt had a hand in your father's death."

"That had nothing to do with you, Michael. Please don't think any of the guilt spills over on you."

"Just the same, Francesca, from this day forward, she's no friend of mine."

"Michael, she's your only relative in this part of the world."

"She's no blood relative," Michael said firmly. "She was married to my father's brother, that's all."

Francesca looked up into his eyes and knew he was trying desperately to make life easier for her.

Francesca picked up the baby and started for the door.

"We're both alone now, Michael. We'll have to stick close together."

Michael's smile spread across his handsome face like sunlight. "I don't think I'll find that hard to do, lass."

It was decided that there would be a funeral in Nassau for the count. A more elaborate memorial service would take place in Venice, after which he would be buried in the family crypt.

Engulfed in the smell of the incense and the candle wax and the drone of the priest's voice, Francesca felt she was in a trance. Why weren't Josie and Marianne there to comfort her? She felt as vulnerable and as helpless as a child, and, like a child, she wanted the priest to be done with it. Nothing seemed to make any difference except to get her father back to Venice where he belonged.

Edward was barely aware of the priest's voice. His eyes drifted from the flower-draped coffin to the pale features and downcast eyes of Carlo Nordonia's daughter, who seemed to have surrounded herself with a wall of secret grief.

As soon as she was strong enough, she had begged Edward to let her take the baby to her father's room, saying she wanted Carlo to bless the child. Edward had refused, explaining that the infant's immature immune system would make such a visit extremely dangerous, and that Carlo spent most of his time in a state of semiconsciousness.

She had gone alone to her father's bedside and had talked to him, telling him about the child, holding his hand.

Edward wondered why Francesca was so desperate for some sign of approval from her father. He had heard about her lonely childhood. A beautiful young mother dead before she was thirty. An imperious, aloof father who kept an ocean between himself and his child. Why, then, was the child so ravaged with grief?

The priest's voice rose in a final blessing, and Edward saw Michael put his arm around his wife and look down at her protectively.

A good man, Edward thought, feeling a tendril of sadness run through him. Francesca was well loved, and the child would have an attentive father. Michael, he knew, had a fondness for drink, but his love for his family would allow him to keep that weakness under control. Francesca had no need to be saved from a loveless marriage by Edward Patiné. Edward shook the thought away and glanced around at the other mourners.

At the edge of the crowd stood a woman in black who seemed actually to be enjoying the subdued spectacle of grief. Edward watched her closely, looking for signs of the madness he suspected was eating away at her brain, the obsession that had made her enter Carlo Nordonia's room and say to him things that had sent him into a final, deadly stroke.

When the difficult morning was over Edward said a few words of comfort to Francesca and then drove back to his clinic, feeling a sense of loss that had nothing to do with Carlo Nordonia's death and burial.

The image of Francesca Hillford was burned into Edward's mind. Her tenderness with her baby son awoke something in his soul. He rarely had time for friendship; he had no real life outside his clinic. Many of his patients were emotionally scarred by debilitating and disfiguring accidents. But Francesca, with her flawless beauty and gentle smile, had moved through the clinic like a spring breeze. Now that she would not come anymore, Edward could not shrug off the persistent sense of loss. But there was nothing to be done about it. He must let her go.

As the plane took off that afternoon with Emilio in charge of his master's coffin, Francesca felt a great weight lift from her shoulders. Now her father could be safely borne to heaven on the wings of the lion. Why was that childish image always so comforting? She leaned heavily on Michael and let the tears flow quietly down her face as he led her to the car.

Edward waited a fortnight, then he swung his car into the long drive again. The small family was assembled on the lawn, which was fragrant with spring. The estate was a startlingly brilliant green and the trees burst with light like fountains. Little Michael slept on his father's breast. Francesca lifted a hand from her needlework and waved at Edward, her mouth forming soundless words. Edward walked quietly toward them with a feeling of mingled pleasure and guilt. He wished that he had found Francesca alone, but it was Sunday; he should have realized that Michael would be home.

"Hello there, Edward. Pull up a chair." Michael was lying flat on his back in the grass, his free arm indicating the expanse of lawn.

"Just thought I'd stop by to see the baby. All is well?" Edward asked lightly, putting his hands in his pockets.

"The wee man is magnificent," Michael said.

Edward sat down on the grass and talked with Michael for a few minutes, making appropriately extravagant comments about the month-old infant. Michael lapped up the compliments as if Christopher were the only perfect creature in the world.

A happy man, Edward thought, as he watched Michael jiggle his son in his arms. He looked up at Francesca and found her smiling down at him. He worked hard to keep his expression casual. "And you, Francesca? You certainly look fit."

"I'm fine, Edward." She rose and beckoned to him. "Come to the garden with me, will you? I have an idea I want to ask you about."

He got to his feet, started to follow, then looked back at Michael. "Not coming?" he asked.

Michael shook his head. "The flowers are my wife's passion. Damn things make me sneeze. Go along with you, if you dare. She'll have you covered with dirt and fertilizer before you know it." He waved Edward away.

"I want to ask you about some flowers, Edward." Francesca led him to her rose garden and plucked a white blossom, then held it up before him. "Notice the fragrance."

"Yes, lovely. Very distinctive."

"This is known as the Lyford Rose. Apollonie tells me it's a local variant of the periwinkle."

Edward listened as she explained that her mother had apparently had a perfume made from the Lyford Rose. "I found a glass vial of it in her bedroom in Venice. It's nearly all evaporated now. I never wear it because I can't bear to think of using it all up. It brings back so many memories of my mother."

Edward watched the play of the sunlight on her delicate face, wondering why she was telling him this.

"Apollonie told me your whole family lives in the south of France, where the perfume factories are, and I—"

"Ah, of course, Francesca." He was delighted that she wanted him to do her a special favor. "I'll have the perfume reproduced for you."

"If it won't be too much—"

"Don't be silly. It will be no trouble at all. It's hardly a secret in the perfume industry that it's remarkably easy to reproduce a scent. That's why there's a constant search for exotic secret ingredients. Let me borrow your mother's perfume, and I'll get to work on this project right away."

The delight in her eyes made his heart turn over, but he cut her off when she began to thank him.

"Believe me, Francesca, I'm delighted to be able to do something for you after all the time you spent sitting with my patients, making them feel that life was worth hanging on to."

She turned away suddenly and busied herself picking dead leaves off a rosebush. "Maybe, if the scent is successful and it's not too expensive to produce . . . well, it might be a way of bringing in some extra money."

Edward glanced around at the lavish estate. The house was too large for the young couple; its spare elegance must, he thought, be full of echoes at night. It was impossible for Edward to imagine that anyone living in the midst of this splendor seriously needed money. But there was something close to panic in Francesca's voice.

"My father's lawyers have just returned to Italy. They were here for three days, and I'm afraid they brought bad news. The estate is in disarray."

"Your father was ill for a long time."

"It went back far longer than his stroke. Apparently he'd ignored the condition of his finances for years. His wineries must be modernized, and that will take capital. He'd been warned to pull his money out of some of his Italian businesses, because of . . . But he refused and insisted on keeping most of his wealth at home."

"How severe is the problem?"

"They advised me to sell the palazzo. The last repairs were done nearly twenty years ago, at my mother's request. Soon it will need a new roof, and the plumbing must be overhauled."

Francesca kept her voice light, but Edward could see the worry in her eyes. "I told my father's lawyers to rent the palazzo immediately but to keep the rentals on a one-year basis. I also authorized them to sell my father's yacht, most of the paintings, and two of his vineyards. That will give me some time in which to get the perfume on the market, or come up with some other way to raise capital."

"Francesca," he said cautiously, "I have another idea. It's been in the back of my mind for months, but I never dreamed until now that it might really be possible."

He took her arm, thinking how fragile it was. "You must realize that I need larger and better facilities as well as another source of income to support my work with indigent patients.'' She started to speak, but he held up a hand, asking for a chance to finish his proposal. ''My dream is to establish a luxurious health spa that would attract wealthy people from Europe and America. People who want cosmetic surgery, who need to lose weight, recover from overwork, change their exercise regimen, or just get out from under the pressure of their daily lives for a while.

''The income from such a facility would allow me to concentrate on helping badly disfigured patients who otherwise could not afford surgery.''

He glanced at her and caught the open curiosity in her eyes.

''I've accumulated almost enough capital to buy a piece of land and put up a small building,'' he went on, ''but that would take me away from my work just when I'm making important breakthroughs in scar-removal techniques. Suppose, instead, that I were to buy this property, or buy into it, let's say. The main house is enormous; it could be converted into an elegant spa, and it's close to my clinic and—''

''And Michael and I and Christopher could live in the beach house. Is that what you're suggesting?''

''It's just that, Francesca. A suggestion. I know I'm asking you to leave your home, which is terrible of me. I would never have mentioned if it you hadn't said you needed money.''

She was silent for such a long time that Edward began to think he'd offended her deeply, but when she spoke he heard no sign of anger in her voice. ''Let me discuss it with Michael. I like the idea, and I think he will, too. He's always complaining because the main house is so big and so far from the beach.'' She dropped her voice to a conspiratorial whisper. ''He also insists the mansion is haunted. He says the ghost sleeps in the wine cellar and sits in his special chair whenever he leaves the house.''

Edward laughed indulgently, ignoring the twinge of jealousy he felt at the obvious fondness with which she spoke of her husband.

She fell silent again, and he guessed that she wanted to say something but didn't quite have the nerve. He waited quietly until she finally spoke.

''Edward, you mentioned buying into the property. That means I would still own a part of it, right?''

"Of course, Francesca. It's your house; you ought to retain some control over it."

"Does that mean I could continue to work with the patients? I mean, you did say I was good at it, and I loved doing it, and it would make me so—"

Edward laughed at her eagerness. "You've got yourself a job, Francesca." He held out his hand. "Partner?"

She grasped his hand firmly. "Partner."

Chapter Seventeen

JOSIE THREW BOTH arms high above her head and spun around, letting the pale blue chiffon skirt swirl high above her knees to show the full length of her shapely legs. Then she faced the audience and smiled before bowing her thanks and walking off the stage.

In the dim hallway that led back to her dressing room, she leaned wearily against the wall, eyes closed, to catch her breath. It had been a good set and a wildly appreciative audience, but it was late and she was beat. She wouldn't need one of Lucas's pills to put her to sleep tonight.

"Josie?"

She opened her eyes and found a well-dressed man standing before her, right hand outstretched.

"I'm Rad Loitner. Your manager sent me your demo tape."

Josie took his hand and regarded him with interest. The man's name meant nothing to her, but if Lucas had sent him a tape, she figured he must be important.

"I'm from Embassy Records in New York," he said. "I'm here in Nassau on vacation, and I decided to look you up. Your voice stuck in my mind, even though the quality of the cassette I received was terrible." He bobbed his head toward the door. "Will you have a drink with me?'

She let him lead her back out into the main room, where they sat down at one of the small tables. Loitner ordered drinks, but neither he nor Josie took more than a few sips. Loitner was so busy asking her questions that he seemed to have forgotten the glass that sat in front of him. Where had she sung? he wanted to know. Would she be willing to work as a backup singer for a while, until she proved her mettle to the record company? When would she be free to come to New York for an audition?

Josie, not quite willing to trust a man who was this smooth and confident, answered his questions honestly without appearing too eager to please. Loitner seemed genuinely interested in her, but Josie was careful to reserve her judgment, restrain her hope. Nothing could be this easy. Loitner said he was about to produce an album for a new rock group. ''They're strictly local right now, but I'm about to make them a coast-to-coast hit.'' He was looking for backup vocalists, and he thought this might be a perfect chance for her to break into the music world in New York.

''Let's face it, Josie, Nassau isn't even the sticks. You'll never get anywhere with this as your base. And you've got to learn, to grow. If you come to New York and do some session work, we can make you a real demo tape, one of professional quality.''

Loitner was eyeing her now with another sort of excitement in his eyes. She decided that if the moment came that he touched her she would know his offer was a lie. She waited for another, less honorable proposal. But it never came. Loitner sent her home in a taxi and asked her to call him at his hotel the next afternoon.

In her room in Lucas's house, she threw herself across her bed, still wearing the beautiful chiffon dress, and let her imagination take her to New York. The stuffy recording studio would be the first step toward the glittering clubs, the gold records, maybe even the Broadway stage. Lucas would die when he heard. After her first few appearances on Bay Street, he had been sharp enough to recognize a gold mine when he saw one. With hardly a backward glance at his own dreams of being a star, he had made a swift and smooth transition from Lucas Caswell, soloist, to Lucas Caswell, manager and backup musician. Anything Josie earned would help to fill Lucas's pockets.

And replenish his supply of coke and dust and rainbow-colored pills, Josie reminded herself. He'd already been arrested once, for selling drugs to tourists, but that hadn't made him any less eager to pass on his pharmaceutical joy to anyone who showed the slightest interest in it. Josie herself had only occasionally let him pep her up or slow her down or chase away the blues with one of his magic preparations.

Still, Lucas wouldn't be able to go to New York with her; he hadn't been invited, had he? Well, she would find a way to explain her absence without ruffling his feathers.

She closed her eyes and made herself a promise. All of the drug-induced highs and lows were over now. She would need a clear head for the adventure that lay ahead. Again the clubs and recording studios began to glitter in her imagination, and, still fully clothed, she drifted into a deep sleep.

The sun was high in the sky when she awoke, and she raced to the telephone. "Rad Loitner, please. This is Josie Lapoiret," she said when the hotel operator answered the phone.

"Our flight to New York will leave Nassau Airport tomorrow at three," Loitner said smoothly. "Meet me in the hotel lobby at two. I've booked a room for you at the Sherry Netherland."

"Thanks, Rad. See you at two o'clock, then." She kept her voice cool and matter-of-fact as she said good-bye. Then she jumped on her bed in her blue chiffon dress, let out a whoop of triumph, and began to bounce up and down joyously.

When Apollonie de Tions entered the great two-story living room, Michael Hillford was standing on a makeshift dais, supervising a group of workmen. He looked more dashing than ever, she noticed, like a pirate captain in a swashbuckling Hollywood extravaganza. She stood absolutely still in the doorway, counting on her green silk dress and thick crown of sparkling white hair to catch his attention eventually.

"Apollonie, you're back!" He strode toward her, holding out his arms. "Hug me, you gorgeous creature. This place has been a wasteland without you." He swept her into his arms and swung her around as if she were a doll.

"Flatterer!" She pounded a fist against his broad chest. "Say it again, and then tell me everything that's happened in the last six weeks."

"It's been desolate here without you," he repeated obediently. "We're booked solid for the next two hundred years, and—thanks partly to your public relations efforts in Europe—we are becoming one of the most famous health spas in the world."

"Thanks in good part to you, too, Michael. I have never in my life met a man who could make workmen hustle the way you can."

"Busy as little beavers, aren't they?"

He threw an arm around her and walked her through the

clusters of chairs the workmen were arranging. "God, how I've missed you, Polly. If I were a few years younger, I'd leave Francesca and the kid and follow you anywhere."

Apollonie ignored his flattery; she was sure he knew how much it pleased her. "You're all ready for the press conference, then. Where's Francesca?"

"She's interviewing job applicants in one of the guest cottages." He led Apollonie to a window and pointed. "Down there among the sheltering palms."

"And Christopher?"

"Playing with his wooden train under Francesca's desk, I suppose. He's with one or the other of us every moment. Can't think why we pay that Bahamian nurse such a large salary." He led her up the stairs and along a hallway. "Come see what we've been doing while you were abroad breaking men's hearts."

Apollonie studied every detail of the new spa with a critical eye. At Edward's suggestion, she had become the third partner in the enterprise. It had been her idea to build private guest cottages near the beach and to keep the living room and the baronial dining room intact for use as social gathering places for the guests. Both suggestions had been adopted, with resoundingly successful results.

She had also recruited Michael to oversee the workmen. With his love of outdoor activity and his strong presence, he made an excellent contractor, capable of motivating workers and commanding respect. He had spent nearly every day on the site, consulting with the architect, overseeing the renovations. He and Francesca had moved into the beach house with the baby, and this suited him as well. He had confessed to Apollonie that the mansion unnerved him. Apollonie was glad to see Michael active and happy despite the fact that his own charter-boat company was languishing. He was better off, she thought, working like this, in the sun and wind every day. Not everyone had a mind for business.

Michael led her into a large room filled with elaborate new exercise equipment. "No question about it," he said proudly. "We've got the best facilities for thousands of miles around, for both the medical patients and the spa guests."

After the tour, he led her back to the living room where the workmen had finished setting up chairs and tables and had begun to bring in huge sprays of fresh flowers.

"I'll leave you to your work, Michael. The room looks lovely already. I'm sure the press conference will be a smash."

"Now that you're here, our success is guaranteed."

She laughed and kissed his cheek. "I'm off to say hello to Francesca and Christopher." As she left the main house and made her way across the grounds, stopping to say hello to guests, many of whom had come here on her recommendation, she was gratified to see a television crew filming the lush gardens.

She found Francesca interviewing a prospective employee in the guest cottage Michael had pointed to. She looked radiant. Apollonie noticed at once the confidence with which she spoke, the assurance with which she questioned the applicant. The old haunted expression was gone from her eyes, and her skin glowed with health and excitement. The responsibilities she had assumed at the spa had been good for her, Apollonie told herself. What with working full time and taking care of an infant, Francesca had no more time to brood over her father's death and whatever else had been on her mind.

"Apollonie! Oh, I'm so glad to see you!" Francesca spotted her as she ushered the job applicant out of the room.

Christopher's laugh came from behind the desk, where he was playing, and Apollonie went to him, picked him up, and hugged him.

"Good news, Francesca," she said. "I've got half the motion picture stars of Europe lined up for visits to the Lyford Rose Spa. And Richard Allerby, no less, is coming to take pictures of you and me for *Vogue*. And we have our pick of the decorating magazines. They all want to publish picture spreads of the rooms."

She sat on the edge of the desk and let Christopher pull her hair. "And, darling, I have a new lover!"

Francesca laughed delightedly. "And he's not a day over twenty-five, right?"

"He's forty-three, way over my maximum, but I'm flexible."

Apollonie spoke excitedly of her handsome racing-car driver and then returned to the subject of the new clients she'd found in France. "The combination is magical, Francesca. My social contacts, Edward's reputation, and the magic of the Nordonia name. Put them all together and you have a can't-miss enterprise. The European movie people are climbing over one another's backs trying to get in here."

Francesca, she noticed, had gone very still. "I hope you don't object to motion picture stars," Apollonie said.

"No, no, of course not. We have several here right now."

"Friedrich Bollner, the German actor, wants to come; he's lost tons of weight and needs some deep rest. And the director Jean-Luc Bernard, from Paris. Oh, and best of all, Nadia Baldini, that beautiful Italian star who keeps committing suicide all over Europe."

"Nadia Baldini."

It was a statement, not a question, and Apollonie hurried to explain. "Poor darling just said good-bye forever to her handsome American husband, so of course she attempted suicide again. Except that she never takes enough pills—or even comes close. The press adores it, though, and it gets her tons of publicity. Actually this last marriage of hers lasted longer than anyone thought it would."

Francesca had sunk down into a chair, and the color had drained from her face.

"Good heavens, Francesca. I've blundered into something, haven't I? Are you all right?"

"I'm fine, Apollonie, really. Just a little tired, that's all. Come along with me to the beach house. We'll leave Christopher with his nurse and get ready for the press conference."

Rad Loitner hadn't exaggerated about Josie's accommodations. Her room in the luxurious hotel looked out on the landscape of Central Park. She had not been surrounded by such discreet wealth since she left the palazzo.

The New York air had a harsh, acrid smell that jolted her wide awake. Below her, cars, taxis, limousines poured along Fifth Avenue like a loose string of jewels.

Loitner had promised to call her today with a session schedule. A wad of bills lay on the dresser; and he had given her an advance of one hundred dollars. She heard a timid knock at the door, and turned away from the window.

A red-suited bellboy stood in the hallway, his arms full of scarlet roses. When she laid them gently on the dresser, a white card fell out. Scrawled on its back was a one-word message: "Welcome." Below was Rad Loitner's signature.

Josie put the flowers in water and stepped back to admire them. The brilliant roses framed her face in the mirror like a lovely and treacherous omen of what was to come. She was in Rad Loitner's territory now, and he would make the rules. Would he do all this for a backup vocalist? Would he provide an airline ticket, pay for an expensive hotel room, and send flowers to a woman he had no designs on?

"He has plans for you, darlin'," Josie told her image in the mirror. "He plans to make you a star. He's interested in your voice, that's all. You'd better get used to the best, because this is what you deserve."

But her performance seemed to lack conviction. The red tongues of the roses ridiculed her, and the face in the mirror stared back at her without expression.

"The trouble with you is that you're not used to getting what you want. Francesca wouldn't expect anything less; she'd take this all in stride. Besides, what if Rad *is* interested in you? That might not be so bad."

But it was no use; the woman in the mirror remained unconvinced. Josie called room service and ordered strawberries and scrambled eggs. After she ate breakfast, she settled back with coffee and the *New York Times,* which had arrived on the tray.

In the entertainment section, a quarter-page ad for a play struck her eye. There, etched in gray ink, was a ghostlike image of Jack Westman, who had apparently come to New York to star in a Broadway play. The advertisement listed the theater and the performance times. Josie looked at it, stunned. She was only a taxi ride from the theater where Jack Westman would perform tonight.

Josie called the desk and asked them to get her a ticket to the play for the following evening.

By late afternoon she had read all the newspapers and magazines the bellboy could find her. She had found two articles about the Lyford Rose Spa and seen countless photos of Francesca in glossy magazines. Francesca looked happy and confident, as if she had finally come into her share of her family's power and pride. When the bond between the two sisters was broken, Francesca had risen as Josie fell. It was as if there were only so much happiness in the world, and one could not enjoy it without depriving the other. Now Josie was on the rise. She lifted a photo and looked into Francesca's face, trying to read her future decline in those eyes.

The telephone's shriek brought her back to reality.

"Josie! Hey, baby. You're not angry, are you? You didn't think I'd forget you?"

"Thank you for the beautiful flowers, Rad."

"Good, I knew you'd be all right."

Josie noticed that Rad didn't really hear or respond to anything she said. Talking to him on the telephone reminded her of the way his eyes slid away from her when they were together, unable to hold her gaze.

"I'm going to send a limo to bring you to the studio. The session starts at seven, and you need to learn the music first. We'll pick up a bite to eat after we finish working."

"Another limousine?" Josie said faintly.

Rad laughed. "I've got to pick up the other line, honey. See you in a minute."

The phone clicked.

When she emerged from the hotel, an impossibly long and shiny limousine was standing at the curb. The driver held open the door and then ignored her, which she thought might be a form of etiquette in New York. She perched on a deep seat of pearl-gray velvet and watched the city glide by. It looked parched and dirty, and its hardness was terrifying. She was thankful for the automobile, which sealed her safely off from the gaudy, hellish colors of the theater district. She scanned the marquees for Jack Westman's name, or the name of his play. But there were too many glittering signs, billboards, pictures of half-dressed girls.

Musicians, Josie had learned, were creatures of the night. She could see that the members of the band had all just gotten out of bed. Her convent-girl courtesy was out of place here, and her pretty dress went unnoticed. The musicians wore torn Levi's and dirty T-shirts; and after they had jammed for a while, the small sound room began to smell of old socks. It was an incense that didn't bother them; Josie knew from their glazed eyes that most of them were at least half-high. Rad handled them as if they were children. He kept saying through his little microphone on the other side of the glass, "Hey, that's inspired," or "Beautiful, baby." But Josie knew he wasn't really pleased. He delicately asked them to repeat phrases over and over until they got them perfect. She saw that he was stifling his own annoyance and wondered if he ever cracked.

But Josie had no complaints. She was singing professionally. Her name would go on the album credits in small print and she would earn residuals. The band members should have impressed her, she knew. After all, they were real artists who had made a name for themselves in the music world. But as musicians, she quickly realized, most of them did not compare to the amateurs she worked with in Nassau. Later, over dinner in a small and expensive French restaurant near the recording studio, she asked Rad about the performers.

"What do they have that other musicians haven't got?" she said.

"Rapport with the audience. Luck. A willingness to turn themselves inside out. That's crucial. You'd be more impressed if you saw them on stage. They're not slick. They lay everything out there."

"But as musicians, they're just not the best—"

"If you want to be a classical performer, book Carnegie Hall. But if you want to be famous, stick with me."

Rad swirled an oyster in cocktail sauce and popped it into his mouth.

Josie squeezed a lemon wedge over her smoked trout. The juice squirted in her eye.

"I'll show you how to get to the top," Rad said, ignoring her squeal of pain. "You'll cut a new demo tape while you're here. Best technicians and backup musicians available. That's a promise. I'll get you some club dates and round up an agent for you. You'll have to work hard and steadily, of course, until your name gets around. Then, when the time is right, we'll cut an album."

Part of Josie's mind refused to believe this was happening, but a small, insistent voice within her exulted. Rad kept moving his chair closer to hers until their knees brushed. She could tell he wanted to touch her, that he needed her affection. She held herself stiffly so that they only touched by accident.

Rad told her about the other stars whose careers he'd helped build. He'd gotten one young woman a small singing role in a Broadway play. She had stolen first her scene, then the show. Another sang on television commercials to pay her rent while she performed in clubs downtown. But then Embassy released a single and it started getting airplay. It was discovered that she was photogenic. Her wide Slavic cheekbones were as much an asset as her voice.

"You're lucky that way, too," Rad said. "You're beautiful. Exotic looking, you know? And mysterious. Not really black, not really white. We'll make up a romantic story about your background. High-society father, island-native mother, something like that. How's it sound so far?''

Josie stared at him incredulously. ''Farfetched,'' she said flippantly, ignoring the irony of his suggestion.

''Would you like dessert?'' he asked her.

''No, thanks.''

''Then let's go back to the hotel.''

The limousine swept them back through the hot, dark streets. Rad held her hand, his thumb circling her knuckles like an insidious question. He wanted her, of course. The airplane and the flowers and the limousine and the singing had been meant to lead inevitably to this hushed ride up through the deserted night streets. New York oppressed her. The things she took for granted in the islands—the gentle air, the pure water, the palm trees, and the wild orchids—would perish under the weight of this harsh city sky in a day. Where were the stars? she wondered. On either side of the car, steep concrete walls soared upward and vanished in a banked, heavy grayness.

''Why so solemn, Josie? Is anything wrong?''

He was sensitive to her moods; she granted him that. He was not a monster, but he was not Prince Charming either. A man composed of slippery talk and trendy images rather than flesh and heart and blood, but still, no demon.

''I'm homesick, I guess.''

He put his arm around her thin shoulders and hugged her. She felt a stirring of feeling for him.

They pulled up in front of the Sherry Netherland. ''Let's have a drink. It'll make you feel better.'' The chauffeur opened the door, and Rad helped her out of the limousine. He held her arm, and she caught a glimpse of that same determined kindness he'd used when he pleaded with the spoiled musicians. Rad was used to getting his way, but with subtlety. And now he was going to finesse her.

Women in gleaming dresses and men in dark suits streamed past them. Josie cocked her head in the warm, pink light of the hotel's canopy. ''Rad, please forgive me,'' she said, knowing that she mustn't argue with him; he would only win. ''I'm not at my best; it's all happened too fast. Please understand. Even one drink wipes me out.''

She was afraid that if she said the word ''no,'' the city, the hotel, Rad, and all he had promised her might disappear and she would drop out of the dream like an abandoned, broken Cinderella.

He let her go when she promised to save the night after next for him. He had scheduled a long taping session for her that afternoon, and she would spend tomorrow rehearsing with a group of studio musicians. He was disappointed, but also slightly intrigued, when he learned she could not see him the next night.

"You tantalize me," he said, kissing her cheek as he left her at her door.

Josie poured a scalding hot bath and soaked in the heat and steam of the large tub. Some new kind of grime clung to her tawny skin, and it would not wash off. *If I pass for white, Francesca's world can be truly mine. There will be no difference between us at all.*

In the morning the bellboy woke her with flowers again, yellow roses this time. Josie sighed sadly as she added them to yesterday's bouquet. Rad's kindnesses were taking too much for granted. The roses, with their brightly unfolding petals, their promises and hopes, tugged at her conscience. They were expensive; they would cost her dearly.

The day was devoted to work. Rad did not appear, although the limousine did. The bored chauffeur under a navy cap avoided her eyes once more and drove her off without being told where to go. She saw him later, when the group broke for lunch, lounging beside the car, which seemed to take up most of the block. He pretended not to know her. Josie identified with him; like him she was now in Rad's employ, showing up at odd addresses on his orders. She knew that if she slept with Loitner without loving or wanting him, that listless, dead look would soon be in her eyes, too. The spiritless chauffeur managed to look as if he were part of the sidewalk.

The studio musicians were friendly. They all wanted to help her; they listened to the tape that had been sent to Rad and gave her advice, suggesting jazz and blues singers she should emulate, songs she should sing. These were real musicians, professionals who made a good living for doing session work. They helped her hone her delivery, and told her what clubs to visit in the city, whom to listen to. Josie could have talked shop to them forever. But at six she left them to prepare for the theater.

There were phone messages from Rad waiting for her at the

front desk, and in her tranquil room the roses had already grown blowsy. She dressed in one of her Venice dresses and swept up her hair. She had no jewelry, but she knew her looks were impressive enough to outshine any stone. Josie was pleased with herself, flushed with anticipation. She looked not just beautiful, but exciting, like the artist she always dreamed she'd become. She twisted one of the rosebuds into her hair as she swept it back in a soft braid. Nervous butterflies batted around in her stomach, and she toyed with the idea of taking one of the tranquilizers Lucas had tucked into her bag. Then she looked at the joy in her eyes. *I don't need it. I'm supposed to feel like this. It's just excitement!* Instinctively she knew she could too easily come to depend on the calm assurance the pills induced in her.

Chapter Eighteen

JOSIE RETURNED TO the theater district. By night this stretch of Broadway was transformed; it was exciting and strange. Fluorescent doorways of record shops swung wide and music blared into the streets. The lights over her head pounded red and orange. People flooded the streets: well-dressed theatergoers intent and single-minded, ignoring the men outside the pornographic theaters who hustled like carnival hawkers; winos crouched in the dusty concrete corners; teenagers bunched in front of the monitors that adorned the wide-mouthed movie theaters. The gaudy clash and grit of the district were foreign to Josie, who was used to the softer lures of the tropics, where the nightlife was mysterious and gentle, a kind of sophisticated child's play. But she found the theater on West Forty-sixth Street with no difficulty. The side street was awash in the light of its many theater marquees. She felt the palpable excitement of the crowds who swelled into their vestibules.

After she had picked up her ticket, an usher led her to her seat. At last she felt some of the magic and ceremony of New York in the elegantly adorned theater, as opulent as the Venetian palazzo, plush with red velvet and gilt scrollwork, and in the parade of beautifully dressed women on the arms of distinguished-looking men. Then the lights dimmed, and the crowd hushed.

Josie was the first to admit she was no theater critic, but it seemed to her that *Partial Eclipse* was a murder mystery without much mystery. It was clear from the moment Jack Westman appeared on stage, playing the new husband of a lovely, young heiress, that he would be made to look guilty, then somehow redeemed. But there was an almost unbearable excitement in his mere presence. Josie couldn't believe the man standing just a few feet above her was Jack. He looked so vivid in the stage light, his hair a shock of gold, his face ruddy from too much sun. He was thinner and gaunter than Josie remembered. The actress who played opposite him could not hold her own in his presence; she seemed to merge with the scenery. Finally the audience tired of the lopsided romance; one wanted only to know how Westman would extricate himself from a murder indictment. The one true surprise of the evening was his last-minute confession in the arms of the pretty girl.

The audience started gathering their coats around their shoulders almost before the last curtain fell, but Josie sat still, reluctant to leave. It seemed disloyal of the others to turn their attention away so abruptly, the play forgotten in the scramble for a restaurant, a taxi. Right now she believed the only reason she had come to New York was to see Jack Westman perform, to imagine herself reaching out and touching him. She forgot all about her own adventure: Rad and his limousine, the Sherry Netherland, the musicians, her tape—how did that compare with Westman? She was still the awestruck girl who had chanced upon him making love one hot afternoon in the children's nursery of the palazzo.

"Spending the night?" said one of the ushers dryly. "I should bring you a blanket and a pillow?"

Josie started up. "I'm sorry. You're probably waiting to close the place down."

"Naw. The actors are still backstage. No hurry. Just didn't want you to fall asleep there."

"Did you say," Josie said, scrambling after the stout woman in thick black shoes, "that the actors are still here?"

"Sure, they're all backstage, taking off their makeup. You can watch them come out, if you want. The stage door's right around the corner." She put her flashlight in her pocket and gave Josie an appraising glance. "First time in New York, honey?"

"Yes. This is my first play."

"Too bad," she said. "I don't want to imply you could have done better, but still—"

There was no point in continuing; Josie was gone.

In an alley beside the theater, Josie saw the plain gray doors that must lead backstage. They burst open and a girl in an old raincoat shot out. It wasn't until she had run out of the alley that Josie recognized the play's female lead. Other actors followed her in a similar rush. Washed of their makeup, they were blank and nondescript. They seemed wary of strangers lying in wait.

At last Jack stepped out into the alley. Josie screwed her courage up and stepped in the light, blocking his path. He put his head down, intending to barge past her.

"Jack," she said, reaching for his arm. "You remember me, Josie. Francesca's friend."

She couldn't believe she was touching him. His build was wiry, even slight, when she was this close. Most of his face was in shadow, but his strong chin was harshly outlined; she could see his emaciated jaw clench in surprise. He stopped short, nearly stumbling over her.

"Francesca?" He turned Josie toward the light so that he could see her face. "Josie! Is that you, really? What are you doing here in New York?"

"I came to cut a demo tape and sing backup vocals on an album."

"So you're a professional singer now. That's good news. Are you here alone?" he asked.

"Yes."

"The cast is running out to the closing-night party. This was our last performance. I've got to put in an appearance for form's sake. But afterward we ought to have a drink together, talk about old times. Can you meet me in, say, an hour?"

"Of course."

"Where are you staying?"

"At the Sherry Netherland."

"Then how about the bar? At eleven-thirty?"

"I'd love to, Jack. I'll be waiting for you."

They walked into the street. Jack hailed a cab for her. "Just tell me one thing," he said as he helped her in. "Is Francesca here in New York?"

"I'm afraid not," Josie said. Then sphinxlike, she smiled and gave the driver her address. He'd have to come to her hotel if he wanted to learn more about Francesca.

When Jack Westman walked into the subdued, elegant bar, all heads turned. From her small, dark corner table Josie saw him approach like a sun god. But when he stood before her, she saw he was tired and drawn, with new age lines in his face that his stage makeup had hidden. He leaned down and kissed her, and she smelled liquor on his breath. He sat down at her side, beckoned the waiter, and ordered a scotch for himself and a split of champagne for Josie.

"Well, I haven't heard a thing about you and Francesca since I read about Francesca's wedding in the newspapers." His voice was slightly slurred. "I was crushed."

"Oh, Jack, you were already married yourself."

"One word and I wouldn't have been. Well, enough of that. Is Francesca well?"

Josie was a little giddy. She knew she'd have to answer questions about Francesca, and decided to get it over with as quickly as possible. "Yes. She's become a businesswoman. Did you know that Carlo died? She turned her father's mansion in Nassau into a health spa. It's become a tremendous success."

"And her husband?"

The waiter brought them their drinks. "Yes. Michael Hillford. He's a sailor, the kind of guy who's better on sea than he is on land. But he's a devoted father."

"They have children?" Jack's face looked pained.

"One. A son, Christopher."

Jack took a long swallow of his drink. "Ah, we should drink a toast." He raised his glass to her. "Here's to your singing career, Josie. I'm afraid I was getting stale with that awful play you saw tonight. *Partial Eclipse*. It should have been a full eclipse. I wanted to do some live theater, and I owed the producer a favor. The reviews were disastrous. I've been slinking around with a hat pulled over my eyes." He laughed, and some fire came back into his blue eyes. "To quote one illustrious critic, 'Westman is stranded in the play like a beached whale gasping for air.' " Jack laughed so hard at this he ended up coughing helplessly. Josie looked on, embarrassed at this extreme reaction. Finally he continued. "I'm amazed we lasted for the full six weeks. I'll be glad to get out of town tomorrow. Meeting you tonight is the best thing that's happened to me since I came East."

She blushed with pleasure. "I don't believe that." The champagne made her a little woozy.

"Why? You know you're gorgeous and you've got a beautiful voice. You're going to be an enormous success, Josie, if you survive the sharks in the business."

"It's all been an adventure, but I'm afraid Rad is going to send me packing back to Nassau at any moment."

"'Who is Rad?"

"The record producer."

"Why? Why on earth would any self-respecting man send *you* packing?"

"Oh, because . . ." Josie hesitated. "Because he is self-respecting, and I may be about to hurt his pride."

Jack threw back his head and laughed. "I see. So he is on your case."

"I'm afraid so."

"Well, hold tight, Josie. Don't compromise. That's no way to do business. The bastard doesn't deserve you."

Josie could not suppress a giggle. "The thought of that little monster daring to . . . It's easy to laugh about it with you around. But I fear for my life after all his generosity."

Jack grinned broadly. "I'll save you. Just let me know if he makes a move, and I'll fight for your honor."

"What a relief." Josie laughed. "Where would I be without my honor?"

Jack became more serious. "I should introduce you to some of my influential friends in the music business. When you get a copy of that demo tape, send it to me. Better yet, why not come with me to California tomorrow? Then I can introduce you myself."

She gasped at the generosity of his offer. He bent closer to her, brushing against her slightly, as he detailed his travel plans, the time of his plane's departure, where she could meet him, as if it were already decided. "Have you got a pen? I don't want you to forget any of this." He wrote down his phone number on a cocktail napkin.

"I can't believe this is happening," she murmured. "I can't leave tomorrow. I have to finish thc album. But I'll come the day after."

"Promise? I've got to get you out of that slimy promoter's clutches." Then he quickly kissed her cheek.

"Where will I stay?"

"There's plenty of room for you in my house in Los Angeles. Have you heard of Benedict Canyon? It's on the side of a mountain overlooking the valley, high above Hollywood. You can stay there as long as you need to. I'll probably have to leave next week, but I'll lend you my BMW. You'll be all right."

"You'll leave?" Josie said wistfully. "I'll be left to rattle around your house all alone?"

"I'd do anything for a friend of Francesca's. I know you two were like sisters."

Josie's face fell. She drained her glass of champagne. So he wasn't interested in her at all. He merely wanted to keep a tie to Francesca.

"I had heard about Carlo Nordonia's death," he said. "Francesca must have been upset."

"I wasn't there when it happened." Josie twirled her glass, trying to think of a way to stop him from talking about Francesca.

"To be honest, I think Francesca's better off without her father standing over her, ordering her around. If it hadn't been for him, she and I would still be together," Jack said quietly. "But I must admit I came to the conclusion myself that I was too old for Francesca and she was better off without me."

Josie thought of the letter she had written and signed with Francesca's name. She swallowed down a lump of guilt. No need for Jack to know that she, not Carlo, had brought the end to that romance. "Jack," she said softly, making her voice sound sympathetic, "wouldn't you be better off if you just made up your mind to forget her?"

"I tried that."

"But you meet so many beautiful women."

He drained his glass and smiled at her. "I've never loved anyone except Francesca." Then he leaned toward her. "It doesn't stop me, though. I enjoy women, all kinds of women. Another drink?"

The waiter brought them another round. Josie and Jack sat shoulder to shoulder. Josie pressed her knee and thigh against his, and he returned the pressure. Summoning up her courage, she said, "I can't understand why she couldn't wait for you, Jack. I would have."

Her words hung between them for a moment, and then Jack slipped his arm around Josie's back, as if to protect her from her own will. "You were always sweet," he whispered, and pressed his lips against her hair.

But the slight caress felt more brotherly than romantic. She refused to let him brush away her feelings so easily. Smiling, she whispered in his ear, "I dare you to do that again."

"What, this?" And he kissed her forehead. She reached up and touched her lips to his earlobe.

As be began to kiss her, her eyes closed on the velvet, whiskey-tasting darkness. "You have the softest skin I've ever touched," he said. His hand brushed her hair out of her face and then he tilted her chin up to his and they kissed again.

Josie felt in some way that she had handed her life over to him in that moment. She knew that he read her desire in her eyes. They separated and he sipped his drink while she straightened her hair self-consciously. But there were only a couple of stragglers left at the bar at this late hour, with their backs turned, their attention on their cupped glasses.

"Somehow I don't want to leave you," said Jack.

"Please don't," she answered, bowing her head. It sounded in her own ears like a pledge.

"Such a beautiful girl, alone here in the city. I can't leave you."

"No, what would I do without you?" she said lightly, but meaning it.

They walked arm in arm to the elevator.

The yellow room opened before them like one of the roses, light and airy and sweet smelling. Josie felt whole suddenly, as she had in Nassau when Marianne was still alive, before they went to Venice, before she learned her true identity. Her own pride had cast her out of the estate into relative poverty. Now, on her own, she had earned once more a position equal to her sister's. She looked around the room, impressed with herself, as Jack must have been. He called room service for a bottle of champagne. Then he sat on the bed and pulled off his shoes.

She stood shyly at the end of the bed. Josie had never made love to a white man before; Lucas and Charles had been her only lovers. She wanted to tell Jack how she cared about him, how she had dreamed about him for years. But she knew it would be wrong. He might leave, afraid of hurting her the way Francesca had been hurt. So she decided she would merely do whatever he asked of her, and say nothing. Suddenly he reached out and pulled her toward him. He reached both hands up, cradling her head, pulling her lips down to his. In Jack's embrace she felt as if she'd at last recovered her rightful home. When he kissed her this time, entwining his arms around her back, there was no need to say anything. Her body spoke to him.

When the waiter knocked at the door with the bucket of champagne, the two separated. Josie went into the bathroom and slipped out of her clothes. She felt dizzy and her body was shaking. In the mirror her eyes shone with both fear and desire. She felt a sense of pleasurable defiance at the thought of what she was about to do. Deliberately taking her time, humming self-consciously so Jack could hear her, she sprayed cologne all over herself and rubbed the refreshing scent into her skin. Then she slipped into a pale pink peignoir and brushed her hair.

The door opened beneath her fingertips, onto the square, perfectly still, perfectly empty yellow room. "Jack?" No answer. She swirled in a panic. There was no sign of Jack anywhere; his shoes were gone and the watch he had so carefully unstrapped had disappeared from the bedstand. Only the opened but untouched bottle of champagne, its wrinkled foil still glittering in the bucket of water, proved that he had ever been there.

Josie poured herself a glass of wine. She turned out the lights and, going to the window, looked out at the magnificent view. She drank until her brain was too muddled to think and her body was too numb to ache. Then she swallowed one of the comforting pills that Lucas had tucked into her suitcase.

Jack Westman wouldn't call the next day or the day after that. If she followed him to California, he would treat her kindly as he had that evening, but he would never take her to bed because he would never see her as anything but Francesca Nordonia's friend.

Even through the buzz of wine and exhaustion, Josie felt the old anger with Francesca rise. Finally, she fell into a drugged, nightmare-riddled sleep.

Sunlight poured through the window as if to mock the darkness that fogged Josie's spirit. The wine and Lucas's pill had kept her imprisoned all night in a grotesque world peopled by caricatures of Jack Westman, Francesca, and Carlo Nordonia. Their monstrously distorted faces called her names. She still felt bruised and defeated.

The shower hadn't helped; neither had the coffee and scrambled eggs. Before her conscience could stop her, she stumbled into the bathroom and swallowed another pill. The good kind. The kind that made her happy. It wouldn't take long to work.

She was staring at the wilting yellow roses when the telephone shrilled. It had to be Jack. He would explain away his desertion. But it wasn't Jack; it was the chauffeur, waiting downstairs to drive her to the sound studio. She was late for her appointment with Rad Loitner.

Josie wordlessly put down the telephone. It was impossible that Jack had left New York without calling her. But if it was three o'clock, his plane must be high above Chicago right now. The night had meant nothing to him. His offer of help was only the babble of a man half-drunk who wanted to sweep a girl off her feet for the evening. When he left her, he ditched those promises and her with them. Josie realized all of this in one splitting minute, and it toppled her. She climbed back into the bed.

Endless minutes passed. With the shades drawn all she could sense of the passing time was an intensifying of the shadows; the room moved in an eclipse from gold to gray. The telephone rang again in the empty air.

"Josie, sweetheart, are you all right? I'm worried to death," Rad Loitner said in a rush. Josie could almost see him struggling to suppress his anger and project sympathy and concern instead. "We're all waiting here for you."

"I'm sorry, Rad, I don't feel very well."

"Should I send for a doctor?"

"No, no."

"What did you do to yourself last night?"

Josie wondered if he suspected drugs. "Nothing. I'll be all right."

"Look, this is the day you've been waiting for. Once you get to work, you'll start to feel better. My chauffeur is waiting for you at the hotel entrance. Come on over here and sing for us, sweetheart."

Josie swallowed down her revulsion. This was the day he would make his move, but she couldn't worry about that right now. The tape was important; she had spent most of the previous afternoon rehearsing for it, and she had to get through today's session somehow. When that was behind her, she'd worry about Rad Loitner. "I'll be right there. Sorry I'm late."

She hurried out of the hotel, glad for the glaring sunshine because it gave her an excuse to cover her red-rimmed eyes with dark glasses. The chauffeur put aside his *Daily News*, opened the door for her, then climbed behind the wheel and sped crosstown to the recording studio.

When Josie walked into the studio, Rad came toward her holding out both arms to embrace her. But she couldn't bear his kindness; she wanted no one to touch her now. She wrapped her depression around her body like a shield, so that his hands barely skimmed her arms as he hurried her into the glassed-in sound room to the microphone.

Josie sang with a new depth and an eerie beauty that she had not possessed before. The musicians moved quickly from one song to another. Behind the wall of glass, Rad's eyes gleamed as he monitored the controls.

Although Josie still felt terrible, she knew she had never sung better; she stood inside the wall of her grief as if encased in ice. Josie thought if she were in her right mind she would have known enough to be nervous, but in her distress nothing mattered to her, not even this chance to make her first professional recording. When Rad finally ended the session, she felt only a numb relief that she would soon be free of the producer's mute scrutiny; she could go back to the hotel and weep in private.

"Let's go out to dinner," Rad said, putting his arm around her shoulders. "I want to celebrate. That went so smoothly. I can't tell you how unusual that is."

"Rad, I really don't feel well. I think I'd better just go back to the hotel."

"What is it, honey?" He hugged her closer and pressed his lips to her hair.

Gently prying herself loose, she said, "Please understand," but before she could go on, he pulled her close and circled her with his arms.

"Don't push me away, Josie. Let me help you." His hands were everywhere, pressing into her spine, her ribs, the sides of her breasts. Rad was not very much taller than she was, but his hold was powerful.

"No." She pushed him away.

"Hey, Josie, it's *me,* Rad. Your friend."

"No," she nearly screamed.

"I like a girl with fight," Rad said, jerking her back to him and kissing her.

Josie bit him. When he yelped, furious, she sprang away. "Can't you tell I'm not interested?"

Rad held one hand over his mouth. He stared at her coldly, then examined his hand for blood. His lips were smeared with it. He slapped her hard with the blood-spattered hand and sent her spinning back against a wall. Momentarily stunned, she slumped forward, eyes shut, one hand holding her cheek where he'd hit her. He pushed her back against the wall

"Why the hell do you think I brought you to New York?"

His voice was hoarse with rage. "Do you think you deserve this . . . all this as a *gift?* I was wrong about you. You haven't got what it takes to make it. You're wasting my time. I think it's about time you went back where you came from. Don't you?" he said.

She stared at him levelly.

"Clear out by tomorrow," he said. Then he strode out of the studio, slamming the door behind him.

The only other person left in the room was the sound technician, who was bent over the control panel. His earphones were in place, but when he looked up, something in his eyes told Josie he had heard Rad's words.

Ashamed, she turned to leave, but he called to her.

"Miss Lapoiret, if you want a copy of that tape, it will be ready for you tomorrow."

She spun around. "Would you do that for me, really?"

"Well, I'm not going to throw it out. I might as well mix it for you. I'm going to bill Rad for the work in any case. But don't tell him I gave it to you."

She smiled at him. "Of course I won't. I'll never speak to him again."

"You can pick it up at one o'clock."

When Josie stepped out onto the street, the long curb was deserted. Even the chauffeur had abandoned her. She walked through the gritty streets to the hotel. No one stopped her at the desk when she picked up her key and asked for messages. The room was as she left it. But the breakfast tray was gone, and a maid had changed the sheets.

That night Josie took another sleeping pill. She needed to still the worries that raced around her head; she needed to forget. At dawn she woke to gray, ashen light, and hurriedly dressed. Rad Loitner's words echoed in her memory: "You haven't got what it takes . . ."

She wandered aimlessly through the crowded streets, not caring where her feet took her. At one o'clock, she picked up the demo tape, thanked the technician, and accepted his "Good luck" with a faint smile.

Then she checked out of the hotel and took a cab to the airport. The demons in her mind kept taunting her with the reminder that she had two chances to grab the gold ring, and both times she had fumbled and let it slip from her fingers. The first chance had been her appearance at Francesca's ball in Venice; the second was Rad Loitner's offer to get her started in New York. Twice she had watched that glittering prize spin away from her and fall to earth for someone else to pick up. Now she had been tossed off the carousel a second time. Once again Josie Lapoiret was being shipped back to Nassau. In a few hours she would be right back where she had started. Nowhere.

"Seen today's paper?" inquired the bartender as he flicked a dishtowel across the display of whiskey bottles.

"No," Michael said.

The bartender finished polishing a glass and dropped the newspaper on the shiny wooden bar. He left Michael alone with it. When Michael was in a bad mood, as now, he spread an aura of gloom around the dark room.

He scanned the paper while nursing his beer. It was not quite yet cocktail hour, but Michael had become less and less cautious about drinking in public. He felt especially defiant when his eye caught the front page headline. Francesca was tied up in a photography session with Allerby and the presence of the famous photographer had so impressed the island natives that the local newspaper had made it front-page news. "Allerby Chooses Countess Nordonia As Cover Girl" the article trumpeted, and went on to detail the successes of the spa and Francesca's latest coup. The famous photographer had chosen her to grace the cover of his new book on beauty. Francesca had briefly described the book to Michael as a good way to publicize the spa. But the article was more explicit. A collection of photographs of the most beautiful women in the world, accompanied with text on their beauty secrets, the book was destined to become a best-seller. It had been bought by book clubs around the world, and an enormous initial printing was planned. Francesca had been chosen to exemplify Allerby's ideal of beauty, of grace and health and vitality. Michael ran his eye down the list of the world's most beautiful movie stars and a prima ballerina whom he had met at the spa. He put down the paper and motioned the bartender to bring him another drink.

"Bushmills straight."

"It must be quite a thrill, having all those beautiful women under one roof," the bartender said lightly as he set down the new glass.

"I really wouldn't know. Nothing's left for me to do there,

now the place is fully renovated. My beautiful wife runs the spa with the help of the duchess and the doctor. They don't need me underfoot anymore.''

The bartender moved down the bar to another customer and Michael looked at his watch. He was waiting for someone. But she was always late, and he was accustomed to waiting.

Finally the door swung open. A young woman with a mane of fleecy black hair held back by a red hair band stood in the doorway. She wore a pale green shift. The bartender looked up, then lowered his eyes quickly.

''Nicole,'' Michael said in a glad voice.

She smiled a shy and pretty smile, and shifted the large leather bag on her shoulder. She swung gracefully up on the stool beside Michael.

''Will you have a drink?'' Michael asked. He looked deeply pleased, relaxed. It was the same expression he wore when he took his first drink of the afternoon. ''No, better yet, let's leave.''

''I want a drink today. Something with lots of ice, like a rum coke.''

The bartender heard this without being directly told, and slipped a slice of lime into a tall glass of ice as he poured a jigger of rum.

''It's getting late. I thought you would never come.''

The amber-skinned woman looked about twenty-five or -six. Her smooth face had an uncanny glow, as if she had been spiritually graced. The bartender had seen the look before on the faces of island girls who had managed to ally themselves with the wealthier natives. The look usually didn't last.

''Can we wait a few minutes? I have a friend who wants to meet you.''

The door swung open and Josie stood, adjusting her eyes to the dark. The bartender's face brightened, and broke into a smile.

''Josie!'' Nicole said. ''We've been waiting for you. This is Michael Hillford—you remember, your old friend Francesca's husband, the one I was telling you about.''

This introduction seemed extraneous. Josie was using her pretty grin on Michael. She offered him her hand to shake, and he raised it to his lips. He was feeling the whiskey.

''Have a drink?'' he said.

''Just ginger ale, Harry,'' she said to the bartender.

"Oh, surely something stronger than that," Michael urged her.

"No, I've got to perform later. I never drink when I have to sing."

Michael pulled up another stool. "Josie. So you're the one she always talks about."

"Yes. Francesca and I grew up together."

Michael was at a loss for words. He suddenly saw an unanticipated problem materialize. "But you haven't spoken in more than a year, have you?"

"No. I'm afraid we parted company after our trip to Venice. I know all about her, of course," Josie said, indicating the newspaper. "Francesca's become quite a star, hasn't she?" Her voice was deliberately light, without a trace of jealousy.

Michael seemed reassured to hear that Josie was not resentful of his wife.

"Do you come to this club often?" Michael asked.

"Yes," Josie said.

"She's just being modest," Nicole said. "She sings here several nights a week. You'd have heard of her by now if you didn't always leave so early."

"Ah, yes, Francesca told me you have a terrific voice."

Nicole laughed. "You should have Michael manage you instead of that Lucas. Stay away from that guy, Josie. He's poison. All this success as a musician has gone to his head. Drugs are glamorous to him. Lucas feels that no self-respecting musician should be without them. He was busted selling dust to some tourists. He's on probation."

"I have only one question," Michael said. "What's dust?"

"Angel dust," Josie said. "It's not fine, like cocaine. Lucas had better drugs in his inventory. Of course, I wasn't interested in them," she added quickly, and then changed the subject. "Francesca's become quite famous, hasn't she? You must be very proud."

"Would you like me to tell her that I met you?"

"No," Josie said, the vivacity dying in her eyes. "I think not."

"I could bring her to hear you sing," Michael offered.

"No, you mustn't." Josie was adamant.

"Do you mind if I come myself, then?"

"I think I'd like that." She smiled softly.

She was still smiling that cryptic smile when Nicole and

Michael left together. The bartender caught Josie's eye in the mirror over the bar. She looked like a cat, he thought, the cat that swallowed the canary.

Francesca was soaking in the bathtub when Michael arrived home. The photography sessions had exhausted her, but she had luxuriated in the photographer's praise. She had not thought about the power of her looks since the night of her ball at the Palazzo Nordonia, when she won the admiration of her father's guests. That wave of attention and the passion she had inspired in Jack Westman had turned her life upside down. It was only now, when her home and her family were secure, that she dared lend an ear to flattery again. Beautiful! The word still astonished her. Her mother had been a great beauty, but Allerby said she surpassed Susannah.

"Bathing beauty," said Michael, reading her thoughts as he lounged in the door.

"Hello, darling." Francesca reached for a towel. "How was your day?"

Michael said nothing, but Francesca noticed the grim set of his mouth.

"We looked for you, Michael. Allerby wanted to talk to you about renting a boat. He'd like to take a short vacation while he's here. But no one had seen you at the office for days."

Michael's voice was colorless. "That's because I haven't been there."

"Michael, I wasn't criticizing you. I'm merely trying to help."

"Merely trying to help. Ah, yes, you're always trying to help everyone, aren't you, darling? Where would any of us be without Lyford Cay's own little social worker? 'The Angel of Lyford Rose,' that's how Allerby should caption his photograph."

"You've been drinking."

"And why not? What harm does it do?" Michael felt his face redden with anger, and knew that his tongue was dangerously loose.

"You promised me you wouldn't drink anymore, Michael."

"Yes, but you made promises, too, didn't you?" he said sarcastically.

"Yes. And I kept them." She pulled on a thick terrycloth robe and began to brush her hair.

"Don't get pious, Francesca. How much of your precious time do you give to this so-called marriage?"

She looked at him mutely. The bitterness in his voice frightened her.

"How much time, Francesca? Five minutes now and then when you're not busy with your rich guests."

Francesca tried to repress the spark of anger that crackled through her. "At least you always know where I am, Michael. While you're out enjoying yourself in some bar, I'm here at home with the guests or with your son."

Michael's dark glare made her stop brushing her hair and study the pain that flashed in his eyes.

"*My* son?" His voice was low, and his expression was cynical. "He's not my son. I've known that all along."

Francesca was dumbstruck.

"You married me because you were carrying another man's child."

She shook her head. "I wanted to marry you, Michael. I love you; you know that." She turned her back on him, unable to bear the accusation in his eyes. "And you know I've never been unfaithful to you. The thought has never even occurred to me." She covered her face with her hands, feeling the security of her happy home slipping out of her grasp. "I'm sorry for what I did, Michael. I wanted to tell you, but I knew you'd leave me if you found out about the baby."

Michael was silent. When she turned around, she saw that he was looking at her fixedly.

"Edward Patiné is in love with you, Francesca."

She shook her head slowly. "I know."

"Is he Christopher's father?"

Francesca went to Michael. "No, he isn't. I didn't meet Edward until my father got sick. And I've never even kissed him, much less slept with him." She took his hands and held them tightly. "Christopher's father is an American. I met him in Venice. He swept me off my feet, I guess, and I had a brief affair with him. Michael, I'll never stop being sorry I let it happen. I haven't seen him in two years. I didn't mean—"

Michael had pulled away from her and was leaning against the sink with his back to her. Now he made a sobbing noise in his throat and, turning, sent everything on the basin's edge crashing to the floor. A hand mirror shattered into a million pieces. "Damn you! *Damn everything,*" he shouted as he strode out of the room.

In the morning Michael had still not come home. Maybe, this time, given the seriousness of their row, he might not be back for days. But then he would circle back to her in longing and shame, like a lost little boy. All right, admit it, Francesca accused herself, Michael was right, you have been unfaithful. Not with your body, but your heart. Michael read your heart like an X-ray. If only his business had not been a failure, she thought, he wouldn't have so much trouble accepting her success. She would have to spend more time with him; he was right about that. Her family had to come before her work, and Michael was her family. She had lost her parents, her lover, and her dearest friend. She could not lose her husband, too.

Chapter Nineteen

JOSIE SAT AT the bar in the cool nightclub, sipping ginger ale. She looked at her watch and frowned slightly. Michael was late; maybe he'd decided not to come today. Still she doubted that. He'd stopped in nearly every afternoon since her return to Nassau almost four months ago. She'd come to rely on her daily conversations with him, just as she knew he counted on her to cheer him up as he enjoyed his two glasses of scotch.

Josie didn't show her unhappiness; she had found a cure for it—Lucas's pills, the ones he was too smart to take himself, the ones that had made him so rich. They came in bright, primary colors—blue and yellow and red, like children's toys. She believed, when she was high, that she was a great singer. She was Billie Holiday or Mabel Mercer. The audience seemed to fall for this charade; her amphetamine-induced intensity impressed them. It was almost as good as inspiration, and in her frame of mind it was all she could hope for. It was how she forgot the past and how she faced the future. Sometimes her true emotions cut through the fog with a clarity that stunned her, but whenever she beheld her own anger and desperation, shining fierce as a blade, she called for Lucas to save her with his dulling medicine.

Josie had sought Michael out deliberately. Michael knew she was alienated from Francesca, but never asked her why. Like Nicole, he kept her a secret from his wife. He liked leading a double life. He solaced Josie in his obtuse way for her loss of Jack. Michael's charm, his deep, joking voice and flashing eyes, stimulated her. They were friends, bonded by a need more important to them than sex. Michael drifted in and out of his relationship with Nicole, but he came to the barstool next to Josie every day. For her part, Josie wanted nothing to do with men physically. She still lived with Lucas, but they rarely made love. She depended on him; his pills were now essential. They worked together. The audiences came to hear her. Lucas seemed to accept this, perhaps because he kept her tethered to him so closely. No one else could have accompanied her so well. He seemed content to coast to fame on her success.

But Lucas couldn't understand her the way someone from Francesca's world could. Michael had suffered, she guessed, in a way she knew well. She had often been tempted to mention Jack Westman to him. They had both been used by the actor, though Michael might not know it. She wanted an ally against Francesca and Jack, against the harm that had been done to her. But some strange reluctance always kept the words back.

Michael came in, heaving his weight across the room. Strong boned and large chested, he looked taller than he was. Josie thought how handsome he was, how naive.

"There you are, lass. You got a start on me."

"You'll soon catch up," Josie said.

He ordered a Guinness, and they began another of their rambling, companionable conversations. "Well, I let the office go today," he said with mock resignation. He had talked for weeks of taking this step.

"No, Michael. That means the end of your business."

"Yes. But I couldn't see the point of it anymore, keeping up the pretense. The customers weren't exactly beating the doors down."

"How are Edward and Francesca doing? Any more excitement out there on the cay?"

"Oh, they wouldn't tell me. I'd be the last to know, wouldn't I?"

She heard the dark undertone of his meaning.

"Strange, I can't picture Francesca with a serious man like Edward. Movie stars are more her sort." She paused. Michael was looking down into his ale, but she knew he was listening. "She and Jack Westman were inseparable."

"Who?" Michael said intently.

"You must have seen Jack Westman's films, Michael. They're popular even in Ireland."

"I have. How did she know him?"

"She met him in Venice, the summer before she married you. That's why her wedding came as such a surprise. They acted like they'd invented love."

"Really," said Michael dryly. His face looked stormy.

"But he jilted her and married someone else, that actress Nadia Baldini. I wonder what ever became of her."

"Fascinating," said Michael sarcastically. "Tell me, was this a serious affair?"

"That's why Carlo sent us back to Nassau. It had all gotten out of hand. Jack was so much older, and Francesca was completely inexperienced. She was heartbroken."

Michael drained his ale, then suddenly got up and flung some change down. "I've got to go, lass. Sing well." He left the bar.

Josie made it through the first act without a pill. But she couldn't trust her performance. She felt flat now, her exultation turned to guilt. One of Lucas's infallible red angels swept her up above the room, and in a blaze of energy she sang her way through her second performance without a thought about Francesca or Michael. In the heat of her performance, she seemed to feel Jack Westman's presence, and she struggled to concentrate enough passion into her voice to make her audience see him there beside her as well.

At midnight Michael drove along the twisting road out to the cay, singing softly to himself one of the rollicking gallows songs of his childhood.

Little did my mother know,
When first she cradled me,
That I'd go be a roving lad,
And hang on the gallows tree.

But he couldn't remember all the words. The car glided along like a boat through the pines. A wind was coming up, he could smell it. Dark clouds billowed across the sky. Hail to thee, Jack Westman, he thought. I've found out the father of my wife's son at last.

There's some come here to see me hang,
And some to steal my fiddle,
But ere they'll play a tune on her,
I'll break her through the middle.

He's a wee blond lad, Jack, you'd be proud, he thought. Then everything went wrong. The car slipped out of the road and into a palm tree, smooth as oil. Michael saw it all happen as if he sat safely in a movie theater watching an accident on screen. The hood loomed up in his face and the windshield cracked ominously all the way across. He stared into its smashed pattern, the fractures bright with the headlights, a web of opaque fissures. After a moment he realized he'd missed one of the last curves, and a palm tree had stopped the Mercedes cold. Luckily he'd been driving slowly. But then he'd always had the luck of the devil. Michael wiggled his toes. All there. He heaved himself out of the car.

Poor thing, it was wrecked. Michael laughed wickedly. What did it matter? Francesca would buy him another.

"Hold on boy," he said under his breath. "Better sober up."

Then he stumbled the quarter mile down to Lyford Rose.

The house was dark at this hour. Michael walked down the graveled drive as quietly as possible. Mustn't scandalize the rich ladies, he thought to himself. When he was well past it, he caught a glimpse of the beach house through the screen of trees. It was dark as a well. Francesca must have given up on him. When he let himself in the front door, it occurred to him that he desperately needed another drink. He was far too sober to face his wife, who was sure to wake up the moment he opened the bedroom door. But as he walked through the still house, some struggle in his soul was won. Instead of opening the liquor cabinet, he stripped off his clothes. A swim in the ocean would clear his mind. When he got back, he'd call the police and report the car accident. Francesca wouldn't like it, but there was no point in making a mistake look worse by trying to avoid it.

He let himself out the screen doors in the living room and ran down to the placid sea. The sandy beach slapped at his soles. He dived into the water as if into a second skin, a new life. Out here, the knot of pain in his mind dissolved. The water was the temperature of his blood. He let a wave wash over his head; he was still deliciously drunk. Far out at sea he could see where the high wind hit the water, making it rough. He would have to keep close to shore, and swim in soon. He faced land. To the west, palms bent in the wind, but the trees around the beach house stood motionless in the silvery light from the moon. The waves began to mount. One swept over his head, and he gulped an unpleasant draught of salt water.

When his head rose clear of the wave, a strange light struck the corner of his eye. At first he thought a streak of lightning had crooked itself over the roof of the beach house. He sped for shore, realizing that the storm was about to strike in earnest. But when he looked again as he turned his head for air, the light was still there, forking into the night. Lurid orange flames began to lick a path over the black roof. Then suddenly the house seemed to explode with light like a blazing chandelier.

Michael swam for shore as if for his life. Then he ran, in panic, across the sand, his one thought now to save Francesca and Christopher.

A figure streaked through the light, as if thrown away from the house. As Michael pounded closer, he saw with astonishment that a woman was crouched on the lawn around the deep shadows at the side of the beach house. His mind registered her presence only briefly before he burst through the front door into the burning crucible of the house. He didn't pause to question the safety of the stairwell; miraculously it held beneath his feet.

Upstairs Francesca pounded at her door. When Michael had not arrived home, she had guessed that he was off getting drunk in some bar. Afraid of his black alcoholic moods, she had locked her door. When she awakened with the stench of smoke in her nostrils, she had tried to turn on the lights, but they wouldn't work. With trembling fingers she had searched the floor in the dark for the key. It must have fallen when she first rattled the door; she couldn't find it. The smoke was too thick to breathe. She began to scream. Christopher was trapped in the nursery downstairs.

Michael smashed through the door with his shoulder, and grabbed her out of the room. Francesca cried out in relief and anguish, "*Christopher!*" They plummeted together down the stairs. Rafters fell around them. One struck Francesca across the face and shoulders, but she barely felt it as she struggled to reach her child. She saw that Michael had taken the brunt of the collapsing beam across his own back. But he, too, stumbled forward. The door to Christopher's nursery was blocked by burning beams.

"You run around the outside and try to get in through the door. I'll try this way," Michael shouted.

Francesca ran from the house and gulped the sweet night air. Her lungs were burning, her eyes seared. The house was an inferno now. She ran around the side to the nursery's sliding glass doors. They were locked. She tried to break the plate glass with her fist, but no matter how she pounded, the panes barely shook. Then she saw Michael moving like an enormous black bear in the room, a few yards away from Christopher's bed. Suddenly he lit up: his hair and beard were on fire, and she could see by the lurid light that half his entire face was a bloody pulp. He moved slowly, cramped to one side. A beam must have fallen on him. As she watched helplessly, he fell. Then he managed to pull himself to his knees, as she screamed at him to rise. He deliberately rolled his burning head and shoulder on the rug, then rose again, this time to his feet. She could see the fire eat his shirt to cinders. He reached into the crib and the enormous effort it took him to lift the crying boy made Francesca understand how badly hurt he was.

Then he was stepping toward her. At last he slid the glass door open. For one second Francesca thought they all three would survive this holocaust, but as the awful stench of the burning room and flesh hit her, the oxygen hit Michael, and he ignited in a burst of light. He threw Christopher into the air as his lungs released a howl. She threw her body over Christopher's whimpering form as Michael turned black before her eyes.

Chapter Twenty

FRANCESCA FELT SHE could not allow herself to let go. She had a son who was severely traumatized; she could not afford to cower before the mirror forever. She was a patient in her own clinic now, and her wounds were beyond even Edward's ability to heal. Every day when she rose late in the room in the ward for the seriously hurt patients, she would stare at herself in the mirror and shudder. The beam that had fallen across her face had left a jagged purple welt, like an accusing finger, seamed on the left side of her face. One profile still shone smoothly, radiant with youth and beauty; but the other profile was hideous and secretive, as scathingly ugly as the dark side of the moon.

With her face carefully bandaged, Francesca emerged from the hospital to walk the well-manicured ground of Lyford Rose. In the evening light the grass looked almost blue. Her mother's flowers gleamed in profusion from the borders and the woods beyond the house. One corner of the property was curiously empty and remote looking, and she stared at it as if she didn't know it. She walked closer, and the ruins, like an enormous charred skeleton, came into view. There was nothing left of the upper story; it had collapsed into the first floor. Francesca felt a premonition that she ought not come closer. There had been evidence from the beginning that it was arson. Who hated them enough to do such a thing? She should have been afraid to walk the grounds alone; instead she felt immune to any future harm as long as Christopher was guarded. She approached the house, or what was left of it.

The fire's damage was haphazard, having struck the house like lightning. The ruin was shaped like a crazy, charred tree, some branches snapped in fury, others left intact. Here and there a wall stood eerily upright like a stage prop, holding nothing, stained with water. The wallpaper was scorched, unfurling like delicate cigarette paper. Francesca realized that when she had remembered the fire, or dreamed it, it had appeared out of nowhere like a curiously cleansing force, and she had imagined the beach house devoured as if in payment for some dreadful sin. But the punishment had not wiped out the evidence. No, it had merely revealed it to the rain and the spoiling sun. All her belongings were tossed about, burnt, then waterlogged, by a giant, callous hand. Nothing had escaped the brand of fire. Nothing had been spared the flood. She saw furniture charred and mildewed, her blackened clothes and papers limp with water. Most awful was the black hole that had been the nursery. She picked up a board and saw a border of hearts and flowers. Michael had painted them on the cradle he had carved for the baby when they were first married. The thick ash came off on her hands and stuck to them like oil.

Francesca recoiled from the stench of the wreckage, felt something warn her away. It was as if this were no longer her property. The very ground seemed to belong to unseen presences, like a graveyard. She was trespassing. She had to leave.

But the haunted feeling didn't leave Francesca. Nearly every night she dreamed of her mother, and in sleep the estate was as it had been before the fire. Though Francesca had lived with Marianne and Josie in the beach house, they did not appear in the dreams, but she sensed their calming presence. In the dream, a beautiful woman would approach the house from the sea. As she drew closer her dark red hair unfurled in the wind, and Francesca knew suddenly the stranger was her mother. But instead of entering the house, she peered through the glass doors, looking for someone. When her eyes discovered Francesca's they filmed with fear, and the woman turned away. Francesca ran toward her, pummeled her fists against the glass. But she could not escape. The glass mirrored back her face, with its hideous welt like a flash of bad lightning.

Francesca would struggle awake, drenched in sweat. For a few wide-eyed but terrified moments, the lightning played over her body and she sensed the fire at her back still, the flames climbing her thighs, her spine. They receded into the darkness of her dream, and the oppressive white dullness of another day spread before her. Francesca knew what the dreams meant. They were records of her guilt for destroying

Michael. The fire began the first night Michael proposed to her, when she did not tell him the truth. Or it began even earlier, in Jack's arms. She saw now that every step she had taken had only brought her closer to the burning house. Michael, always at her side, was the one who had been sacrificed to pay for her wrongs.

She was as guilty as her mother, she thought. No, her mother was innocent. She assumed her mother's blame as well, and imagined Susannah had abandoned her for her indiscretions.

Edward tried to draw Francesca out, but she could no longer talk about her feelings. The litany of losses and abandonment shamed her. Her mother, Jack, Michael and Josie, all seemed to have deliberately turned away. Francesca feared that if she told Edward about her disturbing dreams, he, too, would perceive the flaws in her character, now inscribed in the jagged scar on her face, and leave her.

Edward concluded that Francesca's lingering depression was due to her ugly scar. He decided to take the risk of performing the delicate facial grafts, in hope that whatever improvement in her appearance he could bring about would help her mood to lift. But he was careful not to build up her hopes, and Francesca hardly expected a miracle. She submitted herself to the anesthesia as if grateful for oblivion, not really believing the operation would do her any good. The scar was a part of her now, the manifestation of her guilt. What good would it do to remove it, if beneath it she remained the same woman? When she woke with a start hours later, swaddled once more in bandages, she called out Michael's name. In the lingering shadows of the dream he had seemed, for a moment, still alive. Days later, when Edward removed the bandages, he seemed subdued. Francesca could tell from the way he stared at her scar, with a kind of piercing intellectual curiosity, that it had defeated his art. The wound could not be healed by man.

Francesca received the news in the hospital that Lady Jane had confessed to setting the fire and was being held in custody. Francesca's feeling of foreboding lifted. The mystery was solved and she almost had a feeling of inevitability and relief. That explained why Joe, the gardener, had seen someone before Francesca trying the glass doors to the nursery. Lady Jane had meant to save Christopher, and—the car being out of the garage—she assumed Michael was out. It was only Francesca she meant to kill.

That funeral bell that had been tolling in Francesca's head since Michael's burial stopped at last. The chapter of her life that had been her youth closed. If she could escape her memories and her bitterness, she would be free.

To recuperate, Francesca stayed in a large cottage on the edge of the grounds, far removed from the other guest cottages and screened from view by a small orchard of orange trees. Christopher had his own small bedroom and used the living room as his playroom. Watching over him as he built castles of wooden blocks and played with his miniature trains somehow eased the knots in Francesca's chest. He was so innocent, so pure, she hoped his simple joy would cure her troubled soul. But after she tucked him into his little bed and pulled up the guardrail, the nights were black and lonely. She could not concentrate on the files of spa records her secretary brought her. She'd sign documents and try to indicate correspondence into a tape recorder, but her mind seemed to wander off into some dazed, still point outside the dark windows. She didn't have the heart to send out her usual warm notes to the clients, and she approved plans for publicity and renovation without reading them through. Once or twice it occurred to her that her contribution was inadequate now, and she knew Edward must be disappointed in the way her attention to detail continued to lag. But she never seemed to recover her strength. There was no one on staff capable of shouldering her responsibility.

One day Apollonie burst in on her in a vivacious mood. "Have you seen the papers, Francesca? No, of course not. Here you are alone as usual, without the faintest idea even of what day it is."

Francesca looked up from the couch, where she sat placidly embroidering a pillow cover. Christopher ran trains over her feet. Apollonie's eyes flinched away slightly from the sight of her vivid red scar. Edward had managed to diminish it to a single welted line that stretched along her cheekbone from the top of her ear down across her cheek to its hollow, like a whiplash. But it had seared the flesh too deeply where the golden pigment of her skin prevented it from congealing into a white line. Edward had warned Francesca that the scar was likely to look like a raw wound. *Quel dommage,* the duchess thought. Francesca had a beautiful, fine-boned face. Her clear right profile was like one of Giotto's angels. But the left profile was a shock. No wonder Francesca hid herself away. The welt of her scar struck terror, like the bell of a leper.

"The trial is over. Lady Jane has been sentenced," Apollonie said.

"The poor woman," Francesca said. "How she must be suffering, knowing she killed Michael."

Apollonie looked at Francesca incredulously. Francesca's detachment frightened her. "How can you be so compassionate, considering what she meant to do! And I must say, the judge was also merciful. But what can one hope for, considering she had the best lawyers in Nassau?"

"What was the sentence?"

"In exchange for her confession, the court accepted her plea of not guilty by reason of insanity."

"But she *was* insane, Apollonie. That's fair. She must have been insane."

Francesca knew, underneath, that she and Lady Jane were linked in the crime they had both survived. When she imagined Lady Jane filling the kettle with kerosene and dripping a path around the house, it was as if she herself clumsily prepared a bed for the fire.

"Well, I suppose. After all, there is her cockeyed story about her daughter having been killed in your father's house. I heard she raved about it for days, talked of nothing else when the police questioned her. But no memory of setting the fire? That is very strange. And very convenient."

"What will happen to her now?"

"Francesca, it would be far more natural for you to blame her. Releasing your anger would help you to cope with your loss," Apollonie suggested gently. "Only a miracle saved your son, only Michael's sacrifice. But to answer your question, Lady Jane has nothing to fear from justice. What will happen is she'll probably spend the next seven years in a sanitorium in England. Less, if she suddenly comes to her senses and convinces the doctors she's sane again. Apparently convincing them isn't difficult."

"You don't think she was out of her mind to do that?" Francesca asked incredulously.

"I don't know. All I know is a fine man, a good father, was killed. That woman is far too dangerous to be allowed to go free in seven years. If she can prove she's recovered her sanity, she may be released even sooner. Just look at what she's done to you!'' Apollonie said passionately.

Francesca shook her head. ''All I know is that there's been enough suffering. Lady Jane loved Michael, I know that now. She resented losing him to me. She resented me for everything. For everything my mother ever did.''

''Your mother was a magnificent woman, Francesca. She inspired envy in some lesser souls. I believe envy drove Lady Jane to the verge of madness. But that doesn't excuse her.''

Francesca bent her head back over her embroidery. Apollonie's vehemence exhausted her. For some reason she felt tears welling in her eyes. Perhaps it was the talk of her mother. Once Francesca imagined she could trace her mother's features in her own. That was all she had left of her. But now she bore her no resemblance.

''Francesca, darling, why must I get angry with what's happened for you? You should be outraged at the way the police and the newspapers have covered up for that evil woman! What will become of you here, surrounded by these memories? Won't you consider coming to France with me in the fall? The change of scene is bound to do you good.''

''Are you really leaving so soon?''

''Yes, I've had the letter from Mario. He's coming here to visit, and he insists on dragging me back with him!''

Francesca smiled. That explained Apollonie's sudden exuberance. Mario, Apollonie's fair-weather lover. ''Coming here! Aren't you a little wary of Mario? After all, he's hurt you so many times.''

''He says he can't wait much longer. He's arriving next week! What will I do? I can't just leave you here, darling, suffering like this under the weight of all that's happened. You've simply got to come with me back to France. For my sake, Francesca. Otherwise I'll do nothing but worry about you.''

Francesca, even in her depression, was not immune to Apollonie's charm. ''But who will take care of the spa?''

''Edward, of course. Until you've recovered you can't really shoulder your old responsibilities. Sometimes I think we just get in Edward's way, as it is.''

Francesca looked unconvinced. ''It's not just the spa, Apollonie. Much as I appreciate your concern, there are important reasons why I must say no. Christopher has been through a terrible shock, losing his father and his home. I have no way of knowing how much of that night he remembers. But I worry I might make him more insecure by taking him to a new country.''

''Nonsense. The child echoes your moods faithfully. When you're happy, he's happy. When you're upset and depressed, he feels your sadness. The best thing you can do for that poor boy is recover your peace of mind. You need to get away. It's morbid, this lingering over the tragedy.'' Apollonie spoke with an urgent conviction that almost made Francesca feel ashamed.

''I'll consider it, Apollonie.''

''I'm sorry if I was too outspoken. You understand, I'm concerned about you. Who else do you have to watch over you?''

Francesca smiled. ''You're right. If it weren't for you and Edward, I'd be completely alone.''

''Then think of me as your mother,'' Apollonie said gaily, ''and follow my advice.''

The older woman left Francesca with a kiss on her forehead, sure that she had made some progress in convincing the girl to come home with her to France. But Francesca's smile faded as soon as Apollonie stepped out the door. She didn't have the will to save herself. She knew that if she went to Paris, she would be just as unhappy there as she was now in Lyford Cay. And it was impossible for her to think of Apollonie as her mother, not when Susannah visited her every night in her dreams. She longed to follow her mother into the substanceless blue of her dream world, to travel into blind night.

Francesca was startled out of her gloomy reverie by a rustling near the house. She had the distinct impression that someone hovered close to her, watching her. Christopher had fallen asleep on the rug. She looked down at his corn silk hair and large eyelids, a fragile violet color, and shuddered at the thought that some malevolent, unseen presence threatened him. Then, out of the corner of her eye, she caught a movement in the window. She rose and opened the door.

''Who's there? Who is it?'' she called, stepping out into the garden.

The bushes of flowers were silent.

''I know someone's there. Come out!''

There was a sound behind her. Francesca whirled, and gasped. A dark face was pressed up against the window inside the house, looking out at her. Whoever it was was in there with Christopher. Francesca swung the door open and nearly leaped inside.

A young woman cowered back against the couch. Her hands were trembling and her dark eyes were hollow with fear. The child hadn't wakened.

"Josie," breathed Francesca. And then she said, with no hint of the kindness she intended, "What are you doing here?"

She saw that Josie had grown achingly thin. The small bones in her heart-shaped face were sharply exposed. And there was a darkening in her expression; her green eyes were now shot with red, not gold light.

"I shouldn't have come," Josie said, her hushed voice broken.

Francesca was moved by her frailness. "You shouldn't have left me. Why did you go?"

Josie seemed not to have heard her. Her lips trembled. "Francesca, the police came to see me. About Michael. I told them I never saw him after he left the bar that last night. Do you believe me?"

"Of course I believe you. I never thought you were involved."

"Because sometimes I see the fire. I see the house on fire, and it's everywhere."

"Josie, please sit down. I'll get you some tea."

Josie smiled suddenly. It was a shy smile, with only a shadow of her old warmth and none of the pleasure that used to beam from her face. Francesca thought that the girl had aged.

"I'm so pleased you're here," she continued wondrously. "So much has happened to us both. Come out to the kitchen with me."

Josie followed her warily into the kitchen. Its white counters were cluttered with untouched cooking equipment.

"These days," Francesca said, "I rarely cook, and then only for Christopher."

"Is that your son?" Josie asked.

"Yes."

"Michael told me about him. He was terribly proud."

Francesca put water on the stove to boil. She turned to face Josie. "How did you know Michael?"

"One day he happened to come to the bar where I sang." She bit her lip. "But it was more than that, too. I knew he was your husband from the start. He just wanted someone to drink with, but I wanted something else."

Francesca looked at Josie with deepening misgivings. She thought she didn't really want to hear this confession. She wanted Josie back the way she was before that summer in Venice. But this Josie, with dilated pupils and wandering, unhappy speech, was a stranger.

"But I wouldn't have started that fire," she suddenly said.

"I know that. Of course you wouldn't have."

Josie laughed harshly. It sounded almost evil. "How would you know that, *p'tite soeur?* What do you think you know?"

"Josie, what are you talking about?" In the stark kitchen light Josie's features were almost transparent. She seemed to have starved herself to the point of insanity, but she looked too weak to be harmful.

"I know that you don't mean half the things you say," Francesca said in a barely audible voice.

"I did set that fire. I surely did. It was me."

"How could it be? They already convicted the woman who did it. Lady Jane. Haven't you seen the papers?"

"I heard that," Josie said scornfully, "but I did it. I did it with obeah. I put a curse on you, Francesca."

"A curse? But why?" Francesca moaned.

"Because you're my sister."

"But you were always a sister to me, Josie. That's why it hurt me so much when I lost you."

Josie looked at Francesca for a long, silent moment. "You don't understand. Carlo Nordonia was my father, too, Francesca. I found out about that while I was in Venice. When I came home, my mother told me it was true." She laughed shakily. "All those years I thought my father was dead, but he wasn't. He was just ashamed of me."

Francesca's heart lurched. *Josie was her sister? Her father's daughter?* No wonder the bond between them had been so strong that they could read each other's minds.

Francesca thought of her father. She could see him standing before her, proud, dignified, aloof. His pride had kept Francesca an ocean away from him for most of his life. It had prevented him from acknowledging Josie as his daughter. What else had it done? she wondered. Had her mother also been a victim of Carlo Nordonia's pride?

"That's why I read the curse," Josie was saying. "Even after Jack left you, you went right on being happy. You met

Michael, you were happily married, and you had a baby and a successful business and your picture in all the magazines. Everything was so easy for you. Everyone always loved you."

Francesca had begun to absorb what Josie was telling her. "No. Nothing was easy. I'd say it was a mixed blessing, my parents' love. You had more love from Marianne than I ever had from them. And God knows what I've inherited from my mother. Sometimes I think I have the touch of death. I'm more to blame for Michael's death than you are, surely. Did you love Michael?" Francesca asked Josie.

Josie shook her head. "No. I hardly knew him. Did you?"

"That isn't fair." Francesca felt tears in her eyes. "I was never fair to Michael."

"Nothing is fair," Josie said bitterly.

Just then Christopher stumbled into the kitchen, his hair in his eyes. "Mommy, who's here?" he asked, burying his head in her skirt. Then he looked up.

"Christopher, this is my friend, Josie. Can you shake hands?"

Francesca was struck by the look of astonishment on Josie's face as she shook the little boy's hand. The child was Jack Westman in miniature, but his coloring was so like Francesca's that everyone thought he resembled her. She had long ago stopped worrying that anyone would ever make the connection to the child's real father, but the recognition in Josie's face alarmed her.

Christopher twisted his head into her skirt again. Francesca laughed and handed Josie a cup of tea. Josie reached for it hungrily, and as Francesca knelt to pick up Christopher, she quickly slipped a pill into her mouth. Francesca glimpsed the furtive movement as she rose with the heavy weight of her son pressed against her chest.

"Josie grew up with me. We used to play together when we were as small as you are now."

"I'm not small," Christopher said shyly but firmly.

"You're enormous," Josie said. "Can I try to lift you?" She held out her arms for the boy, but they sank under his weight. How frail Josie was! Vivacious and good-natured, she had always exuded a solid air of well-being. But all that was gone now.

"Run out into the living room and play with your trains

now, Christopher,'' Francesca said. But the reluctant child was curious about his mother's visitor. He dawdled. ''Scoot!'' Francesca said. When at last he was gone, she turned to Josie. ''Are you feeling well?''

''I feel fine.''

''I saw you take a pill,'' Francesca said gently.

''A cold. Antihistamines.''

The two young women stood in the kitchen sipping their tea awkwardly. The old rapport they once shared was gone. Francesca thought that as much as she had suffered, the mental anguish that wracked Josie must be as severe. The trouble in her evasive eyes was as blatant as the red scar on Francesca's cheek.

''May I come and hear you sing?''

Josie smiled sincerely, but it was a smile that didn't touch her eyes. ''I'd like that. I only feel right when I sing. And the club is so fine. It's the best 'over the hill.' ''

She began to describe the band and her life to Francesca, who noticed that Josie's mood had strangely changed. She laughed rapidly now, a nervous, acid laugh that spilled out of her mouth mechanically. She seemed even more tense. ''And Lucas—did I tell you about Lucas?''

''Yes, you just told me.''

''What was I saying?''

''That you live in a beautiful old house near the Seasaw Club.''

''That's true.'' The artificial laughter again. ''My mind wanders sometimes.''

Francesca was hardly reassured. The pupils of Josie's eyes were widely dilated and her brow was rimmed with tiny drops of sweat.

''Francesca, I'm so hyper, do you think I could have a drink?''

''Of course, if you need to relax it will do you more good than tea.'' But even as she opened the small liquor cabinet, Francesca felt she ought not to offer her one. ''I'm afraid I don't have much. Just some wine.''

''Look here,'' Josie said, sorting through the bottles. She pulled out an unopened bottle of Bushmills. ''Michael's?''

''No, but that was his drink. Someone must have brought it over from the main house.''

Josie broke the stamp with her fingernail and poured the

whiskey into a shot glass. Francesca watched her in fascination. She had never seen Josie drink.

"Have a glass?" Josie asked.

Francesca shook her head. "No, you go ahead, though."

Josie hardly needed to be urged. She drank it neat and then measured herself another one with the absorbed speed of a serious drinker. "Here's to sisters," she said.

"Mommy, the train all gone." Christopher stood in the doorway, his face smudged with dirt. Francesca realized she'd left him alone for too long.

"Let's find it then," she said brightly, walking into the living room. She helped Christopher line up his train tracks while thinking rapidly about her unexpected guest. She wanted Josie to stay here with her and Christopher. She did not intend to lose her again. But it was becoming clear that Josie had problems that Francesca had never experienced. She might need professional help. Francesca was afraid she'd get drunk in her kitchen.

There was a loud crash, the sound of breaking glass. Francesca rushed back into the kitchen. Josie was sprawled on the floor, her eyes wide with fright.

"What happened?" Francesca exclaimed. "Are you all right?" She knelt and braced Josie's head with her hand.

Josie's eyes rolled wildly. "Will you forgive me? I never dreamed the curse would work. Oh, Francesca, whatever you do, don't tell Marianne. She warned me. She took me away because she knew I was bad. She saw the way I felt after Venice. She warned me against the obeah."

Francesca helped the raving girl to her feet and led her into the bedroom. She helped her onto one of the beds, and then called Edward.

"I have a friend here who's in trouble," Francesca said quickly. "She's mixed up with drugs. I'm afraid it might be quite dangerous. Can you come now?"

"No, but I'll send an ambulance and we'll treat her immediately. Who is it?"

"It's Josie Lapoiret, my . . ." Francesca's mouth refused to form the word "sister." "My old friend," she finished.

By the time the ambulance came, Francesca had summoned her maid from the mansion to take Christopher away from the upsetting scene. She rode with Josie to the clinic and explained to the doctor in the emergency room that the young woman had taken a combination of alcohol and drugs.

"I want to treat her at Lyford Rose, if that's possible," the doctor suggested. "But what Miss Lapoiret needs now is rest. We'll be in touch in the morning."

She walked back to the estate. It was a clear blue evening. The sea was a deep purple color that Michael had loved. When it was calm as a sheet of dark mirror, he loved to strip off his clothes and swim out half a mile and just float there, looking back at the palm-rimmed shore silhouetted against the golden sunset. Francesca passed the main house before she knew it, and then the newer cabins. The gardens were beautiful in the evening, the flowers closed but just barely fragrant. She strode on as if in a trance to the bluff where the beach house had stood above the shore.

Christopher, whose love for her gave her courage, could not shield her from the ruins of her mind. What is there left of all that glory? she thought. Of the men she had loved, nothing. Of her parents, only broken dreams. First Susannah had died. Then Carlo had bequeathed the legacy of his bastard daughter. Marianne, a better, more constant parent, had died far away from her. But Josie, no matter how shattered, had returned. Francesca felt calm as she had not since the fire. She would not be so lonely now.

Josie—her sister! No wonder Josie had grown so estranged from her in Venice. Everything that had been given to her, the ball, her title, the palazzo, by rights belonged to Josie, the elder daughter. Instead she'd been sent downstairs with the servants and thrown the consolation of voice lessons. So Josie had grown to hate her. The very property I stand on now, Francesca thought, is hers. So much for the famous Nordonia family pride. She wondered if Carlo had loved Marianne, and what he had felt for her own mother. He had scorned Josie. "One *never* eats with them," Francesca remembered him saying. Now must she share everything with her? Francesca had grown too used to being the center of attention, the important one. *Dear God, I don't know if I have the strength to accept this gift. I love her, but nothing is the way I wanted.*

She walked into the rubble of the beach house. As fallen beams blocked her path, she realized that she was standing at the foot of the charred staircase. Half of the twisted stairs still climbed above her head into nowhere. This was where the beam had fallen that had left her scarred and killed Michael. A vine from the overgrown garden had entered a blackened window frame next to the stair, and a Lyford rose, luminous in the blue shadows, bloomed among the leaves. Francesca peered at it. The velvet of one of its petals was smudged with soot. She knelt to blow the ash off, but her breath was of little use. Then she tried to brush it off, but the petal came free in her fingers.

For a long moment she stared at it in the darkening light. Then she crushed it in her hand. Although she dropped the bloom in the rubble, hours later she could still smell its fragrant oil on her palm.

PART THREE

Paris

1973–1974

Chapter Twenty-one

FRANCESCA SAT IN Apollonie De Tions's garden outside Paris and opened the letter from Edward. She skimmed it quickly for news of the spa, but as usual Edward only briefly described the business affairs and the well-being of the guests, and spent most of the letter encouraging Francesca to carry on in spite of her disfiguring scar. "Sometimes I fear you don't realize how beautiful you still are, Francesca," he concluded. Francesca crumpled the letter in her lap. If there were any difficulties at Lyford Rose, there was no doubt Edward—kind as he was—would keep them to himself. His selflessness unnerved her. How vain and self-pitying she was, allowing her problems to ruin the beauty of the day.

From where she sat on a stone bench carved in the shape of a lion, Francesca could look out through a rose arbor onto a broad valley of fields of grain. Bees clambered noisily in the border of lavender and pansies at her feet, and swooped above the pool of overblown yellow tulips across the slate walk. It was late in the spring, and the wall of rosebushes had opened in an ecstatic burst of scarlet. Apollonie's extensive garden had been restored to its eighteenth-century splendor with all the botanist's art she had at her command. The flagstone walks circling baroque statuary had been designed for lovers, and legend had it that here Marie Antoinette dressed as a shepherdess, seduced a flock of lovers. Francesca wondered if she would ever have enough confidence to take a lover again.

Across the garden Josie exulted in the warm sunlight. Francesca had brought her to Apollonie's château, hoping the change would do them both good. Josie had spent several weeks in Edward's clinic, freeing herself from her dependence on amphetamines. But as Josie emerged from her physical addiction with a renewed vigor and determination to develop her singing career, Francesca's unhappiness lingered.

Apollonie had planned a party for this evening, and Francesca dreaded the ordeal.

For the thousandth time Francesca asked herself why she found it impossible to introduce Josie to people as her sister. Was the problem rooted in something as simple as snobbery, or had she still not forgiven her for telling her father (*their* father, she reminded herself) where to find Jack and her that fateful day? She shook her head silently. Carlo had coerced Josie into telling him; of that she was certain. And not for a minute did she believe that Josie's voodoo nonsense had caused Michael's death.

Then why, *why* couldn't she say the words? It should have been so easy: "This is my sister, Josie Lapoiret."

But the words wouldn't come. Not with Christopher or with Apollonie and Edward. And tonight, when she introduced Josie to Apollonie's guests, she would again feel the guilt rush over her at the omission.

And again Josie would keep silent as Francesca repeated the sins of her father. How long would it be before Josie became thoroughly disgusted with the charade and turned away for good?

Francesca closed her eyes against the ugly thought that followed: Josie had become an emotional burden on her. Too heavy a burden in addition to the others she'd had to bear. She knew in her heart that she would be relieved if Josie just disappeared from her life. Eyes closed, she added another layer of self-hatred to the weight she carried around in her mind.

She knew she should go inside and get ready for the party, but the thought of facing Apollonie's guests, and probably more than a few photographers, made her weak in the knees. Tonight, for the first time since the fire, the world at large would see her scarred face. No makeup could conceal the mark; she felt it would be pathetic even to try to cover it up. And the thought of all those people staring at her in horror and shock made Francesca's stomach turn over. She would put off getting ready for another hour or so.

She looked up at the classical facade of the eighteenth-century château. It had a noble restraint and simplicity her father would have admired. Giant Corinthian columns drew the tall bay windows of the two stories together into a single serene unit. The golden limestone building faced and dominated a broad terrace, which sloped gently down to the vast garden's marble fountain. When the sun set in its niche among the low hills, the tall windows became fiery screens, and the finely fluted columns came alive in delicate rhythms. But for all its outward restraint, the rooms within blazed with ornament. Fabulous murals of mythical trysts in elaborate gold tracery spanned the high ceilings above the paneled walls. The arching drama created the illusion of some godly descent from heaven. The opulent chandeliers spun patterns of wavering light on the mirrored and reflecting windows. The large marble-floored rooms were scarcely warmed by their vast baroque fireplaces, but the firelight sent patterns of sparkling light over the gilded furniture. This beautiful stage, set for love, seemed to mock Francesca. Every mirror gave her pain, until at last she fled outdoors to the mute garden, which never echoed her flawed face.

Apollonie had prepared endlessly for the weekend's house party. Tonight guests were coming from all over Europe, and a dozen or so would stay over for the long drive to the car races in Monte Carlo on Sunday.

Francesca guessed the party was actually an elaborate excuse for the Duchess Apollonie de Tions to show off her current beau to society. Mario had been staying at the château off and on for a month while he prepared for the annual car race. He had shown no real interest in the party this evening, and last night he had abruptly announced his early departure for Monte Carlo. Apollonie claimed his indifference arose from his need to practice driving the course. He had not won the trophy in several years, and he hoped to make a comeback. No doubt most of the guests tonight would understand. But Francesca guessed at another reason.

Mario was a tall, blond man of mixed Austrian and Italian ancestry. Although he was in his forties—several years older than the other men Apollonie had loved—his handsome face was unlined. He seemed to have inherited nothing from his aristocratic family except expensive tastes and insufferable pretensions, and he seemed to have no ambition whatsoever beyond racing automobiles. His coldness repelled Francesca. He held himself aloof from everyone except the duchess, and his attentions to her, Francesca had noticed, were studied rather than impulsive. He was being careful to play the part of the devoted lover, but there was no spark of love in his eyes when Apollonie came into a room. Francesca suspected that his sudden attraction to her friend had much to do with her celebrity and her wealth.

Francesca had kept silent, of course. Apollonie could take care of herself. She had cheerfully financed his new racing car and seemed unperturbed by his refusal to attend her party. "But, darling," she had said, "there will be dozens of men at my little gala. Piles of them. We'll be able to take our pick. You wait and see."

Francesca smiled and shook her head at her friend's increasingly cavalier attitude toward love. She herself would never be able to take things so lightly—if, indeed, Apollonie's lightheartedness was more than a pose. She sighed heavily and got up. It was time to prepare for the party.

The excruciating cocktail hour and interminable dinner were over. Francesca hovered near the edge of the crowd, eager to hear Josie perform but feeling an almost desperate need to be away from the curious eyes of the partygoers. As Apollonie's special guest, she had been subjected to the scrutiny of far too many people already; she wanted nothing more at the moment than to be swallowed up by the gleaming marble floor and hidden forever from the pitying eyes of strangers. Another few steps backward took her quietly out of sight of everyone but Apollonie's servants, all of whom had grown used to her during her stay at the château.

Only when Josie began to sing did Francesca forget about herself for a few moments. Along with the rest of the audience, she felt herself being drawn to the eerie vulnerability of the young woman who stood by the piano and pulled the crowd into her spell.

Josie's exotic beauty and the sensuality of her voice galvanized the party guests, as the rich tones filled the rococo music room of the château. Her body was at one with the music; it seemed she was the music. The applause at the end of the song startled her back to herself, and she smiled radiantly. She followed the heartbreaking ballad with a joyous Caribbean nonsense song, taking the guests by surprise. They noisily demanded to hear another.

The rapport Josie built with the audience was palpable back to the farthest corner, where Francesca stood. The sound of her rich, happy laughter reminded Francesca of her own enchantment at her ball almost five years ago. Only now Josie was the center of attention, a newly discovered marvel, and Francesca was the one who lurked on the fringes of the party. As Josie launched into her last encore, Francesca discreetly fled the room.

Silently she made her way out into the deserted garden, where she sank down on a stone bench away from the spill of light from the windows. She had just seated herself, however, when a group of chattering guests burst out of the house and headed toward her. Francesca watched them apprehensively, willing them away from her. She breathed a sigh of relief when most of them walked straight toward the rose arbor without noticing her. Only two men lagged behind, talking together privately. After a moment, they sat on a bench to Francesca's left, showing no sign of having seen her.

One of the men was speaking in a light, somewhat smug voice. His round face, caught in a fall of light from the French doors, could have taken a place among the cupids that winked slyly down from the frescoes on the ballroom ceiling. Nearly bald, he assumed a proprietary air toward the tall, studious young man who sat next to him.

Though she tried to ignore the two men, Francesca could not help overhearing their conversation. The older man was talking about his new novel. Francesca recognized its title. She had heard about the book at Lyford Rose. One of the guests had praised it and had mentioned that the author frequently visited Lyford Cay. But Francesca could not remember his name.

The man's voice droned on in an amusing, if rather sharp-tongued, recital of gossip about various guests at the party, and Francesca's mind wandered away from the conversation. She smiled as she thought about Christopher, asleep now in a quiet room high in the thick-walled château.

". . . the daughter of the Count and Countess Nordonia," she heard the balding man say. "Surely you must have heard of the notorious Susannah! Apparently her poor child, Francesca, has had as tragic a life as she did."

"Converse, don't be absurd," the younger man said good-naturedly. "You're the one who chases after European nobility. I wouldn't know a count if I woke up next to one." He sighed with affected boredom.

Converse Archer? As the well-known name came back to her, Francesca felt a paralyzing chill creep over her body. What kind of a surprise was she in for? she wondered. Still another vicious lie about her mother?

"The Countess was an American. A fabulous equestrienne, quite well known for her horsemanship in both America and Europe, in fact." Archer cleared his throat and went on with his tale. "There were extraordinary rumors about her death. Of course, I was one of the last to see her alive."

Francesca stared at the ground. She could feel her face redden painfully.

The French doors flew open again, and a noisy group of guests burst out into the garden. Catching sight of Josie among them, Francesca sank back deeper into the shadows. She didn't want to be discovered now, just as the writer had begun to speak about her mother.

"Some people thought she killed her lover, a woman named Sybilla Hillford," Archer said, letting his voice linger over the words.

"Converse, you're teasing," the younger man said petulantly. "Either shut up or get on with it. No more of these enticing morsels of ancient gossip."

Josie sailed past Francesca, absorbed in conversation with the handsome Arab prince Francesca had met earlier. Smooth as oil, he had intimidated Francesca with his strong aura of sexuality, but Josie seemed more than a little interested. Clinging flirtatiously to his arm, she passed without glancing away from the prince's darkly attractive face.

Relieved, Francesca strained to hear the conversation about her mother above the chattering of the other guests in the garden.

1955

ALTHOUGH SUSANNAH WAS several years older than Sybilla Hillford, it was clear to a sophisticated observer that the younger of the two was the aggressor, and far from inexperienced, while Susannah was like a child caught in a storm, longing to run for cover. It was fascinating to watch them in public, dissembling as best they could.

Soon after they arrived in Venice, the young women invited Converse Archer to tea. Converse walked into the palazzo with a sense of awe.

With impeccable taste, Susannah had restored the palace to

its Renaissance splendor, and the palace almost overshadowed her, all velvet and astonishing artwork. Archer was shown into a paneled library decorated with tapestries of unicorns and medieval horoscopes. Sybilla sat crouched in one of the enormous carved armchairs.

"Converse, I've invited you here for a reason," Sybilla said in her lively way. "Oh, would you like some tea?"

"I'd love some," he said, intrigued by her brazenness.

"I've just heard from New York that my paintings have been accepted by one of the top galleries. I've been trying to persuade Susannah what a boon that will be. I hope the two of us can live off my work soon."

Susannah put down her cup; her face was unearthly pale. Her attire, a sober gray jumper with a white blouse that buttoned high up to her chin. Her dark red hair was gathered into a chignon at the nape of her neck. "Sybilla, do we have to discuss this now? I'm not questioning your success. I know what this step means, and how important it is for your success."

Converse shot Susannah a look of sympathy. Now he understood everything. Amazingly, Sybilla thought she could support Susannah in New York on the sale of her art. It was a fantastic notion, but it was obvious she had invited Converse here to bolster her case. He tried to think up a tactful escape as he sat there, beneath one of Titian's darkest, most intriguing oils, *The Flaying*.

"My dear," he said amiably, patting Sybilla's strong hand, "it's wonderful news. You have a fabulous talent, and I know you'll be very successful."

"That isn't enough," Sybilla said matter-of-factly, as Converse marveled at her boldness. She was too young to understand exactly what a coup she had made, landing a show at a gallery at the age of twenty-four.

"It is indeed enough," Converse said softly. "For the time being at least, I'd say you're going to have your hands full."

Sybilla gave a short, stark laugh. "Please, Converse, tell her what a good life we'll have in New York." Her eyes were fixed on Susannah. "Carlo will let you have Francesca. He's got to, you're her mother and children that age belong with their mothers."

Susannah looked unconvinced—and embarrassed.

"You haven't even tried to reason with Carlo, Susannah," Sybilla chastised her.

Converse could tell Susannah longed for him to leave, that

she hated this exposure of her problems. Converse took the cue.

"Susannah, I have to go. I trust I'll see you at my ball this weekend. But, on second thought, I wonder if I might have a brief word with Sybilla alone. Just some grandfatherly advice, you understand."

Relieved that he was going to talk some sense into Sybilla, Susannah rose, said good-bye, and left the room.

"Do you know this painting, Sybilla?" he said casually when they were alone. "It's one of Titian's most remarkable works, but it's not as well known as his happier subjects."

"No," she said curtly, resentful of his condescension.

"It's quite odd, isn't it, the way the audience of forest animals is smiling at the sight of the satyr flayed alive, hanging by his heels? It's a scene of unbelievable cruelty. Titian even put himself among them. I have my own theory about it."

Converse paused, waiting for encouragement, but Sybilla looked at him impatiently.

"According to myth, Minerva dropped the flute on the forest floor, where the satyr found it. He ran through the forest piping away on this instrument of the gods until he had perfected his art, and then challenged Apollo to a contest. Imagine the hubris!"

Sybilla looked on stonily.

"To think that he could play more beautifully than the sun god. Apollo won, of course. This is a portrait of the punishment that followed the debacle. Now, why are they smiling to see this suffering?"

Sybilla looked back up at the dark painting. The gold-burnished satyr hung from a leafy tree out of which an audience of wood creatures peeped with enchanted smiles while the god carefully tore his hairy skin. "It's horrible," she said. "Titian was a sadist."

"Oh, no. I think the painting interests us because of the truth it reveals. Apollo isn't just punishing the satyr. He's teaching him the secret of immortality. Remember, satyrs are half-god, half-beast, angels in animal skin. Apollo is releasing him from that animal skin, and his cries are probably inhumanly beautiful. Watchers hear the music Marsyas has at last learned to make, and that's why they smile so dreamily, as if listening to one of the great composers."

"Converse, what is the point of this story?"

"The point, my dear, is one every artist must learn. There is no great, passionate revelation in art that has not first been scored on the human skin."

Sybilla was silent for a moment.

"There is no way to avoid suffering, but the artist makes something wonderful out of it," Converse said gently. "He moves us with what he has learned from his bruising encounter with the gods."

"So you want me to go to New York alone, too?"

"Sybilla, look around you. This is Susannah's home. She created it out of love for her family. What can replace this, and the people it was made for?"

Pride leaped into Sybilla's eyes. "Love?" she said. "Don't you understand what Susannah and I have found?"

Converse thought that he did understand, and so he remained silent.

"We could have a good life in New York. I'll find a studio to work in, but she can have an apartment on Fifth Avenue if she wants one. Francesca can go to the best schools. No one will notice two women living together, no one will look at us askance. In a crowd we'll have privacy. I'll become a success. I practically am already. Money will never be a problem."

"Your paintings will have to sell like Rembrandts to pay for that dream, I'm afraid."

Sybilla was silent for a moment. "I don't need money," she said. "If worse comes to worst, Susannah can always get it from her family. Converse, I can't succeed without her. I've only been painting so well since we've been together. She helps me discipline myself. I'm not capable of happiness, let alone painting, without her. Life after Susannah—I can't imagine the drabness. I'd rather be dead."

Converse looked at her sadly. Perhaps it did her good to confess her love. Usually he envied youth, but now he was glad that he had survived the tumultuous passions of his own early years, which were practically just as miserable. "Sybilla, you may not believe this now, but you'll love again. You will." He rose to leave. "We're deluded when we think we've fallen in love with the most perfect person in all the world, when we exalt a lover's virtues and beauties and vow we cannot live without them. The Greek philosophers understood that the object of our affection had nothing to do with it. Love descends like a sickness, and under its spell we exaggerate our lover's attributes out of all proportion, until the sickness is cured. Then our reason returns and we can go on enjoying life.''

''I know all about the Greek philosophers,'' Sybilla said cynically. ''They're the ones who believed it was impossible to love a woman at all.''

She rose and walked with him down the gleaming marble corridor. They paused in the vestibule while he put on his hat.

''I'm glad you came, Converse,'' she said, her tone patronizing. She often sounded like a much older woman, an effect of her headstrong arrogance.

Converse looked back. The new portrait of Susannah in a bottle-green velvet gown dominated the wide foyer, a luminous beauty suspended just slightly above his head, impossible to forget. It occurred to him that Sybilla had always gotten what she wanted, and done as she damn well pleased. What a brutal discovery she was in for.

But while Susannah and Sybilla agonized over their future together, their indulgence became legendary. Scarcely a day went by without some gossip about the two young lovers from Nassau who traveled through the Venice social whirl like linked comets. On a whim Susannah had her hair cut short like Sybilla's, and the next night Sybilla appeared at Harry's Bar with dark auburn tresses exactly the same shade as Susannah's.

Sybilla had never made much of an attempt to hide her love for the older woman, and now she seemed to fling it defiantly in everyone's face. And Susannah, too, admitted finally her own passion. Her eyes were fixed on Sybilla even in mixed company, and she tenderly touched her on the slightest pretext. As rumor quickly flared into scandal, Sybilla thrived on all of it.

Converse realized she'd gone too far the night of his ball, although at first everyone found the impulsive couple amusing and daring. They arrived, arm in arm, in long-sleeved sequined sheaths on one of those heady Adriatic spring nights when all the romance of Venice gathers in the mysterious air. Most of the other guests had already run the gauntlet of paparazzi up the broad marble stairs leading to the shining Gritti Palace Hotel. As Susannah and Sybilla paraded through the phalanx of photographers, Converse peered down at them from his vantage point in a lounge above the ballroom. He realized he should have hurried downstairs to greet them, but something in their walk arrested him. The two women had their arms entwined around each other's backs. Sybilla's face emerged first from the shadows, and he caught the defiant possessiveness in her eyes. Poor, black-sheathed girl, with her short crown of dyed red hair. She still could not match Susannah's beauty. The countess's sheath, in contrast, was pure, gleaming white. Even without her beautiful auburn hair, she was easily the most striking woman here at the ball tonight. He left his perch and strolled downstairs through clusters of black-and-white-clad guests to play the host for the lovers.

"Countess! Lady Sybilla!" he cried, reaching for their hands. First he bent over Susannah's, then kissed Sybilla's. "At last the ball can begin!"

"I hope we're not terribly late," Susannah murmured.

"I see you've transformed this place. The hotel was always magnificent, but now it dazzles," Sybilla said, looking around at the silver trees festooned with roses. "And everyone has obeyed your instructions and come in black and white, except us."

"You're very naughty, you two. Still, the dresses are beautiful. I recognize Renata's artistry in that stunning line."

Sybilla had a wild look in her eye, and Converse remembered wondering if she'd relapsed and started taking drugs again. She'd been waiting for him to comment on their dresses, and now she rose triumphantly to her cue.

Converse followed them to the ballroom. A few of the guests were dancing slowly to the band music, but most were gathered in knots around the edges of the room, greeting old friends and gossiping. The two women pulled sequined masks over their eyes. They looked like negative and positive images of the same woman. When Sybilla swept Susannah into her arms just within the doorway, he bit his tongue. Susannah seemed shocked at first, but then she looked into Sybilla's eyes and her lips softened into a smile. They went waltzing around the room with a sensuous slowness, smiling at one another like moony adolescents under the spell of first love. Converse watched as heads turned toward the couple in surprise.

"Who are they?" he heard someone say.

With their arms locked around one another in a close embrace, the two women were indeed wearing both black and white; they looked like a pair of happy Siamese twins, beautiful, red-headed freaks. He laughed, and everyone else laughed with him. Whatever the Countess Nordonia did was bound to be spectacular. But there was no harm in it. She could even give scandal a good name.

Strichos, the shipping magnate, strolled over to him. He had broken with his current mistress, and tonight he was here alone. "What are they doing, Converse?" he asked in his thick accent. His brow furrowed. "Women dancing with women?" He shrugged as if to indicate the end of the world.

"It's nothing, Ari. Next week half the women in Venice will have red hair and a female lover. A fad, that's all."

"That's what I mean," he sighed. "That countess, so beautiful. To think of the waste. A tragedy."

Converse smiled as if it were all a joke and joined his other guests. But there was no avoiding the sensation the countess and her young lover made. With her flamboyant, provocative manners, Sybilla didn't make it any easier. She insisted on dancing with Susannah dance after dance, long past midnight, and when the older woman, who grew more anxious and reserved as the hours passed, withdrew at last, Sybilla followed her out onto the hotel balcony. They'd been drinking heavily, and Converse—who could not help but be aware of their movements, for they trailed a wake of tension—followed discreetly. He didn't know what caused his premonition of trouble, unless perhaps it was the strain that now tightened in Susannah's face.

Converse almost stumbled over them, but they were too preoccupied with one another to notice him. He slipped back into the brightly lit room unseen. He did not want them to think he was following them. The two women were silhouetted against the balcony balustrade. Sybilla's form merged with the night, but Susannah in her sheath of white sequins glowed brighter than the moon. At last he knew whom she reminded him of: Diana the huntress, the strong-armed beauty who lived in the forest and whose emblem was the moon. It was not really fashionable to be so classically, vividly strong, not at all the current ideal of womanhood. Not, that is, until Susannah made it fashionable. No wonder she had fallen in love with this impetuous bohemian, this aristocratic rebel. Sybilla, in her dedication to her art, was alone among women Susannah's equal. The girl was even less afraid than Susannah of embarrassing convention. Did Susannah feel so much tenderness toward her because Sybilla reminded her of the self she had suppressed when she became a countess?

Now Susannah was flicking open the Nordonia crest of the

ring on her right hand and raising the ring to Sybilla's face. Converse understood: cocaine. Sybilla inhaled deeply from her ring, and almost immediately she looked more relaxed and happy. But a fury had risen in Sybilla.

"I won't let you leave," she said in her deep voice, and grabbed Susannah by the shoulders.

Converse stepped back farther into shadow. As he watched, Sybilla twisted Susannah beneath her, bending her over the railing. The two women were almost the same height. Susannah had the strong muscles of a horsewoman, but Sybilla's will was stronger, and she quickly mastered Susannah's vainly flailing arms. Then she began to kiss Susannah on the mouth, her black-clad body sliding over Susannah's with the rhythm of pouring oil. Susannah relaxed into the deep kiss, but suddenly her body contracted in a spasm of pain, and Converse heard her stifled scream. She had lost her balance. Converse was frozen where he stood; his mind had already measured the distance to the edge of the balcony, and calculated the fraction by which he would miss saving her from the fall. But Susannah saved herself. One of her hands caught at the railing as she sank backwards, and by tremendous effort she pulled herself level again. Sybilla did not reach out a hand to help. Instead she watched, arms folded severely across her black chest, in defiance or triumph, Converse couldn't tell.

"I lost my balance! You could have killed me!" Susannah said, trying to restrain herself from yelling, from attracting attention. Her lips were bright red. A few drops of blood spilled onto her white dress. She raised a hand to her face. "Look what you've done to me. Why did you kiss me like that?"

Sybilla said nothing.

"Why?" Susannah insisted in a low voice. "You frightened me!"

Sybilla spoke at last. "I meant to," she said.

ARCHER FELL SILENT, remembering the party nearly eighteen years ago, and the silence lasted so long that his companion finally prompted him. "Well, Converse? Surely there's more to this tale."

Converse Archer nodded slowly. ''I wasn't present for the last act, of course. Nobody was, except those two women, so no one really knows exactly what happened. All we heard was that Sybilla Hillford died that same night in the Palazzo Nordonia, with only Susannah present. Died of an aneurism, the newspapers said.'' He laughed quietly. ''No one believed that, of course, but I suppose it saved the Nordonia and Hillford families the embarrassment of an inquest. Poor, poor things. Poor sad little Sybilla with her vast talent and her twisted mind. And poor Susannah with her charm and her confused love for her husband and her daughter.''

''What happened to her? She went free, I assume, since the death was attributed to natural causes.''

Archer nodded. ''Yes, she went free. But it wasn't long afterward that we heard she'd been killed in a riding accident. Somewhere in the mountains, as I recall.''

''God, Converse, what a terrible story! Damn it! You've sobered me up completely, drained me of my party spirit entirely!''

Francesca jumped up from the garden beneath and ran into the house. The impassioned murals flickered past her, their bright colors a streaming blur, as Francesca hurried through the château, hoping to reach her bedroom without having to speak to anyone. Her own scarred reflection kept pace with her as she passed the mirrored walls on one of the hallways, and Francesca felt as if she'd been caught in a fun house where specters waited in the shadows.

As she hurried toward the grand staircase, she nearly collided with Apollonie, who was welcoming a late guest. At first Francesca thought she was hallucinating, but as she swept past them, she heard a familiar voice call out her name.

Chapter Twenty-two

FOR A TERRIBLE moment she stood frozen at the foot of the staircase, unable to run away, terrified to turn around. This wasn't happening, she told herself. It was another illusion; the fun-house mirrors were playing tricks on her mind. She was reliving another ball in another city, a ball that had taken place five long years ago. The man whose voice she'd heard, whose straw-colored hair had flickered past the corner of her eye, could not be the same man she'd danced with in Venice. Such things simply didn't happen.

She picked up her long skirt and fled up the stairs, running as if tongues of fire were licking at her heels. He must never see her face. She flung the door of her bedroom open and slammed it behind her. What hellish fate had brought Jack Westman here? If only he had reappeared before the fire swept away her beauty and her future, he might have regretted abandoning her in Venice. That seemed the cruelest joke of all. In the silence of the large room her ears were filled with the pounding of her heart. He had recognized her; he had called her name. Perhaps he hadn't seen the scar.

Beyond the canopied bed, she saw her reflection in the wavering glass of the large mirrored armoire. The room, decorated in the rich velvets and brocades of the Empire style, seemed impossibly ornate and stuffy to Francesca. She longed for the solace of the clean, bare summer room at Lyford Cay. There perhaps she could restore some peace to her tortured heart.

Her mind quickly compared escape routes. She could change her clothes and hurry down the staircase at the other end of the château. She'd drive one of Apollonie's cars to the anonymous haven of Orly, where she could catch a night flight to New York. Or she could hide in the servants' quarters, where Jack would never look for her.

Her heart calmed, but then she heard a gentle tapping at the thick door. She threw herself on the bed and pulled the enormous goose-down pillows over her ears. Her heart was pounding again, so loudly she thought it was sure to give her away.

"Francesca." His voice was low. He must have pressed his lips into the doorjamb. "Please let me in. Please."

For a moment Francesca feared she would burst into tears. Before the fire, she would have leaped to the door and thrust it wide open, and somehow all the years since she had lain in Jack's arms would have disappeared. She would have had the power to win Jack all over again, and whatever flaw had led him to abandon her she would have overcome. But now she was the flawed one, and there was no cure. She had no power over his heart. All that was left was her pride, and if he saw her face even that would be destroyed.

She remained silent while the knocking continued, harder now, more insistent.

"Francesca, let me talk to you."

She rose and stared at the door in dismay. His voice reverberated through the room like unbearably beautiful music. She remembered that as an actor he would know how to make it resonate on that painful timbre. But she was just as susceptible to its charm as she had been the first time she heard him speak at her ball in Venice.

"Don't let me lose you twice," he said.

Francesca looked at the door in startled dismay.

"Just let me see you for a moment. Just a moment."

She ran back to the high bed and buried her face in the pillows.

He rattled at the knob. It was old and frail, and with a hard jolt he was able to break the lock. The door swung open beneath his hand. Francesca could not bear to look up, but in her mind's eye she seemed to see him there in the doorway, outlined against the light. In the silence she heard him move closer, and then she flinched. His broad hand was on her back. She was sobbing. He meant to calm her, but his touch broke something in her.

"Hush now, darling. Francesca," he said in a low voice, helplessly. Then he tried to get her to smile. "Don't you know I can't bear it when a girl bursts into tears at the mere sight of me?"

Francesca smothered her face in the pillow, squeezing her eyes shut. "Please leave me alone. Please, Jack."

"Ask me anything else, Francesca, but not that, my darling. After longing for you all these years, that's the one thing I will not do."

He slid his hand up into her hair and began to stroke it in the old familiar way. "I know about the fire, Francesca. Apollonie told me how ashamed you are of your scar."

When she didn't move, he took her shoulders and turned her toward him. "Put your head on my shoulder. I won't look, I promise. I just want to hold you."

His arms went around her, enveloping her, pressing her into his hard body, and she buried her face in his chest, inhaling the scent of him as if it were the first fresh air she had breathed in all those years. She let him talk, gently, soothingly, stroking her back and her hair, not attempting to make her lift her face to him.

Slowly her arms went around him. She could feel his breath on her forehead, and she could smell the clean scent of his freshly washed shirt. Everything about him was comfortable and familiar, and she felt herself relax against him. When he lifted a hand to trace the scar with his fingers, she didn't flinch, and when he pushed her away from him and tilted her head up, she looked directly into his eyes. They glowed a deep blue even in the shadowy room, and they didn't flicker even slightly at the sight of her. In his face she saw no pity, no horror. All she could see was his astonishing beauty. Her memory of Jack had blurred in her daydreams. She had not dared to look at his photographs after that one evening of weakness, but she saw now that no photograph could capture the golden texture of his skin, the expression of his deep-set eyes.

Then his mouth was on hers, gently, and only for a second. His lips moved to her left cheek and traced the scar. She raised her hand in protest. Never moving his lips away from her face, he buried her hand in one of his.

"You always were a great one to exaggerate things," he murmured as he lifted his head and pressed her face against his chest once more, still holding her close. He laughed softly, and she could feel the vibration of it rumble through her body. She looked up, startled. "You're still beautiful, Francesca, you silly goose."

He held her away from him and studied her face closely. He shook her slightly, then dropped a kiss on her scarred cheek. "Let me see you smile. Come on." He wiggled his eyebrows at her comically, as if coaxing a child, and Francesca felt the laughter bubble up in her throat and then spill out into the room in ripples.

Jack threw his arms around her, and she could feel the sigh of relief sweep through him. "Good God, Francesca, do you know how many times I've heard that laugh in my dreams? Lord, I've missed you."

Jack pulled Francesca from the bed and kissed her lightly on the lips. As she moved to the dressing table and brushed out her hair, he stood behind her and watched. His adoring reflection in the mirror gave her sudden confidence. There wasn't the slightest hint of the disgust she had imagined in everyone's stare. She smiled in a daze of happiness. Then she remembered Christopher sleeping soundly in the next room, and paused at the door.

"There's just one thing I want to tell you, Jack. I have a son."

Jack remembered Josie had told him about Francesca's husband and son in New York. "Funny, I never thought of you as a mother, Francesca. You'll always be that innocent girl I saw in front of Santa Maria della Salute."

"I'm not, though. I'm a mother now." She looked at him carefully. His face was a neutral mask.

"What difference does it make for us?" he said. "I love you now just as much as I did then. Is he here?"

"He's sleeping in the next room."

"Then let's go."

"Wait just a moment while I check on him. Come with me."

The two tiptoed into Christopher's room and stood for a moment next to the big bed. Christopher's mouth was rosy, his eyelids a faint lavender. Francesca thought this must be complete happiness, to stand watch over her son's sleep with his father beside her. When she glanced at Jack, she saw that his eyes were soft with pleasure, but that she was the one he gazed at, not the child. The resemblance between father and son was startling. Anyone would have guessed that Jack was Christopher's father. Anyone but Jack, that is, who at that moment only had eyes for Francesca.

She held back her words. She knew she must choose the time carefully to tell Jack that Christopher was his son. She calmly slipped her arm into his. They walked down the grand staircase together, and on into the château's ballroom. Francesca's morbid fear of her own ugliness had lifted, and she could look around her for the first time with true appreciation.

Beneath the crystal chandeliers, clusters of people suddenly quieted and parted. Francesca stood in the doorway and savored the beauty before her, and the impression she made. It reminded her of that night in the palazzo when a similar crowd of proud and beautiful people had looked up at her in admiration, but this time she leaned on Jack's arm instead of her father's. There was another change. If she had known then what she had learned tonight, would she have had the courage to face those people, so many of whom were certainly reminded of Susannah and her tragedy?

She wished she had never heard the truth, or the lie, whichever it was. It gnawed at her happiness, burning in the back of her mind like an inextinguishable flame. As she and Jack swirled into a waltz around the parquet floor, she felt herself relax into his arms as if the music and the light that danced in her eyes emanated from another time, from Venice and innocence. Francesca knew that this was what she had been born for.

Only one person was not enchanted by the sight of Francesca sweeping around the ballroom in the arms of the handsome American. Josie looked on in horror, and when Prince Benor Fabi asked if she cared to dance, she mumbled that she had a headache and asked him if he would take her to her room. She wasn't lying; in fact her temples were pounding. The sight of Jack and Francesca plunged her into depression. Francesca was sure to discover that she was the one who wrote that terrible letter, signed Francesca's name, and given it to Jack. She felt a blush of shame creep up her neck when she thought of her spiteful behavior on that long-ago day. Although Francesca could not bring herself to acknowledge publicly that they were sisters, Josie loved her enough to control her envy and hurt. She had learned how to be patient. But now Francesca would discover the ugliest part Josie had played in ending her affair with Jack Westman.

Shaken, Josie leaned on the prince's arm and let him lead her upstairs. Alone in her room, she lay on the bed and looked back on the wreckage she had made of her life.

"Josie? May I come in?"

Recognizing the prince's voice, she called out, "It's unlocked, Benor."

"I brought you some aspirin for your headache, Josie. I

always carry a medicine kit in my suitcase.'' He reached into his pocket and brought out a bottle of French aspirin, then took a prescription vial out of another pocket. ''I also brought this for you, but you must use it carefully. It's an effective painkiller, but it's very strong.''

Josie didn't hesitate for a moment. She took the medicine into the tiny bathroom and opened the prescription vial. She counted the capsules. There were only seven, barely enough to get her through this difficult weekend. She slipped one of the capsules into her mouth, then swallowed another for good measure. She drank a glass of water and began rearranging her hair. A hairpin slipped through her fingers, and as she bent to pick it up, she felt the dreamy, poppy languor of the drug course through her limbs. It couldn't possibly have worked that quickly, she told herself. She opened the door. The handsome Arab prince was still there reclining on the chaise longue, his arms folded behind his head.

''Thank you,'' she said dreamily as she lounged gracefully in the bathroom doorway. She could have purred like a cat. ''I feel better already. But I need some champagne to wash the pill down. I wonder, could you get me some?''

''Of course, my sweet.'' She smiled as he went off to collect a bottle and glasses. Suddenly she felt invulnerable and lighthearted. Her anxiety about Francesca had vanished in a flash, along with the headache. She kicked off her shoes and stockings. She ran her fingers through her soft black hair. She could hardly wait for the prince to return.

Laughing softly, she remembered how one of the party guests had whispered to her earlier that in Benor she had found quite a catch; he was a millionaire many times over, the woman had said. He did not flaunt his wealth and power; his manners were restrained and impeccable, and he was gently self-effacing. He held himself back from the other guests, although he knew them all well; it was as if he, too, felt himself an outsider in this European crowd. Josie knew he was attracted to her. She could read it in his large black eyes.

What was it the woman had said in her glib voice? ''He's trying to prove that the Arabs aren't all rich savages. Most of them think they'll be struck by lightning if they don't fuck seven times a day, but this one's so good he's boring. Never makes a pass at anyone. He's so concerned about his image, he acts like he's been castrated.''

Josie turned down the covers of the bed and slipped out of her dress. "We'll see how virtuous this handsome prince is," she murmured to herself. Maybe it would be for just one night, she told herself, but what was wrong with that? She felt so good she wanted to share her happiness with someone, and a rich Arab prince would serve very well, thank you.

When Prince Benor returned with the champagne, Josie was standing by the bed in her slip, with the light behind her. She knew he could see that she was naked underneath the silk.

The prince let his eyes travel down the length of her body, but he said nothing as he opened the champagne. He was shy, Josie decided confidently. It would be up to her to put him at ease.

"Are you driving to Monte Carlo with us for the races?" she asked innocently.

He gravely poured her a glass of champagne. "No. I must get back to my home in Paris. Besides, the crowds at the races are impossible. The town is tiny, the roads very curved and narrow. There's no room for the natives, let alone thousands of tourists. Anyway, I saw Mario win this race before."

"I'm sorry you won't be coming," Josie said. "Here's to the races." They touched glasses. Her eyes never left the prince's.

"I'm sorry, too," he said, still standing close to her, "because I enjoyed hearing you sing. Perhaps when you're in Paris, you will let me know?"

Josie smiled at him. Unless she was bold, this man would disappear and leave her to an uncomfortable confrontation with Jack and Francesca.

"Take me with you," she said. Her daring took her breath away.

"What will you do in Paris?" he asked evenly, without surprise.

"I'll sing for you." She slipped the straps of her slip off her shoulders. Then she reached over and kissed his full mouth. The kiss was sweet. His lips tightened under hers, and then he was drawing her into his arms.

She pulled away and laughed.

"What is it?" he said, surprised now.

"I've never kissed anyone before with a mustache. It tickles."

He lifted her up and she felt herself fly through the air.

When she opened her eyes she was lying on the bed. The prince's hands were everywhere, all over her body, and she saw that she had been wrong about him. He was not shy at all.

Anything but! she told herself silently as his warm tongue began to send shock waves through her body. When he had satisfied himself that she was more than ready for him, he stood up and stripped off his clothes. She could see that he was wildly aroused and eager to take her. She gazed into his black eyes, too languorous to help him remove her slip.

His hands went not to the straps, she noticed with a sort of vague curiosity, but to the delicate lace over her breasts. She watched, fascinated, as he took the fabric in his strong hands and, with one powerful motion, ripped the slip open all the way down the front.

She stared at him wide-eyed and open-mouthed. This seduction, she realized with a shudder of excitement mixed with horror, was costing her several thousand francs. She laughed wryly as his hands again began to work their magic. Some seductress I am, she thought, lying here worrying about my underwear.

The prince laughed at the apprehension in her face. "You shall have a thousand slips, Josie. More than a thousand, if you wish."

After that, things began to happen so fast that her fuzzy mind couldn't quite follow them. The prince's weight was heavy, his lovemaking punishing but at the same time wildly pleasurable. And, she soon discovered, he was absolutely insatiable. His love was a dark, smothering grave.

Before she slept she thought she saw Marianne, and as she reached out to touch her she heard someone crying. Later, perhaps hours later, she remembered something about Francesca. Josie didn't know why, but she had to flee the château for her life. Murder. She had murdered Michael with her curse. And wasn't the word for what went on between her and Francesca murder?

In the morning the prince entered her while she slept, and she came into consciousness under the spell of that black and brutal ecstacy. He was pounding all the tension and despair out of her body. And when his passion was spent, she gathered what was left of her strength and went into the bathroom. Her face was bruised with lovemaking, her head splitting. She took another one of the pills. Only five left.

When she emerged there was a tray of coffee on the bedside table.

"Pack," Prince Benor said as he poured her a cup and held it out to her. "We leave for Paris in half an hour."

Two months after meeting again in Apollonie's château, Francesca and Jack stood on the balcony of the house they shared overlooking the Seine on the Ile Saint Louis. They were watching the fireworks celebrating the Fourteenth of July, Bastille Day. It was an uncommonly hot night and Francesca had had too much to drink. The house was full of strangers; Jack's movie crowd and their excessive familiarity toward her made her uncomfortable. She sensed it was meant to do just the opposite. Her scar throbbed. In spite of the reassurance of Jack's love there were times when she was still excruciatingly conscious of it. She felt Jack's arm clasp her shoulder too hard. He smelled of liquor and the tension these people always inspired in him. She should have been happy remembering how they had stood just like this on the balcony of the palazzo on the night of her eighteenth birthday. "Oooh . . . ahhh," everyone exclaimed as a spectacular bouquet of colors exploded over their heads and then died slowly. For a moment it was dark and a sudden breeze cooled their faces.

"The lion flies!" Francesca said to Jack with relief.

"What?"

"In Venice when there's an unexpected breeze like this on a hot night, we say it's the lion's wings."

Jack looked down at her blankly.

"Oh, never mind!" She pulled away from him crossly and, pushing through the cluster of people, headed for the bedroom. She really must get into a better mood.

The room was dark except for a light shining in from the bath. She sat down on the bed and lit a cigarette. By the glow of the match she spotted her letter lying on the bedside table addressed to Renata in Venice. It had been returned again. She sat smoking in the dark wondering if she was ever going to find her. Renata, she had concluded, was the only link, the only person she believed could tell her the truth about her mother.

A shout of drunken laughter came to her through the closed door and she got up and turned the key in the lock. She wouldn't be missed for a while. She lay on the wide bed, her eyes growing accustomed to the dark. How lucky they had found a home furnished almost the way she would have done it herself . . . and she loved playing mistress of the house for Jack and Christopher. It was only the heat and the crowd tonight, she told herself, that made her feel so . . . what was it, this oppressive feeling she had of loss? She missed—Josie. The instant she admitted it to herself the swelling in her throat rose and tears of anger stung her eyes; which was worse—that Josie had betrayed her, knowing she was her sister, or was the pain of that knowledge and the way she was treated by their father enough of an excuse for her to behave so miserably? The old question haunted her.

In the first glorious days of rediscovering each other, Jack and Francesca remembered their days in Venice. They went over every detail of the events that led to their separation and Jack mentioned Francesca's letter of rejection that Josie had given him; Francesca would not believe it. She questioned Jack so closely he finally became infuriated and accused her of calling him a liar. Ironically, they fought over the old misunderstanding. Old wounds opened and were deepened for Francesca as she learned the extent of Josie's treachery. How that would have pleased Josie, Francesca thought disgustedly. No wonder Josie had disappeared with that Arab. At least she had had the decency to be ashamed, or was she just a coward? She didn't want to think about Josie and yet it was there, the old need for her: for her humorous view of life, her trick of making Francesca stop taking herself so seriously. That's exactly what I'm doing now, Francesca thought impatiently. If Josie were giving this party she would be out there having fun instead of sulking in a dark room. Francesca jumped up and turned on the lights. After she washed her face with cold water, she put on fresh lipstick and combed her hair. Then she marched out of the bedroom with a big phony smile on her face; sometimes you had to work from the outside in. That's what Josie had always said and sometimes it worked.

Everyone she had asked who might know of Renata thought the famous dressmaker was dead. Even in Jack's arms the recurring nightmares that Converse Archer's conversation had provoked continued to wake her. She lied to Jack that it was Josie's treachery in Venice she dreamed of; he told her to put the past behind her. She wondered why it was a point of honor with her to keep her mother's secret.

* * *

Now it was the end of October. She and Jack passed the summer happily enough once Paris had become quieter and they were alone. Though her search for Renata had remained fruitless, still she persevered. Francesca held the old-fashioned phone receiver away from her ear, and, as she gazed helplessly out the frost-rimmed windows of the library, Paris was a study in black and white. People walked alone or in pairs along the narrow sidewalk, holding their hats, ducking their chins down inside their raised coat collars. Overhead the gnarled and leafless boughs of an ancient chestnut tree made a trellis under the gray sky. Between the babble of the French and Italian telephone operators and the deafening static, she couldn't understand a word. Finally the line cleared and a distinct voice told her crossly that Renata's number was still disconnected. Francesca insisted, but the voice repeated the same old message. Then there was a click and she was cut off.

Francesca turned away from the window and moved a bowl of pink tea roses from the coffee table to the mantel. Above the ornate mantel, Pan-like statues framed a huge old mirror. The fireplace itself was carved with stone fruits and plants; a spilled cornucopia. Francesca found herself attracted to the blue vacuum of the distorted mirror despite herself.

Her own seared face, caught in the rose stems in the antique glass, was as dubious a work of art as the domineering fireplace. In this light it was pale gold, with its broad scar tissue flaring across the cheek like a livid purple flame. She could have been the garish paramour of one of those coy, half-naked statues.

"Don't be hard on yourself," she whispered into the glass. Today she noticed a slight change, an improvement in her appearance. The scar had not diminished; there was no hope of that. But once she thought of herself as meek; now her eyes seemed brave, focused on an inner strength. And her slight limbs were no longer fragile, but knifelike in the slanted afternoon light. Her beauty now struck her as odd, as exotic as these carved boys who guarded the mirror. It was strange to meet them in her own library; stranger still to try to claim the marked face that regarded hers from the other side of the roses. Yet it was she. Because Jack was willing to claim her, to love her at least, Francesca no longer cringed at the scarred vision of her own reflection.

Francesca meandered into the living room, looking for a spot for the cool irises. They suited the paneled room, with its brilliant oriental rug and deep aubergine velvet couches. This house was like an enormous dollhouse for Francesca, perhaps, she thought, because she was not its owner. She was glad that Jack was still adamant about not returning to America, where two recent box-office hits had greatly augmented his already enormous popularity. His fans had become hysterical and obsessed. Like crazed fanatics in the presence of a saint, they clutched at him, tearing at his clothing in the hope of obtaining a relic that would work their salvation.

''You have no idea what it's like,'' he had told Francesca. ''Some of them actually camp outside my driveway gates in California. They pore through my garbage, try to break into the house. I had to hire a security guard, and I gave up going out in public long ago. Now they've invaded my home. I can't even enjoy my own swimming pool. They've got telephoto lenses.''

The price Jack had paid for box-office success was too high, Francesca thought. He valued his privacy. He had never needed noisy approval of his work, and the attention he received embarrassed him. He wanted to develop his own film projects, but all the adulation distracted him. So he had closed his Malibu home and rented this eighteenth-century house on the Ile Saint Louis in Paris.

The graceful old house on an island in the Seine was like something out of Francesca's girlhood fantasies, with its overgrown garden in back and the tiny courtyard between it and the cobbled street of town houses. An ornate cast-iron fence with a creaking gate separated the courtyard from the narrow thoroughfare. On the other side the windows looked out on the river directly below. All of the houses on the street were small and delicate, with enormous casement windows and gabled roofs from which tiny lights winked in the night. Built centuries ago, they seemed to huddle together on the small island like birds crowded on a stone above the water. From the upstairs windows Francesca could see the majestic bulk of Notre Dame. She found the urban night sounds of the Seine eerily soothing. The rippling, slapping water, the occasional reek of fish and kerosene, and the foghorns and distant bustle of chains and tugs reminded her of the mysterious night traffic in Venice. She seemed destined to live near the water.

Jack, too, was happy in Paris. At first he could walk the

Paris streets almost unrecognized, and he and Francesca had dawdled in the Left Bank cafés and shopped unselfconsciously in the open fish markets near their home. After his films began to appear in the French theaters, however, he began to wear sunglasses again. One afternoon he had put them on and taken Francesca to see how one of his films played in French. The little theater near the Sorbonne was crammed with thin, intent students. Jack had laughed out loud when he heard himself speaking dubbed-in French on screen.

"I talk like Donald Duck. Do I really sound like that when I speak French?"

"Not too much," Francesca had said slyly.

An angry student swore at them the next time Jack laughed.

Jack quickly led Francesca out of the dark theater. "What did that guy say to me?" he said.

"I'm afraid it wasn't very pretty. He called you some kind of farm animal, I think."

"Did he really?" Jack looked pleased. "Delightful."

But as the winter deepened, Jack's exuberance had begun to diminish. He had read countless scripts but found none that he wanted to do. He met with producers and directors—endlessly, it seemed to Francesca. But still, she could see the restlessness in his eyes.

One afternoon she was curled up reading when he burst through the door, exuding energy, his coat open in spite of the frigid weather, bursting with excitement as he stepped over the threshold.

"We're invited to an opening at the Arneau Gallery tonight, Francesca, and to a bash afterward. Please say you'll come, darling. Everybody was talking about it this morning. Friends will be there. I told everyone you'd come."

"Aren't you going to say hello?" She placed her hands on his shoulders and stood on tiptoe to kiss him. "Do I have to share you with all those social butterflies?"

As she brushed her lips against his cheek and inhaled the clean smell of his skin, she toyed with the idea of seducing him on the spot. That, she was certain, would take his mind off the opening.

As if he'd read her mind, he put his hands on her shoulders and pushed her away from him. "You're not going to distract me into forgetting about this party, my love, so don't even try." He assumed an exaggeratedly pained look. "You keep me in bed all the time, Francesca. You're going to wear me out."

She broke into a peal of laughter, but he clamped a hand over her mouth.

"We'll have years to sit at home together after we're married," he continued. "But right now I want to take you out, see some people, have a little fun."

"You know it'll be painful for me," she said, suddenly serious. "I still dread facing strangers. I always will."

"Poor darling. Don't you see, that scar only makes you more remarkable?"

Francesca was unconvinced. She blushed under his stare. "I don't want to be remarkable."

He lifted her chin. "But you are, Francesca. And very beautiful, too." He bent to touch her mouth with his. "I want everyone to meet the extraordinary woman I'm going to marry."

Francesca lowered her eyes. Whenever he mentioned marriage, she felt suddenly afraid. She wanted it too much to believe it would really happen. She wished she were more like her mother, a woman who knew she deserved love. Francesca couldn't shake her insecurity, no matter how Jack bolstered her ego. When she lost her beauty, she seemed to have been abandoned by some essential part of herself. The dream of becoming like her mother was lost forever. Even the dream of being Jack's wife seemed impossible.

She forced herself to look up into his eyes. "Jack, those people won't be comfortable with me. They'll take one look and think, 'Oh, that poor, poor girl!' It'll be terrible."

He dropped his hands from her shoulders and kissed her quickly, trying for a lightness of tone that his disappointment made unachievable. "Okay, Francesca. I understand, really. I shouldn't have mentioned it." He tugged off his coat and hung it up. "What's for lunch, lady?"

"Grilled cheese sandwiches, American-style." She caught his grimace and shrugged. "I told you years ago that I never learned to cook."

"Right. Let's sit ourselves down to another one of your god-awful rich-girl specials. Cook's day off, I take it."

"She'll be in later. She went to the dentist."

Francesca led him into the kitchen. All during the meal, he talked pleasantly, asking about Christopher's school, as he did every day, then listening with apparent interest as she described the child's latest experience.

She still hadn't told him Christopher was his son. She wanted to wait for a special moment, a time when Jack and the child fell into a rapport. But the time still hadn't come, and she knew Jack's interest in the boy was feigned, for her sake.

They moved on to other subjects—Jack's meeting that morning, Francesca's shopping expedition the day before—but never once did Jack mention the party she'd refused to attend. She searched his eyes for a sign of resentment or sullenness, but she found nothing except kindness and love. But by the time the meal had ended, the familiar fingers of guilt were clutching at her stomach.

"And to show you how much I love you," Jack said cheerfully, "I'm going to help you wash the dishes."

"So good of you, sir." Francesca flung open the door of the dishwasher and watched admiringly while he put the dishes inside and pushed the starter button. "Well done! And so quickly."

"I'm going upstairs to change into some comfortable clothes. Be down in a minute." He turned and left the kitchen.

"Jack," she called.

He turned at the door.

"I'm going to try on a new dress. Will you tell me if it's all right for the party tonight?"

"You don't have to do this for me," he said quietly. "I didn't mean to push you."

"I want to go to the party, Jack."

"No, you don't. You're just afraid I'll stop loving you if you don't bend before my will." He walked over to her and took her hands. "I won't, you know. I'll never stop loving you, no matter what you do."

Francesca felt the tears well up in her throat. "Thank you for that. But I do want to go to the party." She flicked away the tears and tried for a mischievous smile. "So, if you won't take me, I guess I'll have to go by myself."

"You've got a date. Now, show me the dress. Maybe I'll hate it."

He followed her up the stairs and watched her change into an amethyst velvet dress that gave a glow to her red-gold hair and brought out the green in her eyes. He stepped back, away from her, and regarded her critically.

"Turn," he commanded.

She slowly did.

"Put on your shoes."

She slipped her feet into high heels and anxiously faced him. "Will it do?"

"Great legs," he said. "Your legs will do fine."

"I wanted your opinion on the dress, professor."

"The dress is fine. It's what's underneath it that impresses." He approached her and touched her face. "Lift your chin."

He turned her so that she faced a full-length mirror. "Look at your face." His finger traced the thick scar from her ear across her left cheek. "It's not ugly," he said. "It gives you panache. It makes you interesting. Your face was too beautiful before, too perfect. But now you look fascinating."

She looked at him in anxious disbelief. His own craggy blond countenance was full of admiration.

"You ought to play with the scar, Francesca. Don't let it depress you; master it! Look." He rummaged through the old tin makeup box full of his stage makeup and pulled out a tube of thin white paste, which he applied lightly to her entire face. Then he took a deep red lipstick from her dressing table and carefully darkened the welt so that it looked like a tattoo.

"War paint," she said with a slight, unconvinced smile.

"Why try to hide the scar with makeup? It can't really be camouflaged. Instead, you should emphasize it like this."

She stared into the mirror with fascination while he finished painting the scar. She looked like a mime in whiteface. A strange feeling came over her, as it did in her dreams when her mother walked toward the beach house. It was like seeing Susannah, peering through the window, gazing out at her from the mirror. Francesca did not flinch or look away, but faced her own reflection boldly. The scar was almost black now, like a brand. Jack had molded her a new face, a new identity. A fractured beauty oddly stitched together with a hellish seam, it was the face she suddenly wanted to bare to the world, one that had seen and comprehended a life as tragic as her mother's.

"Do you like it?" Jack said, his eyes excited.

"Doctor, I think you've healed me," Francesca answered slowly.

That night marked the inevitable beginning of Jack's popularity in Paris. The couple entered the gallery easily enough, borne forward on a tide of guests. But when word spread that Jack Westman was present, by the time the couple was ready to leave, a crowd was pressed against the security guards positioned at the glass doors. Francesca was dismayed. She had had more excitement that evening than she could bear. Friends rushed up to her all night to tell her how much they loved her "new" look. One art critic, looking at Francesca more closely than the paintings, remarked that her astounding, flamboyant scar had not detracted from her beauty, but emphasized its perfection. Strangers stared at her in fascination.

"I love it," gushed the gallery owner, a short woman with perceptive, Gallic green eyes, when she accosted Francesca and Jack in the hub of the crowd. "The only problem is, everyone is staring at *you*! No one is paying any attention to the paintings I've hung on my walls."

Francesca thought uneasily that that was certainly true of Jack. He paid no real attention to the paintings at all, although he professed to be a connoisseur of contemporary art. Francesca had already discovered that his knowledge was shallow, and used for show; he was not well educated enough to really appreciate or judge modern art. Instead, he had come here to be appreciated himself. He was electric with excitement. Francesca suddenly realized that he must secretly crave fame; the phenomenal power of his personality and looks made him feel secure. At last he had conquered Paris the way he had Los Angeles and New York. He seemed pleased and amused that the gossip columnists and journalists who shadowed his heels at functions like this now swarmed around Francesca as well, but he quickly acted as buffer to ward them off when their assaults became too strong.

"Now that you see what fame is like, have you had enough?" Jack said. "Let's leave and try that restaurant Marion recommended. I'm famished."

Outside the front doors the crowd of paparazzi jostled and shouted. The gallery owner showed Jack and Francesca out a back door that led to a twisting, deserted alley. It would allow them to elude the photographers and make their escape by way of a back street. Collars up, they ran out into the darkness together, holding hands. They made their way through the maze of ash cans, quiet as the cats that prowled the cobblestones, and after a false turn, found themselves in a narrow driveway blocked by a high iron gate. Jack tried to open it in the dark; it creaked, but it held. A chain rattled coldly.

"Damn! It's padlocked. Come on, let's jump over." Jack put his hands around Francesca's waist and lifted her to the top of the fence, where she clung helplessly. He placed her knee on his shoulder, and she pulled herself up and over. Jack followed in a neat vault, arching over the fence just as Francesca's feet touched the pavement.

A quick flash of lights told her that the photographers had caught them climbing over the fence like kids playing hooky. She ran wildly, but could hardly keep up with Jack.

"Which way?" he said as he paused at a corner.

"Into the metro," she said, and they were off, clattering down the stairs, out of breath now, but not daring to slow down.

"We're running like a couple of thieves," Francesca said. "People are staring at us." But the bystanders were smiling indulgently.

As a train slid into the station, a lone photographer descended onto the platform and looked around. Jack and Francesca leaped through the doors.

Exhilarated by the chase, they collapsed into seats and laughed.

"Still game for that restaurant?" Jack asked.

"No. Look at us! Your coat is torn. I've got a hole in my stockings, and there's dirt all over your face." Francesca wet a handkerchief with her tongue and dabbed it at Jack's face.

He was staring down at her as she tried to clean his chin. "Was I right?" he asked. His lips brushed her scar gently.

She took his hand and kissed it, thinking how good it had felt at the gallery to be looked at again with admiration instead of pity and embarrassment. She held his hand as the train slid to a stop.

"Tell me," he said in a low, desperate voice, "is there anything at all in the refrigerator at home?"

Francesca laughed. "I think so. Some strawberries, some champagne. Maybe a frozen steak."

"That settles it. We're going home."

Jack smiled down at her and Francesca was warmed by the desire in his eyes, his conspiratorial smile.

"I can't promise the steak. I'm not sure."

"What can you promise?" he asked, kissing her gently.

"Strawberries," she said.

"That sounds exciting," he said in a low voice.

A wave of fear and desire broke over Francesca. Jack's eyes were amused but also devouring; and she knew that part of his amusement derived from her confused longing, as if she were still a child, an innocent, in the grip of a passion she didn't understand. He would like to prove to her she was not quite the dignified young lady she had been brought up to be. He made her body respond despite herself; she had no control in his presence, not even here, on a metro seat, surrounded by curious strangers. She broke off his stare and looked around. The eyes of the passengers, still and focused, were all fixed on them.

"Jack," she whispered. "I think you've been recognized again."

A couple of young women were pressing down on them. One began to giggle, and the other asked Jack in French for an autograph.

"I don't speak French." Jack shrugged his shoulders and smiled innocently, and suddenly a new crowd began to gather. They started, awkwardly, to besiege him in bad English for his signature.

The train stopped, and Jack shot out of the doors, dragging Francesca after him.

They took a taxi the rest of the way to the Ile Saint Louis. Francesca sent the housekeeper home and went upstairs while Jack headed for the kitchen. Christopher was sleeping soundly. She dropped a kiss on his forehead and hurried into her bedroom, where she took a quick shower and slipped into a warm cashmere robe. When she went back downstairs, she found that Jack had taken over the kitchen.

"Steak and champagne," he announced, setting a tulip-shaped crystal glass before her.

"Am I to eat in solitary splendor? What are you having for dinner?"

He kissed her scarred cheek. "You."

She smelled the steak broiling. "But you said you were starving. Isn't there enough for both of us? I'm not that crazy about steak." Jack, a confirmed American in his tastes, liked simple meals of steak, potato, and salad. He was easy to please. She tried to get up, but he held her down and kissed her again. "Let me set the table."

"Nope. I've got everything under control."

He set two salads and a loaf of bread before her, then

sliced the steak and presented it with a flourish. She laughed and gave him half.

"Now tell me," she said as she sipped the champagne, "what's behind all this special service?"

Jack smiled cryptically. "Lust."

"No, seriously."

"Well, since you ask, there is something we should talk about. I've been offered a chance to direct a really good picture. That's what my meeting was about this morning. It'll be shot in the States, so we'll have to go there if I decide to do it."

Francesca opened her mouth to speak, but he cut her off, as if anticipating her objections.

"Until tonight, I was pretty sure I'd have to turn it down, because I didn't think you'd be able to take the kind of scrutiny you'd get in America, but you were so great tonight that I think you're ready to take on the whole world. What do you say?"

Francesca's mind was reeling. "How soon will all this happen?"

"Hard to pin them down, some time in the late spring." There was a note of excitement in his voice. "I'm beginning to get too much recognition here. Soon Paris will be as impossible as Los Angeles, so I might as well go back and face it. Besides, an actor has to ride the crest of his popularity. They've just found out about me here in France, which means people are already starting to forget me back home."

"But I thought you wanted to be forgotten."

He ran a finger over the back of her hand. "Never." He gave her a puzzled smile, as if he didn't quite understand himself.

"But you claim you hate all the publicity."

He took another bite of steak and shrugged. "It's a necessary evil, I guess. I'd probably hate it more if they ignored me."

Francesca studied Jack's face uncomprehendingly. His hair was beginning to gray slightly at his temples and she noticed the deep weathered lines around his eyes.

"Besides, it's time I changed my image," he went on. "I've got to appeal to a broader audience. Right now people see me as a happy-go-lucky playboy type, because that's the way the media have portrayed me. That image limits the types of roles I get offered as well as the kinds of movies I'm asked to direct. It's time I presented myself as a serious person, a family man."

Francesca found herself staring at him. "Are you telling me you want me to go to Los Angeles with you to improve your image?"

He looked shocked, but she suspected he was acting.

"I don't *believe* you!" She put down her fork. "You intend to palm me off on the American press as the little woman who's going to make a serious family man of you. And you intend to use my son to enhance that same false image. You have *got* to be the most self-centered man I have ever met, Jack Westman!"

He was laughing. "Come on, scarface. You know I'm crazy about you. I'll even turn this picture down if you really don't want to come to the U.S. with me. In fact, that's what I intended to do until tonight. I'm honest enough to admit that you and Christopher would do my reputation good, but you know damn well that's not my main reason for wanting you to come with me."

"Jack, I don't know if it would be good for Christopher. I'd have to take him out of school just when he's getting used to it and making some friends. I'm not sure we should uproot him again. He's been through so much since the fire." The disappointment in Jack's face stunned her. She leaned her elbows on the table and covered her face with her hands. "I can't make you happy, Jack. Everything I do is wrong for you."

He reached out and took hold of her wrists, pulled her hands away from her face, and looked at her hard. "Listen, Francesca. You're the *only* one who can make me happy. Please believe that." He pulled her to her feet and took her into his arms. "We'll work this out, darling. We're both tired now, but in the morning we'll talk it over, and we'll figure out a way to make things all right." He began to kiss her, stifling her words.

She wanted to talk to him, but she felt her resolve slip away as his lips claimed hers. She struggled briefly to break loose, but she was too weak and she gave it up. She opened her eyes to halt the dark rush of passion, and saw Jack's burnished skin, the slant of his high cheekbone, and his shoulders pressing toward her. She felt the flame of desire arc up in her body.

He carried her upstairs, eased her down on the bed, and

opened her robe. In the dark her ears filled with the sound of the river, flowing along in the pursuit of its own inscrutable purpose.

He undressed, then covered her with his body and held her as if his love would end her doubts at last and forever. Her body was pulled taut with anxiety, and he began to caress it, easing away the tension. She felt his warm mouth on her breast and gave herself up to him. They would work things out; he would make her life all right again just as he was making her body whole again. She urged him inside her and watched his face in the darkness as he swiftly brought her to fulfillment, taking his own pleasure only when he was sure she could go no higher.

The next morning the newspapers were full of their photographs. Jack and Francesca sat on the Oriental rug in the library with the papers spread out on the floor around them. Christopher sat between them, eating toast with strawberry jam and exclaiming over the pictures of his mother. There was Francesca in a close-up, staring wide-eyed into the lens as if she'd never seen a camera before. And there were the two of them climbing over the fence in a picture captioned "Le Leapfrog." Other photographs recorded their headlong flight down the dark streets. One paper had made up a new name for Francesca: *"La Comtesse Marquée,"* the branded countess.

"I don't know if I approve of this," said Francesca, putting the papers down and walking over to where Christopher had gone and was staring out the window. "They've given me even more space than you."

"That suits me fine, darling. I'm old news. Maybe I'll just retire and let you take the heat for a while."

Francesca laughed, then sobered quickly as she caught sight of a man standing motionless before the front gate, staring at the house. She seized Christopher and hurried him to the other side of the room, out of the intruder's line of vision. "Jack, come over here, quick. There's a strange man standing outside the gate trying to see into the house."

Jack stood up and peered out the window, then laughed softly and closed the blinds.

"What should we do?" Francesca asked, shaken.

"Nothing," Jack answered laconically. He kissed her lightly and headed for the kitchen. "Welcome to celebrity."

* * *

One of Josie's greatest pleasures was the Olympic-size pool in the basement of Benor's house. In Nassau she had swum almost every day. The first time the prince took Josie down to see the pool, she heaved a great sigh of pleasure, stepped out of her clothes, and dived in. When he saw that she literally was as happy in the water as out, he decided to surprise her. He forbade her to go into the basement for a week, and when he finally took her down, the pool had been transformed into an underwater paradise with plants and tropical fish, coral formations and giant shells, lit strategically to resemble sunlight playing through the water. Speechless, Josie slipped out of her evening dress and handed it to Benor. Naked, she lowered herself into the water. Benor pulled up a wicker armchair and turned on the speakers to the record player. Ravel floated softly up to them. Benor smoked his pipe of kif and watched her as she snaked her way underwater through the coral, investigating her new domain. Finally she burst to the surface, laughing.

"Oh, Benor!" She could not resist jumping out of the pool and giving him a great wet kiss. Benor, chuckling with pleasure, gave her bottom a spank as she dived back into the pool. There was a passageway down around the side of the pool with large windows so Benor could watch his newest acquisition from every angle. The pool was perfectly planned; there weren't so many fish or plants to make swimming uncomfortable. It was as natural an underwater environment as it could be without being below the surface of the sea itself.

Josie imagined the pleasure Benor derived from watching her lithe body swimming close to the glass, never looking him in the eye, but brushing her body against the window, close to his face and away again exactly as she had watched porpoises do in the aquarium. When she surfaced he was at the edge of the pool.

"Out!" he commanded.

"Oh, no, *chéri*. Not yet." Josie smiled teasingly, floating on her back just out of his reach. They had found a game, a very original game. One she was in control of, but that she always let him win.

That had been three months ago; now it was becoming more and more difficult to invent new games to play, Josie thought worriedly as she walked down the endless corridor to her room, pulling off her gloves, exhausted from rehearsing all day. All she wanted was to relax alone in a hot tub. She walked into the high-ceilinged bedroom, taking pleasure as usual in its beauty. The air was filled with the scent of the vases of fresh flowers. A tiny spotlight lit the Bonnard over the mantelpiece, and apricot moiré curtains cascaded onto the floor on either side of the French windows opening onto a garden below. Redon's pastel flowers hung on the pale wood paneling between the windows, emphasizing the delicacy of the room.

The bed was covered with a darker shade of apricot velvet and piled high with soft, inviting pillows. Out of the corner of her eye she saw the vicuña rug at its foot come alive. An orange-colored long-haired kitten uncurled out of the fur and stretched toward her, yawning. Josie gave the animal a quick hug. "To go with the room," Benor had laughed when he had presented her with the tiny animal.

She opened the door to the bathroom. It always gave her a slight jolt, it was in such contrast to the subtle elegance of her bedroom. Its Chinese-red laquered walls were decorated with a collection of sexually explicit etchings by famous artists, and over the tiny marble fireplace in which a crackling fire burned, hung the pièce de résistance: one of Picasso's convoluted ladies being ravaged by a satyr. Opposite the fireplace, "center stage," was an old-fashioned black enameled bathtub with gilt claws for legs. Yellow and black silk curtains were held back on either side by grinning three-foot blackamoors. The floor was entirely covered by a white fur rug. The whole room was camp, very expensive camp.

She had just come out of the little toilet adjoining and gotten her clothes off when a veiled Arab woman entered the room. Josie sat naked at the dressing table in front of the large, ornately framed mirror. The maid took the brush from her hand and began to brush her hair expertly up from the scalp in long strokes. The water ran in the tub and the fire warmed her back and finally she began to relax.

As the maid helped her step into the tub, Benor entered. He was wearing his dressing gown and, loosening it, he lay down on the red velvet chaise near the fire. There was something in his manner that suggested to Josie that this was a ritual, one she was not the first to have endured.

The woman poured sweet-smelling oil into the tub and turned off the tap. Josie sank down into the water but she was only allowed to soak in the warmth for a moment when she saw Benor make a small gesture with his hand and the woman gently urged Josie onto her knees. Slowly she began to soap her in a soothing manner that was nonetheless calculated. The soft sponge circled Josie's high round breasts until the nipples were erect. She swept down between her legs, up over her belly, and back to her breasts. Josie was aroused in spite of herself by the rhythmic movement. She wanted to sink back into the tub but the woman made a small sound of warning and instead lifted her to her feet. Benor's eyes were slits. He inhaled his pipe of kif and smiled. The maid turned her so that the prince would get a full view of her back. The sponge circled her buttocks. Finally she was allowed to sink back into the tub. Benor gestured impatiently and the woman took Josie's arm and helped her out of the tub. She wound her around with an enormous white towel and rubbed her vigorously until Josie's polished body had a rosy glow. Then, whipping the towel away, she stepped back as if presenting a finished piece of porcelain.

The room was hazy with kif and the perfume of bath oil. Benor poured a glass of champagne and brought it to Josie. He signaled to the maid, who was tidying the room, to leave. She was barely out the door when he pulled back his dressing gown and pinned her against the high edge of the metal tub. Quickly she gulped her champagne. A little voice warned her he was not in a gentle mood. She braced her arms in back of her; he had already pushed her thighs apart and was entering her. Oddly, perhaps because of the warmth of the bath, instead of the pain she usually felt when he was so abrupt, she felt a strange new pleasure. Her head buzzed with the wine. She opened her legs wide as her belly relaxed. She pushed against him, seeking her own pleasure for once. She heard herself groan. It was unbearable; she was getting closer and closer. But it was over; Benor pulled out of her roughly while she was still yearning toward a climax. Her arms shook from bracing herself against the tub.

"Benor," she murmured pleadingly.

Through half-closed eyes she saw him grin disdainfully. He tied his robe and left the room. She heard the door of the bedroom close and she sank down next to the tub on the snowy fur rug. Curled up, she stared into the dying flames of the fire and her fingers found the wet mossy place he had left throbbing, the promise of ecstacy with him just out of reach.

She closed her eyes and felt herself catapulted over the shimmering waterfall of pleasure into a warm sea of peace. Totally relaxed, she dozed.

When she awoke she stretched luxuriously and got up. She felt much better, almost gay. Humming a little tune, she washed and splashed herself with eau de cologne; then she slipped on her favorite nightie from back home. It had been washed so often it was as soft as a handkerchief. Marianne had painstakingly embroidered flowers around the neckline. As she opened the window and climbed into bed, she thought, life was not so bad. She had a lot to be grateful for. She had beautiful clothes, and a place to live that would have impressed even Marianne; she had her swimming pool; and, most important, chances to sing for important people at the parties Benor gave in the town house or that they attended in other people's homes. Her career was at last beginning. Tomorrow she would think of something new and exotic to keep him happy. Until she was established as a singer and able to support herself, she had to keep Benor too engrossed in her to think of tossing her out in favor of a newer model. She had to do that; she knew it. She stared at the Bonnard in the moonlight until her eyelids closed, and she was a child again, skipping across the sand in Nassau.

Chapter Twenty-three

"It's urgent, madame," the maid said as she summoned Francesca to the telephone.

Francesca immediately thought of Jack as she rushed for the receiver. He commuted to Los Angeles now, working on the new script he meant to direct, and he must be on his return flight this very second. Francesca half expected to be told that his plane to Paris had crashed. Failing that, there was always bad news from the spa to expect. Edward sent her increasingly troubled letters about the perilous fall-off of business. Francesca's new, sudden notoriety had had a disastrous effect on the clinic's business as her clients realized she would not be found hostessing activities at Lyford Cay. Her scar and her liaison with Jack, however, had combined to enthrall the public's imagination. Francesca's memorable face looked out from every newsstand; her activities were chronicled glowingly in every gossip column. The public had an insatiable curiosity about her, and although her impulse was to become more and more retiring, Jack, when he was home, insisted on squiring her to every important social event.

"I've finally found someone who's more famous than I am," he would chuckle. "You're my lightning rod. Next to you, I'm practically anonymous."

He was not, of course; far from it. His exile in Paris had turned out to be a great way of flirting with the media by playing hard to get. Now that he was embarking on a new career as a director, publicity mattered to him again more than ever. He thought about it as a kind of insurance.

"As long as they talk about you," he would say, "good or bad, it doesn't matter what they say."

But as usual, the mere thought of Jack made her pulse pound. He had given her her face back, her self-confidence. Besides Christopher, loving him was the sole purpose of her life, and the hungry horde of the media he courted like a cruel lover only made her jealous. She missed him dreadfully and hated sharing him with the public and his producers. No matter what flaws she had managed to find in Jack's perfect veneer, she knew she could not live without him. If she lost him, now, she would never be happy again. Francesca thought she must be the flawed one, who needed love so desperately, like a crutch, and whose moods were so dependent on another's. But that need was ineradicable, knit into her marrow from the time she lost her elusive mother. In Jack she had found that excitement again.

"Francesca," gushed the musical French voice. "Have you seen the new *Vogue*? Oh, but you must. What a surprise!"

Francesca groaned silently and the fear drained from her body. It was Apollonie. Ever since the older woman had allied herself with Mario, she talked in this breathless, slightly excited tone of voice, as if always on the verge of announcing that her lover had won another race in one of his shiny, low cars. Her calm, professorial dignity had vanished.

"This is an emergency?" said Francesca in an amused voice. "French *Vogue*?"

"*Mais oui*, if your picture is on the editorial page! If they write an editorial about Francesca Nordonia and the meaning of beauty! Darling, you are *l'exemple par excellence* of the new, independent woman. They have designated you *'La Muse Américaine.'* But why are you laughing? Doesn't this make you proud?"

"Oh, Apollonie, of course. Of course I'm thrilled, in a way." But Francesca felt she was hardly an example of anything. "The next time I'm feeling low I'll go out and buy a copy. Thank you for telling me about it."

Apollonie seemed disappointed at this reception to her news. "Well, Jack will be thrilled, at least. There is one small thing before I let you go. There is an emergency, it's true." Apollonie's voice was sober now, and uncharacteristically timid. "Edward called. He's coming to Paris to talk to me. I'm afraid there's been a misunderstanding about the spa."

This seemed inevitable. Francesca guiltily thought that she had shamefully neglected Edward and her duties. It would make for an awkward meeting. "Poor Edward," Francesca said, "having to travel all this way when he's so busy. I know I've been too lax, leaving it all to him. I feel so awful."

"It's not your fault, Francesca. He wants to talk to me

about something that I did. That is, that Mario did, but I must take responsibility."

"Good heavens." Francesca had no idea how Mario could possibly be involved with the spa. It was nearly impossible to pry him away from his cars for long enough even to attend a dinner party, and then he had no other conversation than automobiles.

"Some money is missing from our joint account. By mistake the publicity budget for the spa was deposited in my personal, joint account, not the business one. And now it is gone. It was all a terrible mistake."

Francesca noted that Apollonie kept repeating the word "mistake" with an odd stress. Still, it didn't sound like a serious problem.

"That's dreadful, Apollonie, but surely not irreparable. We'll just cover it until Mario can return the money." She knew Mario and his hot streaks of luck. Surely he would win it back, as he had the first year at Cannes.

"If Mario *himself* will return," Apollonie said. "I wish it were that simple, *ma fille*. Unfortunately the bank covered a large overdraft from our joint account. I lost more than I care to admit."

"But surely it can't be that dire, Apollonie. Jack and I will help you. Don't worry about the spa."

"That is what I must talk to Edward about. But I have a favor to ask you. Will you meet with us as well? I need your help once again, Francesca. You have a way with Edward, you know that."

Francesca was just barely aware of the power she held over Edward, and was a little surprised to learn that Apollonie had divined it. "Of course, I'd be happy to. When is he coming?"

"Right away."

"Right away? Surely it isn't urgent."

"Oui, ma petite," Apollonie said sadly. "It's that urgent."

The next morning Edward rang at Francesca's gate. Jack was out at a meeting with one of his producers, who had returned to France with him for business discussions. Francesca looked out the French windows and beheld Edward standing there, his raincoat scant protection against the cold and wet March afternoon. A rush of warmth made her smile to herself. Edward looked so natural standing at her gate, as if he belonged there. After all, she told herself, this was Edward's country, his real home, and his dignified and intelligent face suited these surroundings. Francesca compared every man she met now with Jack, usually to their disadvantage. Among Frenchmen Edward was tall, but compared to Jack he was slightly stooped and almost delicate. His handsome features and dry expression were full of life and refinement. He lacked Jack's magnetism, but she felt a pure, uncomplicated joy at the sight of him. She ran to let him in.

Edward looked drawn and slightly weary, and Francesca quickly learned it wasn't because of jet lag. The doctor's own clinic was busier than ever, but expanding his services for the spa had strained his resources to the breaking point. He had hired a manager to replace Francesca, but still had to provide training and supervision. And now that reservations were down, Edward felt compelled to pick up the pieces of their enterprise.

"Francesca, this is very difficult for me. I've never failed before. Every one of my endeavors has been completely professional, and I've never been able to tolerate any falling off from that level. And now I'm afraid that for the first time I, or I should say we, are going to fail. The quality of our service has already begun to suffer badly." Edward crossed his legs and rapped his sensitive hands on the arm of the Louis XVI chair. It was the least comfortable chair in the living room, and Edward looked very ill at ease.

"Surely we can't be that close to failure."

"You must come back to Lyford Cay and look at the books. We've suffered an enormous loss this winter."

"But the profits—"

The bell rang again. Francesca leaped up to usher Apollonie into the living room.

Apollonie came slowly and tentatively, and her face, partly hidden under a silk scarf, was crestfallen. Francesca took her coat, and then brought her into the living room, where Edward rose to take her hand. The three of them sat down together. After a moment of silence Francesca realized Apollonie was on the verge of tears. But she was too proud to cry; she stifled her sobs in a handkerchief and then was still.

"I can't help but think of the last time we three were together. Lyford Rose brought us each a new life. Now look what I have done."

Francesca suppressed an urge to comfort her. She sensed

that Edward had an agenda planned in his head for this meeting, and she allowed him to lead it.

"No point in talking about blame now, is there?" Edward said.

"You made a mistake in judging Mario, that's all. Whatever possessed you to open a joint account, if you weren't married?"

"We've been living together for a year. It was my idea. I felt so awkward giving him money all the time, forcing him to ask for it. It will destroy the pride of a man like that."

"A man like that has no pride," Edward said angrily, and Francesca frowned at him. He was being far too harsh.

"At first he deposited his winnings from Cannes and other races, several hundred thousand dollars," Apollonie said. "I put in far less, I assure you. Then he began to lose, he needed a new car, a new engine. I did not want to hurt his pride by making him account for every penny. I let him handle the money. He is so much better at it than I am. Once I started my lectures in the fall, I was relieved to have his help." She opened her hands in her lap to indicate that Mario's behavior was a mystery to her.

"But how did he get his hands on the Lyford Rose money?" Edward's voice was patient, but Francesca could tell from the annoyance in his eyes that he despised Mario.

"Edward, I am just as distressed about this as you are. I gave it to him to deposit. He deposited it in our joint account. All he needed to withdraw funds was a signed check. He left for the Mexican road race, and I discovered the withdrawal. He hasn't returned."

Edward turned to Francesca. "The problem, Francesca, is that Apollonie has not reported this as a crime."

"Of course I haven't," she broke in. "He'll call me soon. He'll explain. I know that he considers this just a loan."

Francesca was astounded at Apollonie's ability to deceive herself about Mario. "Has he done this before? Run off without calling?"

Apollonie looked at her helplessly, her large blue eyes filled with tears. "Yes," she said in the defeated voice of a little girl.

"We might as well consider the money lost for good," Edward said. "We've got to notify the police, see if your insurance covers it, or if ours will. And finally, we've got to find an immediate way to make good that money. Without some new and very effective publicity, Lyford Rose is going to fail."

Francesca looked at Edward guiltily. She knew he was right, and had a right to be angry. In fact, he had suppressed his feelings too long. But before his disappointment she felt nearly as helpless as Apollonie.

Apollonie leaned over and pulled a long magazine out of her large leather bag. Francesca's heart sank. It was the French *Vogue* that extolled her shallower virtues. She knew that Edward would not be impressed by it.

"Edward, I brought this magazine to show you. There are three entire pages of pictures of Francesca. *La Comtesse Marquée!* And they mention Lyford Rose here at the end. How is that for publicity?"

Edward took the magazine from her and looked at it incredulously. He had a strong puritanical streak, and it offended him just as Francesca predicted.

"This is how you spend your time now?" he said to Francesca in a voice as hurt as it was scandalized. "I didn't realize you courted the press for your own sake. I thought last year you posed for all the fashion magazines in order to help Lyford Rose.This is useless as publicity for us. Everyone who doesn't know already will learn that you're no longer managing the spa. Francesca, don't you understand? They flocked to us because of you, to see you, to enjoy what you created. You aren't 'the branded countess' or any such nonsense. *You* are Lyford Rose."

Apollonie could no longer hold her tongue. "Edward, please. You've gone too far."

"I cannot warn you strongly enough about the financial condition we're in. You are my partners, but you're living lives of useless frivolity. Unless you're willing to work, we owe it to our clients to close the spa down."

Apollonie rose to leave. "Give me a week, Edward, to find Mario. You have my word that I'll make good the loss."

"I strongly urge you to come back to Lyford Cay as soon as possible, Apollonie," Edward said. "I know I've been more severe than I intended, but I feel your presence there is crucial, for your sake as well as the spa's." He shook her hand and gave her a begrudging smile.

When Francesca returned from showing Apollonie out, she found Edward standing before the fireplace, examining its incredible sculpture. He turned to her. "Francesca, I'm sorry I had to come bearing such bad news."

"Is it really that bad?"

"Yes. And for Apollonie it's worse. Part of the reason I want her to come back so strongly is because she's suffering a recurrence."

"No," Francesca said, shocked. "Why didn't she tell me?"

"For the same reason she hasn't told anyone. She doesn't want to undergo chemotherapy again, or more surgery."

"How long has she known?"

"Several months. Her doctor in Paris is a friend of mine, and since she is also still my patient, he contacted me. But Apollonie refused to return to the cay where I could treat her, or to undergo therapy here in Paris."

"What will happen to her?"

"It depends on how far the cancer has spread. She's been complaining of severe stomach pains. Her doctor has advised a CAT scan. We'll know when we get the results. Francesca, you've got to talk to her. She's throwing her life away on this scoundrel. There's a chance if we hurry we can still save her."

"I'll do all I can. To think she never told me! She must have known I'd want her to go back to the clinic."

"Will you come home with her?"

The question stymied her. Home was here, where Jack was. "I'm not sure, Edward. Jack needs me now. I may be able to get away for a weekend or two. But I'm not sure how soon I can move back for good."

A nerve in Edward's cheek flinched. "That's not enough," he said.

"Please, Edward"—she was desperate now—"I know we've let you down. I'll borrow some money and cover Apollonie's losses and I'll hire a public-relations firm here in Paris. At least I can handle that aspect of it. Please don't make any drastic decisions based on this one mistake." Then she made a desperate promise. "It means a lot to me to be with Apollonie. If she returns to the cay, I'll try to talk Jack into making Nassau our home base." But she knew she had little hope of influencing Jack, who wanted her to uproot Christopher and bring him to California.

"Something tells me that Jack doesn't want you to work."

"Edward, you know me better than I know myself. Jack is

terribly possessive. In Paris my life revolves around his. Even if I could convince him to come to Nassau, I don't know if he could accept my working full time. But we could try."

"I can't give you any advice because I'm too involved. I need you back in Nassau. And I can't believe the life you're leading here is worthy of you." He raised her hand to his lips and kissed it. "But whatever you do, I want you to be happy."

Later Francesca telephoned Apollonie. "Oh, Apollonie. Edward told me. I'm so sorry."

"I wish he hadn't. It's my secret."

"But why?" Francesca was bewildered.

"Because the cure is worse than the disease. How can I undergo chemotherapy now, when I'm in love? It weakens you terribly, and ruins your appearance. Last time all my hair fell out! What chance is there of getting Mario back then?"

Francesca was suddenly furious. "What chance is there now! And is he worth dying for?" But then her anger changed to sadness. She didn't know what to say to this woman.

"I prefer to live the rest of my life the way I choose," Apollonie said levelly. Her calm dignity shone through again. "I made my decision last fall after a lot of hard thought. Besides, in the last six months Mario has given me more than I ever could have desired."

"Why is it the end? If you get treatment now, you can beat the cancer again."

"Perhaps, but I think not. There are signs, pains in different places. I have no choice now, though. The pain is too severe. I'm putting myself in the hands of the doctors at last. Isn't it amusing, Francesca? I feel like a criminal turning himself in. At least Lyford Rose is a beautiful prison."

"Christopher just came in," Francesca said. "I'll have to call you later." She hung the telephone up abruptly. She didn't want Apollonie to hear her cry.

Late in the afternoon, Francesca's hairdresser arrived, and she began to prepare for a party that evening. Jack would be home soon. Francesca made sure Christopher was playing happily with his nurse, and then took the hairdresser upstairs with her. Ferdinand was short and wiry, with astute eyes and the sensitive hands of an artist. He was scrupulously polite, but critical. His salon in the sixteenth arrondissement was the most successful in Paris, and he was a businessman as well as a hairdresser; his clients considered Ferdinand a magician. But he still came to Francesca's home as a special favor to prepare her for parties. To Francesca, Ferdinand was priest and confessor, and she poured her heart out to him while he shampooed and set her long, wavy hair. But today as his firm fingers massaged her scalp she closed her eyes and tried to surrender her tension. His touch failed to work. She sat stiffly in a chair before the broad mirrors in her dressing room.

"A difficult day?" Ferdinand asked.

Francesca grimaced slightly. She could not bear yet to talk about Apollonie's illness and she had no desire to tell Ferdinand about Edward's visit. Edward's criticism gnawed away inside her.

A life of frivolity. Those words said in his slight French accent emphasized his contempt. Ferdinand began to brush her hair with a stiff brush.

"Ouch," Francesca said loudly. "Must you *yank* at my hair, Ferdinand?"

"I'm sorry."

He had barely pulled at a small tangle, and she knew it. But there was no point in trying to relax. She hadn't even the patience to endure Ferdinand's calming presence.

"Please be more careful, Ferdinand. I'm not a rag doll. My scalp is quite sensitive, and I feel it when you pull that way."

Ferdinand stood poised behind her, his hand with the brush frozen above her head. His startled eyes met hers in the mirror.

"I'm sure I didn't intend to hurt you. I apologize."

"Go on, then," she said, a little ashamed of herself.

Ferdinand slowly and cautiously began to brush out her hair again. She caught a gleam of resentment in his eye.

"I'll need you next week. Thursday evening Jack and I are going to the theater."

"I'm afraid I'm busy that night," said Ferdinand.

"You promised two weeks ago that you'd be available when Jack was in town. I was relying on you, depending on you. What shall I do? It's too late to get anyone else now."

"You can come into the salon, if you like. I'll arrange an appointment for you," Ferdinand said gently.

Francesca felt suddenly he had deliberately thwarted her.

"You know I never go out to have my hair done. I'm far too busy. Do you think I'll wait in line with your everyday customers?" she said in an imperious voice through clenched teeth.

"I didn't mean to offend you," he said, abashed.

"It's worse than an insult. You've ruined my schedule. Who do you think you are?" she thundered.

Ferdinand drew back. Now his anger showed openly in his face. "If you're unhappy with me, Francesca, perhaps you'd rather I leave."

"No, you can't go now," she said arrogantly. "All the photographers will be there tonight. I have to look perfect."

"*Alors*." The hairdresser put the brush down. "Shall we wash the hair?" He took her into her bathroom, positioned her before the sink, turned on the tap, and with a hose wetted her hair down.

But Francesca could not bear to lose the argument. Her hair foaming with white suds, she rose up like an implacable Medusa. She eyed him squarely in the mirror. "Ferdinand, you must come next Thursday. I simply won't have this unreliability."

"But we had not set the date—"

"If you give your word, you must keep it. I won't be treated like a customer off the street. Don't forget who I am."

"I haven't, I'm sure. But unfortunately I have obligations to my business that come first."

"*You* have obligations! How dare you be so self-important."

"Really, Francesca—"

"I need a hairdresser, not a businessman," she interrupted him. "If you can't keep your word, you ought not to be in business. Do you think you'll be in business for long if word of what you've done to me gets around?"

Ferdinand's patience broke at last. "Madame, don't forget who *I* am. I come here to help you, to do a favor for you, because once I found you charming."

"How dare you speak to me that way!" she cried, outraged. Water dripped down her face, soap blinded her eyes. She cried out against the burning suds. She could no longer see Ferdinand but she could feel the heat of his pride.

"*I* am Ferdinand," he drew himself up and said. "And madame, you are no one. A freak. A one-season joke. The mistress of a movie star. He is what keeps the paparazzi on your scent. Without him, who would pay attention to you? What have you achieved, what have you done? I leave you to your lover. He apparently finds your rudeness bearable."

Ferdinand washed his hands and snapped them clean in a towel. Then, before Francesca could wash her eyes free of the stinging soap, he was gone. She ran blindly out of the bathroom, into the bedroom, her arms flailing the air. "Ferdinand," she called vainly. "Where are you?"

The bedroom was silent. She stumbled back into the bath and stuck her head in the shower. Hot water cascaded on her, soaking her robe. Then, sopping wet, she ran through the house calling out the hairdresser's name. But it was no use. He was really gone, the wrought-iron gate fastened shut behind him.

The housekeeper met her in the kitchen with Christopher. "Is everything all right, madame?"

"Did you see where Ferdinand went?"

"He let himself out a moment ago, madame."

"But he can't leave me like this," Francesca wailed.

Christopher stared at her dumbly. "Mommy, Mommy, look!" he cried suddenly. "Bare feet!"

She looked down. She was standing barefoot in a pool of water. She always forbade Christopher to go barefoot, afraid that he would catch a chill from the cold stone floors and the river damp. Now he began to laugh at the sight of her breaking her own rules. "You're all wet," he said.

Suddenly Francesca was crying. She lifted him into her arms and kissed his face. He was so heavy now that she could only hold him for a moment without straining. "I guess I'm breaking all the rules, aren't I, darling," she said. She had behaved despicably toward Ferdinand. With a rush of horror she thought of the spectacle she had made of herself in Paris; it was as if she stood at Jack's side naked before the public, a vain and foolish woman who refused to accept the truth about herself that was so astonishingly clear to everyone else.

She left the kitchen. Slowly she mounted the marble staircase. As exaggerated as Ferdinand's statement was, there was a germ of truth in it. She closed the bedroom door and lay down across the wide bed. Was her self-image so fragile it could be shattered by a few words from a hairdresser? Well, why not? Who had she been all her life but a mirror obediently reflecting what others told her she was. As she was growing up she had thought she was plain. Then in Venice, society and Jack had told her differently. After the fire it was only Edward's eyes and voice that convinced her she wasn't repulsive. And in Paris, without his reassurances, she had been crippled again until Jack rescued her and, reflected in his eyes, she thought she had found herself once more. In the final analysis she was totally dependent for her self-esteem, her happiness, on how others saw her.

Francesca began to realize that their hedonistic way of life had not been a solution but a subterfuge. Though Jack had transformed her scar into a beauty mark superficially, she knew its ugliness and every day it penetrated and poisoned her being more. Disgusted with her self-pity, she disguised it with her short-tempered and imperious behavior.

When Jack come home, he found Francesca upstairs in bed. At first he was afraid she was ill, but the petulant set of her mouth warned him of an emotional storm. He sat on the end of the bed and with one hand shook her feet from side to side as a kind of greeting.

"Hello, scarface," he said.

Jack's fond nickname made something in Francesca shudder. She turned her face toward him but said nothing. She was pale without makeup. Her reddish gold hair lay in damp tangles around her shoulders and breast.

"The party's in an hour."

"I'm not going," she said flatly. She could not help but be aware of his presence, for Jack, rising to tower over her, could not be ignored. But tonight she found his beauty, his long, taut body and handsome face a nuisance.

"I'll pick out your dress," he said.

"Don't bother."

"Why don't you want to go to the party?"

"Can't you go anywhere alone!" she suddenly cried out. "Why do you drag me around after you? Everyone stares at me, at my ugliness. What am I compared to you?"

Jack ruffled his hair in confusion. He never knew how to respond to Francesca's outbursts, and so retreated into his boyishness.

Francesca recognized Jack's retreat as a pose meant to placate her, and it infuriated her all the more. At least Ferdinand had had the honesty to tell her the truth about herself, but Jack meant to manipulate her back into passivity. She sprang from the bed.

"What are you? Aren't you human? Does everyone have to

be perfect? Can't you realize I'm not! Why do I have to expose myself to everyone's ridicule for you, just so you can keep your picture in the paper? So you can sell tickets to your movie? Why must I make a fool out of myself?''

Jack caught her fists and held them. ''I'm not asking you to do anything,'' he said. ''What's this, *making a fool out of yourself*? What does that mean?''

''Don't pretend, Jack. Look at me.''

Francesca turned toward the mirror. ''Look at me!'' she insisted.

Jack didn't look at her face in the glass. He stood looking at her back, which was turned to him, until his stare seemed to pull her attention back to him. ''I think you're beautiful,'' he said.

She shook her head.

''What do you care what strangers think?'' he asked, stepping toward her and sweeping her hair away from her face. He held her head with his hand.

''I don't know. But I do care. Oh, Jack, I can't handle this life anymore! I want to go away . . .''

Jack pressed his mouth to her brow. For a moment she sobbed in his warm arms, until he stifled her cry with his mouth. It was as if he tried to patch together her skin, her torn spirit, with his body. But the flaw was too deep, deep into the root of her being, and the man whose kisses were meant to heal her could not fathom its hurt.

Chapter Twenty-four

JOSIE WOKE IN a glow of cold March light. The high casement windows of her bedroom on the top floor of the large town house faced south, and the sunlight reflecting from the rooftops dazzled her. She lay on the fur-covered bed for a moment in suspension between sleep and wakefulness. Then she felt the tenderness between her thighs and remembered the dark lovemaking of the night before.

The fragments of a strange dream also clung to her: She was in her apple-green bedroom in the Palazzo Nordonia in Venice, high above the gnarled trees in the courtyard. In the dream, she had been happy to be there because Francesca was with her. She had looked and looked through the palazzo for Francesca, calling her name, wanting to talk to her, wanting to confess to her the aimless and sybaritic life into which she had fallen.

But of course that was impossible, Josie realized as she lay staring at her reflection in the mirrored ceiling. Francesca, of all people, would be the one least likely to understand.

Josie felt a blush creeping up her neck, and nearly laughed aloud at the odd sensation. How long had it been since she'd last been embarrassed? Months! Certainly not since the prince had installed her in his town house and devoted his evenings to the sensual enjoyment she was expected to provide.

And yet the thought of Francesca did make her blush now. Pure, innocent Francesca. How could she have been so foolish as to dream of confessing her sins to such a woman? She lived in dread of running into her.

Josie got up and took a shower, letting the hot water soothe her love-battered body. Thank heaven the prince had left before dawn, for once, and let her sleep peacefully until almost noon. She had an important singing engagement that night, and she needed to feel, and look, rested.

Tonight her talent would go on public trial. For months she had been working for this chance to perform before the best European critics and producers, but outside the prince's social circle, her talent had gone largely unnoticed. After all her hard work, at last she was ready for the public performance that would bring her the acclaim she needed. The prince had decided that she'd sung at enough private parties and was now ready to dazzle the critics and bring more honor to his name. He'd reserved a popular nightclub for the evening and had mounted a production especially for Josie. His money and her talent, she was sure, would raise the show above the level of a vanity production and ease any prejudice the critics might feel against the consort of a rich Arab prince who could afford to put on such a show for a novice. Josie had arranged all the details, selected the costumes, and hired the backup musicians, who included both Charles Cash and Lucas Caswell. Charles, who had been working in Paris for the past year, had happily agreed to accompany her in a series of tender love ballads. And Lucas, whom the prince had flown to Paris at Josie's request, was the key to the success of her calypso numbers.

The prince, of course, would fill the nightclub with his influential friends, who would bring a contingent of critics in their wake. Josie had been rehearsing for two weeks; she had no doubts about her talent or about the quality of the production. It would be superb. If . . .

Josie put on a beige tweed skirt and a cashmere sweater that was exactly the same color as her tawny skin. She forced herself to meet her amber eyes in the mirror, a task that grew harder with every night she spent in Benor's bed. Then she forced herself to voice her reservations out loud.

"I'll be all right tonight if I can forget for two hours what I have become. If I can present myself as Marianne Lapoiret's carefree daughter and Francesca Nordonia's loyal childhood friend. If I can erase from my mind for just one evening the knowledge that I've traded away my integrity in exchange for Benor's money and sexual favors . . ."

The face in the mirror, she noticed, bore only a trace of resemblance to the one that had looked out at her from the mirror in her bedroom at the beach house all those years ago. The soft, round curves of that young Josephine had been hammered into the planes and angles and hollows of a mature woman.

The jaded misery in the mirror-eyes made Josie turn away, shaken. She gathered up her purse and gloves and headed downstairs. When Josie went downstairs the prince was gone; he left every afternoon. Taciturn and driven, he would be dining with opinion-makers of any stripe, perhaps the editors of a few scandal sheets or the publisher of *Le Monde*; entertaining the odd members of royalty passing through Paris like diminished comets or useless, unstoppable orbits, whom he knew from his prep-school days in Switzerland; consulting an armada of investment bankers about new companies to buy. He patronized the arts and attended charity functions, primarily to further what he regarded as his "mission"—to rectify the distorted image of Arabs in the West as rich but primitive nomads. Soft-spoken and refined, with languorous dark eyes, he glided through his privileged life in impeccably tailored London suits.

The first time he heard her sing at Apollonie's château, he had decided that Josie was a living work of art, and he had simply acquired her the way he would have bought a Matisse or Degas; and because he was an astute businessman, he expected a return on his investment. He made himself clear when he first brought her to Paris: He would introduce Josie to influential people—critics, nightclub owners, wealthy members of the international set—and would arrange for her to sing at private parties; in return, Josie was to entertain him each night in a new and sexually exciting way. Like Scheherazade, eternal narrator of the Arabian Nights tales, she would enjoy his patronage only as long as she could keep him from being bored.

She had stuck to her end of the bargain, racking her brain for new ways to excite him. She did so mostly because she knew he would turn her out if she didn't please him, but she also hoped to beguile him into pleasing her as well as himself. Often she succeeded.

Josie smiled as she entered the dining room and watched a servant lay out her breakfast. She put aside her purse and gloves and sat down to enjoy the meal, remembering the last time the prince had pleased her, just a few nights before.

She chewed contemplatively on a piece of bacon, smiling at her own deviltry. Well, she thought, he deserved it. The prince had ignored her all evening while he entertained a roomful of wealthy guests. Then, after everyone else had left, he had closeted himself in the library with a stack of financial documents.

Bored and in need of attention, Josie had burst into the library and leaped onto the huge oak table. She had been wearing an expensive gown designed for her by Givenchy to the prince's specifications. Tight and silky, it glittered with green and blue iridescence, like the wings of the Nassau dragonflies. She had peeled the dress off her body inch by inch until she stood naked before Benor except for high-heeled gold sandals and diamond earrings.

The prince, thoroughly distracted at last, had put aside his papers and turned the lights higher.

"Turn," he had said at last, and she did, slowly. She could feel his dark eyes boring into her back. Then, just as he reached for her, she had run laughing from the room. By the time he caught her in her bedroom, he had been fierce with desire; she could no longer tease him; he overwhelmed her. A large-boned man, he was a mass of rippling muscles; Josie sometimes felt there was simply too much of him to make love to. He flung her on the bed and stood silently beside her. Her heart pounded so rapidly, she thought it might explode. She had lain still for the cool inspection of his hands, but while he stripped off his clothes, she had run away again, making him chase her through the suite and then repeat his caresses. Only when she felt truly eager for release did she allow him to pin her down on the soft, thick rug. Hungrily he had stroked the satiny skin of her breasts and stomach before arousing her with his lips and tongue until the rockets went off inside her head.

When he was sure she was totally satisfied, he had taken his pleasure from her and then started all over again from the beginning.

It had been a very good night, one that Josie would not soon forget. She sighed as she turned her attention to the excellent coffee, doubting that even Benor could perform that wholeheartedly two nights in a row. She wondered idly where he had taken himself off to. Once, on a whim, he had disappeared for a week, to announce upon his return that he had bought a wild-animal preserve on a mountainside in Kenya. The park contained, he told her, five hundred lions. It seemed a fabulous number, a symbol of his incredible wealth. She had thought about those lions for days with a kind of envy. They were free in their mountain preserve, to hunt, to stalk, while the prince kept her in a tight cage of lust where she could not forget her subservience for a second.

Wherever he went, though, he never forgot her; she had to give him credit for that. He would return to Paris laden with gifts for her, full of new ideas about how to promote her career. How many audition tapes had he arranged for her to make? Four? No, five. He had sent copies of them to producers all over Europe.

She poured more cream into her coffee and opened the papers with a flourish. They were in French, her mother's native language, which made Josie feel comfortable. In fact, everything about Paris comforted her. She felt much more at home in France than she had in Venice. Here at least people pronounced her name the way Marianne had meant for it to sound—Jho-*see*, with the accent on the second syllable. Benor, too, said her name correctly. And, like Benor, Josie now spoke French like a native. The years of self-teaching and the months in Paris had stripped away all traces of the Haitian accent and idioms that Carlo Nordonia had ridiculed.

But the thought of Marianne made her feel a wave of vanquishing guilt, and she forced the memory from her mind. She turned to the entertainment pages of the newspaper to check the announcement of her performance that night, but found it dwarfed by a photograph of Francesca. The blowup of her scarred face covered nearly a quarter of the page. The caption said that a famous Parisian photographer—Josie had met him at one of Benor's lavish parties—had chosen Francesca as his muse and was creating a series of portraits of her, all of which emphasized the cruel beauty of her scar. In this portrait, the eyes above that scar were as clear and as beautiful as ever, glowing with triumph and happiness.

Josie fought down a small surge of old resentment and forced herself to think objectively. Francesca, in spite of the suffering she'd been through, had managed to make something of her life. She had lost Jack, her father, and Michael; even her own porcelain-perfect beauty had been destroyed. And yet she hadn't turned to drugs; she hadn't tried to escape from herself as Josie had. Nothing in Josie's experience—except her mother's death—could even compare to what her sister had been through. But in Francesca's eyes, she could still see integrity while her own gaze reflected only decadence.

But with a slight tremor of surprise, she realized the old resentment was nearly gone. She felt more shame than anger when she thought of Francesca. How could she ever face her sister again, after selling her soul to Benor? If Francesca had been unwilling to acknowledge their blood ties before, Josie had now given her the best reason in the world to keep their sisterhood a secret.

Josie folded the paper and went to the hall for her coat. She was to spend a part of the afternoon with Lucas, running through the lyrics of the island songs for the performance tonight. She would need all of her concentration for this session, so it was important to put Francesca out of her mind. Fighting down the first wave of stage fright, she walked through the great hall and out the front door.

The prince's marble town house exuded elegance, but it was as cold and quiet as a cemetery. Its windows were shrouded. The gate was guarded by a soldier with a fez, a ceremonial sword, and a heavy pistol. The prince lived in fear of a jihad by the religious fanatics who were a tiny minority in his country, who had believed that the country had been corrupted by the Western progress he had encouraged. The new windfall of oil profits was stirring revolt; materialism and modernism were deemed grave sins. The prince, who had grown up in Europe, would have been considered the devil incarnate were he closer to the throne; there was danger for him even though he would not inherit the crown.

Josie rummaged through her purse in search of the directions Lucas had given her. She had been to the rehearsal hall twice before, but had been taken there by the prince's chauffeur. Today the car was nowhere in sight, so she decided to walk. She had plenty of time, and the chauffeur had apparently taken Benor out for the afternoon. She found the sheet of note paper on which Lucas had scrawled the directions, and she set out toward the appointment at a brisk pace, enjoying the tangy bite of the March wind.

After ten minutes or so, she found herself facing a complicated intersection of small streets. Consulting the directions again and finding them unclear, she decided to walk down the widest street until she found someone who could tell her which way to go.

The neighborhood, she noticed, was not as elegant as Benor's, but it was older and more private. The houses were walled off from the street by high gates, inside which trees sheltered private gardens. There were no kiosks or vendors as on the Left Bank, nor were there any other pedestrians, unless she counted the white pigeons waddling across the cobblestoned street. Josie recognized the area, however, as one the prince frequently visited. Sometimes the chauffeur dropped him off before driving Josie somewhere else. She turned into a narrow street near the corner where the chauffeur often left him, letting her curiosity lead her forward. In a row of parked cars she saw the prince's chauffeur seated in the black Mercedes. He was sound asleep, a toothpick balanced on his lower lip, his cap on the seat beside him. Josie turned to face the residence before which the car was parked. Behind the open iron gates stood an unimposing old building with shuttered windows. Overcome with curiosity now, she stepped through the gates and walked up to the door. She peered through the narrow windows that framed the entrance.

She saw nothing, but while she was bent awkwardly forward, the front door opened as if she had inadvertently touched it. Surprised, she looked up.

"Who are you?" said a tall and very slim young woman in accented French. She was quite beautiful, her long, honey-colored hair swept up in curls on her head. Her elegantly ruffled cream silk blouse was tucked into a deep blue velvet skirt. She was dressed to receive guests for dinner, say, or to attend a reception at an embassy. Josie could not place her accent, but guessed she was English.

"I'm sorry," Josie murmured, stumbling back, dying suddenly to run down the short path and out the gate. "Is the prince here? I saw Prince Benor's car—"

But she was talking to air. The girl had vanished and the door swung shut. Josie turned away in relief. She had not taken three steps before she heard the door open again, and suddenly another stranger was beside her, reaching for her wrist. Josie swung around, desperate now to get away before the prince realized she was outside.

"I'm sorry, I've made a mistake, I was just passing," she said to the middle-aged woman who held her now quite firmly. Small and delicate, with a charmingly pretty face, she did not look like she had the strength to restrain Josie. She wore a light blue Chanel suit with long gold chains around her neck, and elegant high heels. But her hand was like an iron clamp. "Just a mistake," Josie repeated.

"Someone sent you," the woman said, her eyes searching Josie's face.

"The prince is here . . ." Josie began. Josie had the

sensation that the woman was reading a blueprint of her soul as she drew her back toward the front door.

She looked Josie swiftly up and down. "You are an actress," she announced.

"No." Josie quizzically shook her head. "I was just passing by, and thought a friend of mine might be here—"

"Prince Benor Fabi?" The woman raised a faintly penciled eyebrow.

Josie grew afraid.

"Eleanor told me you mentioned him. Yes, he is here. I am Simone Deloup," she said in a cordial voice. "Do not be shy. You must come in and have some tea. Often the young girls are shy, but you see, there is no need to be."

Before Josie knew what had happened, she was standing in a narrow, dark foyer, introducing herself. She thought that whoever owned this house must be serving the prince lunch. They were all dressed to receive royalty.

"The prince sent you," Simone said in her presumptuous way. "Not an actress? A model, then?"

"No, I'm a singer."

"Ah," said Simone, as if that explained Josie's sudden arrival on her doorstep and no more questions were necessary. "I can help you, then. If the prince sent you, that is a good enough recommendation. I see you are quite lovely," she added disarmingly as she guided the reluctant Josie into a large living room.

After the austere appearance of the outside of the house, this room was a shock. It was walled with enormous mirrors in heavy gilt frames, and lushly carpeted. There were basins of tropical fronds and a silvery white stuffed peacock on a pedestal by the draped windows. On a couple of overstuffed velvet couches sat pretty girls; after a moment Josie blinked and realized that if she did not count the reflection in the mirrored ceiling, there was only one girl. Simone shooed her away. The girl rose, bone thin in a narrow evening gown that was beautifully, expensively cut, and moved her head jarringly for a moment from side to side, as if getting the kinks out of her neck. Her hair was also beautifully cut in a straight line, and each hair fell into place with a silken shimmer. After this dramatic pause, she gave Josie an odd, sly look as she passed her in the doorway.

Simone chuckled when she was gone. "You can learn

much from Marie. She hardly moves a muscle, like a cat, but each stretch vibrates in the man's spine."

Josie had no idea what this meant. "Where is the prince?" she asked.

"You do not want to disturb him now. Next time he comes, perhaps. He comes here often; you won't have to wait long. Nearly every afternoon, perhaps tomorrow. I always save him a room. Do you have clothes?"

"Of course," said Josie, now thoroughly confused.

"Because all my girls are beautifully dressed. I have only the best. They are all like you, struggling young actresses, singers; they meet many important men here, and when they are ready to fly away, I let them go. I wish them well—"

Josie backed away. Now it was Simone's turn to look at her quizzically, but before she could reach out with her iron grip again, Josie was running down the dark corridor. She burst out of the house, into the sunlight, and never stopped running, past the sleeping chauffeur, down the narrow street, until she reached a little square. A bus was passing; Josie jumped on it, out of breath and half expecting, when she looked back, to see a string of beautiful girls in evening gowns like unholy debutantes in full pursuit. But the streets were quiet, wrapped in a noon sleep. Only Josie was fully alert, running as usual, for her life.

Chapter Twenty-five

LUCAS'S HOTEL NEAR the Sorbonne was a dingy, charmless building. It stood in a row of other faceless buildings that were cheap enough for students to afford. Lucas let her into his small room, and then sprang back onto the wide, rumpled bed from which she had wakened him. He wore a pair of Levi's shorts and nothing more. She paused in the doorway. The room's only asset was a large window that looked out on a low monument; there was nothing in the room besides the bed and an uncomfortable, straight-backed chair. Its starkness depressed Josie. Once she would have thought such a room in the heart of Paris a splendid find. The air was heavy with the smell of marijuana.

"What brings you here, princess?"

Lucas's voice reassured her. At least she could always depend on his friendship. It had been the one constant in her life, ever since her mother's death. But although she basked in that veiled love, she could not return it.

"Lucas, I need your help. I'm so nervous about the performance tonight, I couldn't sleep. The prince doesn't understand me, he ought to keep away from me . . ." Her voice trailed off plaintively. She suddenly found herself explaining something to Lucas that was better left unsaid. Her self-pitying tone sounded false, but she dared not betray the real reasons for her distress.

"What's the matter, baby? Don't tell me when you kissed your prince he turned back into a frog."

"Don't laugh at me now, Lucas, I need help."

"You always need help, don't you, princess?" he said in a sly, light voice. "I guess you think I'll be your nursemaid forever." He pulled deeply on a cigarette.

Josie stared at him in confusion. "No, I'm sorry to barge in on you. It's just this awful pressure today, I feel like hell.

You said I should always come to you, I should count on you if anything happened.''

''Right. So now you think my world revolves around you. Well it doesn't, and I haven't got any pills left. I got rid of them all last night. A big sale.''

''Lucas, that's a mistake. You'll get caught. Dealing is a game of Russian roulette—''

''I'm not dealing. I'll never deal again. I got enough for my flight back to the islands; that's all I wanted. Besides, do you think I can spend the rest of my life playing backup for a would-be jazz singer? There's nothing in it for me.''

Josie was startled by the drawling defiance in his voice; yet part of her had always known that Lucas harbored a deepening hostility toward her. ''Tonight's your chance, too, Lucas, you'll have a solo. You don't know what it could lead to.''

''Nothing.'' He grinned at her. His large teeth were yellow, like the dirty color of his bloodshot eyes. He stomped out the cigarette. ''It'll lead nowhere, princess, because I ain't gonna be there.'' He said it proudly, as if privately laughing at her. ''I don't need to. I like playing in the Seasaw Club, under my own name. I like being the main attraction. Does that surprise you, princess?''

Josie's head reeled. She badly needed Lucas to accompany her on several of the island songs she intended to sing. No one else knew them, or if they managed the impossible feat of learning them in an afternoon, could deliver them with his inventive virtuosity. Losing Lucas would mean losing half her repertoire, the distinctive, unique half. The enormity of his betrayal at this late hour stunned her. She said in the helpless voice of the already defeated, ''You can't ditch me now. It's too late to get a replacement.'' Then Josie was suddenly furious. ''It's a filthy thing for you to do after all of my help. Why do you want to destroy me?''

''You destroyed yourself, sweetheart. Or did the prince accomplish that for you, too?''

''You hate me. You're jealous of him.''

''Jealous? Girls like you aren't hard to come by. Not in this town. I see them on every corner. Oh, poor baby. Look, I'll help you. I'll try to find some of those magic pills for you.'' He drew his large, rawboned body up. His chest had a yellowish, unhealthy pallor, and his ribs fanned through the skin. He shambled to the armoire and began to scrounge around in the pockets of his clothes. "It's not going to cost you a dime. Call it a parting gift. Because you did so much for me." His voice was drenched with sarcasm.

Something in his tone sparked Josie's remaining pride. She snorted bitterly. "Forget it, Lucas. I don't want your help. I don't need your music and I don't need your chemical inspiration. Maybe this is all for the best. I'll do just fine without you."

As she walked out the door she heard the mattress groan as Lucas threw himself down on the bed again. And then, echoing down the staircase after her, rang his deliberately loud, hollow laughter. He meant it to shake her, and it did. How could she have earned such an enemy? Without Lucas, tonight was bound to be a disaster. Josie couldn't sing; she wanted to scream.

She secluded herself in her bedroom in the prince's town house, thinking she would plead sickness and call off the performance tonight. In fact, she did feel ill. She had never faced the extent of her addiction to amphetamines, though she knew it went deep. But the pain was as nothing compared to her anger, which gouged deep in her mind and released a surprising energy. Every night she practiced singing, accompanying herself on her guitar. She knew all her music backwards, and her fingers were limber. She got up and before she realized consciously that she had decided to accompany herself, she was practicing. Even the sense of her impending failure no longer shook her. She would face the audience with pride, as herself, and their judgment would not harm that new feeling. And tomorrow she would fly back to Nassau.

Just four hours later, the pianist and bass player filed onto the tiny dais at Lilo's nightclub. Josie stood backstage, behind a maroon velvet curtain, and looked out on the dark mass of faces. Slivers of light lit up crescents of heads and arms, but nothing came to her whole, and she recognized no one. Worse, the audience was solemnly quiet. That meant that the prince's invited friends had come here not just to greet one another and be seen, but to listen. Josie felt tension pull the skin of her face as taut as her guitar strings. Now adrenaline had taken the place of speed; she wanted to race through the act and get it over with. The worst the critics could say about her was that her act was a vanity production for the prince's girl friend; and somehow Lucas had forced her to face that truth this afternoon. It was a suitable finale to her sojourn as a royal consort in Paris. The pretender was about to be deposed.

Then she was bathed in rosy light. The glimmering lights in the black sea of the audience were as unreal as starlight reflected on water. The pianist played a note and she tuned her guitar. The strings leaped to her fingers, weaving a sound that she found oddly consoling in this lonely light. So the guitar, at least, would not betray her. It would absorb her nervousness and turn it into song. She followed that comforting sound, and began to sing.

At first her voice sounded hoarse as her tight vocal cords tugged at the air, but suddenly she remembered her lessons in Venice, and let the breath flow unimpeded from deep in her stomach. Then something marvelous happened: The air cleared a bright space around her, transporting her to the golden Adriatic of her memory, of her dreams. She had recovered the beauty she brought as a gift to Venice. The innocent happiness of her earlier life wafted out and filled the room until there was no escaping its spell. She sang a song she had not intended to sing, an island song that imitated bird calls, and her happy, leaping shouts more than made up for Lucas's absence. It was as if a bird within her throat had opened its throat, and she found that she could radiate bands of emotion like the lights that peel from shooting stars. Lucas didn't matter at all now; what mattered was her happiness, finally remembered, and her sadness, an exile about to end. She launched into the blues, stunning the audience with her masked, cavalier intensity.

But for her the audience no longer existed; her voice had pierced them, and the lights shattered around her like a thousand shivering bits of broken mirror. She sang for herself now, and then for Marianne. Her mother knew what it was like to live so many millions of miles beyond the earth, among the vacant amnesias of the stars. She was alone now; she had never been so alone. What did wealth matter, or all the glitter of fame, compared to the lonely singular melody of this song, to the unheard sound of a girl singing? She floated the song out onto the air, not caring whether anyone understood, or would want to understand, what tonight's performance had cost her. She sang not to impress, but to tell the truth to herself. She sang of the prince lolling in the temple of her body, rutting in it; of Francesca craning on her slender swan's neck the perfect side, then the degraded side of her moon-white head for the enthralled artist; of Lucas showering her with his little death pellets in a paroxysm of envy and anger and love. She sent these images out from her breast, and then she grew still while the piano player played a solo. After that a happy calypso song, the dream of her future at home, of the traveler returned safely to the center of herself. It was over.

The audience roared with applause and kept her onstage for four encores. Josie was cold suddenly with sweat, and now that she was released from the need to perform, her body no longer resisted the effects of her strain. But she sang with a true, sudden love of performing. The audience loved her for the real self she had finally revealed. The sense of freedom that gave her was exhilarating. She took her last bow beaming with pride, stepped backstage, and collapsed.

When Josie regained consciousness, she found herself lying in the prince's bedroom. It was daylight, and the room was filled with the sweet, cloying odor of orchids and roses. The prince had never before allowed her to spend the night in his private sanctuary. He was gone, and sunlight glazed the dozens of pots of flowers. Josie reached for the bell.

A maid entered with a breakfast tray. She wore a look of awe.

"Where did the flowers come from? Did the prince order them?"

"No, mademoiselle. His friends sent them for you. They are still arriving downstairs."

"Where is the prince?"

"His Highness was called away to London this morning. He'll be back in a week. He said to tell you he will call."

"Thank you."

The maid waited in the doorway. "Can I bring the doctor upstairs, mademoiselle? He's been waiting."

"The doctor?"

"Yes. The prince insisted," she said in her musical French, and disappeared.

Josie poured a cup of coffee from a silver pot and lifted the covers off the plates. A warm croissant and scrambled eggs were on a plate, and beside it on the white linen napkin lay a very large emerald. Josie picked it up in wonder. It was held on a delicate prong of gold, suspended on an antique gold chain. Its clear green facets seemed to hold a small sea in which a heavy sun had just set. There was a note. In the prince's scrupulous, tiny print she read, "The color of your eyes." She knew that this was his way of thanking her for not disappointing him, or embarrassing him in front of his friends.

A timid knock on the door announced the doctor bearing a black bag. He looked at her in consternation as if she were very ill, when in fact she was overwhelmed with relief. He examined her, listened to her heart, measured her blood pressure, peered into her ears and eyes. He took her into the enormous bathroom and weighed her on the prince's scale. Then he admonished her to gain weight, and took away urine and blood samples. He left her with a vial of tranquilizers and a prescription for more. Josie smiled at the little blue and red bottle. With doctors like this, she would have no need for Lucas. When he was gone, the maid came once more to deliver newspapers and mail.

Josie had never gotten mail in Paris before, but she turned to the entertainment pages of the newspapers first and scanned them for reviews. Each paper carried a small review of her act, and one printed a photograph the prince must have had his public-relations firm send out. In the blurry photo she grinned stupidly out of the newsprint as if she had never suffered for a moment in her life. The reviews made her sound like an *objet trouvé*, some fabulous shell picked up off a Caribbean beach, a primitive native girl. But they were more than patronizing; they praised her skill and gracefulness, and one suggested that she must have had instruction from a master; to sing with such perfect intonation and phrasing was unnatural. Both reviewers predicted that her performance at Lilo's had been the debut of an auspicious career, and hoped to hear more from her. It was overwhelming. Josie sank back into the high pillows. It surprised her to read about the way she sounded to others. (To herself she sounded discordant.) But in spite of her success, she longed to go back to the islands. She knew now that she could not go on with this artificial life. Even this sudden, small flurry of fame could not compensate for the damage her so-called career had caused her.

The letters the maid brought had been delivered by messenger. They were notes of praise for her performance of the night before, and each enclosed an invitation to dinner. It was almost as if all the prince's guests had had the same thought, to send bouquets and offer hospitality. She wrapped her emerald in a handkerchief and laid it in the compartment of her jewelry box. Then she dressed. The maid summoned her to speak to the prince on the telephone.

"You pleased me very much last night," he said.

She was suddenly shy, as if his opinion mattered terribly to her. "Thank you," she mumbled. "I loved the necklace." Then she ran out of words. She always felt awkward before the prince, as if she were in fact some creature of a lesser order.

"Unfortunately I've been called away. But when I return next week we'll have a grand party for you and invite all of Paris to celebrate. My secretary is making all the arrangements."

"But Benor, there's something I have to tell you. I've been longing to go back home. I'm very grateful, believe me, but I'd feel better—"

"Nonsense," he interrupted her. "You can't leave now. You've got an engagement to sing at Lilo's for the next two weeks, and several offers after that. All my friends in the music industry are coming to hear you sing, all the way from America. Your tape may be pressed into a record. You have no time for shyness now, Josie," he said firmly but kindly.

"A record? But I don't know anything about that. I didn't authorize it."

"That's all right. I did."

The phone clicked dead in her hand. The prince did not mean to be rude, she knew; his attention had merely passed on to other matters. Her stay in Paris was settled as far as he was concerned.

Downstairs there was a commotion at the front door. The butler was haranguing someone in rapid Arabic. Josie heard a goat's ragged whiny with surprise. As she watched from the top of the staircase, two men in Arab dress managed to lead a pair of white goats halfway into the foyer. The butler's face went from red to purple, and he swore loudly. The goats tried to break loose from their tethers. Sliding on the marble floor, they bucked and pranced on sharp heels, backing out the door.

"What's going on?" Josie asked one of the servants.

"They are trying to deliver another gift for you. Two goats from one of the tribes in our country."

"But surely not into the house."

"Yes, they are sacred to that tribe."

"Well, send them back, for goodness' sake. That's what the prince would do."

"No, no." The butler overheard her. "We dare not send them back. It would be too great an insult."

"But they'll ruin the carpet, they'll eat it! Lead them around the back to the garden. I'll send someone to unlock the gate."

The butler looked about to cry.

"Let's donate them to the zoo," Josie suggested. "There must be a zoo in Paris."

"You don't understand these matters, mademoiselle, if I may say so," the butler said as he passed her to get the keys to the iron gate that surrounded the garden. "A display of proper gratitude is essential, at least until the donors come to visit. These goats are worshiped in some parts of the country."

The butler's attitude somehow made Josie feel that the arrival of the goats was all her fault. She saw the foyer was filled with bouquets of flowers, still unwrapped, and there were more messages for her on the table. The front bell rang again and the butler hurried to open it.

"More flowers! We shall have to feed them to the goats. We should be thankful they did not send a bull."

Lady Jane handed the nurse an extra pound note and took the brown paper bag from her. "You are a dear," she murmured as she pressed the note into the woman's hand. The nurse smiled and put her finger to her lips. Then she left the room.

Out of the bag Lady Jane pulled a copy of the *Paris Herald* and a *Vogue* magazine. Her only treat, this forbidden glimpse of the outside world that she had smuggled in to her once a week. She glanced at the headlines and then with a sigh of pleasure began to flick through the magazine. Something caught her attention and she turned the pages back quickly. She could not believe her eyes. It was Francesca staring out at her, brandishing her scar like a medal of honor. Beautiful as ever, more so for being brave. She threw the magazine down, her heart beating wildly. Anger lifted the cloud she had been living in since her arrival at the sanitarium. She got up from her bed and walked to the window. She gazed across the vast green lawn at the sprawling Gothic buildings. The institution bore a distressing resemblance to her husband's estate not far away, the same English countryside. Well, she had a reason to leave now. Francesca, whom she had believed to be crippled by the fire, was alive and thriving and that was not to be endured . . . not to be permitted . . . not while she had a breath left in her. How dare she look like that with Michael in his grave. She went back and, snatching up the magazine, quickly found the page again and started to read the text carefully. At the same time a plan, a very clear-cut plan began to shape in her twisted mind.

Later that afternoon Lady Jane's psychiatrist congratulated her on a "breakthrough." "We are making progress at last," he said patronizingly, patting Lady Jane on the back as she left his office. Lady Jane resisted the temptation to shake the man's hand off and merely smiled. It would not be difficult to get around these fools, now that she had made up her mind. They had promised her freedom if she would pass their tests. She had failed them thus far because she hadn't cared to pass. The next time would be different.

Francesca let herself into the house and dropped wearily onto the couch. Jack followed, with Christopher at his heels, both of them laden with her suitcases and garment bags.

"Where's Marie?" she asked Jack.

"I gave her the day off."

The two of them thundered up the stairs, and a moment later Francesca heard them opening closet doors and slamming drawers shut. She closed her eyes and let herself drift off into a half-sleep.

This, she decided groggily, was not working.

She felt her head fall back against the soft velvet upholstery as the lonely, frustrating days of the past three weeks began to fade from her mind.

"Wake up, scarface. We have a surprise for you."

Francesca opened her eyes and blinked sleepily up at Jack.

"We made cookies," Christopher said proudly. "They're a homecoming present. We're glad you're back." He leaped up onto the couch and leaned across her to plant a kiss on her cheek.

Something in Jack's smile made her glance warily at the tray he placed on the coffee table. It held a small silver coffee-pot, a glass of milk for Christopher, and a plateful of dull lavender disks with oddly shaped bulges. "Cookies?" she said weakly.

"*Chocolate chip* cookies," Jack replied helpfully. "Don't they look good? Christopher and I worked extremely hard all afternoon baking them especially for you."

She stared stonily into his laughing blue eyes. "I can't wait to see the kitchen."

Christopher reached out, grabbed one of the lavender disks, and stuffed it into his mouth while his mother looked on warily. "Have one, Mama," he offered.

Francesca took a cookie and ate it valiantly, washing it down with black coffee. "These contain some sort of secret ingredient, don't they? Let me guess what it is."

"Grape jelly," Christopher said, "and chocolate-covered cherries. Jack chopped them up real small, and I stirred them around with the other stuff."

Francesca began to laugh, then forced herself to look solemnly at her son. "I have a terrible feeling you didn't miss me one bit while I was in Lyford Cay."

He tried to look grave. "I missed you the first day. But after that Jack and I went to the movies every night."

Francesca clamped one hand to her head and closed her eyes. "I will not lose my temper," she muttered between clenched teeth.

"Time for bed, Christopher," Jack said cheerfully. "Run upstairs and get ready. Your mother and I will be up to say good night in a minute."

Christopher kissed Francesca and then obediently went up to his room.

"Francesca?" Jack said, too sweetly.

"Don't speak to me."

"Look, honey, I'm sorry Christopher and I didn't miss you, but—"

Francesca started to laugh, tried to stop, and failed. "You are the most dreadful man I have ever met! There I was all by myself, an ocean away from Paris, worrying myself sick about having left you behind, and you and Christopher were living the decadent life of two bachelors on the loose in gay Paree."

Jack took her hand and raised it to his lips. "Well, maybe we missed you a little bit now and then." He put one arm around her and pulled her to him, pressing her head into the hollow of his shoulder. "Francesca, tell me you love me and that you hated being away from me." He smoothed her hair back from her forehead and dropped a kiss on her nose.

"I adore you, and I couldn't stand being away from you," Francesca admitted. "That's why I came back early."

"What have you arranged about the spa?"

"They need me. There's no getting around it. People expect me to be there to greet them personally and see to their needs. Unfortunately there is no one who can replace me."

Jack got up angrily and crossed the room for a cigarette. Francesca was too tired for an argument.

"I discussed it with Apollonie and Edward for hours."

After being with Edward for the last ten days, Jack seemed even more boyish and immature, she thought guiltily. Edward had made it clear there was more for her to come back to than just the spa.

"It's as important to me as your career is to you," she said defensively. "If I could be there just six months a year—you don't want to be in L.A. more than that, anyway. At least come and see Lyford Cay—"

But he was already starting up the stairs. "I've been to Nassau," he said curtly.

"Well, I've seen Paris!" she shot back. "And I don't like it," she finished to herself. A door slammed above her. She rose with a sigh and turned off the lights. Upstairs she went in to say good night to Christopher, who had fallen asleep waiting for her. She looked down at him.

They had gotten along well together, Christopher and Jack. That single fact, for some strange reason, made her uneasy. Always before, the two of them had maintained an amiable truce, but they had never been intimate. There had been no fights, no bitterness between them, but neither had they been truly bonded.

And that, Francesca knew, was neither Jack's fault nor Christopher's. It had been Francesca herself who had interrupted the occasional father-son talk or play session, who had discouraged Jack from taking Christopher on outings without her, who had attended to her son's needs without ever asking Jack's help. The new intimacy between them frightened her;

she could feel the hard, cold mass of anxiety forming inside her.

She tried to convince herself that it was wrong to insinuate herself between them, but their closeness threatened her in a way she did not understand. She closed her eyes against the brightening light and tried to analyze her feelings.

Christopher, she knew, was the one absolute in her life. He was her son; he would love her forever. Even when he grew up and left home, he would hold his mother's image in his heart. And about him Francesca had no doubts. She never questioned his love for her or her own for him. She didn't worry about his abandoning her, as Susannah had, or disapproving of her, as Carlo had. Francesca loved him unconditionally, just as he loved her.

But Jack might do just about anything. He might grow impatient with her excuses and walk out on her, fly back to Los Angeles and devote himself entirely to his work. He might begin to feel envious of Francesca's new fame. He might get tired of her unwillingness to marry him. He might just wake up one morning and say to himself, "This woman isn't worth all the trouble I go through for her."

Francesca wondered why Jack hadn't figured out by now that Christopher was his son. Was it because her own coloring was so much like his? Did Jack simply assume that Christopher had Francesca's light hair and eyes? That, she knew, was the reason no one else had questioned the child's parentage. No one except Michael.

The old gnawing pain of guilt joined the anxiety that had seated itself inside her. She had tried to deceive Michael, assuming he would believe Christopher was his son. Now she was doing the same thing to Jack.

And while she was keeping the truth from Jack, she was destroying her own chance to become the kind of person she knew he deserved. He wasn't perfect. Far from it. He was egotistical and shallow. He lacked Edward's selfless drive to serve others. He had not been endowed with Michael's refusal to be beguiled by his own charm and good looks and he lacked Carlo Nordonia's seriousness of purpose.

Francesca closed the door to the nursery. When would the right moment come to tell Jack that Christopher was his son? He made it impossible for her to decide to marry him; perhaps intentionally, she thought cynically.

In their bedroom she looked down at Jack. He was sleeping

as peacefully as Christopher. As usual their resemblance touched her heart and she bent to kiss his forehead. Two strong arms reached up and grabbed her. ''Gotcha,'' he said and she let out a shriek. He rolled her over and over on the big bed, kissing and tickling her until she was laughing helplessly. His blond hair fell over her face. She swept it back and they smiled into each other's eyes. Imperfect as he might be, there was no doubt about it . . . she adored him.

Chapter Twenty-six

JOSIE GLIDED THROUGH the drawing room flashing an automatic smile at the occasional guest who looked her way, trying desperately to quell that panic that had seated itself in the pit of her stomach. Why, she asked herself, had she thrown away the doctor's tranquilizers? What a stupid thing to have done! Had her success blinded her so completely that she really believed she would never again feel this cold terror?

The prince's press-party luncheon seemed ridiculous today, although she had thoroughly enjoyed the others he had held since her triumphant appearance at Lilo's several months before. Even Benor's elaborate entertainments and colorful guests could not take her mind off the fact that she would be performing on the stage of the Olympia, France's most prestigious showcase for popular singers, in just a few hours.

Concentrate on the people around you, she commanded herself, forcing her eyes to focus on Benor's guests. Half of Paris seemed to have shown up. Standing together in a quiet corner were three of the most influential men in the French government. Opposite them, in front of a gigantic vase of wild orchids, stood the owners of several large Parisian nightclubs. Benor himself was seated on an upholstered love seat, deep in conversation with the manager of the Olympia. Models, painted and dressed to look like statues, posed in the corners of the huge room. The goats wore bells and stood quietly to one side with the goatherd Benor had flown in from the Middle East to watch over them. Photographers jostled one another outside the gates as even more celebrities descended on the town house to partake of the prince's hospitality.

But Josie couldn't seem to focus on any of it. Her mind had closed down, and no matter how much champagne she drank, she couldn't quench the thirst that made her throat scratchy and her mouth dry. Fleetingly, her thoughts went to

Lucas. Who else could help her get through this terrifying evening?

Again she shook her head. Mustn't think about such things. She would get through this performance just as she had gotten through all the others. The terror would threaten to consume her until she began to sing; then, magically, she would feel at one with her audience, and she would be all right. She straightened her shoulders and reached for another glass of champagne. The worst part—the waiting—was almost over. She would calm herself by thinking about her phenomenal success during the past three months.

The papers blazed with photographs of Josie in slender satin gowns that encased her sensuous body like tulip petals. The great jazz musicians had sent requests to have her appear with them when they performed in town. Josie had even sung with Count Basie, who was so impressed with her talent and stage presence that he dubbed her "The Countess." Josie smiled dryly at the irony of the title. Mabel Mercer and Ella Fitzgerald had come to hear her perform. She was still a jazz musician's musician with only a French following, but the groundwork was being prepared for a breakthrough that would make her an international star.

As a result of her sudden popularity, her two-week engagement at the Olympia had sold out the day tickets went on sale. Her new friends had helped her rebuild her self-confidence, and in the warmth of the stage spotlights, she had slowly recaptured the effervescence of her childhood and the belief in herself that had once rung in her infectious laughter. Her personality and her beautiful voice were both unique. She knew this phoenixlike ascent from despair would not have been possible if she had not been forced to depend less on drugs and more on her own inner resources.

This terror had begun when she had opened the note from Francesca that morning saying that she and Jack would be in the audience at the Olympia for her performance. They must have decided to forgive her. Josie realized they had undoubtedly heard of her success and who her "patron" was; their worlds were not that far apart. But Josie could not bear to face them. Not while she lived in Benor's house.

A waiter passed with a tray of champagne, and Josie reached out for a glass. Her hand was trembling so violently that she spilled the wine on her soft blue dress. Slamming the glass down on a table, she fled from the drawing room, ran up the stairs, and flung herself across her bed.

The champagne had dulled her brain just enough to make her feel depressed as well as frantic. She closed her eyes, trying to lose herself in sleep, but she kept seeing herself on the stage of the Olympia, frozen in terror. She could hear the audience tittering out there in the dark. Then the titters turned to open laughter, finally erupting into jeers as Josie tried to sing but found herself unable to do more than croak through the dry tightness of her throat, paralyzed with fear.

Then, in the horrible scene that played itself out behind her closed eyelids, she saw Francesca in the audience, her face glowing in the penumbra of the stage lights. Her sea-colored eyes were filled with pity for this misbegotten half sister who had sold her soul for an emerald pendant and a now-ruined career.

Josie opened her eyes, hoping to banish the vision of failure. She tried to breathe deeply and relax, but the knot in her stomach simply tightened itself and her throat seemed to close completely, cutting off her breath as well as her voice. She lifted a trembling hand to finger the emerald, but its icy coldness only reminded her of the prince, who was as inscrutable as ever. He did not love her for herself; he was attentive only because he enjoyed her eroticism. At least he allowed her to plead tiredness before his physical assaults now that she was working constantly. These days he saved most of his royal seed for his ball-gowned whores. Josie was no closer to him than they, although he respected her more. It was not the same as love, as what Francesca had. Jack loved Francesca for nothing more than a glimpse of her sailing past in a gondola. He loved her for herself. Benor was incapable of loving anyone that way, least of all Josie.

Josie rose and slipped out of the blue dress. Maybe a long, hot bath would relax her. Naked, she walked into the bathroom and turned on the taps. But, as she started to climb into the tub, she caught sight of her reflection in the mirror that hung over the sink. Stunned, she froze for an instant, staring into the glass. The skin on her neck, arms, and breasts was covered with ugly red welts, as if she had been beaten with a thick whip.

She walked over to the doorway where the light was stronger and looked down at her body. Her legs, thighs, and abdomen also bore the marks of her fear. She touched one of the welts on her left arm; the skin was raw and tender. Hurrying to the full-length mirror in her bedroom, she turned away from it and looked over her shoulder. The skin on her back was raw, red, and ugly with the same rash that had turned the rest of her body into a grotesque parody of her former self.

Josie began calling musicians she knew, backup players in jazz bands, white English rockers staying in a Left Bank hotel, anyone, searching for help. She had to get something to calm her nerves. By four o'clock one of the English rockers had arrived with a couple of friends. She knew them vaguely as friends of Lucas, who sometimes dealt with him.

"What did you bring me?" she asked them, helpless.

"Just the thing. It'll put you right," he said and held up a syringe and a little packet of powder.

"I don't do that," she said, backing away from him.

"One time won't hurt." He cooked the drug with silent efficiency, then delicately traced a point for the needle on the large veins in her arm. She watched abstractedly as if the arm belonged to someone else. It was so thin and vulnerable, its warm amber skin defiled by the red welts of panic. She felt a sudden prick of pain, and then an incredible floating feeling, as if her tense body had suddenly turned to air.

"That should get you through the night," the musician said.

The next three hours wafted past her, and the ugly red welts gradually disappeared, leaving her skin as smooth and unmarked as it had been that morning before the panic had set in. When Benor's chauffeur dropped her at the Olympia, her throat was completely relaxed and the knot in her stomach had disappeared.

Only when she walked out onto the stage did she begin to realize that too much of the deadly tension had been sapped from her body. Now she was as limp as a rag; she could sing, but she had nothing to say. When the band insisted, and the audience was hushed, she forced herself to look out beyond the lights at the thousands of people who expected her to sing for them. Confused, she put a hand up to her eyes to block out the glare. The band was playing something; she tried to turn and tell them to start over, but the words were trapped inside her head.

She stood in the spotlight, staring down at the musicians in the pit, her face blank with puzzlement. The band stopped playing, and she heard the audience tittering uncomfortably.

Why, she wondered, was that sound so familiar? She looked at the bass player, Manny. He raised his right hand in a thumbs-up gesture, then smiled and nodded. She saw him mouth the words, "You can do it, Jo. Go get 'em."

Numbly, she looked out at the audience and told herself that Manny was right. She *could* do it if she wanted to. The magic of her voice had always worked before. It was the one thing she could rely on.

Josie began to sing. She sang like a record played at too slow a speed. Her scraped and tortured vocal cords, strained raw from the tense assault of too much practice, made an inhuman croaking sound. It took her a few minutes to realize that the sound she heard amplified over the loudspeakers emanated from her own throat. Baffled, she lapsed into silence and looked out into the crowded theater, trying to spot Francesca in the audience. The faces blurred before her eyes so that she couldn't tell one person from another, but she could hear the coughing above some tense laughter and a great deal of shuffling. Out of the corner of her eye, she saw several people get up and leave. Not quite understanding what was happening, she looked again at the bassist. His face was almost blue in the glow from his music-stand light, and his eyes had turned to orange fires.

Horrified, Josie backed away, knocking over a vase of blood-red carnations. She tore her eyes away from Manny's face and looked at the other musicians. They, too, had been transformed into grotesque monsters with orange eyes. From somewhere far away she could hear people shouting, jeering, cursing.

Then, very slowly, the floor floated up at her, offering a lovely, waxy oblivion. Nothing, not the shouts in the audience or Manny's strong arms, could get her off the floor. She cowered there until the stage manager bent over her. Then she grew afraid, and tried to flee. This man was a danger to her. His eyes, like those of the musicians, were filled with orange fire. His hands were scratchy, like sandpaper, when he touched her bare shoulder. Frantic, certain he meant to kill her, she scrambled away from him toward the apron of the stage.

Out there in that vast darkness were people who would help her. Francesca was calling to her, standing in the back, telling her to come to her. Desperate, she heaved herself to her feet and began to run toward her. Behind her, someone shouted, but she kept running.

As she hurtled off the stage and plunged into the orchestra pit six feet below, she heard people screaming, shouting for an ambulance. Then a great darkness closed itself around her and she knew she was safe at last.

Francesca was out of her seat and running down the aisle before Jack had a chance to stop her. Breathlessly, she hurled herself into the crowd that had formed behind the barrier that separated the front rows from the orchestra pit. "Josie!" she called, needing to say the name even though she knew her voice would be lost in the shouts of the musicians who were trying to help Josie and the theater personnel who were calling for a doctor.

"Francesca!" Jack's voice, behind her, sounded close to panic. A moment later she felt his hand on her arm. "Go back to your seat, darling," he said, pulling her away from the crowd. "You can't do anything for her, and you're going to get hurt. Francesca, please come away from here," Jack urged.

"No. She saw me, Jack. She was looking straight at me when she started to run."

"That's impossible, Francesca. We were ten rows back. No way could she have seen you beyond the lights. You're getting upset for nothing."

"For nothing! How can you say that? Josie's my—" She broke off, still unable to admit the truth. "My friend," she finished.

Shouts rang from the back of the house, and Francesca looked up to see four men running down the aisle with a stretcher. The audience had started to leave the theater, buzzing with ugly speculation, but they squeezed in among the seats to let the ambulance attendants through.

"Such a shame," someone said. "The poor girl seems to have been in some sort of panic."

"The poor girl," her companion replied cynically, "is stoned out of her mind."

"Jack, I've got to find out where they're going to take her." Francesca tried to break Jack's grip on her arm.

"Stay with me." Jack moved in front of her. Francesca saw it was impossible to get to Josie through the crowd. Police were now ushering the fans, who were turning angry, out of the theater.

"I never wanted this. Never, no matter what she's done to us. I wanted to see her to make amends. You know that," Francesca said when they settled in a cab. "We'll lose her for good; I know we will."

"No, Francesca. She'll get better, and when she does, she'll find you." He put one arm around her shoulders and pulled her against him. "In the meantime, we'll find the name of the hospital. I'll even try calling Benor, although I have a feeling he won't tell us much."

"What on earth ever made Josie run off with him, I wonder."

Jack gave her an incredulous look. "You can't be serious!"

Francesca didn't meet his eyes and fell silent, lost in her own thoughts; she wondered how much she was to blame for the sad twist Josie's life had taken.

Chapter Twenty-seven

JOSIE FELT THE old tightness grip her throat and stomach as she walked up the stone pathway to Benor's house. On either side of her, the grass had grown long, its verdant perfection spotted with weeds and litter. Her mouth grew dry as she looked up at the blank windows, dulled now with a layer of streaky dust.

She had been spared most of the ugliness of the aftermath of her collapse at the Olympia. She had slept through the news of her failure in a small private hospital. The prince had taken care of the police, of course, and although the newspapers screamed of a drug overdose, the case was never officially investigated. She had seen little of the sensational journalism—just enough to know she had been ludicrously described as the "*Piaf Noire*." But she had suffered nevertheless, as if every word were printed on her skin.

The months of evanescent fame had crested that night at the Olympia, and when she plunged from the stage, she fell into the depths of her being. Her fleeting success had not saved her from her demons, and could not. Recovering from the nervous breakdown had taken almost three months. Then the doctors had released her, and she had taken a cab back to the prince's town house.

But the town house was deserted. The armed guard was gone, and no one answered the bell beside the handsome oak door. She let herself in with her key and walked from room to room, listening to the hollow silence. The furniture was sheeted, the valuable paintings gone. Upstairs, none of the prince's clothes remained in the closet, and the desk drawers were empty. Only Josie's belongings were still there. She found her suitcases and numbly began to pack. Down from the rack came the couturier gowns she had performed in, and her Venetian ball gown. She had few clothes besides these beautiful dresses, and she was afraid she would never wear them again. Her jewelry box was undisturbed. She fished out her emerald and with it came Francesca's note with her telephone number at the bottom. Josie shoved it into her pocket, picked up her two suitcases and her guitar, and walked to the doorway. Slowly she turned around to look back into the room. Nothing remained here of Josephine Lapoiret.

She remembered the day in Lyford Cay when she had returned to the beach house after her mother's death and stripped the rooms bare of every trace of herself and Marianne. Bitter and alone, she had meant to start a new life, away from Francesca and away from her own memories of the past. The bare, impersonal room in Benor's house would mark another beginning for her.

She heard a rattling sound in the back of the house. Frightened, Josie looked out the window as she descended the elegant stair. There were the twin goats, calmly nuzzling the grass. One butted a tin can with his head. They had eaten their way through the fruit trees and the borders of flowers, ruining the paths with their excrement. It scarcely seemed to matter. For half a second Josie envied them the security of their existence.

As she left Benor's house, Josie knew where to go, to Lucas's working-class neighborhood, where drab student hostels cost only a handful of francs a night. The local cafés allowed their patrons, who lived in small, single rooms and had nowhere to relax, to linger for hours. But she did not direct her cab to Lucas's hotel, avoiding it as if he were still sprawled on a bed upstairs.

The hotel she chose was buried even more deeply in the working-class area, away from the busy tourist streets. On a slight hill above the Seine, it was boxed in by taller buildings, but her small room's eastern window overlooked a tiny, ancient alley that trapped the sunlight every morning. Here Josie vowed to break her destructive dependencies on lovers and drugs. She unpacked her opulent dresses carefully and hung them in the old armoire with a cracked mirror. She would have to earn those iridescent butterfly wings all over again—but this time they would be hers, fair and square. She pulled out her hidden handkerchief and unwrapped the emerald, its green radiance glowing indestructibly with a self-containment that captured the light and bent it in its own unique pattern. That was the gift she had been born with. She must rediscover it. She promised herself that no matter what happened, she must never sell this stone, as she had sold herself. She must never fall low again, alone in this room without money or a friend. As she rewrapped the stone, the scrap of paper that bore Francesca's telephone number crinkled in the linen. Francesca had left messages at the clinic for her but Josie was too proud to take her calls. Josie paused for a moment, and then folded up the jewel in the paper and hid them away in her jewelry box at the back of a bureau drawer.

Josie might have been ready to start anew, but none of the club owners who had once dubbed her "Countess" and promoted her appearances in the past would see her now. "They don't trust you, *ma petite*," one manager explained to her. "Look what happened to the Olympia. Two weeks of tickets gone. Who do you think covered their losses?"

Josie felt her face punched in with every word. She had never given a second thought to the financial responsibility she had borne; she had been protected from financial problems. In that Benor had been like the count; loveless, he spoiled her with money. Lucas had always provided jobs for her, handling the club managers and negotiations. It never occurred to Josie that the theater might have suffered more than an embarrassment because of her disastrous performance. Like a child, her mind groped hopelessly with the reality of money. She had no way to earn a living, other than her voice. Because she had always had someone to depend on, her own poverty now was all the more frightening.

"No one needs you, Josie!" the manager said, not unkindly. But then it was clear that he didn't expect much from artists. He was looking at her as if she were some caged curiosity in the zoo. "Let me give you a piece of advice. You can break every promise but one. No matter what happens, you show. You can get high, sing off-key, make a spectacle of yourself, so what? They don't care if you stand there and hum with your thumb in your mouth, so long as the audience doesn't wreck the place. But you show."

Josie didn't know what to say. She was about to turn to leave, but the manager was enjoying his lecture. "Don't worry about the bad publicity. They loved that. Your name in all the papers, comparing you to Piaf—it was worth a million, and they would have upped your salary if you'd arrived the next night on a stretcher. But you didn't show." He shook his head in regret. "What a chance you missed. Too bad, Countess."

She turned and fled.

After two weeks of trying, Josie gave up. The man's words were true; none of the clubs where she used to sing would take a risk on her. A couple of the small jazz clubs that catered to a student clientele, where she had gotten her first break, promised to find something for her if a slot opened, but Josie could tell the managers didn't intend to push very hard for her. As far as they were concerned, she was strictly a pinch hitter now, untrustworthy but perhaps, in a crisis, useful.

On the eighth day of her search for work, Josie let herself into her hotel room. Sitting on the bed, she thought, "They are going to turn me out on the street." She began to practice the guitar. The reassuring sound usually relieved her tension, but tonight not even her guitar could console her. She stretched out, exhausted. The money Benor had left for her, "severance pay," as she had come to think of it, was gone. She had spent the last of it on a late lunch of fried potatoes and coffee. For a moment just before she fell asleep, Josie thought of Benor's favorite whorehouse and realized that Madame Simone would welcome her with open arms. Josie felt a surge of pride when she realized that she dismissed the notion automatically. She was too good for that sort of a life.

She awoke from a dreamless sleep and lay staring out the open window at the black sky of late summer, listening to the sounds of people talking as they passed on the street below. She imagined them, walking in twos and threes, through the balmy Parisian nights, on their way to dinner, heading for the theater, searching for a taxi to take them to a party.

Suddenly she sat bolt upright. She ran to the window and looked out at the sky. It was clear, filled with the tiny nailheads of northern stars. They were nothing like her native stars. In Nassau the stars bloomed bright and large as camellias in the tropical night. She had never been able to chart her destiny by this pinched, northern starlight. But since the weather was warm and clear, perhaps she could take her fate into her own hands tonight. She dressed in a short, sexy pink shift and made up her face.

Then she picked up her guitar and walked several blocks to a busy corner on the Boulevard Saint-Michel, or the Boul' Mich, as it was known. She chose that particular intersection because it was dotted with jazz clubs, ethnic bistros, and dark underground nightclubs that were open and busy almost until dawn. Many people would pass by this spot, and most of them would be in search of entertainment.

She found a niche in the outside wall of a building, set her open guitar case before her, and began to sing softly. People hurried past, ignoring her, not stopping to listen; but after a while, as her voice warmed up, she found herself enjoying the warm August night. She felt loose and free, and she began to sing at full volume, sending her rich voice out over the crowded streets in mellow ripples. Occasionally her songs were punctuated by the metallic clink of coins being tossed into the guitar case. Sometimes a passerby would speak to her, and she would smile pleasantly in reply. A man offered to buy her dinner, but she shook her head. It grew late, and the crowds thinned. Josie's feet hurt, but she sang on. At last she was alone. She picked the coins up and walked home.

Back in the room with its watermarked wallpaper and dim light, she counted out her earnings with shining eyes. For the first time since she came to Paris, she felt she had really earned her pay, and although it was meager, it made her curiously proud.

Piaf Noire indeed, she thought, remembering the stories of the young Edith Piaf singing for coins on the streets of Paris. Those critics hadn't known how apt their comparison had been.

She changed into blue jeans and left the hotel, suddenly hungry and eager for the sight of people, even if they were total strangers. She walked to a small café and ordered steak, *pommes frites*, and a glass of red wine. It was the best meal she had ever tasted, she realized, as she paid for it with the coins she had earned. She went back to her hotel room and slept in a glow of warmth and peace.

The next evening she returned to her spot. A few people remembered her from the night before, and rewarded her by tossing contributions into her guitar case. She smiled at them, and her rich voice and cheerful warmth soon attracted a small crowd. She sang French ballads and American blues songs, enjoying the pleasure reflected in the faces of her listeners. Occasionally someone would recognize her, but after the first time it happened, she stopped being afraid. There was no contempt in their faces, only interest and honest enjoyment of her music.

One young woman knew instantly who she was and had apparently heard her sing somewhere. She clapped her hands and shouted, "Jho-*see*, Jho-*see*. Sing caleepso!"

Touched by the request, Josie lit into a series of island songs that drew an audience so large and appreciative that two gendarmes appeared and stood nearby, watchfully eyeing the clapping crowd.

Each night for a month she counted her earnings, spending only what she needed and saving the rest toward a day when she would be able to move to a nicer hotel. And each night she returned to her doorway to welcome the crowds who had learned to shout, "Caleepso, Jho-*see*!" She learned to recognize the faces of the people who were her neighbors, and for them she sang her heart out, loving them for their loyalty even though many of them couldn't afford to toss coins.

Occasionally a car or a taxi would drive up to her spot and someone would get out, listen for a while, throw her some money, and then drive away. She wondered how they had heard of her and what made them go out of their way to hear her sing.

Every morning she would awaken and feel a warm pride flow through her as she remembered the crowds of the evening before. Her new success, she knew, had little to do with the money she earned. The triumph this time was in the faces of her listeners and in the joy that had slowly settled in her heart as she came to realize that she was good again, that she had begun to win back her soul.

Then, one morning at the very end of that enchanted September, Josie sat outside a café eating a croissant and drinking thick black coffee. When a newsboy passed her, she handed him a coin and spread the paper open before her. She turned the pages, reading a paragraph here or there, looking at the ads and some of the pictures. Then, like a spray of icy water, her own face jumped out at her from a photograph in the entertainment section. Beneath the picture was a long story that related every detail of her life from her first appearance at Lilo's through the night of the Olympia disaster and on to her appearance on the Boul' Mich the evening before.

She glanced through the article hurriedly, then went back and read it slowly, feeling the old fear wrap itself around her heart as her eyes took in the damning words.

A nurse at the private hospital had sold her story to the press. Josie hadn't even been aware of some of the incidents the woman had described—her raving about Marianne and Michael, her hallucinated fears of obeah. Tears gathered in Josie's eyes. Dredging up the past just to sell newspapers seemed needlessly cruel. The reporter, having done some rather casual research, made much of Josie's rise from "a ghetto in the Bahamas" to the "harem" of a "notoriously decent Middle Eastern sheikh." He even went so far as to mention the name of her little hotel. Josie covered her eyes with one hand, feeling the hopelessness embrace her like a shroud. Why had this happened now? she asked herself silently. Just when she had finally begun to heal herself and recover her lost honor, the paper had held out her shattered life for all to see. The crowds would now flock to see the crazy, degraded black addict, not the strong island girl who at last had stopped spitting on her own talent. She closed the paper in shame and despair.

That night Josie did not return to the Boulevard Saint-Michel. She huddled in her room in a deep depression, determined not to give in to the urge to find some pills, some wine, some ticket to oblivion. She could not bear to go back and face the passersby who were now her sole means of support.

When a faint rain began to fall, she went out and walked through the wet streets, wandering aimlessly. When she came to the Seine, she stared down into its gray depths. Downriver loomed Ile Saint Louis, where Francesca lived. An odd emotion tensed in Josie's heart. Francesca, too, must have known this kind of despair after Michael was killed, when she looked into the mirror and saw her ruined beauty.

They were both scarred now. Francesca's mark was on her face; Josie's was on her soul. They were, after all, sisters.

Josie turned away from the river and walked back to her hotel in the still, gray dawn. She slept restlessly for a few hours until she was awakened in midmorning by a knock on her door. Opening it, she found the pleasant old concierge holding out a note. He handed it to her and chatted for a few minutes before returning to his post.

As soon as she was alone, Josie opened the envelope and read the note. It was an invitation to sing at a small club in Montmartre. Josie had never heard of it, but that scarcely mattered. Instead of telephoning the manager as the note requested, she dressed carefully and set out to inspect the club and its environs.

Montmartre was the part of Paris where she felt most at home. Unlike the Latin Quarter or the proud and sedate arrondissement where Benor lived, it had the ragged air of a neighborhood that is not on display and would not pretend to be other than itself. Those who couldn't be bothered with pretense lived here: immigrants from more hospitable climates, many of them Arabs and Spaniards; artists, like Picasso in his early poverty, had always come here. Life seemed harsher here because nothing was hidden from the eye. And yet its little cemeteries, their graves sunken with age, had a melancholy beauty. The wide vistas of the city below gave Montmartre an air of openness, and the steps of Sacré Coeur, rising high over Paris, seemed a monument of pride on a mythical scale, however faded.

Josie found the little club in the shadow of Sacré Coeur on the Place du Tertre. Chez La Lune's entrance gave nothing away. There was not even a sign to mark the establishment, just discreet brass numbers too high above the doors to be seen easily. The old gray stone building rose directly from the curb above the cobbled street. Its vaulted double oak doors with large iron hinges were polished with oil. There were no windows; just a tiny opening the size of a letter slot carved out of one of the doors.

Apprehensively, Josie knocked on the door and waited. After a moment she heard sounds from inside and knew that someone was watching her through the slit. After a moment, the huge door swung open. A middle-aged woman in a loose shift led her into a room that made Josie think of an underground chamber in a monastery. It was extremely dark, but she could make out a few details as the woman led her to a dais at one end of the main room. There were heavy oak tables, polished to a high gloss; some had been screened to make them resemble confessionals. The ceiling was low and peaked, bolstered with beams of dark wood. She liked the club's air of mystery, its deliberate obscurity. It seemed less like a bar than a setting for a religious rite of some cryptic sect.

"Here's Bette," announced the woman who had led Josie through the club.

Josie looked up at the little stage as a handsome woman with a crop of shiny black hair stepped forward and held out her hand.

"Bette Diamant," she said, as if to confirm the other

woman's words. "I am the manager of La Lune. You are Josie Lapoiret."

Josie nodded and shook the woman's hand.

"I saw you at Lilo's at the insistence of a friend of mine who has a good instinct for talent." Bette Diamant led Josie to a table in front of the room and gestured for her to sit down. "At that time I knew I couldn't afford you. Then I heard about your misfortune and feared you were lost to all of us."

She picked up the pain in Josie's face and reached out to pat her hand. "Please, Mademoiselle Josie, don't look at me that way. I saw the story about you in yesterday's paper. It was a cruel article put together by cruel people. But it made me think that perhaps I might be lucky enough to get you to sing for me now."

"Madame," Josie began, "I am grateful—"

"Such talk!" the club owner interrupted. "If you will sing on my tiny stage and accept the meager wages I offer, it is I who shall be grateful. When I heard you at Lilo's I was sick to think I could never offer my patrons a chance to hear you. But now that I have found you, I can please my customers and make them love me more than ever."

Josie smiled at the mischief in the woman's face, though she suspected that her offer was motivated by kindness as well as self-interest. That, she decided, was all right. Kindness was not the same as the stifling charity that others had offered her. She had only one reservation, and she voiced it tentatively. "I wouldn't want to be primarily an object of curiosity, Madame Diamant . . ."

The club owner smiled again; the skin crinkled around her dark eyes. "My customers are mostly professional women, Josie. Many of them have been through struggles that would make your life look like a bed of roses. If you sing well—and I know you will—the patrons of this club will see to it that your reputation is redeemed in the best restaurants and clubs in Paris."

Josie listened while Bette talked about salary and schedules, insisting that she take supper at La Lune after her last performance. As the woman talked on in her low, soothing voice, Josie kept wondering about the patrons she had mentioned. Why, she asked herself, would so many successful professional women come to this tiny, dark club tucked away in Montmartre?

As Bette Diamant stood up to lead her out of the club, a young woman strode into the room and took up a post behind the bar. Something in her carriage and in the movements of her hands as she arranged glasses and bottles caused a light to dawn in the back of Josie's mind. So, she said to herself. That's the way it is.

"I am not going to press you, Josie," Bette Diamant said as she let Josie out through the heavy oak doors, "but if you could see your way clear to start performing tonight, I would be very, very happy."

Back on the street the bright sunlight seared her eyes. Josie hurried to the hotel and took her evening dresses out of the armoire. She washed her hair, letting the short black curls dry naturally; then she put on a long full skirt and a silk peasant blouse. As she slipped gold hoops in her ears she felt a buzz of excitement as well as the old familiar stage fright.

Chez La Lune was a club so exclusive that even the press seemed not to have heard of it. A few neighborhood people filtered through the darkness for Josie's first, early show. They were artists and workers, with a few young career women, expensively dressed, taking the front tables near the dais. When they offered to buy her drinks after her performance, she turned them down. She was afraid now of her own capacity for addiction. By the second show, the dark room throbbed with a strange clientele.

Josie had never seen women like this, alluring women aware of their own power, who frankly sought out the company of other women. They exuded self-confidence, a kind of electricity that made them stand out in the crowd. Some were dressed as executives in expensively tailored suits, but others came as exotic bisexuals embodying secret dreams. Josie recognized a famous American actress. Other women came with men, who seemed to find the atmosphere erotic and intriguing. And the poorer, more natural-looking neighborhood people, though eclipsed, still held their own at the bar. No one gawked, except Josie, until she realized that these were the people, uninterested in passing moral judgment, who would accept her most readily. She noticed she felt at ease and really at home. She sang her heart out for them.

Chapter Twenty-eight

As the weeks went by, the crowds at Chez La Lune grew larger and more varied, but Josie quickly grew to recognize the regulars. Some of them came once or twice a week, to hear Josie sing or to meet with their friends. Others came only once a month or so. But the ones Josie came to know best were those who stopped by almost every night, stayed to hear one set and have one drink, and then drifted home to bed.

Josie would occasionally accept an invitation to join one of the regulars at a table between sets. She became fast friends with a group of young men from the neighborhood who came in every night at eleven-thirty on their way home from work at a hospital. She also got to know a great number of young singers who had heard about her on Paris's vast music grapevine and made the pilgrimage to Montmartre especially to hear her sing. And she found, to her own surprise, that she genuinely liked those patrons she had come to think of as "Bette's women," even the ones who tried to disguise their femininity by wearing male attire and short, masculine haircuts. Bette's women, she discovered, were infinitely kind; it seemed never to occur to them to pass judgment on other people. And it took Josie only a very short time to realize that one of the things they accepted instantly was her own lack of interest in their kind of sexuality.

Josie would smile whenever she thought of her suspicion in their company during her early days at the club. What on earth had she been afraid of? she asked herself. How naive she had been to see a come-on in every compliment.

One of Bette's women, she noticed, always sat in one of the booths that was done up to look like a confessional. She would come in during a song, silent and unnoticed, stay for an hour or more, and then slip away during the next set, as if she didn't want anyone to see her. Bette always joined the woman for twenty minutes or so; Josie would see them talking quietly between sets. Very occasionally the woman would bring a friend, and the two of them would sit together in the confessional, their faces shrouded in darkness, never talking to anyone but each other and Bette Diamant.

Only once did Josie catch a glimpse of the mysterious woman's face, on a night when she came alone and arrived a bit early, before Josie began to sing. She stood inside the door, her back against the wall, waiting for the lights to be turned down for the next set of songs. Josie watched, fascinated, from the dark room offstage. The woman was in her fifties or early sixties; small, thin, and plain, but with a dignified bearing. There was something oddly familiar about her, not so much in her face as in the extreme straightness of her posture, as if she were trying to compensate for her lack of height.

Intrigued by the woman's apparent passion for anonymity, Josie asked Bette about her, but the club owner reverted to an uncharacteristic vagueness. "An old, dear friend. Just a friend. No one important," she said.

"She seems so reclusive," Josie said.

The club owner suddenly remembered she had to talk to a certain patron. Muttering, "She's shy," Bette wandered off.

This served only to whet Josie's curiosity. On a cold, rainy night when the crowd was thin and the bartender was not busy, Josie sat down at the bar between sets and ordered a soft drink.

"Slow night, Thérèse," she said.

"It's the weather, Josie. Boring, isn't it?"

"Dreary." Josie waved her glass to indicate the occupied tables. "The regulars never fail, though. Rain or shine, they show up, bless their hearts."

Thérèse smiled. "Yes, they're very devoted. Most of them live nearby, so it's easy for them to come here." She stuck out her chin to indicate the far corner of the room where the mysterious woman was sitting in her confessional. "Her, for instance."

"The shy woman?"

"She never used to be shy. She's been coming here for a couple of years. She used to mingle with the crowd; she even came to the bar sometimes to talk to me. It's only the past few weeks that she's taken to hiding back there in the corner." Thérèse shrugged. "Maybe she's getting eccentric in her old age."

"Who is she?"

"An old, old friend of Bette's. She was a couturière. Still is, they say, but she's semiretired now. *Riche d'un million,* people say. She has a little shop just outside the Place du Tertre where she works in the mornings. They say she designs clothes only for a few special clients, although she was once extremely famous. She speaks with a slight accent—Italian, I think."

Josie's head snapped up as the realization hit her. Of course! The exceedingly straight posture, the high chin. "Renata?"

Thérèse nodded. "Renata. You've heard of her?"

"I met her in Venice years ago; she made a beautiful dress for a friend of mine. What on earth is she doing in Paris?"

Again the bartender shrugged. "Josie, you know it's not my place to ask questions. How would I know such a thing?"

Josie hurried to her hotel as soon as her last set ended. What would Marianne have done? she asked herself as she entered her room. Josie knew the answer and quickly retrieved Francesca's telephone number from its hiding place, where it lay wrapped around the emerald, and called her. Francesca was excited to hear her voice.

"We were so worried about you. We've left messages for you at the clinic. I was afraid you'd never phone," Francesca said.

Josie was both elated and uncomfortable. She should have called her long ago; soon all her guilt would be assuaged.

"Could you come and hear me sing tonight?" Josie asked, then gave her the address of the club. "Please come, Francesca. I have a surprise for you."

"I wouldn't miss your show for the world," Francesca said.

She was a little afraid of what Francesca would think of Chez La Lune and its seedy environs, but she shook off her doubt and practiced a new song on her guitar all afternoon. By evening she was glowing with anticipation. It made her tense, but it was not crippling tension, the kind that had killed her voice before. It was a mild rush of adrenaline that would enable her to sing her best. At the thought of seeing Francesca again, Josie felt a stirring of her old happiness and pride.

That night her voice was clear and bell-like, her delivery assured. As usual, the woman was shown to her half-secluded table before Josie's performance. Before the first set was finished Francesca arrived.

She walked through the gloom. In this rare, unnatural milieu, Francesca's appearance created a sensation. Her gold hair was massed on top of her head and she wore a blouse of shiny black charmeuse with elegant slacks. The crowd, which had not yet swelled to its usual unmanageable proportions, parted for her with an almost imperceptible murmur of approval. Her scar was traced in dark red. It was a hieroglyph, a sign language those present understood. She was wounded yet invulnerable, proudly marked as an alien, a psychic state they shared.

Right behind her walked Jack Westman. The crowd seemed to make him nervous, but he was clearly proud of Francesca. They sat at the reserved table and looked up at Josie and saw immediately she was distraught. It hadn't occurred to Josie that Jack would come along. She might be ready to face Francesca, and all that she had done wrong to the younger woman, but Westman's presence weakened her resolve. She simply could not talk to them.

So Josie went on singing, but turned her head from side to side to avoid eye contact. Finally she ended the song before its refrain and leaned over Francesca's small table. Francesca rose to kiss her, and as she did so, Josie whispered hoarsely, "It's not me you're meant to see. Look over there." She pointed toward the half-hidden table only a few steps away.

Francesca looked curiously, and, seeing no one, turned back to Josie in puzzlement. Josie had already begun to pluck out her next song on the guitar. She felt she should leave Francesca alone now to whatever privacy she could manage to find in this fishbowl of a club. She ignored Jack's smile and turned her attention back to the audience.

Francesca peered back at the half-hidden table and noticed someone sitting quietly in the shadow of a tapestry that was pulled back like a drape. In the dark room it was hard to see.

She looked up to find Bette Diamant standing beside their table. "Excuse me for disturbing you," she said, "but an old friend of mine would like to speak to you, Francesca, and it would make her very happy if you would sit with her for a moment."

"I would be delighted, Bette. Will you take me to her?"

She followed Bette to the dark, shrouded table in the corner; her heart thumped wildly. "Renata! I can't believe it." Francesca stared down at the older woman. Renata did not appear to have changed an iota. She was looking at

Francesca as matter-of-factly as if she had been sitting here just waiting for her for a lifetime. "I'm so glad to see you," Francesca said incredulously. "May I sit with you for a minute?"

She sat down in the chair Renata indicated. "Every time I think of my ball in Venice, I remember you. My happiness that night was your doing, Renata."

The older woman looked at her steadily, as if searching for something. "You are different now," she said in her low voice. "Still beautiful, but a woman, not a frail little girl."

Francesca found herself chattering nervously, not wanting to frighten Renata away with questions about her mother.

But Renata interrupted her with a blunt invitation. "Will you come to see me at my home tomorrow morning? I want to tell you about your mother."

Francesca stared for a moment, astonished to have her wish granted so readily. God bless Josie Lapoiret, she thought, with a shiver of gratitude.

Renata coolly gave her her address and told her how to get there. "Ten o'clock would be a good time for me. I usually drink some coffee about then. Perhaps we could have a cup together."

She spoke as if she were suggesting a perfectly ordinary social call.

Trying not to show undue excitement, Francesca merely nodded and said she would be there at ten.

The dressmaker continued to regard her steadily. "I couldn't talk to you about your mother when Carlo was alive. Such a tyrannical man, your father—if I may speak ill of the dead. Anyway, in those days you were too young and naive to understand Susannah." She squeezed Francesca's hand and smiled faintly. "I think you are different now. It is time for us to talk."

Recognizing this as a dismissal, Francesca stood up and took Renata's hand. "I look forward to visiting you tomorrow."

As she sat back at the table with Jack, as she listened to Josie's next few selections, Francesca let her eyes wander around the club. At a nearby table two young women were holding hands, and as she quickly turned away, she found herself looking directly into the face of a woman who was contentedly smoking a cigar. Embarrassed, she looked down at her drink.

Jack leaned close to her, and she heard the laughter in his teasing voice. "Finally dawned on you, has it?"

"You knew all along?"

Francesca found herself remembering Lady Jane's wild accusations on the day she burst into Carlo's room at the hospital in Lyford Cay. At the time, the charges had sounded like the ravings of a madwoman. But then she had overheard Converse Archer's conversation about Susannah's passion for Sybilla Hillford.

Was it actually possible, Francesca wondered, that her mother had been like these women who sat at the tables around her? No, she told herself, that wasn't possible. She remembered Susannah as an extremely feminine, almost girlish woman.

Her eyes wandered of their own will to the two young women who were holding hands at the next table. They, too, were feminine, she noticed with a sinking heart. Everything about them was soft—their hair, their voices, their clothing.

That night Francesca told Jack everything she could remember about her mother. And as she spoke, she realized that part, at least, of what Lady Jane and Converse Archer had said must be true. Susannah and Sybilla had been more than friends; they had been lovers.

"Why is that so hard for you to accept?" Jack had asked her. "Think about it, Francesca. Just a few years ago, you and I would have been ostracized from society for living together without benefit of clergy. Think how horrified your mother would have been to hear that you and I are lovers. And think what it must have been like for her to be married to your father. Imagine how hungry she must have been for a bit of simple, uncomplicated affection."

That, more than anything else Jack said, had made Francesca realize that Susannah had simply responded to love, just as she herself had once.

But Susannah's love affair had ended with Sybilla's death, and that one cold fact struck fear into Francesca's heart.

1955

DESPITE SUSANNAH'S WISHES, Sybilla wanted to stay at Converse Archer's masquerade ball even after most of the guests had filtered out the doors of the Gritti Palace. Susannah had been embarrassed by the girl's loud presumptuousness, the way she swayed and knocked her hips against Susannah's suggestively as they walked down the long corridor, passing chandeliered rooms sumptuously decorated in silks and brocade. Susannah knew she was deliberately trying to provoke her, but she could barely hold her temper in check and the deep despair they both shared about the position they were in made it unbearable for her to look Sybilla in the eye. She could feel the other guests watching them, discussing them. And although she knew anything that she, Susannah Nordonia, did or said or wore was thought to be amusing and inspired simply because she did it, she felt tawdry and ashamed. When she glanced at Sybilla her guilt made her look quickly away again.

"Don't walk like that, for God's sake," she whispered hoarsely, unable to hear the anger in her own voice, as they walked down the broad steps to the canal and slipped into the Nordonia gondola.

Directly across from the Gritti Palace stood the Church of Santa Maria della Salute. Susannah looked up at its domed facade and whispered a small prayer to herself. "Help me do this kindly." She thought for a moment. "And cleanly. A clean break, once and forever."

Sybilla was already reclining on the velvet pillows within the small cabin of the gondola. She reached out for Susannah's arm and yanked her down imperiously.

"You've been cold to me all night," she pouted.

A cool wind stirred through, bringing up the smell of the Adriatic's salt depths. As the gondola cut smoothly through the water, rocking gently, hidden within the cabin Sybilla pressed her lips to Susannah's hair, then her ear; her tongue touched the delicate folds of Susannah's earlobe. Seeing the gray distance in Susannah's eyes, she began to kiss her lips. Susannah moved her mouth away.

Suddenly Susannah was grieving for her loss, for what her life would become when Sybilla was gone. It was not the same, to kiss a man. Sybilla's lips were soft and lush as blackberries, her kisses the taste of sweet water. Carlo was a skillful lover, proud and affectionate. But even his warmth could not compare to the girl's tenderness, her languorous, gentle rhythms, and her passion that burned but never hurt. And what man could understand Susannah's exasperation with her feminine restrictions, her need at times to take power into her hands? People sensed the conspiracy of her relationship with Sybilla, its subversiveness, and were outraged; but finally—for them at least—it was the bond of laughter, of complete freedom between the two women that society would not tolerate. That laughter mocked Susannah's role in society as a wife, and more importantly, as a mother, and she shuddered when she realized that as terrible, as isolating as losing Sybilla would be, to lose her child would be worse.

Wiping her mouth on the back of her hand, Susannah collected her thoughts. She eyed the gondolier's impassive back nervously through the window in the small door. He was a mere boy Emilio had found, and she didn't know if he could be trusted. She wanted no one to hear what she told Sybilla now. Measuring her words carefully, she began to talk in a low voice. "You terrified me tonight."

"I know that."

But Susannah ignored the glinting challenge in Sybilla's eyes. "It's gone too far, Sybilla. Please understand. We'll destroy each other this way."

"Why not?" The young girl tossed back her head defiantly, but Susannah sensed the paper-thin bravado was about to collapse.

"My God, Sybilla. I could have been killed up on that balcony. Think of what you're doing! You nearly killed me then, and you're pushing me to the brink now." Susannah's voice rose too high and she saw Vieri's neck tense.

Sybilla looked chagrined. She said nothing. The black canal slid by. A few lights were reflected on the surface like oily waterlilies.

"You've got to admit there's no future for us. Converse was right, you've got to devote yourself to your career now if you want to make your mark as an artist. And I can't leave my family. Please understand."

Sybilla looked out the window at the glassy black water and then faced Susannah. "I thought you were brave."

"I'm not self-destructive. Nor do I want to see you change like this, but can't you see you're destroying me?"

Sybilla began to cry suddenly. Susannah moved to her and put her arm around her shoulder and in a moment they were hugging, both their faces wet with each other's tears. They kissed each other so deeply they didn't notice that the gondola had stopped moving.

Suddenly Susannah sat up with embarrassment. Vieri was

studiously looking away, down the canal. When Sybilla saw the twin lions at the landing she giggled and jumped out of the boat, agile despite her hip-clinging dress, and offered Susannah her hand, pulling her up. Susannah dismissed Vieri for the evening and turned to Sybilla.

"Our last night," Sybilla said in a voice full of daring.

Susannah moved toward her slowly, hypnotized by Sybilla's narrow, sinuous hips, and as they walked into the palazzo together they saw that all the servants had been dismissed for the night. Sybilla chased Susannah up the marble steps. Laughing, Susannah took the stairs in leaps of four. She barricaded herself in her large marble bath and turned on the gold spigots. Steam clouded the room as Sybilla pounded for admittance until Susannah finally opened the door and backed off toward the huge sunken tub. Sybilla, grinning and out of breath, approached her.

Susannah groped backwards with her hands and heels, suddenly frightened, giggling nervously. When Sybilla saw how close she came to the edge of the large sunken tub, she grew still and smiled. Susannah fell backward with a splash and knocked her head, and Sybilla leaped after her.

Almost before she could rise, Sybilla was kissing her, her wet hands sliding all over her body. Susannah was dazed, her head throbbing. At last Susannah gathered enough strength to struggle away from her.

"Why didn't you warn me?" she said in shock, raising her hands to the injured side of her head.

"Is it hurt? Shall I get you something? Let me see." Sybilla parted Susannah's abundant red hair and saw a broad purple welt. "It's going to be nasty," she said with concern.

"I don't understand you," Susannah said.

Sybilla reached over and slid Susannah's ring off her hand and put it on her own. "Will you give me this to remember you by?"

"I can't. It's Carlo's."

Sybilla sulked. Susannah still moaned softly and held her head. Her skin was whiter than Sybilla's and her body fuller and softer. Sybilla looked at it with longing. Susannah had large breasts, with nipples crinkly and soft as poppies, and her arms were rounded with her horsewoman's muscles. It was a painterly body, at once feminine and strong. She wanted to memorize it. Suddenly she brightened. "I know what will make you feel better." She flicked open the secret latch under the crest of Carlo's ring and poured the remainder of Susannah's cocaine onto a small hand mirror among the collection of antique toiletries arranged around the edge of the tub. Then she divided the crystals with a silver Byzantine dagger and offered them to Susannah to inhale.

Susannah flung her head back and then tried to rise. "God, my legs are bruised. I must have knocked them, too. I didn't even feel it. I wonder if I can walk."

She tried to rise but Sybilla pulled her down and began to caress her. She ignored Susannah's protesting hands. "They're mine."

"What's yours?"

"Your breasts." Sybilla suckled them like a child.

Susannah tried to push her away again. "Come on, now. Let me go. I've got to see how badly I'm hurt."

Then Sybilla was on top of her, pulling her under the water. Susannah's arms flayed in the air in disbelief. "No, Sybilla! Not here! Not like this. You'll drown me."

"I want to make love to you," Sybilla said through clenched teeth.

They fought as Susannah went under and after a moment she rose and bucked, nearly pushing Sybilla off.

"You'll kill me with your damn passion," she shouted.

But the girl clung to her slippery skin, and she was under again, breathing water. Susannah suddenly realized that this was what Sybilla wanted: to end their affair, their passion, with their lives. She had often talked of suicide.

Her hands pounded against Sybilla's back and she felt her strength surge. But she knew the adrenaline of fear would only last a minute before her body gave in. Her hand groped for something to defend herself with and felt the blade of the antique dagger. Susannah managed to grab it blindly. As her vision blackened and the water roared in her ears and poured into her throat, in a burst of terror she plunged the knife into Sybilla's back.

Sybilla's grip went slack and the bathwater turned red. Susannah surfaced, gasping for air and gulping it down with a final, relieved surge of strength. After a minute her dizziness subsided and her vision returned to normal. She found herself staring at Sybilla in disbelief. Her face was down in the water, her dyed hair eerily coagulating the blood that gathered between her shoulder blades. The dagger stood straight out of her back as if it had pierced her like a spindle.

"Oh, my God, Sybilla, breathe," she moaned, trying to lift Sybilla's head. But her head was lifeless, like a heavy rock. Susannah managed to turn it; when Sybilla's glassy white eyes met hers she dropped the head back in the water.

"Jesus, what have I done."

The girl lay stomach down in the red bath like a dead crab, all heavy body and weightless appendages. Yet she might still be alive; scarcely two or three minutes—though it seemed like an eternity—had passed since Susannah's fingers curled around the dagger. But she didn't know how to save her. She lifted the limp girl up again, a process that took precious minutes, and pulled the dagger out of her back so that she could brace the rag-doll body against the tub. Sybilla's head rolled to the side. Susannah dragged her out of the tub by her armpits. Several more minutes had passed. Too many, Susannah frantically thought. She tried to remember how to perform artificial respiration, working over Sybilla's slender chest as if it were bread dough. Her skin felt curiously springy and cold; her lips were frozen and sharp.

"Sybilla, come back, you never wanted to go alone," Susannah addressed the blind girl. Then she shook her shoulders in fury. "Live! You can't die on me."

Then Susannah felt her own bruises, the throbbing head and scraped leg bones. Fear and cocaine had blocked the sensation, but now pain flooded back. As she rose from the marble floor she saw that she'd been kneeling over her lover in a pool of blood. Nothing, no feat of breath, no will of love, would bring the girl to her senses.

Susannah felt a wall of pain crush her as she rose. Yet she stood and somehow washed the blood off her body. She stepped over Sybilla, went into her bedroom, and threw on some clothes.

She let herself out of the back of the palazzo and made her way as quickly as she could through the familiar but dark streets to Renata's small house. She knew she could trust Renata, who had done so much for her already. Renata knew all her secrets and counseled her on her affair with Sybilla. She would not have trusted one of her own social circle with such intimacies; there was too much rivalry. But Renata was like an aunt or a grandmother. Her love was unconditional.

She roused Renata from sleep and the story of Sybilla's death poured out of her. Renata looked at the young woman, her hair falling wildly around her grieving face, and judged the terror in her eyes.

"The police are coming for me," Susannah moaned, clinging to Renata.

"No. Carlo will handle the police."

"Carlo isn't in Venice," she gasped, her voice rising. "The police—"

"No one will find you here," Renata reassured her. "Come, lie down, I'll give you something to help you rest."

Renata sat by her bed until Susannah's breathing was easy and deep with sleep. As dawn gilded the windowsill, Renata knew what she must do. Cold practicality guided her. She returned to the palazzo and rang the bell until Emilio awoke and clattered downstairs, swearing and puffing loudly.

"In the name of God!" he greeted her.

"We must call Carlo," Renata said to him.

He looked at her in confusion.

"The English lady has bled to death in your mistress's bathroom."

Emilio was speechless. Then he muttered to himself, "Is this a nightmare? Am I really awake?"

"Come," said Renata, stepping across the threshold. "Quickly."

For the rest of the morning she took charge of the household. No maid was allowed to enter Susannah's suite. She washed and arranged Sybilla's body as if she were an undertaker; then she scrubbed out the bathroom rapidly. And she managed all this by noon, when she scurried back home to attend Susannah. When Susannah woke Renata gave her another sedative, helped her into her Peugeot, and drove her far out of Venice and into the alps of Northern Italy, to a mountain farm where she had been raised. Her immediate family were all dead now, and she owned this home, using it for vacations only two or three weeks a year. Rustic and isolated, it was as much a part of the landscape as the bluffs of dolomite. Her relatives lived nearby. She asked an aging cousin, who always wore black widow's weeds and filled her days with knitting, to care for Susannah. Then Renata hurried back to Venice, in time for Carlo's arrival from Nassau.

Renata had hoped that the clear mountain air and a simple healthy life among the villagers would help restore Susannah's sanity. But the more lucid Susannah became, the more she suffered. She grew to blame herself completely for Sybilla's death, and Renata's report that Carlo had taken care of the police provided no relief from her guilty conscience. Carlo knew the chief of police well, and since there was no autopsy, the public accepted the story that Sybilla had died of an aneurism. But Susannah kept believing that she would be discovered and tried for murder. She was too fearful to return to Venice. She could not face Carlo.

In the meantime, Renata turned over most of her dress business to her assistants and spent as much time with Susannah as possible. Only the reminder of her young daughter made her smile, but it was a smile that quickly faded. A doctor, whom Renata brought from Trieste, examined Susannah and told Renata—without knowing what had happened—that he felt the young woman was deeply depressed.

"She seems to have lost all affect," he said.

"What?" said Renata uncomprehendingly.

"The capacity to feel. Sometimes after a terrible tragedy, such as the death of a loved one, a person will be unable to feel again. It's as if their emotion dies as well."

"Is there any cure?" Renata asked.

"Sometimes a cure is spontaneous. We don't know what makes them snap out of it." He advised a healthy diet and lots of exercise, and recommended a psychoanalyst.

Renata telephoned Carlo and reported this opinion. His response was as cold as ice. "I don't want to see her. Do you understand, Renata? I don't care what you do with her."

"That's too cruel," Renata gasped.

"If I find her, I'll have her institutionalized."

"You wouldn't do that to your own wife."

"I should. It's easier than you think, and far preferable to prison."

Renata, thinking of how weak and disoriented Susannah had become, felt tears spring to her eyes. "If you could only see her now, Carlo, how she suffers . . ."

"She must never set a hand on my daughter again. Hasn't she destroyed enough lives?"

"Surely you don't blame her for saving her own life."

"I blame her for bringing shame and dishonor to my family. For years, Renata. For years she's been heading for this. If I had only banished her right from the start . . ."

Carlo's voice was like iron. Renata hung up the telephone in bewilderment. Perhaps he felt that Susannah's sexuality or despair was contagious. Or perhaps he feared that somehow Francesca would learn that her mother had killed the girl in self-defense. But surely Francesca would suffer the most for her mother's dilemma. Carlo, being a man, might not understand that a child's emotional life was so delicate and dependent it could easily be destroyed by the loss of a mother.

In the meantime, in an attempt to help Susannah recapture her sense of accomplishment and master her feelings of guilt and grief, Renata encouraged her to ride again. But Susannah had no real desire to ride, and while she was willing to give it a try, she dressed sloppily, as she did every morning she managed to get out of bed, and didn't bother to groom herself. Renata brought her her riding clothes, helped her dress and brush her hair into a chignon. Then she drove the mute woman to the stable.

The stable was part of a grand resort that had few guests this time of year. Its view of the gorges and valleys below was spectacular. The air was cool and bracing, the fields white with a carpet of tiny mountain flowers. Overhead the sky arched a pure arctic blue; it was no longer an Italian sky, but a Swiss or Austrian heaven, with white, starched clouds.

Susannah was oblivious to the beautiful panorama. But when the groom led her horse out of the stable, for the first time since her accident she seemed animated again.

"Not that one," she said. "Can you saddle that horse that's kicking his stall? That's the one I want."

The groom frowned. "No, ma'am, you don't. No one wants him. We don't ride him. We just brought him up here to breed with one of the mares. He's wild, barely broken."

"*That's* the one I want to ride."

Renata knew that tone of voice, and silently rejoiced. It was hopeless to argue with Susannah now. At last Susannah actually wanted something. She looked beseechingly at the groom, who still shook his head.

"I'll saddle him up myself," Susannah said.

"He'll bite your hand off."

In the end the groom reluctantly saddled the red stallion. He snorted and pawed in his stall, but when the groom let him out on the lead he was quiet and proud. He seemed to strut. Susannah watched him with a gleam in her eye.

"Yes, boy," she said.

Only later did Renata realize that this change in Susannah seemed too abrupt. There were clues, and she ignored them stupidly because she so badly wanted to see signs of improvement in Susannah. Of course Susannah chose that wild horse, a horse whom even she could never master if she lost her nerve and regretted her decision. She hoped to ride him into the grave of one of the gorges. The horse would end her suffering once and for all.

Susannah cantered the stallion around the paddock twice and then galloped him past Renata and the groom for the freedom of the open fields.

"Don't take him far," the groom shouted after her, but she didn't seem to hear.

For the first time Renata felt afraid. "You'd better go after her."

The groom shrugged. "She's a stubborn one. Stubborn as he is."

Renata walked back to the lodge and sat on the terrace. A waitress brought her coffee. She stirred it absently and stared out at the fields, hoping for a glimpse of Susannah. From time to time she checked her watch. After an hour, when she was about to go back and beg the groom to look for Susannah, she saw the chestnut stallion cantering across the field, headed for home. His stirrups flapped against his sides, glinting silver. Renata blinked her eyes. The horse was riderless.

Later that afternoon they found Susannah unconscious beside a trail. She had fallen on her head and fractured her skull. Apparently the horse had dragged or trampled her; one leg was seriously damaged. By the time they found her she had lost a lot of blood. But she would live; whether she would gain her mind back was doubtful.

Renata called to tell Carlo what happened. "Then she might as well be dead," was his only remark.

A short time later Renata saw, to her horror, an announcement of Susannah's death in the newspapers. Defiantly she sent Carlo the bill from the hospital where Susannah—under an assumed name—lay in a coma. And that day marked the start of a new life for Renata. She decided to keep Susannah with her as a daughter for better or for worse. After all, someone had to take care of her.

Susannah came back to life but her reactions were slow and, mercifully perhaps, her mind remained cloudy. The only indication that Carlo knew she was alive was his check twice a year. He paid generously to have the secret kept.

When Susannah was well enough to travel, Renata brought her back to Venice and installed her in her small house. She needed to build up her dress business now to pay her own bills. Eventually Susannah learned to walk again. But although she had once been a fine athlete, she gave in to her illness and let her body deteriorate. She aged more rapidly than Renata, to the older woman's horror. Yet Susannah's leg eventually grew stronger; her body healed itself despite her neglect. She was still fairly lame when something happened that gripped her at last.

Francesca walked into Renata's shop to be fitted for a dress.

As Susannah hid behind a door and watched her daughter spin before the mirror, her face seemed to thaw and tears streamed from her eyes. Afraid that she would betray her presence, Renata called the fitting off and sent Francesca away, though after that Susannah's progress was amazing. She seemed, in a matter of days, to revert almost to her former self. Her energy was unflagging. She even insisted on sewing her daughter's dress herself. Soon she began to prepare for another opportunity to see Francesca sometime over the summer—though of course the girl must never recognize her. Susannah could not bear to face Francesca's scrutiny. So she and Renata made endless plans for her seeing Francesca from a distance. They had to be especially careful, however. One word to Carlo and he could have Susannah committed for life.

In the meantime, the newspapers blazed with stories about Francesca that made her mother laugh with joy, but suddenly Francesca disappeared, and Renata was able to learn through the palace grapevine that she'd been sent back to Nassau. Susannah assumed that somehow Carlo had got wind of their schemes, and once more she blamed herself. She didn't dare travel to Nassau to revisit her old home. Francesca was sure to recognize her there. So, brokenhearted, Susannah suffered a relapse.

One day in one of the gossip sheets Renata read that Francesca was in Paris. There was a picture of the young countess with the shocking scar across her face, marring her perfect beauty. She was hesitant to show it to Susannah, but in the end she did.

"I must go to Paris," Susannah announced, putting the paper down. "I must see her again."

Renata had a lesbian friend, Bette Diamant, who had recently invested in a building in Paris. She had started a club and was converting several small apartments into cooperatives. Renata called her to ask about coming for a visit. Susannah packed, her eyes bright, her voice excited.

It was easy enough to glean news about Francesca, Jack, her child, and her house from the Paris newspapers. For months Renata and Susannah walked along the Seine and lingered in the cafés that lined the Left Bank near the Ile Saint Louis, hoping to catch a glimpse of Francesca. Hope itself seemed the best tonic for Susannah, who was driven to the point of obsession to be near her daughter. One day she saw Christopher and his nurse enter Francesca's house. She came running home to Renata with the news that she had seen her grandson. After that, she always took her camera with her on what she called her "visits" to her daughter.

"Such a beautiful blond boy," she would shake her head and say.

Renata thought her obsession had reached the point of insanity and that finally it might be best to arrange a real meeting with Francesca.

THE MORNING AFTER meeting Renata at Chez La Lune, Francesca took a taxi to Montmartre. She was so nervous and excited her hands were like ice as she shook hands with Renata. She was not surprised the room she was led into was almost identical to the tiny studio in Venice where Renata had fitted her for her ball gown years ago.

Renata gestured to a chair and brought in a tray of coffee and croissants. "Nowadays I work only to keep my skills sharp," she explained. "Only a few of my dearest ladies know my whereabouts."

Francesca stood frozen.

"But my dear Francesca, it's time you learned the truth. Please sit down," Renata insisted gently. As Francesca perched on the edge of the chair opposite her, Renata looked into her eyes with an intensity that filled her with an almost unbearable suspense. "My dear," she began, but Francesca's lips started to move as if she were in a trance.

"It's about my mother, isn't it?"

"Of course it's about your mother—"

Francesca's face had grown so pale Renata was afraid she would faint, but she knew the time had come. She must tell her. "Your mother, my dear, is alive."

As Renata spoke, Francesca realized that this was what she had never stopped believing since she was a tiny child. At the same time, the tears slid down her cheeks. Renata slowly nodded and leaned toward her. As Francesca's tears fell on their clasped hands she began to laugh apologetically and tried to wipe them away with her skirt. At last she took a deep breath and, letting go of Renata, she leaned back in her chair, sat very straight, and met the old woman's eyes calmly.

"Before I see my mother, I want to know the truth about everything."

"I will tell you all I know, and in time your mother will tell you the rest," Renata answered.

It was almost noon when Francesca and Renata emerged from the tiny studio. Susannah was standing in the sunlight in Renata's tiny garden, her red hair like a beacon meant to guide Francesca through the long hallway and out into the little courtyard. She stopped and watched her mother bend down to tug a tall weed out of a patch of marigolds. Susannah wore a denim skirt and a soft white cotton shirt. The sight of her made Francesca's heart turn over. Except for the soft lines of middle age, her face was exactly as Francesca remembered it, and she looked, astonishingly, like an ordinary Parisian housewife tending her garden.

Renata opened the door and stepped outside, pulling Francesca behind her. "Susannah, I've brought your daughter." She spoke softly, but her words made Susannah start. "It's all right," Renata said reassuringly. "She understands; she wants to talk to you."

Francesca ran to her and took Susannah in her arms. The

woman's bent shoulders were shaking. The thought of her mother's vulnerability made Francesca sob until at last Susannah's hand began to pat her back and comfort her. Nothing had ever felt so right in the world.

Chapter Twenty-nine

FRANCESCA WOKE JACK early the next morning, and while they were still in bed the argument began. "You can't take your mother back to Lyford Cay, Francesca. She's hardly a charter member of the jet set now. Apparently she's gained some ground here, but if you take her to Nassau, she might have another relapse." Jack's voice was patient but strained. These days he often spoke to Francesca as if she were an exasperating child. "She'll have to face everyone she used to know. How do you explain away a couple of decades? It will be very awkward for her."

Elated, Francesca ignored his objections. "No one need know until she's ready to come out in public. I want to get her safely installed incognito as a patient at Lyford Rose. I know once she's back on the estate, in her old home, she'll come around. She can stay there forever in private if she wants to."

Francesca and Jack had brought her mother home to Ile Saint Louis the night before. She was sleeping upstairs in a guest room now. Not even Christopher had awakened yet. But Francesca could not contain her happiness. She had roused him out of his deep sleep to discuss the future.

"Then where will we spend Christmas? Are you going to move back to Lyford Cay, and leave me to rattle around this enormous house alone?"

She saw his point. Francesca laughed nervously. If she knew Jack, he wouldn't be alone for long; the last time she'd left him, he'd impulsively married someone else. "I'm not going to desert you, darling," she said hurriedly. "But please understand. I've got to take care of my mother now. I can't imagine the life she's led for the past nineteen years." Her exhilaration of having her mother back from the grave was sobered by the thought of all the woman had endured.

"Granted, she needs help. But you can get the best there is right here in Paris. There are excellent sanatoriums in Europe, and some, believe it or not, are nearly as good as Lyford Rose."

Francesca knew it was pointless to argue with Jack once he had his mind made up; and he was determined not to understand her reasons, her need, to take her mother back to her real home.

"What's the matter? You're so quiet."

"Oh, Jack, my mother doesn't need doctors. She needs her home. She loves Lyford Cay. She built our house there. I've got to give that to her."

"But not if it means deserting the man you're going to marry. You can't sacrifice your life for her just because she finally decided to walk back on stage."

"I love her," Francesca said intensely. Her fists were clenched. She was so worried about Susannah. She had been barely lucid last night. The strain of rediscovering her daughter might be too much for her. She needed help, and quickly.

"What about me? I'm not some ghost from your childhood. I'm real flesh and blood. And I don't like to be alone." Jack was aroused by her anger. He lifted her white-knuckled hand and kissed it. Then he slid closer to her under the covers.

"Don't make me choose," she said as he kissed her.

"I'm going to make it impossible for you to leave me," he said, pressing himself between her closed legs.

She tried to speak, but his lips were insistently kissing her. She could see under the rumpled sheet his long golden torso smothering her white skin. She felt so helpless before the strength of his passion. But as much as her body wanted to yield to him, her mind could not. She knew better than to struggle; that would only increase Jack's desire and her own body would collaborate with him against her. Her mind, still and fixed above the sheets, seemed to watch him caress her breasts from another room. Her detachment frightened her. It had never happened before. She watched Jack bury himself in her passive body, inert and lifeless. It gave, and she felt, as she always did, that some endless hunger was finally assuaged. But she didn't reach out to caress his beautiful body in love as she had always done before. Suddenly his passion seemed impersonal. He might have been anyone satisfying some natural urge; the fact that it was Jack, her first and real love, the father of her child, no longer touched her.

"You're wonderful," he murmured in her ear.

His face was flushed, his blue eyes wild with the heat of his passion. She looked away.

"I'll never have enough of you," he said.

She turned her head and watched the tips of the bare trees rock against the window. November in Paris was damp and cold. How she longed for the yellow sun, the glaring white beaches, the clear water of her real home.

He rolled over. After a moment he said, "What are you thinking?"

She glanced at him quickly and turned away. His lips were pinched in a thin line and his eyes were troubled. He could tell something had changed in her.

"I was thinking of a cove at home where the water is so clear you can read the ocean bottom like a book. There's nothing like it in Paris. Here the waters are murky, and the shapes you see through it are fantastic and delicate and highly evolved. But nothing is innocent or pure."

"I don't know what you're talking about," Jack said after a moment.

"I guess I'm trying to say that I can't be everything. At heart I'm not very sophisticated. I'm like Josie, I'm an island girl."

"So you're going back to Nassau." Hurt and anger rose off his hunched shoulders as he sat at the edge of the bed, his back to her.

"Come with me. Please. You'd love it there. You and Christopher and I would have such a wonderful Christmas together. It's the best time of year, and Paris will be so dreary. And I want to spend some time with Apollonie while I can."

He stood up and walked into the bathroom. She heard him turn on the faucet. She rose and followed him. He was washing his face with cold water.

"Jack. I can't bear to hurt you." She placed a hand on his shoulder. He shook it off with a shiver.

"You can't even stand to make love to me anymore," he said bitterly.

"That isn't true."

"What was that performance a minute ago? I felt like I was lying on top of a glacier."

Francesca was silent.

"Francesca, I rented this house for you. Living here with you was my dream. Not with your mother. Not in Nassau. Don't forget, I've been there. It's pretty, but it's a backwater compared to Paris or New York or Los Angeles. I can't make my home base some far-flung island in the Caribbean. For God's sake, that's where people go when they want to be forgotten about. The last thing I need now is to go into hiding."

"Then I promise I'll fly back to be with you as often as possible. If you'll spend Christmas with us."

He dunked his head into the water and then patted it dry. "Are you giving me a choice?" he asked, leaving the bathroom.

When she emerged from the shower she heard Christopher on the stairs. As she gathered her bathrobe around her, he pushed the bedroom door open and stood on the threshold, his eyes round with wonder.

"Mommy, something happened! There's a woman upstairs!"

Francesca smiled. "Yes. That's your grandmama." As she gathered the boy in her arms, she explained, "She's *my* mommy, Christopher. Come on. I'll take you to see her."

The little boy clutched her hand and together they tiptoed up the stairs, both concerned about their guest. Christopher felt she was some kind of captive wild animal, and Francesca was worried about her mother's state of mind when she woke up under her daughter's roof. Christopher had left the door to the guest room half-open. Francesca knocked timidly. "Mother?" she said in a low voice.

"Come in," a tremulous voice answered.

Francesca stood back and gave Christopher a small push forward. He bashfully lingered in front of the door and then said in a loud, clear voice, "Are you really my grandmother?"

Susannah smiled broadly, enchanted by the little boy. "Yes. I really am."

Christopher decided that this strange, red-haired woman was more friend than foe and impetuously flung himself forward onto the bed. "Will you take me to the movies, then? Jean's grandmother takes him to the movies every Saturday afternoon."

Susannah stretched out her arms and pulled him to her. "Of course I'll take you to the movies. And to the park, exploring." She smiled down at him and minutely examined his face as if it were some lost, beautiful treasure. He squirmed, allowed himself to be kissed, then jumped off the bed to escape.

As the child ran across the room to his mother, the two women's eyes met. Christopher buried his head against his mother's stomach. Then he ran out onto the landing.

"Francesca, he's an angel. He must make you so happy."

"He's very pleased to discover he has a grandmother." Francesca sat on the bed and looked at her mother. "Can I bring you breakfast? Or would you like to come downstairs?"

Susannah stared at her daughter as if she hadn't heard the question. Her eyes welled with tears. "You've managed so well, Francesca. Here you have this beautiful home, and you've brought up Christopher to be such a delightful child. All these years I never dared dream that our lives would turn out this way. Right now I'm the proudest grandmother in the world."

Francesca gave her a hug. "I'll run you a bath, Mother. Then we'll make plans over breakfast."

"I'm so grateful to Josie," said Susannah. "What a marvel she's become."

In the excitement of last night's discovery, Francesca had forgotten about Josie. "I must call her and invite her here. Oh, Mother, Josie and I have been terribly estranged."

"But why? You two were always like sisters when you were children."

"Yes." Francesca didn't know where to begin. "Marianne was like a mother to me," she said delicately. "And Josie helped raise me as if she were my older sister. In fact" —Francesca paused and nervously reached for her mother's hand—"we *are* sisters." Susannah, she noticed, was watching her oddly. "Mother, you've known all these years that Josie is . . ." Francesca let her voice drift off, unable to believe her mother knew the whole truth about Josie.

"Of course I know, darling, but I didn't want to stumble into something you hadn't found out about."

"Oh, I found out, all right," Francesca said. "I found out about a lot of things as a result of that very educational summer I spent with my father."

"I think the news came as more of a shock to you than it did to me, Francesca."

Francesca felt herself coloring under the force of her mother's understatement. "You think I'm rigid, don't you, Mother?"

Susannah nodded almost imperceptibly. "Perhaps you find

it harder to bend with the wind than I did at your age. But Francesca, I would never ask you to accept anyone else's moral code. That's something you have to develop for yourself. And of course your father was hardly the kind of man who would teach a child to be forgiving.''

''Don't, Mother, please.''

''Listen, Francesca. I know you have a hard time accepting the way I chose to live my life, and I find that totally understandable. Does Josie know she's Carlo's daughter?''

Francesca nodded slowly. ''She found out when we were in Venice. It was very hard for her, especially since Papa treated her like one of the servants.''

''And you, darling? How did you treat her?''

''Not as well as I should have—then or later.'' She looked at her mother as if in search of the kind of guidance no one had ever given her. ''I find it hard to accept what my father did. Sleeping with a servant and then pretending that he was no relation to Josie.''

Susannah said nothing, and Francesca felt an accusation hanging in the air between them. ''I love Josie, Mother, but I can't stand to think that she's my—my older sister and that she's the one who should have been given everything.''

''No, Francesca. Those things were due to Carlo's legitimate heir, and that's you, not Josie.''

''But it's not fair, really.''

''No, but since when has life ever been fair? Josie is your half sister. Why is that so hard for you to accept?''

Francesca shrugged. ''I'm not sure. I think about it a lot, and I feel terrible for not being able to come right out and tell the world we're sisters. But when an opportunity to do that arises, I just can't get the words out of my mouth.''

''Maybe you'll be able to do it someday,'' Susannah said.

Christopher accepted Francesca's preoccupation with Susannah more easily than Jack did. Still, no matter how he felt, Francesca was determined that her mother regain her whole mind and spirit, and her labor of love seemed to increase her own strength as well. She refused to go out on his cocktail-party rounds, warning him not to try to make her feel guilty. After all, her mother was an invalid.

Eventually, Jack grew petulant, then distant. Francesca felt the strain, but at a fortnight's end Susannah seemed well enough to keep up with the energetic Christopher and help Francesca pack. That was reward enough. Realizing he had lost the battle for her attention, Jack sulked.

"You've left me many times," she reminded him. "I've always given you freedom."

"Only because you wouldn't come with me. Remember? You were afraid to uproot Christopher."

She sighed, tired of arguing. If only Jack were less insecure, he would not mind sharing her with her mother. But just as he had been jealous of Christopher, he now saw Susannah as a rival. "Join us as soon as you can," she said fervently.

He eyed her suitcases lined up at the door. "You've taken enough to last you six months."

"No, I haven't." But she knew it was true; she wouldn't be back soon. "It's just that sometimes we dress in the evening at Lyford Rose. I have to play the part of the grande dame, you know," she said, trying to make a joke of it.

Jack took her in his arms and kissed her cheeks, her forehead, and finally her lips. "Promise you won't forget me," he said.

"Darling, of course." She smiled. "I couldn't look at anyone else if I tried."

She pushed back his hair and gazed into his blue eyes. He was always trying to force her to see behind that beautiful face, into the depths of his loneliness, his isolation. At last she felt sorry for abandoning him. He needed her as much as, or even more than, her mother did. Once back in the warm sun of Nassau, Susannah would cure herself. But Jack would never heal. The wound was too deep. And now she, too, had harmed him.

Josie swept her arms out in a wide circle, then bowed deeply to her cheering audience. "Thank you. I love you!" she shouted, knowing they couldn't hear her over the applause. "I love you!" Then she turned and strode off the stage into the little dark room where she often sat alone, getting her mind ready for another performance at Bette Diamant's little club. She fell into the one comfortable chair and let herself relax totally, rotating her head in a full circle to loosen up the muscles in her neck.

What a week this had been! The word had spread quickly through Montmartre that Bette Diamant had found a jewel in

Josie. Then, gradually, the news had been carried to the rest of Paris. On Saturday night of the previous week, a critic had sneaked in unrecognized. The next day he had printed a review so filled with praise that the telephone in Josie's tiny apartment had not stopped ringing since.

She had moved the month before into a more comfortable hotel, and had begun to enjoy the money she was earning, but it was Bette's audiences that made her glow with happiness. These people had saved her life. They had accepted her totally and made her feel whole again. All week long, lucrative offers had been coming in. She had regretfully given Bette her notice, but had assured her that she would come back whenever she could for a week at Chez La Lune for the usual wages.

Tomorrow she would begin a two-week engagement at a chic hotel near the Louvre. When that was over she had an engagement in Orléans. The following month she was scheduled to cut a record and then, best of all, she was going back to Nassau to sing at The Seesaw Club, a triumphant return! Josie stretched happily as she anticipated swimming in the warm island waters again.

Only one thing marred her happiness: Francesca's continued refusal to acknowledge Josie as her sister. Although they had kept in touch, the old ease of conversation was gone. No longer could they shut themselves in a room and talk for hours, confessing their deepest, darkest secrets and desires. The fact of their sisterhood, and Francesca's inability to acknowledge it, stood between them like a dark shadow.

Otherwise, Josie told herself determinedly, things were going beautifully.

PART FOUR

Lyford Cay, Commonwealth of the Bahamas 1974–1975

Chapter Thirty

LADY JANE HAD become the star of her exclusive sanatorium. Here among the pale and ineffectual, the hysterical and paranoid, she discovered she was in her element. Skillfully she worked among the other patients, playing Mother Superior to her postulants—who looked to her for a daily injection of the dignity they had lost when the gates of the institution closed behind them. For years, as Lady Hillford, she had enjoyed playing the role of the thoughtful and correct hostess, until her husband locked her up to keep her from carrying out her "wild threats," as he had called them. Now she discovered once again that she was good at making people feel at ease.

Each afternoon during what the staff called "free time" —Lady Jane had smirked contemptuously every time she heard the expression—she would gather a group of patients around her and put her social graces into operation. Lady Jane had gained permission to serve tea in the afternoon, inviting certain patients in person and sending written notes to others. She knew, of course, that the doctors were aware of her kindness to the other inmates, and she was fully aware that her actions worked to her advantage. She did enjoy her afternoon teas, though, and she was pleased that they had a slightly beneficial effect on the other patients. Besides, it was almost possible, Lady Jane discovered, to pretend for a while that she was not in a hospital at all.

She submitted herself to a session with her therapist every day as if she were talking to a priest in a confessional. She held back no sin, no grim fantasy, no longings for revenge. For months, day after day, she talked of nothing but Susannah and her daughter, admitting her envy of Susannah's youth and beauty, her rage when she learned that Francesca had survived the fire. The therapist probed her for memories of her childhood; she offered them up, along with detailed descriptions of her dreams.

He was impressed with her candor, her concern for the other patients, and her new acceptance of the tragedies of the past, and he praised her lavishly for her hard work and long hours of self-examination.

Trembling with excitement and the exhilaration that follows a hard-won victory, she listened to him announce that she was well enough to leave the institution.

"But you must continue to receive treatment as an outpatient," he warned. "We cannot risk a relapse."

"Am I truly well enough to leave, Doctor?" she had asked humbly.

He had nodded benevolently, confident that he had saved still another patient's sanity, and totally unaware that Lady Jane regarded him as a pompous and incredibly stupid functionary.

Her release was discussed, approved, and signed without further delay, and she hurried back to Lyford Cay to face the task ahead. She did not venture off the grounds. She did not want to call attention to herself. The maid shopped for her, or she ordered groceries to be delivered, and although many of her friends were returning for the winter season, she avoided the club and none of them knew she was living among them again.

She found her binoculars and quickly fell into her old routine, going up to the attic window several times a day to sweep the grounds of the adjoining estate. It was interesting to see how Francesca's amusing little spa had grown in the years she'd been away. There were several new buildings now.

For the first month, she saw no sign of Francesca, but early one morning she caught sight of the familiar thatch of bright hair. Carefully, she focused the lenses until the magnified face below her stood out sharp and clear.

Lady Jane began to tremble and then, for the first time, to doubt her own sanity. Surely, this was not possible. She put the glasses down and closed her eyes, but she knew her vision hadn't failed her. This woman was not Francesca but her mother. When she looked again, Susannah was still there, still beautiful. Still alive.

"I told Cyril she was alive," she said aloud. "Twenty years ago I told him, but he said I was insane." She began to laugh, softly at first, then wildly, nearly doubling over with the force of the joke she'd allowed the Nordonias to play on her. "And they think they got away with it! They think they're going to live forever." She had been pondering what her next move against Francesca would be and now here the solution was presented to her on a platter.

She shuffled among the labeled boxes and trunks until she found what she wanted. Wrapped in tissue paper and yellowed, crumbling newspaper, the stained knife was filthy, but it had not been touched. As she unwrapped it, she remembered her shock on seeing it the first time.

Through a blur of tears, she had gathered up Sybilla's scattered belongings in the palazzo that morning, and thrown everything in a suitcase. And days later, at home in England, when she could bring herself to, she had unpacked it, and there, inexplicably, it had gleamed up at her from the jumble of Sybilla's clothes and jewelry. Immediately, she recognized it for what it was, and at the time it seemed like a plea from her daughter for her to act. She had run to Cyril with the evidence to avenge their daughter, but he would have none of it. She knew the futility of trying to fight the Nordonias and the Hillford clan, but secretly she kept the weapon near her. Until now; now she was finally going to be able to use it, as it should have been years ago, against Sybilla's murderer. The knife glinted dully through the rusty stains. What had the clever Nordonias been thinking of, to have made such a dangerous oversight? They could only have assumed the dagger was safely in the traditional Venetian repository for such items: at the bottom of the canal.

Was it possible that Susannah's fingerprints were still on the dagger? Perhaps not, she thought, but even after nineteen years an autopsy would reveal the traces of a knife wound on the bones of a skeleton. It would be easy to prove that Sybilla had been murdered. Even without the fingerprints, there was enough evidence that Susannah had killed her.

She wrapped the knife carefully and tucked it back into its box. It would be safe there until the moment came for her to produce it. Then she put her binoculars on the ledge next to the window and went downstairs, into the drawing room. Standing in the center of the meticulously tidy room, she made a mental list of the things she would have to do in the next few days.

In her closets she sorted through to find the clothes that would best become her and that would at the same time be sober enough for court appearances. She would have to get her hair cut; it had grown dull and wild during her incarceration. But first, she decided, she would start making the long series of telephone calls that would be necessary to put Susannah Nordonia behind the iron bars of an Italian prison for the rest of her life.

Lady Jane swept across the room and sat down at one end of the chintz-covered sofa. She picked up the telephone and called her broker, informing him that she wished to sell certain bonds, since she would need a large amount of cash for a project she had in mind. Then she called her lawyer and informed him of her plan.

"Send someone to Italy," she said in a tone that brooked no contradiction. "Tell the officials in Venice that I wish them to charge Susannah Nordonia with the murder of my daughter."

The attorney, stunned into a brief silence, finally found his voice. "But, madam, your daughter died nearly twenty years ago of natural causes! And the countess is dead as well."

"On the contrary. The countess is here in Lyford Cay. My daughter was stabbed to death by Susannah Nordonia," Lady Jane said calmly. "I have the dagger with which she was murdered. I have kept it in a safe place all these years."

"But, Lady Jane, surely this should have been done long ago."

"My husband was afraid of the scandal," she explained. "Then Carlo Nordonia spread the lie that his wife had died. But she is alive. Scandal means nothing to me now. I will welcome the publicity; it will restore my good name. I want to see justice done."

"Justice, Lady Jane? Or vengeance?"

"A murder has gone unpunished," she snapped. "If you are unwilling to help me bring this woman to justice, I shall find another attorney."

The lawyer sighed and promised to set the wheels in motion.

Lady Jane went upstairs and to her bedroom and took a stack of old magazines down from a shelf. Somewhere in here, she remembered, was an article about a forensic archaeologist, a man who could read skeletons the way a coroner could read a body for clues to the cause of death. She had read the article perhaps ten years before and had saved it for just such a moment as this.

She pulled a magazine out of the stack. This was it, she

was sure. Flipping through it, she found the article; it said the archaeologist worked for a number of police departments in Europe. Lady Jane picked up the telephone again.

It had been Edward's idea to sail out to the island off the shore of Nassau, and hold their business discussion on a quiet beach without interruptions from their offices. Christopher wiggled in Francesca's lap in expectation. He had brought along an armada of toy boats, and he imitated Edward's movement at the rudder with them.

Francesca dragged a finger through the water as a breeze swept the boat quickly across the bay. She felt so relaxed and happy with her old friend, she had let her mind wander over her problems.

Edward stripped off his shirt. A battered straw hat protected him from the strong sun.

"You look like Huck Finn in that hat," Francesca said. "It's a sieve. Careful you don't get sunburned."

Edward's shoulders and torso were white, but strongly muscled. She could have traced his ribs with a finger, and for a moment she felt the urge to. Edward's bones were finer than Jack's, long and narrow. His body was lean and hard and disciplined; like his mind, Francesca thought. She had never really allowed herself to think of what Edward was like as a man. Now she wondered how she had ignored him for so long.

"Mama, look! Jellyfish!" Christopher pointed into the shallow water, and Francesca held him tight so that he wouldn't jump overboard in his excitement. In a moment Edward had pulled them toward the shore. Francesca lifted Christopher out of the boat and, while Edward hauled it up to the beach, she deposited her son and the picnic basket on the sand. Then she surveyed the woods and seagrass above the narrow beach. She found a knoll overlooking the sea not far above the beach.

"How's this? Come and see, Edward."

He rolled his khaki pants up to the knee. Christopher came running, waving a stick, and Edward followed with the picnic basket. For a moment they looked like father and son moving through the panes of sunlight toward Francesca. She held up a hand to shade her eyes. Then they came clear of the blur of light, Christopher with his hair bleached white from the island sun, his tanned skin, and Edward with his Gallic darkness, his face hard and intent. They were nothing alike, not at all.

Francesca spread a blanket and laid out the sandwiches, cheese, and fruit. Christopher, forgetting his manners, gobbled down his sandwich and swallowed a glass of lemonade while the adults talked of budgets and publicity plans. Then he was off as fast as his little legs could propel him. First he chased sandpipers down the beach. Then he collected a pile of dried starfish and pink-bellied conch shells. Now he was probing the sand with a stick.

"But you still haven't answered my question," Edward was saying. "Why so somber on this beautiful day?"

Francesca turned her gaze away from her son, back to Edward. "Well, for one thing, Lyford Rose needs so much work. I hadn't realized, despite all your letters, how much the place has fallen behind. I feel so ashamed, especially after such a smashing start. It makes me look like the kind of person who can't follow through."

"But you've known that for months. It can be corrected easily enough now that you're back. We've pulled together a lot of loose ends this afternoon. No, I think something else is troubling you."

Francesca squinted across the bay at the purple hills of Nassau. Already Paris seemed more than an ocean away. Jack gave her everything she wanted except independence. And that was what she wanted most. She knew now she loved Lyford Rose, the green land and stunning white rim of beach, the buildings she'd designed, the ideals and goals of the place that meant so much to her. She loved sharing her home and helping others get well and improve themselves. The feeling of having done her job well was as gratifying as love, and as necessary. In comparison to her work at Lyford Rose, her life of leisure in Paris with Jack was a bore, shallow and insubstantial. She was even embarrassed now by the thought of their shameless quest for publicity. Surely she hadn't deserved all that attention—her hairdresser was right. *La Comtesse Marquée* indeed! Even Edward must have thought her a fool.

"Edward, I've needed to come back here so badly."

"I know. I saw the way you and Jack were living. Exhilarating for a while, perhaps, but not very nourishing in the long run."

"I was mortified," Francesca said, "when Apllonie showed you the pictures in *Vogue.*"

Edward only shrugged. "You are very rare, Francesca. *Ravissante.* Of course society would take you into its orbit. And you even managed to turn your scar into a sensation. Perhaps you needed to prove to the world that you're still a great beauty."

"Perhaps. But I haven't given my scar a thought since I arrived back here. It's as if it never happened. I'm nearly healed, even if my face doesn't show it."

Edward smiled. "It shows. But something else . . ."

"You're right, as usual. Sometimes I think you can read my mind. It's Jack, of course. He's terribly upset about our separating, even for a short time."

"But surely he understands about your mother needing you."

"Yes, but sometimes I think he needs me just as much. There's gossip in Paris that we've separated. It depresses him. He's afraid I won't come back."

Edward said nothing. He gazed out at Nassau and rocked his bare feet in the sand.

"Oh, Edward, if only I could talk to him the way I talk to you! Why is it so hard to be friends with your lover? Why must we always put people and our emotions in compartments, so that we can't share it all with one person . . ."

"I don't know," said Edward quietly. "It's not that way with me. I can love a friend. Love is easier between equals."

Something in his voice made Francesca stare at him as he faced away. She wondered suddenly what life was like for him in Nassau. Constant work, and few real friends, or lovers either. Edward's name had never been romantically linked with anyone's. His wife and son had been killed in an airplane crash the year before Francesca had met him. After once stating this fact, Edward's attitude made it clear to Francesca that it was a subject he preferred remain closed. He hadn't time for romance. If there were a woman now, Francesca supposed she would lose some of her easy intimacy with him. That would make her sad. She had been through so much with Edward: her father's death, the birth of her child, her troubles with Michael, the building of Lyford Rose, and finally the trauma of the fire and Michael's death. Edward had helped her survive those crises like an older brother or the close and loving father she had never had.

"Are you in love with anyone, Edward?" she asked shyly.

He didn't turn around but his shoulders hunched eloquently. "Sorry. Those are my company secrets. I can't divulge them."

"Then you are," Francesca crowed. But underneath she felt something fall away within her. To hide her panic, she smiled.

"I'm only human," he said. Suddenly Edward stood up and shook sand off his legs. "Where's Christopher?" he said. The alarm in Edward's voice brought Francesca back to reality. He stood up and turned around. When he faced her again, he looked worried.

Francesca looked down the beach. It was dazzling white and deserted. A sandpiper ventured down to the water. "There's his pile of starfish. Where do you suppose he's gone?"

They got up and walked along the beach together. It curved slightly, and as a new stretch of sand came into view with no sign of the small boy, they began to call out his name urgently. Edward ran ahead, disappearing around a far bend. Instead of following him, Francesca moved inland toward the grassy fields and woods, combing them as she called out her son's name. Her heart began to pound wildly in panic when Edward reappeared, running swiftly, out of breath.

"I walked about a mile, but no Christopher," he said. "He couldn't possibly have wandered that far in such a short time. He must be in the woods somewhere. Perhaps he lost his way."

Francesca shouted Christopher's name until her throat was raw. Staying several yards apart but always within sight of each other, she and Edward combed the woods for more than an hour. When they came to a narrow creek, Francesca said, "He loves to explore. Do you suppose he followed the stream?"

Edward joined her and pointed inland. "Let's go that way. Maybe he decided to trace the creek to its source."

He waded to the other side, and they began to trudge along the banks of the stream, pushing undergrowth aside, looking in clumps of long grass. They had gone about a mile when Edward called to her. "Francesca, look there! Up ahead there's a waterfall. I saw a flash of red near the cascade."

"Yes! That's Christopher's shirt. It has to be!" She set out at a run, ignoring the pebbles and roots that tore at her bare feet. "Christopher!" She kept shouting his name, although she knew he was too far away to hear her. Finally, as she approached the roaring little waterfall, the child looked up.

From a distance she saw his mouth form the word "Mama," and then he started to run toward her, waving his arms excitedly.

"Slow down, Christopher," Edward shouted. "Don't run! It's dangerous."

Before he'd finished the warning, Francesca watched with horror as her son tripped and fell headlong into the stream. When she finally reached him, he was still lying facedown in the rocks, his head in the water.

She screamed his name, lifting him up gently. In a moment Edward was beside her, releasing the child from her grip.

"Let me get him breathing."

"It's my fault," she said numbly. "I wasn't watching him."

Edward didn't answer. He just kept breathing, steadily and forcefully, into Christopher's mouth. Water gushed out after the first few breaths, then nothing. As Francesca watched, Edward began to tire.

"Let me take over for a few minutes." She knelt on the other side of Christopher. "I'll start on the count of three." She began to count out loud. As Edward raised his head after the third breath, she lowered hers and breathed into her son's mouth. She was surprised at how exhausting it was. After only a few minutes, she was worn out. Edward realized it immediately and, after another orderly count, he took her place.

How long had he been unconscious? Francesca asked herself as she watched Edward try to revive her son. And how long had he lain facedown in the water while she ran toward him? She and Edward had been a good fifty yards away from Christopher when he fell, and the rough terrain had slowed them down. She closed her eyes and prayed silently.

Again she took Edward's place. When she began to falter, he replaced her. The minutes ticked past, and with each one she became more certain that she had lost her son.

Then Edward froze, his face just inches from the child's mouth. "Come on," he said softly. "Come on!" He looked up at Francesca, his dark eyes brimming with relief. "He's breathing!"

Francesca leaned forward, but Edward held out his arm to prevent her from hugging the child.

"We've got to get him to the hospital, Francesca. Lead the way back. I'm going to carry him."

"Why doesn't he open his eyes?"

"He will, Francesca. Please don't worry about that now. He'll live; I promise you that."

She reached out and took Edward's hand. She knew she would never be able to express her gratitude to him. He had saved Christopher's life. Alone, she could never have kept the resuscitation up long enough to get her son breathing again.

Shakily, she stood up and led Edward back to the boat.

The rest of the day and all that night, Francesca lived in a kind of limbo. All was not lost, since Christopher was in no danger of death. But while they tried to revive him he had been unable to breathe for a long time, and the unspoken fear of brain damage hung in the air of the hospital like a hideous apparition.

Edward drifted in and out of the solarium where Francesca waited, forcing her to talk, to eat, to drink water, bringing Susannah and then Apollonie to sit with her.

It was almost five o'clock in the morning when the neurologist sat down beside her and assured her that Christopher was as sound as a bell. "No brain damage whatsoever," he said. "He'll be a little vague for a few days, but trauma always does that. Don't let on that you notice."

He had led Francesca to Christopher's bedside and let her look down at his sleeping face for a few minutes, drinking in the sight of him, her legs trembling with relief and exhaustion.

At dawn Francesca and Edward left Christopher with a nurse at his bedside and walked slowly out of the hospital. Edward drove her home, the convertible with its top down swinging through the deserted island streets. The air was cool and the bushes and grass, still colorless with night, were loud with the calls of birds. Edward did not speak as he pulled the car out onto a hill overlooking the beach.

"Let's watch the sunrise."

She nodded. In a moment their shoulders were touching. Francesca did not pull away. A red horizon line sliced the blue world in half, and the dark sea separated from the brightening sky. Then the clouds boiled up, and the first rays of the sun gilded the water.

Edward was kissing her. His lips were soft yet demanding. As her eyes closed, the incredible spectacle of the sky became part of his kiss. Her lips parted beneath his. It did not feel wrong. Edward drew back and looked at her, his eyes intent.

The sea seemed to brim over as the sun's flat rays struck the peak of each wave ripple and turned them to gold.

"Good morning," Francesca said.

He kissed her again, tenderly yet coolly. "You hold yourself back from me," he said.

"No, I don't mean to." She looked into his gray eyes, wondering if she could learn to love him as more than a friend. He was, she knew, the perfect man for her. His life was serene, dedicated. When she needed him, he would be there; he wouldn't be making a movie in Spain or talking with a theatrical producer in New York.

His head bent forward and their brows touched. He laughed a little. "I'm too selfish. I won't pressure you now." He turned back to the driver's wheel. "Let's go home and get some sleep."

Chapter Thirty-one

"JOSIE! LONG TIME no see! Where were you last year?" a customer shouted. "They tried, but they couldn't find anyone to replace you."

"Thank you," Josie said, smiling at the garishly dressed tourist, one of many who had gravitated toward the long, curved bar early in the evening. "Happy New Year. I hope you enjoy the show."

"If you're singing, we'll enjoy it," another man called.

Josie felt a tingle of excitement. Her return to the club after a long absence had done more to rebuild her faith in herself than had the whirlwind of club dates and recording sessions she'd been through in Paris during the preceding two months. This was where she had been given her start. Returning here as a newly acclaimed star was rich, delicious food for her battered ego. Since the drugged-out nights when she'd sung here with Lucas, she'd shed several skins. She had worked her way back up on her own, without Carlo, without Lucas, without Benor. Her natural confidence had returned in force. She was pleased with herself as she had never been before. Yet she'd lost none of her passion and emotional depth; her access to her deepest feelings was effortlessly fluid. She was not afraid to dredge up her memories of loss and self-hatred because she knew she was in control of them now. Nothing stood in the path of her joy.

Except Lucas's bitterness, she reminded herself as she made her way through the bar, heading for her tiny dressing room in the back of the club. He blamed her for all of the misfortunes that had befallen him since his return from Paris. The Seasaw Club wouldn't give him back his old job. The manager had told Josie he didn't trust Lucas because he'd been arrested for drug dealing. But Lucas stubbornly insisted that Josie was to blame for his career failures. "You've been talking against me,'' he'd insisted, when she ran into him on the street her first day back in Nassau. ''And now you've taken my job at the Seasaw.''

She had offered to take him on as her backup for the calypso set, but he had refused, saying he couldn't work with anyone as ''white'' as Josie. She had shrugged that off, telling him she wasn't interested in the racist slogans he had adopted since his return to the island.

''You're ashamed of your black skin,'' he snarled. ''All you do is toady up to white people.''

Furious, Josie had lashed out the palm of her hand, catching Lucas across the cheek.

She had not seen him since that day, and she knew she would be better off if he stayed out of her life for good. But she couldn't forget the early days. It had been Lucas who gave her a place to stay during those dark months after her mother died, and a chance to work with his combo.

Perhaps she would call him and try to mend fences with him before she left the Bahamas for her tour of Italy.

Josie held her purse extra tightly as she made her way through the New Year's Eve crowd. Tucked inside the leather handbag was a letter from a record company, asking her written permission to press the tapes of her Paris nightclub performances into an album. She'd called the company president that afternoon and promised to meet him in Rome. ''I have another idea,'' she'd said. ''If the first album does well maybe you'd be more interested in some tapes I made when I was singing at Chez La Lune in Monmartre.''

''Sounds like a great idea,'' the record executive had said. ''We'll call it 'Josie Lapoiret Live at Chez La Lune.' We'll leave the applause on the track . . .''

Josie had hung up the telephone, eager to leave the Bahamas and get down to some hard work in Europe.

''Full house tonight,'' the bartender called to her as she approached him. ''Break a leg.''

Josie smiled and thanked him. Some of the patrons, she knew, had come to the club especially to see her, but most had come because it was New Year's Eve. They had heard about the holiday celebration that had become a tradition in Nassau.

The natives had already begun to flock into the streets. Later on, they would don enormous masks fashioned from painted boxes, and parade through the streets. Already the town had turned into a carnival of steel bands and swirling, unorganized throngs of shouting adults and children. Tourists, as drunk as the natives and eager to join in the revelry, had armed themselves with confetti and cameras.

Josie glanced uneasily toward the front of the club. There was something sinister about the crowd of painted revelers this year, some new anger she had never noticed before. In addition to the usual noise and color, she sensed a hard edge to the celebration. The eyes of some of the costumed natives were filled with a zeal that frightened her.

Earlier, when she entered through the front door of the club, she'd had to push herself against the huge plate-glass window that faced the street. The crowd, she noticed, was noisier than it had been in previous years, and there was a nasty ring to the shouting. "Too many Rastafarians," the manager said when he let Josie in. "I'm keeping the door locked tonight, not letting anybody in who doesn't look right. I don't trust those loonies."

Now, as she headed for the door that led to the back corridor, she cast an apprehensive look at the bartender. He gave her a worried frown. "Too much politics going on out there, Josie. Makes me uneasy."

Josie stopped at the bar to nod her agreement. "Some of those guys act as if they're out to hurt people."

The bartender looked toward the front door. "I'll ask a couple of the waiters to hang around the entrance. Go change for your act. We've got things under control."

But as she walked down the narrow rear corridor and entered her dressing room, she knew somewhere inside her that everything was not under control. She'd seen dozens of New Year's crowds, but never one as hard-edged and wild as this one. She flipped the switch to turn on the lights around the dressing table mirror, sat down before the mirror, and went through the practiced ritual of applying her makeup. Then she slipped out of her street clothes and into the floor-length gold lamé sheath she would wear for her first set.

She was buckling her sandals when the bartender pounded on the door.

"Josie, open up! Everyone's being sent home!"

She ran to the door and swung it open to stare wide-eyed at the shaking bartender. "What?"

"No time for questions, honey. Get your butt out of here. Phil's sending the customers out the back door a few at a time. That crowd out in the street has lost control. If they decide to come through the big window, we are gonna be in big trouble. Don't stop to change your clothes. Just split."

"But they'll trash the club!"

"Uh-uh. Phil's got a shotgun. First head of dreadlocks comes through the window will be one dead Bahamian. Now, you get out of here, quick." He turned and fled toward the front of the club.

Through the open door, Josie saw a group of tourists hurrying toward the rear exit. She snatched up her purse and followed them out into the dark alley. She had almost reached a deserted back street when someone grabbed her around the waist from behind and hauled her through a doorway into a dim foyer.

"Where do you think you're going, girl?"

"Lucas! Let go of me."

"You've got to let me buy you a drink, baby. It's New Year's."

She could smell liquor on Lucas's breath, and his slurred speech told her he was blind drunk. She wrenched away from his grasp and backed toward the door, but he grabbed her arm and held a bottle of rum up to her mouth.

"Drink up, Josie. This is the good stuff. You did me a favor when you made sure I wouldn't get any more gigs in Nassau, Josie. After you dumped me, I had to find a new way to support myself. I don't play anymore, but I make a much better living using my brains than I did using my fingers."

"Don't tell me how you make a living, Lucas. I'd rather not know. But I don't think it's with your brains."

Lucas slipped her dress strap off her shoulder. She looked at his narrowed eyes, his clenched lips, and suddenly she knew this was no coincidental meeting with a former friend. Lucas had been waiting for her in the alley, and he intended to take out his anger on her. Slowly she began to back away from him. She had gained no more than six inches when one of his long arms whipped through the air, and his fist caught her under the chin.

Josie forced her way back through a tunnel of darkness and found herself lying on the ground with Lucas standing over her.

"That's just the first thing I owe you, bitch," he said. "You've got a lot more coming. Stand up!"

She felt him take hold of her shoulders roughly and haul

her to her feet. Then he had his arms around her and was trying to kiss her. She tensed with all her strength against him, and bit his neck hard. Lucas reared back in surprise, and hit her again. Darkness cracked across her face, followed by another pain, dull but persistent.

"Don't you ever do that again, bitch." Lucas gave her a malevolent look, which she barely saw.

She held still for a moment, trying to clear her head then shuddered as she felt Lucas's hands pulling the narrow skirt of the lamé sheath up over her hips. She used all her strength to push him away, but he simply stood at arm's length, his hands holding her skirt up around her waist, his eyes roaming over the lower part of her body. Josie swallowed her revulsion and stood absolutely still until he raised his head to leer at her. She braced herself against the wall and jammed her right knee violently into his groin.

Lucas doubled over and let loose with a stream of obscenities, but Josie didn't stand still to hear it. She was running down the back street before Lucas came out of his crouch. Still clutching her purse under one arm, she pulled the lamé skirt down over her hips, but kept it high enough to free her legs to run.

She heard a crash, as if someone chasing her had tipped over a trash can. Her heart was pounding hard, and her breath came in painful gasps, but she kept running, even after she felt the heel of one of her sandals slip out from under her. Carried forward by the same fear she had felt when she saw the violent hatred in Lucas's eyes, she flew around a corner at full speed and found herself in a blind alley.

Footsteps behind her told her that Lucas was following. Terrified, she threw herself back against a damp wall, then held her breath as the footsteps reached the mouth of the alley and then stopped.

She waited, heart in her throat, for Lucas to snatch her by the hair and drag her to her feet. Eyes closed, she fought back the urge to dissolve in tears. But the silence went on and on until she summoned up the courage to open her eyes and peek cautiously out from behind the crates. The mouth of the alley was deserted.

Josie pushed herself upright and crept forward until she could peek out of the blind alley. There was no sign of Lucas. She crept away from her hiding place and made her way slowly along the littered back street until she could see, ahead of her, the crowd of revelers flowing along the street. Creeping forward, she waited for a break in the mob. Then she scrambled into the midst of the crowd and let it carry her forward.

She glanced around wildly, unable at first to get her bearings. Then she caught sight of the boarded-up entrancc to the club she had left only a few minutes before. Standing near the doorway, his eyes narrowed, was Lucas Caswell. Josie could see him searching the faces in the crowd as it surged toward him. She edged her way toward the opposite side of the street, staying close behind a group of teenage boys who were walking close together.

The throng flushed her along on its buoyant tide. She could see hundreds of people lining the streets and balconies, watching the noisy spectacle. The air around her was heavy with the smell of sweat and whiskey, and the shouts of the celebrants rang in her ears. Before her eyes, the colorful horde of ragged revelers began to blur into a kaleidoscopic nightmare. The people became indistinguishable from one another as the dancers' limbs snaked out toward her in reptilian circles. Their grotesque movements had a malevolent grace that made Josie think of a dance of death.

She watched Lucas until she was sure she had passed him unnoticed. Then, driven by an uncontrollable panic, she fought her way forward through the crowd and, when it passed a side street, bolted for her hotel.

She was pumped so full of adrenaline that she was still running when she burst into the lobby. She sprinted for the elevator and then ran along the upstairs corridor. Seconds later she was standing alone in her room, her back against the double-locked door trying to catch her breath. Slowly, the blood stopped pounding in her ears. Shakily, she walked to the bed and sat down. The sounds of celebration that came to her from the street and through the thin walls of her room only served to make her feel more isolated. Nassau was no longer home. Josie clicked the phone for the operator and asked for Francesca's number. She was surprised to hear Jack's voice answer. Pretending not to recognize it, she quickly left a message for Francesca that she was going away and would not be able to see her. Before he could speak, she hung up the phone.

Francesca had read she was in Nassau and had telephoned, insisting that she spend New Year's Day with them. Well, she didn't need that anymore . . . to wait in suspense until Francesca deigned to recognize her. She had evened the score for what she had done in Venice when she had led her to her mother. She quickly dialed the airlines and made a reservation for the next morning. She would begin the New Year in a place she had never been . . . Rome.

Chapter Thirty-two

It was after midnight. Fireworks burned and dazzled the sky. The parade of costumed natives had begun in earnest, but the crowds seemed exhausted, sodden with drink, too tired to stop celebrating. Men and women staggered through the streets, laughing as explosions punctuated the reggae music that clashed from steel bands and ghetto blasters. Francesca had driven Apollonie to the airport. "I'm going home," the woman told her. It meant she was ending the chemotherapy that was keeping her alive. "I want to spend some time in my château while I still have the strength to notice its beauty. Will you visit me?"

"Yes, before the spring," Francesca said.

Apollonie had hugged her resolutely when the passengers began to board the plane. "*Ma fille,* you bring others so much happiness. My wish is happiness for you." Francesca kissed her and stayed at the window until the plane disappeared down the runway.

Francesca maneuvered her car slowly through the scattered revelers and out onto the cay. She put the top down. The silence stunned her; there was nothing but the sweep and hush of the ocean. In the moonlight the breeze turned the grass silver.

She wished Jack was there to share the beauty of the night with her. He had surprised her and arrived a week earlier than expected for Christmas. Since the moment he had set foot in Nassau, he had been more than she had ever hoped for. Curious and enthusiastic about Lyford Cay, the spa—her work—unresentful of her mother . . . If he was playing a role, it was the best acting he'd ever done.

He was ready now to adjust his life in order to share hers in Nassau instead of insisting, as he had always had in the past, that she give up everything to lead his life. And Francesca no longer avoided the subject of marriage. They had even begun to look for a site to build a new home. On the other side of the island it would have a different feeling entirely from the houses she had shared with her parents or Michael. Francesca suddenly felt a shiver of apprehension that left gooseflesh on her arms. And yet, out here, in the moon's pale light, she was far from human harm.

Unless, of course, the danger was within herself, in her own heart. No, Francesca's lips moved soundlessly. She loved only one man truly. Then why did she have this fear—this premonition? Just when everything seemed to be so perfect.

The lights were out in her cottage. Francesca let herself in quietly and tiptoed into Christopher's room. Jack had taken the boy out to see the parade and the excitement had exhausted him. Christopher slept soundly. Francesca pulled the sheet to his shoulders and turned to her own bedroom. In the dark she could just make out the outlines of the furniture. Moonlight pooled in the white drapes on one side of the room. Careful not to wake Jack, Francesca undressed in shadow. Then she stepped toward the bed, and drew back in surprise. She saw for the first time that it was empty. It was still made, the covers stretched flat to the pillow beneath the chintz bedspread.

Francesca switched on the lights and looked for a note. Jack could not have left Christopher alone. The kitchen, stark with fluorescence, gleamed emptily, the finished champagne bottles lined up, the only reminder of their festive New Year's Eve supper earlier. There was a liquor glass on the counter next to an empty bottle of scotch. Francesca had a resurgence of the panic that had gripped her whenever Michael caved in to his alcoholic urges. But Jack's excesses were worse because they were so rare. He never allowed himself to let go. He needed to be in control too much to succumb to liquor. Something had gone wrong.

"Francesca?"

She swirled around. Her mother stood in the doorway, hugging a robe around her. "I heard you come in. I fell asleep on your couch. What happened? You look frightened."

"I had to drop in on the New Year's Eve celebration at the spa and then I took Apollonie to the airport. I left Jack here with Christopher. Do you know where he's gone?" She held up the empty bottle of scotch. "I'm afraid he's been drinking."

"No. I sent him off to talk to a friend of mine, who called while you were out. He left me to babysit. He had a tiny drink, but I don't think it did much harm. Otherwise I wouldn't have let him drive."

"But why would he go out at this hour?"

The two women sat in the living room. Susannah grew agitated as she talked. "There's something I must discuss with you. I received a telephone call from Italy warning me that Lady Jane is opening up a legal proceeding against me."

"Good heavens, what are you talking about, Mother? Against you! After all she's done!"

"Yes. In Venice." Susannah's face was tense. "She's charged me with the murder of her daughter, and sent lawyers to press the case in Italy. They've already gone to England to exhume poor Sybilla."

"Oh, my God. But surely too much time has passed . . ."

"No, the statute of limitations is twenty years for murder," said Susannah, getting up to pace the small room. "I'll have to go back to Venice and clear my name. I won't hide. It will be better for you and Christopher."

"Oh, my God." So this was the impending danger she had sensed. Francesca realized she was shaking. "I think it would be the worst thing possible for Christopher. Not to mention you—you can't go back there in your condition. Lady Jane wants to start a witch hunt. Think of the publicity, the scandal."

"Think of the scandal if I don't go. People will assume I'm guilty of murder. Perhaps I am guilty of something, but not that. You see, I loved Sybilla."

Francesca sucked in her breath. "Oh, Mother, I know you did. They'll crucify you for that."

Susannah looked down at her with mingled sadness and resolve. "I know it will be a horror for everyone concerned, but darling, it was bound to come out someday. Surely you knew, when you came to me in Paris, what the truth could do to us."

"Why must it come out? Why turn all our lives into a spectacle?"

"For people who live in the public eye as you and I have, there's no escape." Susannah was nearly trembling. She sat down on the couch and reached for Francesca's hand. "Do you know, all these years I've hidden from the truth? And now I see I've wasted the best part of my life. I missed watching you grow up, marrying, having your beautiful boy. It's wrong to cower away in darkness."

"We'll hire lawyers, too. We'll find a legal way out."

Susannah continued as if she had not even heard Francesca's objection.

"And it drove Lady Jane mad as well. The anger festered away inside her, rotting her mind. Apparently she's boasted that she saved the murder weapon—or what she calls the murder weapon—all these years like some precious relic. My God! I can't believe she's had it all this time. I could never remember what had happened to that knife. Carlo and Renata each thought the other had taken care of it. They say it's still covered with Sybilla's blood and my fingerprints. Can you imagine?"

"That woman is evil. God help us, she hates you."

Susannah smiled wanly. "At least I have you. That will help. Jack's gone to talk to my old lawyer friend, Anson Prescott. He was afraid he might distress me so he's reciting all the horrors I've got to face to the man of the household. But he underestimated me."

"Well," said Francesca, "I can see why Jack had that drink."

Susannah rose. Her face wore her old, familiar determination. "I know this will turn out for the best."

"I don't," said Francesca. "How can I explain this to a five-year-old boy?"

"Don't explain it to him. Tell him only what you must. But for his sake, I've got to clear my name."

Francesca sat, transfixed with fear, while her mother left for her own cottage.

When Jack arrived home some time later, he found her still sitting there. Gently he opened the clenched palms of her hands and bent to kiss her.

"Everything is happening so quickly," said Francesca, clinging to Jack's arms. "I feel like everything I've worked for is being taken away from me."

"Mother," Francesca said quietly but firmly, "cannot go to Venice, and that is that."

They sat at the kitchen table drinking coffee while he told her one terrible fact after another.

"Francesca, I don't think your mother is fully aware of the trouble she's in. The inquest won't be scheduled for weeks—if there is an inquest. And until then we're going to have to keep her pretty much out of sight."

"That's not going to be easy, Jack."

"No, I'm aware of that." He reached across the table and took Francesca's hand. "Right now, Francesca, I'm more worried about you and Christopher than I am about your mother."

Francesca looked up at him, surprised. "Why?"

"I don't think you're safe here, darling. I can't forget what Lady Jane did to you four years ago. She's got to be even crazier now than she was back then; God knows what she has in mind for you this time." He reached up to touch the long, jagged scar that marked the left side of Francesca's face. "I'm not willing to take any chances this time. I want you and Christopher out of here before that lunatic thinks up another method of retribution."

"But surely if she pressed this case, that will satisfy her."

"Prescott doesn't think much of anything will come of the case. Your mother's guilt or innocence hardly seems to interest him. He says this case will threaten to expose the corruption of Italian police and city officials. Lady Jane contends that your father bribed a good many highly placed cops and city brass. Even the death certificate was phony. Prescott thinks we should call their bluff. In all likelihood the Italians will let the case blow over or tie it up with so much red tape that Lady Jane will have to give up."

"My mother wants to go to Venice, Jack. I think it's a terrible mistake. She'll only make things worse. But she won't listen to me. She thinks it's the only way to clear her name."

Jack shook his head. "That's a bad idea. I think we ought to get her out of Lyford Cay immediately, but Venice is not the place for her right now. God knows what the Italian press would do to her, to say nothing of what they'll do to the rest of us."

"Let's not worry about the damned press!" Francesca felt a sudden flash of rage. "My mother has been charged with murder, for God's sake. She could be sent to prison. A few sneering stories in the newspapers shouldn't concern us."

Jack sat down and spoke quietly. "In the real world, darling, the press is important. You should know that as well as I do." He poured milk into his coffee and stirred it absently. "Let's get our priorities in order. First thing we have to do is get you, Christopher, and your mother the hell out of Lyford Cay. It's clear that Lady Jane is just as vindictive as she was when she set the fire."

"But the guards, Jack, and the security system."

"Francesca!" He let go of her hands and pounded the table with his fist. "Please, darling, just this once, please don't argue with me."

The urgency in his voice had intensified into something close to panic, and Francesca forced herself to be silent.

"You," he said carefully, trying to calm himself, "are in danger of being murdered! Can you get that through your stubborn skull? This time, Francesca, I'm not asking you to leave Lyford Cay for my sake. I'm trying to save your life and the life of my son!"

He pushed away from the table and slammed out the back door, leaving her to absorb the implications of what he had just said.

She sat at the table, staring at her trembling hands. After a few minutes, she got up and poured some scotch into the glass Jack had left sitting on the counter. She drank it slowly, hating its taste but appreciating the warmth it brought.

She heard the screen door open again slowly. "Why didn't you tell me about Christopher?" Jack asked quietly.

"I didn't tell you because you and Christopher didn't get along very well, at first," she said. "When we started to live together in Paris, most of the time you acted as if Christopher was in the way. I always meant to tell you the whole story as soon as you started to get along together." But Christopher and Jack had been thick as thieves for several months, she thought. Why, she asked herself, had she been unwilling to share her son with anyone, even his own father? Had she been afraid it would force her to commit herself to marrying Jack?

When she spoke, her voice was dull and lifeless. "I'm sorry. I can't even give you a sensible reason for the way I've acted."

"I wish you'd told me from the start."

"How could I? By the time I realized I was pregnant, you were married to Nadia."

"You wanted Christopher for yourself. You were afraid I'd take too much of his love away from you."

"No!" Francesca felt the blood drain out of her face as she recognized the brutal truth of his words. Christopher had seemed to her like a special gift God had sent her to make up for all the love her parents and Jack hadn't given her. Christopher had been hers, to make her life complete.

Numbly she admitted the truth for the first time. "All right. I was afraid of losing part of his love to you. He's all I've ever had, Jack."

"Stop it, Francesca. You have me. I've always loved you, from the first time I laid eyes on you that day in front of Santa Maria della Salute. Why can't you accept my love?"

Francesca didn't answer.

"It's just that you don't, and you can't, love me the way I love you," Jack said, finishing the explanation she had been unable to give.

"No, please don't say that, Jack. You must know I've never loved anyone the way I love you."

"What about Edward Patiné," he said bitterly.

Francesca felt her breath catch in her throat, but she said nothing.

"You think about him a lot, Francesca." Jack's eyes were steady, but there was a tightness around his mouth. "If you just say the right words at the right time, you'll be able to live the rest of your life here in the sun on your safe little island, away from the dangers of the big, bad world. Well, my darling, if that's what you want, I'm not going to try to wrench you away from it. But understand this: Christopher is *my* son, and I won't let you hide that fact from him or from the rest of the world any longer."

"How long have you known?" she asked.

"Since the first March we spent together in Paris. You celebrated his birthday, remember?" He smiled grimly. "I can still count, Francesca."

"Why didn't you tell me?"

Jack looked around the kitchen. "Is there an echo in here? Wasn't that *my* line?"

Francesca covered her face with her hands. "Oh, God, I feel so awful, Jack."

"So do I, Francesca. I've felt awful for a long, long time. It started when I realized you didn't really trust me, and it got worse a couple of weeks ago when I realized I was going to lose you to a man who will never love you as much as I do."

Francesca swallowed the lump of despair that threatened to send tears spilling down her cheeks. It wouldn't be fair for her to cry now; it would look like a bid for sympathy.

Distraught as she was, she knew that it was Jack, not she, who needed sympathy tonight.

"Let's get some sleep, Francesca." Jack stood up, took her hand, and pulled her to her feet. "We've both had enough for one day. Maybe things will look better in the morning."

She let him lead her into the bedroom and ease her down on the bed. After he undressed and stretched out next to her, she expected him to turn his back on her and go to sleep. But he pulled her close to him and held her comfortingly until she fell asleep in his arms.

Chapter Thirty-three

"FRANCESCA?"

"In my office," Francesca answered, looking up from her desk, listening to Jack's footsteps pass through the kitchen and along the corridor to the office at the front of the cottage. "Any luck?" she asked as he threw himself down in the chair across from her.

"I think so. I sure as hell tried."

Francesca smiled. "Oscar-winning performance?"

"Mmm, except that I wasn't acting." He ran a tanned hand through his hair. "Your mother is one damned tough customer, I'll tell you that. I spent all day yesterday describing every possible horror that could befall her, you, Christopher, and the world at large if she insists on running off to Venice. And she said, 'Thank you very much, dear, but I'll do it my way.' " Jack nodded. "That was yesterday. This morning I decided to get tough; I tactfully pointed out to her that twenty-years-to-life in an Italian prison is probably not all cocktail parties and gardening."

"Well done, Jack." Then a furrow appeared between Francesca's brows. "But why didn't you make that your first line of attack?"

Jack shrugged. "I assumed it would have occurred to her, but I guess she's never considered the possibility of losing the case."

The telephone rang, and Francesca picked it up.

"Francesca? It's Josie."

"Josie, I can't believe it's you! We didn't know where you'd disappeared to."

"I'm calling from Rome—I just arrived here—and I've got bad news. The Italian newspapers are filled with Lady Jane's lies about your mother."

"One second." Francesca gestured for Jack to go and pick

up the extension in the bedroom. When she heard the click, she said. "Go ahead, Josie. Jack's on the other phone."

"They've virtually convicted your mother already. It's awful, Francesca. The front pages are covered with twenty-year-old photographs of Susannah and Sybilla. There are even pictures of Carlo."

"Josie," Jack interrupted, "before this mess is over, somebody is going to connect you with Francesca. You're on your way to the top. There's no way we can let you get involved in this mess."

"But I might be able to help."

"No. Stay out of it. Don't even tell anyone you even know Francesca. If you want to talk to her, call from a pay phone, understand? I know these scandal journalists. They'll do anything to get a story. Please, Josie. Stay out of this."

Josie started to argue, but Francesca broke in on her. "Do as Jack says, please, Josie. Promise?"

After a short silence, Josie agreed.

"Now," Jack said, "let's hear the gory details."

"Lady Jane has supplied the Italian authorities with a gruesome autopsy report on Sybilla's skeleton. She had found a forensic archaeologist who could find clues to a murder on the decaying parchment of bones. But just as her own lawyers predicted, nothing happened; the Italian police had plenty of new crimes to concern them. In an apparent attempt to make the authorities pay attention, Lady Jane told her story to the press in London. According to the rag I'm looking at right now," Josie said, "that was yesterday. I guess it took the story twenty-four whole hours to find its way to Italy. Listen to these headlines, Francesca: 'Famous Lost Countess a Murderess?,' 'Alleged Murderess Reappears After Nineteen Years.' Sybilla is being eulogized as 'a lovely and promising young English artist who was sacrificed to an older woman's lascivious passion.' And Susannah is described in Gothic detail as an overprivileged, drug-crazed socialite who went on a rampage, dagger in hand, in their Venetian palazzo. Francesca, of course you know there's going to be an inquest. But the main reason why I called you: I think you—all of you—ought to get out of Lyford Cay right away before the newspaper vultures arrive."

"Josie, do the stories mention Jack or me?" Francesca was clutching the telephone so hard that her knuckles had whitened.

"Yes, they dug up all the old publicity about you both and about the spa."

Francesca and Jack thanked Josie and said good-bye.

"I give them twelve hours," Jack said as he rejoined her in her office. "By midnight the grounds of this spa will be crawling with reporters. Pack your bags. We're getting out of here." Jack leaned over the desktop, his face just inches from Francesca's. "Like it or not, I'm taking the lot of you to California. Later on, when this mess dies down, you can come back here, and live quietly ever after, Francesca, but for the moment, you're coming to L.A. with me." He straightened and left the room, yelling over his shoulder, "I'm going to round up Christopher and your mother."

Francesca didn't stop to argue with him. She fled into the bedroom and started to pack. There would be time later on to make up her mind about the way she wanted to spend the rest of her life. Right now, she had to agree with Jack: California would be a safer place for all of them.

She was still throwing clothing into suitcases when the first reporters arrived. Jack's estimate had been off by nine hours. She wondered at first how the newsmen had penetrated the security system, then realized that the methods they had used simply didn't matter.

The spa phone rang, and she snatched it up.

"They've got us," Jack said on a note of hopelessness. "I'm at the main house with your mother and Christopher. Can you get up here without being seen?"

"I'll try sneaking out the back way."

She hung up, tied a scarf over her bright hair, and walked casually out of the cottage, forcing herself not to hurry. The main entrance to the mansion was swarming with reporters; she quietly strolled around to the garage, walked through it, and let herself into the kitchen. A minute later, Jack was at her side, hurrying her up to a deserted exercise room on the second floor.

"Your mother insists on going to Venice for the inquest," he said after he had shut the door. "I told her we could get Prescott to figure out a way of avoiding extradition, but she won't hear of it."

Francesca nodded silently, not at all surprised. "Then I'll have to go to Venice with her, Jack."

"She doesn't need you." Jack's voice was compassionate. "I know that's hard for you to accept, because you really want to serve her in some way, but you're kidding yourself, Francesca. Your mother will be just fine without you."

"I know that, but *I* won't be just fine. Can you imagine how I'd feel sitting safely in California while my mother is being tried for murder?"

"Francesca, we have no other choice. We can't take Susannah away from here by force."

"I have to go with her, then," Francesca said stubbornly. "I can't let my mother go to Venice and face the inquest alone. If she ever needed me in her life, Jack, it's now."

Jack was silent for a moment. Then he sat down on an exercise bench and pulled her down beside him. "Consider what this will do to your life, Francesca. Think what it will do to Christopher and to me. And to the spa, for that matter. If you get involved in this inquest, your name will be splattered across the front page of every scandal sheet in Europe, and probably America, too. Everybody will suffer."

Francesca felt a sort of numbness creep over her. This moment, she knew, was the final test she had always known would occur in her relationship with Jack. "I can ignore the scandal; so can my mother. By the time Christopher is old enough to understand all this, the whole mess will have been buried and forgotten. Granted, there will be hard times for the spa while the story's in the headlines, but we've endured troubles before, with no lasting ill effects."

She stood up and walked away from him, not wanting to see his face as she asked him, "So just what do you mean, Jack, when you say that everybody will suffer? You mean *you* will suffer, don't you? You're thinking about your image, aren't you, Jack?"

"Francesca, I've never even pretended that I don't value the reputation I have as a squeaky-clean American hero. That's been my bread and butter, and this scandal can ruin me."

"And your image is more precious to you than Christopher and I are!" She turned on him.

"Never."

"Then come to Venice with me." She held her breath, waiting for the answer she wanted to hear, knowing it wouldn't come.

"I can't, Francesca." He stood up and walked over to her. "Listen to me, darling. I have to try to make you understand that if you go to Venice you'll destroy both our lives, and you won't help your mother one bit. You'll only make her worry about the effect the trial will have on you and Christopher."

"Stop talking about me and Christopher and my mother. You're not thinking about us, Jack."

"Francesca—"

"My mother is supposed to go on trial all alone, with no one to support her, simply because you're afraid of a little bad publicity?" Francesca knew as she spoke that she was treading on dangerously thin ice, but her anger wouldn't allow her to be silent. "You've always thought that way, haven't you, Jack? Your reputation first and above all. And then, if there's time left to consider anything else, maybe you'll spare a thought for someone else. You don't care about Christopher or me!"

Jack grabbed her shoulders and shook her hard. "Stop it, Francesca! That's crazy, you know damn well I care about you." He pulled her against him and held her firmly, ignoring her attempts to push him away. "Honey, there is no way your mother can beat Lady Jane's charges, not after the hatchet job the newspapers have done on Susannah. That inquest is going to be step one in a long murder trial that will stay in the headlines for years, and the first mention of my name in connection with a lesbian murder will destroy me at the box office."

He took Francesca's shoulders and held her slightly away from him. "Look, I know I sound shallow and cruel to you, but please try to understand the position I'm in. No matter what I do right now, I'm lost. If I let you go to Venice without me, I'll lose you, and I don't think I could bear that. But if I go with you and the scandal spills over on me, I'll be out of work, Francesca. Then what kind of a life will I be able to give you? I'd have to live on your money, like a gigolo, because I don't know any business other than motion pictures. And there's no way I could ask you to love me if I became that kind of man. Given a choice between those two nightmares, I'd have to let you go, Francesca. Please don't make me do that."

Francesca found herself thinking about Edward. The scandal would threaten the spa, and if the spa fell into financial difficulty, Edward would have no means of support for his surgical clinic. But she knew he wouldn't let that possibility stand in his way. If she asked him to come to Venice with her, he would do so in a minute.

"I know what you're thinking, Francesca." Jack let go of her shoulders and walked away from her.

He didn't say anything more, and she wondered why. Jack could have argued that the scandal wouldn't do as much damage to an obscure plastic surgeon as it would to a world-famous actor.

Francesca couldn't give up the notion that if Jack loved her he would be willing to make this sacrifice for her. Even when she knew that she had finally succeeded in driving Jack away, she couldn't admit that she was expecting too much of him. Instead, she pulled around her the protective shield that had hidden her emotions after the fire. The only way to endure the unendurable, she had learned, was to put all of one's energy into the tasks that presented themselves with each new moment.

"I have a great deal to do before my mother and I leave for Venice," she said coldly. She was astonished at how well her defense system worked. She wasn't even close to bursting into tears. Even as Jack kissed his son good-bye and walked out the door late that night, she felt no inclination to cry.

All night, Francesca sat staring into the darkness, hating Jack for making her choose between himself and the mother she had worshiped all her life.

On the day they left, Edward took a couple of hours off from his work and drove Francesca, her mother, and Christopher to the airport. He had not spent time alone with Francesca since Jack's arrival in Nassau. They lingered alone together in the car while the others went ahead. Edward was formal and distant toward her, yet somehow deeply involved at the same time. Jack's departure had surprised him, but he asked no questions about it. "Would you mind if I came to Venice for a few days?" he said to Francesca as she reached for a bag she had put under the seat. "I haven't been there since my student days." He said this tentatively, almost wistfully, as if their night of shared panic over Christopher had never happened.

Francesca's invitation sounded so forced and rigid even to her own ears that she smiled in dismay. "I won't be the best hostess, but I'd appreciate your company." Impulsively she leaned over and kissed his cheek. He put his arm around her for a moment.

"I want to make sure you're all right," he said.

"I could use a guardian angel right now," Francesca said lightly.

After they were settled in the plane Francesca looked out of the window to see Edward standing apart from the crowd waiting for the plane to take off. She took Christopher on her lap and gave him her white handkerchief to wave, hoping Edward would spot them. He did, and as he waved back, she had the same warm, deep feeling for him she'd had the night of Christopher's accident. She hugged Christopher to her as the plane roared down the runway and lifted off.

PART FIVE

Venice
1975

Chapter Thirty-four

FRANCESCA STOOD IN the back of the motor launch, holding Christopher's hand, and watched the golden buildings flow past. She pointed out the gondolas to the boy, who looked at Venice with wide-eyed amazement. Susannah, sitting quietly, was trying to get used to this city of memories again.

"Why can't we have boats like this in Nassau, Mama?" Christopher asked.

"A gondola wouldn't be much good in the ocean. The streets aren't made of water in Nassau."

"We could have a boat like that in Paris. We could go up and down the Seine," he said.

"Yes, I suppose we could." Francesca smiled slightly. She didn't want to tell Christopher that they were not going back to Paris. She wanted to shield him from the uncertain future; there were things she wanted him never to know.

Christopher's little face looked pinched and pale under his tan. In spite of all her efforts to be cheerful, he seemed to have picked up her anxiety by osmosis. "Where is the lion, the lion with the wings, Mama?" he asked her for the tenth time.

"He's there, sweetheart, but it's too foggy to see him from here. I'll show him to you, I promise." Francesca warmed his hands with her own.

"I want to see him now." Christopher rubbed his eyes and began to cry. Francesca turned him to her and tried to hold him against her breast and comfort him, but he squirmed away.

Again, the flat miles of salt marshes, the sharp smell of the Adriatic, the eastern sky and the city that floated over the marsh like a mirage. A city on stilts, Francesca thought, an artifice such as only the mind of man could devise. She had once been crowned here as its most exalted daughter, heir to Venice's history and beauty, and basked in the city's admiration as a living work of art. Now she would see Venice's medieval, cruel face, the scarred, vengeful face of a people forced off the very edge of the land into the sea. There was a ceremony of crowning, and a ritual for a crown's removal. Francesca had come back to Venice in her mother's shadow to be shorn of her glory.

Not even Venice's display of beauty could lighten Susannah's somber mood. She had known a different Venice. "The houses, the facades are all the same. But the feeling is different. Of course, I was never here in winter," she said. "But still, how could I have ever left?" Francesca could not bear to see the puzzled hurt in her mother's eyes.

They sped down the Canalazzo, past the Gritti Palace and the Church of Santa Maria della Salute, toward the Palazzo Nordonia.

"Even the tourists can't ruin it. It's so beautiful! I never thought I'd see Venice again," the older woman exclaimed. Surely Susannah had never expected a homecoming like this.

At last the launch swung in front of the palazzo. The driver leaped out to tie the prow to the ring in the stone lion's mouth. Christopher's eyes widened at the sight of the ferocious-looking twin animals.

"Are there real lions in Venice, too?" he asked.

"No, but stone ones are everywhere. It's the sign for Saint Mark the Evangelist, who's buried here."

"What's an evangelist?" he asked, saying the strange word slowly as Francesca helped him out of the gondola.

"It's a long story," she said. "I'll tell you tonight. Now, be careful, go slowly."

Christopher, defying her, jumped onto the marble landing.

"Is this Grandma's home?"

"Yes. This is the house where I was born."

The front of the palazzo rose steeply from the landing, and Christopher had to crane his neck to look up to the top stories. Susannah and Francesca exchanged a glance over his uplifted face.

The gondolier unloaded their luggage onto the landing. Susannah turned to Francesca impatiently. "I'd love to just go up and open the door, but I feel I can't barge in on the tenants. Would they mind? Do you suppose we could go up the grand staircase?"

Francesca had rented out the bottom two floors of the palazzo to a wealthy German family. She and her small family planned to stay on the top two floors, an inconvenient arrangement but the only one possible. The upstairs tenants had recently vacated, but the Germans' lease ran for another six months.

"No, I think we'll have to do what the former upstairs tenants did, and climb up the back staircase. I'm sure the Germans will let us take a look later, if we ask very politely. I've heard they're terrible ogres."

"But you own the palazzo, darling; you're their landlord. They've got to respect you."

Francesca sighed. The prospect of sharing the grand palazzo depressed her. She could tell it diminished her mother's happiness as well. Francesca had not come back to Venice before in part because she couldn't bear to see strangers living in her father's home.

As if they had never left, Emilio was there to meet them at the upstairs door. The tenants had kept him on as a servant. But now, years later, his proud posture was ruined, his shoulders stooped with arthritis. Yet he held the door for them spryly, his eyes gleaming with light as he beheld Francesca.

"Contessina," he said in his deep voice. "Welcome home at last!"

Then he saw Susannah moving slowly up the steps. Tears pooled in his eyes and, embarrassed, he stepped back in the shadow. "In the name of God, can it be?" he murmured, almost in shock.

Susannah, out of breath, paused at the top of the stairs. "Well, this will keep me in shape. No more of those one-story cottages that spoil you so," she said, squinting into the darkness. "Who's there? Who *is* that? Is that really you? Emilio?"

In a moment Emilio was bending to kiss her hand. It would have been awkward for him to embrace the countess, and so she put her hands on his shoulders and squeezed them.

"After all these years, Emilio, you're still here. Thank God some things don't change."

Emilio was too moved to speak. "So it's true. A miracle," he said at last. "Now I go to help with your baggage."

"No," said Francesca, thinking he might be too weak. "Is there anyone else here? Vieri, perhaps?"

"No, no. Vieri works at a hotel now, not far from here. But there is no one else here. I am alone."

Francesca carried the last suitcase up and closed the door. Before her the long corridor gleamed darkly. She walked through the lavish rooms, all gilt and velvet and heavenly Tiepolo ceilings. She found Susannah and Emilio in the rose room where she had stayed seven years before.

"Mother, I wish you could have seen my face when I first came upon this room. You decorated it for me, didn't you?"

Susannah hugged Francesca to her. "Emilio was telling me about your beautiful ball. We'll have another one, one day. Now, where shall I stay?"

"You will stay right here," Francesca said firmly, "and I will sleep in Josie's old room with Christopher just across the hall."

Francesca took her small case from Emilio, her face troubled.

Emilio's eyes met hers. "I have read the newspapers, Contessina. Please know I am here to help you in any way that I can. You have only to ask."

"You can help me with my son, Christopher, Emilio. I will be very busy with my mother in the next days."

"Oh, that will be a pleasure." Emilio's face broke into a broad grin. He bowed low and left the room with a new spring to his step.

Alone now, thinking of where she was again, Francesca felt she had walked through a door and found herself in a distorted room, corners not quite square, the walls moving imperceptibly. Logic didn't hold in this shifting world. Like the palazzo, it seemed the same from a distance, but it was no longer hers. Strangers made the rules, had all the rights. Everything was happening so fast. One day she had planned her marriage to Jack, uniting her family at last. And the next, it seemed she was leaving for Italy, and Jack was already at the other end of the world.

That first evening back in Venice Susannah had in her head that she must walk through the palazzo, not just through the upper stories, but through the grand piano nobile where the Germans lived.

"Oh, Mother, I'm afraid to call them. Let them get used to us first. They're terribly formal. We'll have to make an appointment," Francesca said.

"They're probably using the furniture for firewood and have knocked down all the walls. Perhaps it's best we surprise them."

"Just let me call."

To Francesca's relief, the wife, Frau Gegenschatz, invited them downstairs without delay. "I'm so glad you've come to Venice, Mrs. Hillford. I will unlock the door for you."

Susannah went first down the grand staircase. The Germans, a heavyset, middle-aged industrialist and his tall, blond wife, waited for them at the foot of the stairs. They stood very erect and surveyed the descending procession with mingled suspicion and pride. Susannah walked across the marble floor to the portrait of herself in a green dress. She stood silently before it for a moment, then turned to face the tenants.

There was not a trace of recognition on their faces, she realized with a combination of hurt pride and amusement. Francesca, standing behind the Gegenschatzes, looked relieved. Her and her mother's pictures had been plastered all over the Italian scandal sheets for days. Luckily the German couple seemed oblivious.

"You have left the house intact?" Susannah said.

"Mostly. We did not want to move that portrait because it's so lovely. We believe it's a previous owner of the palazzo. She must have been very grand. Somehow she seems to be the presiding spirit of the place, the household god, as it were," the industrialist said in correct, heavily accented English, hooking a hand in his vest pocket. He obviously relished the role of guide. "Let me take you on a tour of the place. Have you been here before?"

"Yes," Susannah said simply. She winked at Francesca.

Their self-appointed guide walked them through the magnificent rooms, pointing out the treasures Susannah had brought here.

As she wandered through the rooms, Francesca felt the magic of the old palazzo wrap itself around her as it had during that fairy-tale summer when she had met Jack and then lost him for the first time. She stood in the center of the ballroom, letting the ghosts of kings and princes waltz around her, remembering her happiness as she danced in her father's arms and her joy as she looked into Jack's eyes.

"You'll forgive the mess," said Frau Gegenschatz.

Francesca smiled. The rooms were as spotless as they'd been when the staff polished and dusted every day. The woman was a real German hausfrau and she knew it. "You've kept it the way I would have," Francesca said.

"Come down and have tea with us one afternoon." The woman beamed.

Susannah smiled at her pleasantly. They all knew they'd never sit down over a cup of tea or anything else. Still, the meeting with the tenants had been at least a partial success. As soon as the door was shut behind them, mother and daughter flew laughing upstairs.

"It seems impossible they haven't read the papers about us," Francesca exclaimed. "But they're entirely oblivious to local life. Imagine, my tenants are the only residents of Venice who don't know what a scandal is brewing under this roof."

The topmost floor of the palazzo, which had been storage rooms and Francesca's nursery, had been converted into a small servants' quarters. Its kitchen now served as cooking facilities for the upstairs tenants. It was a bare room, large enough but plain, with marble tiles on the walls and a harsh overhead light. But the stove was new and the refrigerator a rarity in Venice. Francesca began to prepare a supper of Spanish omelettes with some of Emilio's prosciutto and tomatoes. Tomorrow she would go shopping. Christopher played in another room with Emilio, who had already fed him his favorite spaghetti supper.

As she set out wineglasses she turned on the radio, adjusting the dial until she heard a familiar melody. It was a song Josie had frequently sung. She turned the volume up a little and froze in shock. She stared for a moment at the radio in wonder, then turned it louder still and went running down the hall.

"Quick, Mother, Josie's on the radio," she yelled.

Susannah hurried quickly to the kitchen. While they listened silently, Francesca poured out the wine.

"It's beautiful," breathed Susannah.

"It's the first time I've heard a recording," said Francesca.

The song ended and the announcer described Josie in Italian as the cabaret singer who had been a sensation in Paris. An album had been released of her Parisian nightclub performances.

Just as the next song came on the pounding began downstairs. It sounded like a crowbar smashing against the ancient pipes. "In Gott's name, quiet!" came the distant roar of the German paterfamilias.

"The truce is over," Francesca said. Susannah burst out laughing and for a moment it seemed their real troubles were forgotten.

* * *

On Monday morning, the Nordonia attorneys arrived at the palazzo and insisted that they be allowed to speak with Susannah alone. The bored and weary attitude with which they set about their duties increased Francesca's suspicion that they were not up to the job she and her mother had been forced to entrust to them. She wished Anson Prescott could have come to Italy to take these men in hand, but he had been forced to stay out of the Italian proceeding by his inability to practice law in Italy. All morning long, messengers and deliverymen arrived with flowers for Susannah, letters of encouragement from friends on two continents, promises of support, win or lose. But, much as the messages buoyed up her spirits, Francesca kept thinking about Jack Westman, alone in California, and herself, alone once again in Venice.

Francesca longed to go outside and walk through the streets until she felt exhausted, but the canal was lined with paparazzi. Like vultures, they hovered around the neighborhood, waiting for a member of the Nordonia family to appear in the doorway.

She looked around as the three lawyers came out of the room in which they had been sequestered with Susannah.

"We have asked your mother to study the written materials we prepared for her," the oldest of the three said to Francesca. "And we must insist that she stay away from the journalists."

"Did you think that such advice was necessary?" Francesca asked sarcastically.

"We have advised the contessa not to admit to having been the victim's lover," the youngest one said coolly, ignoring her question entirely. "And, of course, she is not to speak of the murder to anyone, nor are you."

Outraged, Francesca flared up at the three of them. "*Murder*! How dare you use that word?"

"Ah, the incident," the lawyer amended, obviously finding it hard to correct his own blunder.

"Understand, signora," said another member of the team, "that we are working under a distinct disadvantage. We have no witnesses to testify in your mother's behalf. Therefore, it is most—"

"What are you saying, signor?" Francesca's voice was trembling with outrage. "Are you telling me that you haven't bothered to listen to one word I've said to you?"

"No need to become upset, signora. If the inquest leads to

a trial, we shall win, provided you and your mother are willing to cooperate with us."

Annoyed by his complacency, Francesca ordered him and his colleagues into the ivory-paneled reception room, ignoring their protests and informing them imperiously that they were her employees and that they would do as she asked them if they wished to remain in favor with the Nordonia family.

After asking them to sit down, she said, "When I spoke with you on the telephone last week, I gave you a list of names of former friends of my mother's who might be effective witnesses. One of them was the novelist Converse Archer. Have you been in touch with him?"

"Well, now, signora, you must understand—"

"What I understand is that you might not be good for this case. I suspected that from the beginning, and so I've done a good deal of your work for you." Quickly, trying to hide her anger, she explained what she, Susannah, and Edward had accomplished on the telephone.

Francesca remembered Converse Archer's pleasure in telling his story to a friend in Apollonie's garden during the party at the château. She suspected that the novelist would enjoy being the center of attention in a courtroom. She had called the Gritti Palace on her first afternoon in Venice and had not been surprised to learn he was registered. No doubt he had come to Italy to observe the end of the Nordonia tragedy. To play a part in the melodrama would thrill him, even if, as Francesca had begun to hope, the outcome disappointed him.

"Mr. Archer will be present at the inquest on Thursday," she said briskly. She went to the small rosewood desk in the corner and picked up a manila envelope. From it she removed several sheets of typing paper. "Here is a list of questions you will wish to ask him."

"But, signora—"

"Don't interrupt me." She watched them look at her unhappily, then continued, her voice cold with fury. No wonder, she thought, the Nordonia estates were in such disarray after her father's death. Carlo's attorneys were idiots. "Here is a list of the servants who worked here at the palazzo during the years before Sybilla Hillford's accidental death. I provided you with these names over the telephone." Francesca leaned slightly forward and spoke very slowly. "I expect you to find them before Thursday. All of them."

Susannah, she noticed, had entered the room and was

standing motionless near the door. Totally wrapped up in her work, Francesca ignored her.

"These servants did not witness the accident," she went on, "but they will surely remember Lady Sybilla's odd behavior during the days that preceded it. I want every one of them to take the stand during this inquest. If a single servant is absent, I will expect you to provide me with proof that he or she is dead."

From the doorway she heard a slight choking sound. She paid no attention. From the manila envelope she took another sheaf of typed papers. "This is a deposition from Dr. Edward Patiné and also one from a nurse who was working at a clinic in Lyford Cay, New Providence, Bahama Islands, when Jane Hillford, in an insane rage, burst into my father's sickroom and upset him so violently that he died soon afterward. You will present this as evidence of Jane Hillford's mental incompetence. This"—she wielded another sheaf of papers—"is a transcript of the trial in which Jane Hillford was found not guilty by reason of insanity for maliciously setting the fire that killed my husband, Michael Hillford, who was also her nephew."

Standing in the doorway of the ivory-paneled room, Susannah Nordonia proudly watched her daughter fight against the incompetence and complacency of the lawyers. Jack had been wrong, after all, Susannah realized. She did need her daughter's help. Even Susannah herself, with all her courage and strength, could not have worked up enough anger to bully these men into defending her effectively. It had taken Francesca—with the bitter knowledge that, for this, she had lost the man she loved—to frighten these little men into doing their job.

Chapter Thirty-five

THE MORNING OF the inquest dawned bleak and oppressive. The chill wind that blew in from the Adriatic made Francesca retreat from the balcony and pull the door shut. As she stared out the window, she realized that all of the fury she'd let loose at the lawyers during the past three days had left her exhausted and emotionless. Before her, the cold winter sun sent bars of gold flickering across the gray canals. She could see no trace of the fairy-tale city that had welcomed her seven long years ago.

Francesca turned away from the window when Christopher tapped on the door. "Jack's coming today," he shouted, running across the room to hug his mother impetuously. "I know he is."

Francesca got down on her knees and took her son in her arms, wondering if he, too, had dreamed that Jack was here in Venice with them. "Probably not, Christopher," she said carefully. "But when we leave Venice, you can visit Jack in California."

"Disneyland is there," he said. "Jack told me all about it when we were in Paris."

"Come along, Christopher," Emilio said, glancing at Francesca. "We'll spend the morning playing in the kitchen, if it's all right with your mother."

Francesca nodded. "I know it's hard on you and Christopher to stay cooped up inside, but things should calm down a bit after a few days. If it warms up this afternoon, you can go out into the courtyard, but don't open the gate, all right?"

"'Say good-bye to your mama, Christopher," Emilio said.

Francesca went off in search of Susannah. The telephone rang as she walked down the hall. It surprised her; it was only eight o'clock. "Hello?"

"Is this Francesca Nordonia? Perhaps you remember me, Antonia Olmi. I was your father's researcher."

"Antonia. How good of you to call."

"I saw your ad in the Rome newspaper. So I telephoned."

Francesca quickly explained that she was looking for her father's previous employees, but only those who worked for him years before Toni had.

"Yes, I have read about the inquest. I am so sorry. I know your mother is innocent. You see, your father told me things, and others I learned. I have something that belonged to Sybilla Hillford. I think it's important that you should see it."

"I am most anxious to, but we'll be at the inquest all day."

"I will meet you there and show you. What is the address?"

Francesca gave it to her, wondering whether some piece of Sybilla's clothing, or stray belonging, would do much good at this point.

"I know that this is what your father would want. But you must not tell your mother. Not until you see. Please?"

"Yes. I promise."

Francesca put on her hat and coat. She found her mother already waiting downstairs.

"Good morning, Mother," she said, kissing her. "Good luck today. I'll be right behind you."

Susannah smiled. "I'll make sure those lawyers are aware that my daughter is watching them. Come along. Time to face the unknown music."

"Can we walk to the courthouse?" Francesca asked.

"Yes. It's a hike, but we have plenty of time. We can go out through the garden and perhaps avoid the photographers."

"Let's do that, then." Even through the closed doors, they could hear the gnatlike whine of the paparazzi's motorboats.

Tense and exhausted from three days of riding herd on the Nordonia attorneys, Francesca let her mother lead her into the leafless olive orchard, through the heavy gate, and into the winding streets of Venice. They walked briskly, not looking at the people who passed them, speaking very little.

When they finally arrived, they were led into a mahogany-paneled room at the end of a maze of imposing marble corridors. Susannah sat with the lawyers, just in front of Francesca. Almost as soon as they were seated, the judge entered the room and called the inquest to order. After a long, chilling preamble, Lady Jane was called to testify. Francesca saw the judge, a taciturn man who wore thick horn-rimmed glasses, study the witness as she began to speak.

She sat with moist, clasped hands and watched Lady Jane intently. She no longer bore the scars of her institutional stay; she looked like a well-preserved society matron who was about to preside over a meeting of the garden club. It was impossible now to believe that she had once set fire to her neighbor's house. She was rational and calm, and when she spoke of beholding the body of her dead daughter, her aggrieved voice was controlled. She paused every sentence or so, and a young man translated her testimony into Italian. The delay increased the suspense of her testimony, and the repetition seemed doubly damning, an echo of outrage. The courtroom was so quiet that the spectators could hear the reporters' pens scratching. The judge listened impassively, and then asked Lady Jane a series of questions about the condition of the body, the appearance of the bathroom, the behavior of the police, and finally about Susannah.

"She took my daughter away to Venice although I forbade it," Lady Jane began.

Francesca saw her mother shudder and reached out for her hand as Lady Jane calmly lied her way through the first hour of the session. Unless the Nordonia lawyers conducted a brilliantly ruthless cross-examination, and Francesca had little hope that they were capable of that, Jane Hillford's calm, clear lies would prevail over the less deeply involved witnesses who had been rounded up to testify in Susannah's defense.

The judge called for the retired chief of police to come forward. The morning had already passed, and Francesca saw that the inquest could take several days. A guard tapped her on the shoulder, and pointed to the door. When the judge announced a recess until after lunch, Francesca rose and left the room. Antonia stood in the hallway.

Antonia greeted Francesca with her serious smile and a warm handshake. She had grown heavier than Francesca remembered. Her black hair had grown long, past her shoulders, which made her look girlish. But she wore a Chanel suit with a silk blouse and several strands of pearls. Her hand flashed with an emerald and gold wedding band.

"You're married now," Francesca said.

"Yes, after your father died I went to Rome to work. I teach art history at the university there. My husband is a banker. We have a baby daughter." She smiled shyly. "I'm afraid I know much about your life, Francesca. You're always in the newspapers."

"Surely you didn't come all the way from Rome."

"Yes. I drove here last night. I knew that what I have brought would be terribly important for you. Come over here behind the pillar and I will show you."

Francesca watched as Antonia slipped an old book bound in cracked and faded red leather from her purse. The book was slender, the pages painted in gold leaf.

"What is it?"

"Sybilla Hillford's notebook. It's a kind of diary of events and ideas and sketches she kept the last few months of her life. The last pages are filled with drawings of Venice and of your mother."

Francesca took the book from her, the worn leather still warm from Antonia's hands.

"It would hurt my mother terribly to see this," Francesca said as she flipped through the yellowed pages. The paper was heavy and expensive, and had borne the years well. There were quick sketches of Venetian churches and medieval houses, impressions of people's faces and hands, studies of Madonnas with their sweet, doomed, and joyful expressions. Then, at the end of the book, followed page after page of drawings of Susannah, her face, her profile, her nude body, her legs. "She was obsessed," Francesca said in a shocked whisper.

"Yes."

"I had no idea that Sybilla was so talented."

"Yes, she was very gifted. That's why I was so interested in her. I found this locked away in your father's desk. I didn't mean to steal it, or even see it," Antonia said in an apologetic voice. "I had the key to the desk because sometimes I would write out checks for him, and that was where he kept his checkbook, in another drawer. After he died, I went through the desk to find my love letters. I knew that he had saved them."

She looked with embarrassment at Francesca. "Did you know?" she asked.

Francesca nodded her head.

"I'm afraid I'll have to tell the court all this."

"Tell me first."

"In one of the drawers there was a pistol, loaded, and this book. You know how fascinated I was by artists. I read it, of course, and realized what had happened. I knew that I must keep it, and the checkbook as well. Your father would not have wanted anyone else to read it."

"What do you mean, 'read'? There's nothing to read, although the meaning is clear. I don't see how this will help us."

"You only looked at the front of the pages. Turn the book around and look through it again. Sybil wrote out a diary on the back of every drawing. Do you see? First she lists the name of the subject, or the place, and then writes about her artistic plans or problems and how to resolve them. Some pages are lists of inspirations and increasingly, toward the end, it is the story of her love for your mother."

Francesca bent over the cramped writing. Sybil wrote in a careful block print, so small it could hardly be read.

"The Venice chapter at the end first tells of how your mother was her real subject, the inspiration of her art, and how, if Sybil lost her, she might as well have her right hand cut off. Then it begins to rave about plans for a double suicide. She tried to talk Susannah into it, apparently with no success. But Sybilla thought it the highest honor to die for her art. The last page gives the details of the plan, which was set for that night. She thought she lacked the courage, and dared herself to accomplish it. But she needed practice. And so, in the morning, she drowned one of the palazzo's cats in the canal."

"No," Francesca breathed.

"*Sì*. She wrote about its dying struggle with fascination."

"She meant to drown my mother."

"Yes, if your mother would not go to New York with her, yes. And then she would slit her own wrists. It seemed, to her, a noble decision. She had left a record of her love for Susannah in her art, and she thought the double deaths would make her name."

"How awful."

"So I had to bring this to you. I knew it would exonerate your mother."

"I'll get our lawyer to come out now and talk to you. But tell me, why did you take the checkbook?"

"When I pieced the story together of what had actually happened, I understood why your father wrote out a large check to Renata twice a year. Once I saw one of the checks and I wondered what in the world he paid her for. When I asked him if it was a mistake, he told me never to speak about it, never to tell anyone. At first I thought she was blackmailing him. But now I realize that the payment was for the upkeep of your mother."

Susannah and her lawyer were just coming out into the hall. Francesca signaled to them. After introducing Antonia to her mother, the three women and the lawyer went back into the now-empty courtroom and sat huddled together over the notebook in the back of the room.

Stunned, Susannah murmured, "My husband kept hidden away in a locked drawer the evidence that would have cleared me of a murder charge nearly twenty years ago!"

Francesca's eyes widened. "But why? Why would he have done such a thing?"

"He must have been thinking primarily of his own reputation," Susannah said. "You see, he had already gone to the trouble of bribing all those officials. If the notebook had turned up, his illegal actions would have become common knowledge. Your father prided himself on his reputation as a man of honor, and charges of bribing public officials would have put him in prison. And then, of course, there would also have been a trial. The notebook would have cleared me, as you now know, but my relationship with Sybilla would have been publicized. Imagine what that would have done to my husband's pride. And his famous Nordonia name."

Susannah looked at Antonia and smiled kindly. "I'm sorry to speak of him this way in front of you, Antonia. It must hurt you to hear such terrible things. I think you saw a better side of him than I did." She waited for Antonia's nod of acknowledgment, then spoke to Francesca. "I suppose Carlo was also thinking of you when he hid the notebook, Francesca. He was a rigid man to whom adherence to convention was more important than love. I'm sure he believed no mother at all was better for the daughter of Carlo Nordonia than a mother who behaved as I had."

Susannah stood up and pulled her coat around her shoulders. Then she held out her hand to Antonia. "I can never tell you how very much I appreciate what you've done for me today."

"Contessa," Antonia said quickly, "I must explain one more thing. When the count showed me where he had hidden the notebook, I picked it up and leafed through it. But when I started to study the pages, he took it out of my hands and locked it up again."

Susannah nodded. "You're telling me that you knew it contained fine drawings, but you didn't know about the notes Sybilla had written on the backs of the pages. Thank you. I'm glad to hear that."

"I would have told Francesca, if I'd known, but I never thought to study the notes until I read about the inquest. I still thought you were dead, Contessa, but I would have told Francesca about the notes anyway. It's important to me to know that you believe this."

"I believe you," Susannah said.

Antonia offered her hand to Susannah, who shook it, then dropped a kiss on the younger woman's cheek.

Antonia acknowledged the gesture with a smile. "I'll be here tomorrow," she said, "in case they want me to testify." She shook hands with Francesca and left the room.

Immediately after the recess ended, Susannah's lawyer asked for a conference with the judge and explained to him the new evidence. The judge asked to read the notebook overnight, before any more testimony was given. The inquest was adjourned until the next morning.

The spectators filed out of the courtroom decorously enough, but once in the hallway they began to buzz with rumors. The reporters crowded around Francesca and Antonia, shouting questions. Lady Jane emerged last, looking confused and harassed. Francesca felt that she could read the woman's mind; Lady Jane felt she might be cheated once again of the vengeance she deserved. Francesca turned away in horror from the ugliness of those thoughts.

Surprisingly, the afternoon had turned bright gold and the water blue as the sky. Susannah held her head high as she pressed through the mob of reporters outside the building.

As they walked out together, Susannah turned to look into Francesca's eyes. "You must think I'm trying to make you hate your father's memory. I don't mean to do that, Francesca. In fact, I've never been able to hate him myself."

"That's because he loved us," Francesca said, realizing with some surprise that she believed her own words. "He was a harsh man, but he did love us. And I loved him, in spite of everything." She put an arm around her mother, feeling better than she had felt since her world fell apart on New Year's Eve.

Chapter Thirty-six

FRANCESCA STOOD IN front of the full-length mirror in her bedroom at the palazzo, examining the scar on the left side of her face. When had she stopped emphasizing it with makeup? How long had it been since she had leaned close to a mirror this way to examine the flaw? Francesca couldn't remember the last time. The brand of the fire had become just another detail of the reality with which she lived. It had ceased to distress her or even to hold her interest.

Francesca started to turn away from her reflection, but stopped. Another question occurred to her. How long had it been since Jack had called her "scarface"? She couldn't remember exactly when she'd stopped hearing the pet name, but it had been around the time she had stopped thinking about the scar. Had Jack perceived the exact moment when she began to accept herself as she was, without the old self-pity and regret? Had he seen the change in her behavior or in her eyes?

No, she told herself. He had no special talent for reading her mind. If he had, he would have come to Venice with her instead of leaving her to deal with the lawyers and the press alone. It was time to put him out of her mind once and for all, she told herself.

She turned away from the mirror and walked out of her bedroom. A look into the room next to hers showed her that Christopher was contentedly playing with a deck of picture cards.

In the small sitting room nearby, she sat down at the elegant rosewood desk, and began to sort through the stacks of papers she had compiled for her mother's attorneys. She hoped the judge, after looking over the notebook, would decide in favor of a quick dismissal of the charges against Susannah, but she didn't dare count on such a move. With a weary sigh, she began to pore over the depositions she'd collected, remembering the disgust she'd felt at the attorneys' failure to mention them to the judge that afternoon. A knock on the door brought her head up sharply. "Yes?"

"May I come in or are you still feeling fierce?"

"Come in, Mother." She waited until Susannah stepped into the room. "What do you mean, fierce?"

"You can't deny that you've been ruthless and savage in your dealings with my poor attorneys, Francesca. You absolutely terrify me these days."

Francesca laughed. "Are you trying to tell me I'm overdoing it?"

"No, no, no. Really, Francesca, I don't think I've ever enjoyed anything so much as your new and terrifying fierceness."

Francesca pulled a wry face. "Mother, if you tell me I get my fierceness from my father, I am going to scream."

Susannah shook her head. "It's true, you know. You really have inherited some of the Nordonia ferocity, but I know you'll never abuse it, as your father occasionally did." She walked over to Francesca and tucked a finger under her chin. "During that summer when you were in Venice, and later when you lived in Paris with Jack, I used to comb the newspapers for photographs of you. When I found them, I would cut them out and look at them for hours. 'My beautiful daughter,' I used to say to myself over and over. 'My lovely, beautiful child.'

"But now, today, you're more than beautiful, Francesca. You have strength of character now, and integrity and grit." Susannah was smiling, but her green eyes were misty. "And I am so proud of you that my heart is threatening to burst."

"Oh, Mother . . ."

Susannah's laughter rippled through the room. "I love the way you say that, like a teenager. I missed those years, Francesca; were you a brat? Did you drive Marianne crazy?"

Francesca smiled and nodded. "Both of us did. Josie was even worse than I was. You'd have hated us."

"I seriously doubt that." Susannah took both of Francesca's hands and shook them slightly. "Edward Patiné just called. He's here in Venice."

"He did decide to come then, after all. I told him his deposition would be enough."

"He needs a vacation, darling. I called his hotel and

nvited him to have dinner with us. I've given Emilio the evening off and so I shall prepare my famous Linguine alla Susannah!"

Francesca screwed up her face. "Ugh."

Susannah's eyebrows shot up in mock outrage. "Bite your tongue, ungrateful child."

She followed Susannah to the kitchen, where she watched without comment as her mother prepared dinner, both of them trying at least briefly to put the trial out of their minds.

At eight o'clock, Edward appeared at the courtyard door of the palazzo with a bottle of wine and a bouquet of roses. At Edward's arrival, Francesca felt a flow of strength. She showed him through the upstairs rooms with exuberant pride. In the nursery they looked in on sleeping Christopher.

"Poor thing. He seems to absorb my moods by osmosis. He was so upset on the plane coming over, perhaps because he sensed I'd broken off with Jack," Francesca said.

"Have you, really?" asked Edward in a light voice.

"Well, he'd certainly be pleased if my mother were exonerated tomorrow. But a basic trust is lost," Francesca said slowly.

"Maybe if you tried," said Edward. "It's not what I want for you, but I can't help playing devil's advocate."

They both had the same thought. Jack should have been standing beside Francesca and the hushed child in the dark.

Edward took her hand and led her from the room. While Francesca set the table, in the small upstairs sitting room, Edward made a fire.

Over dinner Francesca and her mother told him about Sybilla Hillford's notebook. Caught up in their excitement, Edward started to raise his glass in a toast but Susannah caught his wrist. "Don't, please. It's premature. God knows what can happen. Remember we're in an Italian court and Lady Jane may still have something up her sleeve."

"We can still drink to good fortune," Edward smiled and they touched glasses.

Francesca watched Edward, amazed. Socially he had always been hopelessly diffident, but now he was transforming their little supper into a cozy lark, entertaining them with tales of his exploits in medical school. How right he looked in the great eighteenth-century armchair, his long legs stretched out in front of him. This elegant and ancient setting suited him. Watching the firelight play across his sensitive features,

she was tempted to reach out and trace a finger along the dee
laugh lines that ran down along his cheeks. If they'd bee
alone, she might even have curled up in his lap.

Francesca smiled to herself; she'd had way too much wine

Edward rose. "Francesca, you're about to fall asleep o
us. I'll be off to my hotel now, but I'll pick the two of you u
tomorrow morning and escort you to the hearing. Eight o'cloc
sound all right?" He kissed her mother's hand, dropped a kis
on Francesca's cheek, and let himself out of the palazz
through the rear courtyard.

His departure was followed by a long moment of silence
Francesca could feel her mother's eyes on her.

"He's an exceptional man . . . Edward."

"Yes," Francesca murmured, meeting her mother's eyes
Even more exceptional than she had given him credit for, sh
thought. As always he was there trying to make it easier
although now everything that could humanly be done ha
been done. Once in bed, she calmly prayed for guidance an
the good will of the judge, then closed her eyes to sleep.

Chapter Thirty-seven

LADY JANE WAS shown to a seat in the front row on one side of the narrow aisle, and Susannah was seated on the other. The spectators and witnesses, Francesca noticed, had arranged themselves as if for a wedding, with the Nordonia supporters seated on the left side behind Susannah, and Lady Jane's friends and lawyers on the right. She recognized Converse Archer, prim in a robin's-egg-blue sweater, as he took a seat diplomatically on the aisle. Suddenly he leaned over and waved at Susannah. Lady Jane turned her neck for the first time and gave Susannah a look of sheer hatred, as if insanity had seized her again.

The judge entered and his expression, too, was changed. He looked more involved, somehow, and Francesca knew he had begun to form his decision. They would all be judged today—her mother, the corrupt police, Renata, who had helped hide the murder and the accused murderess. The press seemed to sense the mood of impending doom. They sat erectly on the edges of the uncomfortable courtroom pews.

The door opened and a last spectator walked in.

"Josie!" Francesca sprang to her feet, feeling her heart leap with a combination of joy and despair as Josie Lapoiret walked straight down the aisle, looking neither right nor left. When the court officer tried to direct her into a pew on the right side of the room, Josie shook her head and walked straight toward Francesca. Josie quickly sat down in the pew next to Francesca.

"Oh, Josie, you can't imagine how I've longed to see you." Francesca took her hand and squeezed it. "But you really shouldn't have come. The newspapers will crucify you for this."

"I couldn't let you go through this alone," she whispered.

Antonia was the first person called to give testimony as,

page by page, the judge took her through the events chronicled in the slender notebook. The press was mesmerized by the important new evidence, their pens flashing across their pads; and through it all Jane's face looked tortured with shock as she heard Antonia's story. When Antonia had satisfied the judge and he allowed her to step down, the red notebook was placed in evidence on a table before the bench along with the bloodstained knife.

"Susannah Nordonia," the judge said.

Susannah rose, took her oath, and began to tell the story of her week in Venice with Sybilla.

Lady Jane stared at her. Francesca felt the woman's frustration at not being able to absorb the exact meaning of every word. She would want to dispute Susannah's testimony if given a chance, but in spite of the interpreter, Susannah's Italian was an unexpected barrier.

Susannah was describing Sybilla's behavior at the ball at Gritti Palace. The press churned through their notebooks. Then Susannah described the events in the hushed palazzo. She told of Sybilla's frenzied, murderous passion in the bath; how she held Susannah under the water; how the knife blade met Susannah's grasping fingers; and how, in another moment, Sybilla's arms went limp, and Susannah surfaced into the nightmare that changed her life and the lives around her forever.

"I never meant to harm her," she said in a voice quiet with dignity. "I panicked when I realized she meant to kill me. I tried to save her. I loved her, and I did everything I could for her. But it was too late. I ran for help to my friend Renata."

"Why did you go into hiding instead of facing the police?" the judge asked.

"I wanted to die myself. My husband would not have me back. He would not allow me to see my daughter, to write her or call her. I had nothing left to live for."

After asking her several more questions about the night on which Sybilla died, the judge asked Susannah to step down. He called Renata to the stand and began to question her fiercely. Francesca watched admiringly as the tiny woman, her eyes sparking with outrage, snapped out her answers, meeting the judge's eyes with courage and purpose.

Apparently satisfied with Renata's testimony, the judge asked her to step down. She walked proudly past the table on which the court officers had placed the evidence: the bloody dagger and Sybilla Hillford's notebook.

After a long moment during which he looked down at his gnarled hands, the judge lifted his head and addressed the courtroom.

"I strongly believe," he announced, "that Susannah Nordonia acted in self-defense on the night of Sybilla Hillford's death. In light of the testimony of several witnesses and the evidence provided by the diary of the victim and the handwriting which has been certified by two court-appointed experts to be that of Sybilla Hillford—I have decided to pass this case on to a panel of judges to whom I shall strongly recommend dismissal. Countess Susannah Nordonia will remain in Venice until the final decision is announced. This hearing is adjourned."

"All rise!" shouted a court officer as the judge strode out of the courtroom amid the deafening cheers of spectators. The reporters leaped out of their seats and surged toward the doors. Francesca stood and opened her arms for her mother, who had paused in front of the evidence table. Tentatively, Susannah reached out as if to touch the cover of Sybilla's notebook.

"Keep your filthy hands off that!" Lady Jane shouted. Then, before anyone could restrain her, she jumped to her feet and lunged toward the table.

Taken off guard, Susannah turned to face her. "Lady Jane, I—"

The rest of Susannah's words were lost as Lady Jane's right hand snaked out, seized the dagger from the evidence table, and raised it above her head. The weapon flashed brilliantly. Then, just before the dagger plunged home, Josie lunged forward, flinging Francesca out of Lady Jane's path and hurling herself against Susannah, who fell backward, away from the knife.

Someone was screaming. People surged forward. For a moment Francesca could not see. When she pushed forward, she wondered crazily why Josie had crumpled to the floor. Then she understood: Lady Jane had plunged the knife to the hilt into Josie's back. She lay there without making a sound, her amber cheek pressed against the marble. Her eyelid flickered, then opened, and Francesca, looking into the deep, green pool of pain, realized that Josie was still alive.

The room exploded with noise. Edward was shouting at

people to get back, away from Josie. Converse Archer and a reporter were holding the struggling Lady Jane at the door.

"Susannah's daughter for mine! That's justice!" the woman exclaimed in a frenzy, insisting she had stabbed Francesca.

Francesca bit her lip as she watched Edward tear Josie's blouse open at the wound. All the while the pain in Josie's eye darkened like a hole boring deeper and deeper underground. Josie was slipping through it. Francesca wanted to follow her, but the weight of her mother in her arms held her back.

Chapter Thirty-eight

FRANCESCA SAT ALONE in the hospital waiting room long past midnight, well after Renata had taken her mother back to the palazzo. A fan spun lazily from the big ceiling. She could hear a child crying down the corridor. An hour slowly passed, then another. Francesca watched numbly as the hours of Josie's life ticked away on the huge old clock that hung accusingly on the opposite wall, as if to remind those who sat watch here that time was running out.

Like a film being run in reverse, as the exhaustion of the day overcame her and she drifted into sleep, she saw her life with Josie flashing past in clear, painful images on the walls of her memory.

Josie hurling herself forward to take the dagger that was meant for Francesca.

Josie at Chez La Lune in Paris. She knew almost with a certainty that she would never have found her mother without Josie's help.

Josie in Venice, on the landing of her palazzo, jumping up and down with excitement. "Francesca, why didn't you tell me your father was a king?" Francesca repressed a giggle as she remembered the happiness of that long-ago spring morning just before the golden years of their childhood ended.

Josie in Lyford Cay years ago, giving her sister the courage to dive off the high rocks and swim out into the deep waters, teaching Francesca to laugh at a stubbed toe, to thumb her nose at a thunderstorm instead of cowering under the bed.

Was it Josie, all those years ago, who planted in her soul the seeds of courage that had enabled her to be strong?

Early the next morning Francesca let herself out of the palazzo and boarded a vaporetto on the canal and sat facing front, anxious to get to the hospital again. Suddenly she heard Josie's voice. Someone was playing a radio. She looked around. A short man in an ill-fitting brown suit was walking toward her with a radio in one hand and a suitcase in the other. It seemed so macabre; for a second Francesca had the horrible conviction that Josie was trapped in the small box of transistors. Francesca was filled with dread, suddenly convinced that Josie had not survived the night. The sound floated around her like an insidious perfume. She was paralyzed with memory; Josie stood laughing beside her. Then the voice faded as the man with the radio got off the vaporetto. The boat moved on and the air was filled with bells. Francesca was reminded of the first morning she and Josie traveled down this canal, in the opposite direction, six years before. Now she realized she had come full circle, her family reunited. She said a small prayer for Josie as the vaporetto passed the winged lion in the Piazza San Marco. "Don't take her. Please don't take her."

When she disembarked she bought an armful of roses at a flower stall. Then she hurried through the twisting streets, past the courthouse, to the hospital. The nun at the visitors' desk looked at her inquiringly.

"I'm here to see Josephine Lapoiret."

The nun, blank-faced and meek, looked through a long list. Her fingers moved slowly over the pages as if reading Braille.

"Room two twenty-six," she said at last. "The elevators are across the hall."

But instead of waiting for the elevator, Francesca ran up the wide marble staircase to the first floor. She was already breathing hard. She started up the second flight, her heart pounding as the stairs seemed to extend in front of her endlessly. The more she climbed, the more frightened she became. The landing was still not in sight, only the wide marble steps up and up leading to nowhere . . .

"Josie!" she screamed, and the ringing in her ears woke her as she opened her eyes to find herself in the hospital waiting room; Edward was shaking her gently.

"She's dead! . . . I know she's dead!" Francesca began to sob.

"Shhh, Francesca . . ." Edward put his arm around her. "She's alive. With a little luck Josie is going to be fine. Come on . . . you can see her for just a minute. She's still in the recovery room."

"Is she really going to be all right?" Francesca asked him, still crying.

"I was only allowed to observe. She did not have the greatest surgeon and she's lost a lot of blood, but the blade didn't damage any vital organs." He tried to smile, but couldn't quite succeed. "Of course she's in danger of infection, so she'll have to be watched very closely."

Francesca watched him run a tired hand over his red-rimmed eyes.

"How that thin old woman managed to drive the dagger straight through Josie's shoulder I'll never understand," he said. "Only thc superhuman strength of the insane could have made such a thing possible."

"Edward, are my mother and Christopher safe at the palazzo? If Lady Jane gets loose, she won't miss her target the next time."

"Don't worry. She's locked up. Her actions today made a mockery of the Venetian legal system and security in the courtroom. The city officials don't take that sort of thing lightly. I doubt if any of us will ever see Lady Jane again."

Francesca followed him down a narrow hallway. Josie lay on her back in a high hospital bed, her eyes closed. An intravenous tube ran its way from a bottle of fluid into the crook of Josie's elbow. On the opposite side of the bed stood a watchful nurse.

"She looks so little," Francesca murmured as she approached the bed. Josie's face, drained of all its vitality, was gray, and there were new planes and angles in her beautiful face.

The Byzantine dagger, with its accumulation of grime, had done its job well. Francesca wondered how often over the centuries that sinister weapon had found a home so close to the human heart.

Almost as if she knew someone was watching her, Josie feebly opened her eyes. "Francesca?" Her voice was thin and reedy; she cleared her throat and tried again.

"Francesca? The lion didn't fly, *p'tite soeur*."

Francesca's voice came out halfway between a sob and a shout of laughter. "You remember . . . How do you feel?"

"Numb. God knows what they've given me."

"I heard your song on the radio. It must be a smash hit."

"It is. Thank God Lady Jane missed my vocal cords."

The nurse made a low sound of disapproval, but Francesca

looked up quickly and caught her eye. "She's my sister," she said to the nurse. "I have a right to be here."

And then Francesca realized that the word "sister" just came out. The word she hadn't been able to say for all those years. With what little strength she had, Josie clutched Francesca's hand as if she were holding on to it for life.

"Let them have another minute," Edward told the nurse as he stood in the doorway.

Josie winced slightly and pulled Francesca closer. "Come here . . . secret."

Francesca leaned over the bed to hear Josie's whisper.

"Did you know a famous American movie star is in Venice, *p'tite soeur*? He was in court today; I saw him sitting in the back."

The nurse circled the bed and planted a hand firmly on Francesca's elbow. "Enough, signora. Come along."

"Bye, *p'tite soeur*," Josie said dizzily.

"See you later. I love you, Josie," Francesca replied.

Josie nodded sleepily. "I know, Francesca."

Francesca took a rose from the dozen Charles Cash had sent, and placed it in Josie's hand, then bent to press a kiss on her forehead. Her sister's eyes, she thought, were as clear and guileless as they had been when they were children racing across the grass toward the sea.

She left Josie's room and let Edward lead her along a hallway.

"The main entrance is mobbed with reporters," Edward said. "I'll show you how to get out through the back."

"No, Edward, let's face them. It's the only way to get rid of them."

"Are you sure, Francesca? There were at least fifty of them outside the last time I looked."

"I'm sure."

She let him lead her toward the main entrance. Just inside the door, he stopped for a moment and looked into her eyes.

"Is Jack out there, too?" she asked.

"I sent someone out to tell him he was welcome to join you in the hospital, but he said he'd wait."

As her heart lurched with the anticipation of seeing Jack again, she looked up at Edward as if to search his sensitive face for the right words to say to him. She saw no signs of pain in Edward's eyes, only concern and compassion. He raised a hand and placed one finger over her lips.

"Just be happy," Edward said, reading her thoughts.

At the top of the steps outside, she stopped and stood absolutely still, letting the cameras flash and pop around her. Far out beyond the crowd, she could make out Jack's blond hair gleaming in the early morning sun as he stood in a motor launch. A microphone was pushed under her nose.

"Is Josie Lapoiret alive?" one reporter asked.

"Why did the signorina risk her life? Who is she to you?" Instead of being offended by their insensitivity, Francesca threw back her head and laughed.

"Yes, she is alive. She is in stable condition. And to answer your second question, Miss Lapoiret is my sister."

There was a shocked silence. "You mean 'your sister' in a manner of speaking?" a reporter demanded.

"No, in actual fact. She is a Nordonia, like myself."

Edward gave her arm a surprised little squeeze. She looked up at him.

"Yes," she said. "It's true." She felt as if a mantle of lead had been lifted from her shoulders. For a euphoric moment she was oblivious to everyone. She was a bird floating high above them, acutely aware of the smell of the cool, clean air and the sight of the magnificent city, her birthplace. Tears of happiness stung her eyes. The world had come back into focus.

She kissed Edward lightly on the cheek and walked down the steps. Then, with the reporters at her heels, she ran to the canal where the motor launch was waiting. Taking Jack's outstretched hand, she jumped in as the crowd cheered and clapped.

The boat swept out into the bay. As Jack wrapped her in the warmth of his arms, the bells of San Marco pealed in the distance. Francesca began to laugh.

"What is it?" Jack asked.

"I'm so happy the lion didn't fly!" she shouted over the sound of the motor and hugged him hard, knowing she would never let him go again. Then she turned and faced into the wind. She tasted the sea spray on her lips and murmured the words "my sister" to herself, "my sister."